MAÑANA MAN

The troubleshooter who thought he'd hung up his guns and his alias for good.

MAÑANA MAN

Fired by vengeance, he'll track his man into the center of Central American espionage and intrigue.

MAÑANA MAN

The pulse-pounding new thriller by the author of *Sixth Precinct,*

CHRISTOPHER NEWMAN

MAÑANA MAN

Christopher Newman

FAWCETT GOLD MEDAL • NEW YORK

A Fawcett Gold Medal Book
Published by Ballantine Books
Copyright © 1988 by Christopher Newman

ISBN 0-449-13173-4

Manufactured in the United States of America

First Edition: May 1988

For my wife, Susan

Whoever fights monsters should see to it that in the process he does not become a monster. And when you look long into an abyss, the abyss also looks into you.

—NIETZSCHE

ONE

A steak sandwich smothered in melted cheese lay half-eaten on Jack Terranova's plate. He took another swig of the pungent local beer as a fly, buffeted in the gusts of an overhead fan, dove crazily for his brow. In preoccupied irritation, he swatted it away. Across the street, in a similar open-air cafe, a pair of men conspicuously avoided the appearance of caring whether Jack Terranova existed. He knew differently, and, as always, the knowledge was a source of irritation. He'd first noticed them yesterday morning as he strolled down the Sexta from his hotel, stopping at the *libraria* for a copy of the *Miami Herald*. It was the younger one who actually caught his eye. American, definitely, and working to look both local and preoccupied. No matter how hard he'd tried, he'd gotten it wrong. The little things. The shoes and haircut. A confident, even cocky, G-man walk. His partner, an older guy, was much better. He dressed and looked vaguely Colombian, until you found cause to squint and study him carefully. His Ivy League pal was plenty cause enough. Who did they think they were fooling?

Without appearing to, Terranova studied them now. Picking up his sandwich, he bit and chewed slowly, the *Herald* folded back on itself at his elbow. Football season was just getting started back home. The way both Jack and the writers saw it, Shula had his work cut out. He flipped over to the results

1

from yesterday's action at Hialeah. The taller of the two guys, the kid, seemed to have a pretty decent build. Real prep-school look. Probably played squash to stay in shape. Jack smiled to himself. College boys. There was a sort of perverse satisfaction in going up against a man with an expensive education.

The older man was different. Short. Maybe just five-eight. He was built like a nose tackle standing in a ditch, with an air of the journeyman about him. Jack knew all about nose tackles. They weren't as much fun as college boys. Nose tackles could be dangerous. This one had steel-gray hair, greased back like all the rest of these fat farts who seemed to have nothing better to do than to sit around and drink coffee all day. He had a sun-toughened face that looked like it had gotten in the way of a docking freighter. His hands were big for his size, with thick, gnarled fingers. Competence. Jack could read it as easily as if they'd hung a sign across his wide, heavy shoulders.

There wasn't much question about whom they were ultimately working for. But which agency? In his line of work, the FBI had been a constant pain in his ass, but this was foreign soil. They weren't likely to be DEA. Jack had made it a point to stay off their turf. These guys were spooks, then, and that gave him a little charge. He liked the idea that he was probably up against the CIA. He'd never had that particular pleasure.

Some of this wasn't much of a surprise; surveillance of one sort or another had become a fact of Jack Terranova's life. The presence of this pair on his tail wasn't jeopardizing anything just yet. He hadn't made his contact and wouldn't for another day. This was how he always worked. Come around, hang out, get a feel. Anticipate trouble before it became a factor. Deal with it. Late tomorrow afternoon he would meet Diego somewhere down around Popayan. There was plenty of time between now and then to clear the way.

Slowly, Jack finished his sandwich and the sports section. Even though Cali was only a stone's throw from the equator, it was far enough up above sea level to enjoy a hot but relatively dry climate. Jack liked the way it managed to cool right off toward morning. He understood that once he started climbing further up into the Andes toward Popayan, it would

2

get even cooler. He liked that. Right now, in Miami, the air was muggy and stinking hot.

Carl Stickley hadn't wanted to take the kid into an actual surveillance operation. All charged with puppy-dog energy and full of training-school idealism, the guy could prove unreliable in a tight spot. Back at Langley, Virginia, they never got it through their thick heads that training a man and then sending him directly into the teeth of the storm was no way to ensure he would live a long, healthy life. This wasn't the military. One firefight didn't make you a veteran. Throwing out the book and learning to stand on your own two feet made you a veteran. Playing on the Princeton lacrosse team, as noble an enterprise as that might be, didn't make you anything but raw, untested meat once you were dumped on the jungle floor.

The honchos back at Langley thought Carl Stickley was some sort of a miracle worker with these new kids. Recruited while still operating a Navy SEAL unit in Indochina, *Commander* Stickley had been something of a legend in certain tight little circles. His kids had gotten the job done back then. Dirty jobs of long-range recon and covert political assassination. Fruitless, perhaps, in the end, and sixteen long years in the past. It seemed to him that the kids they were recruiting now were different from the ones the Navy had given him back then. If he had to put his finger on it, he might call it a sort of political naivete coupled with a physical softness. Too much emphasis was being put on IQ. Shit, you got in a tight jam, you couldn't clobber some asshole with your IQ.

Stickley was sure the target had made them. What the hell; this man was supposed to be the very best, his bodies stacked under the Triborough Bridge in New York like cordwood. Although theirs had been designated a simple passive action, a guy like Jack Terranova didn't go to Colombia for his vacations. The company wanted him watched, and they'd saddled Carl with this kid Tanner as if it were going to be some sort of picnic. Like maybe along the way the boy could get his feet wet in the kiddie end of the pool.

"How're you supposed to drink coffee like this?" Tanner

3

complained. He was peering disgustedly into his demitasse cup at a syrupy black liquid.

"You asked for coffee, sport. That's coffee. You want something you can drink, you ask for *cafe con leche*."

"Why didn't you say something?"

"You're a South American *expert*," Stickley grunted. "The U.S. government done pried your mouth open and poured money down it. I'm interested to see how badly inflation has eroded the dollar's purchasing power."

Tanner looked at him blankly, ready to ask what any of this had to do with ordering coffee. After reading the look of irritation on the older man's face, he thought better of it.

"You aren't too thrilled about my being assigned to you," he mumbled instead.

"I'm getting too old, sport." Stickley probed his omelet with his fork and sighed, losing interest. "It ain't you any more than it was the last six of your kind. It's like getting a new puppy every couple months. Just about the time he learns to shit on the newspaper, they take him away and give you another one. Some asshole in Washington got the idea wedged sideways up there that Carl Stickley can teach a kid the ropes like nobody else."

God, Carl missed the old days. It had been different once, back when they'd sent him kids like Henry Bueno. Young guys with saavy, guts, and immense physical prowess. Bueno, a California kid, had been the best of them all. The ideal protégé. After nearly twenty years, Henry'd gotten out. Stickley wondered if it was envy he felt when he thought about him. Maybe it was at that. Henry was off on some beach somewhere now. He probably didn't even *know* any assholes like Scott Tanner.

"He's moving," Tanner announced under his breath.

As Jack Terranova rose from the table gas rumbled up from his gut and erupted in a soft, cheek-cushioned belch. This food down here didn't agree with him, even if the beef was supposed to be some of the best. He strolled now, thinking about the two spooks and how he was going to deal with them. Diego had been adamant that he arrive at the contact point without being followed. There was no way to know whether these two were working in tandem with another team, switching off. They were the only ones he'd spotted so

4

far. Still, the only thing that made any sense was to draw them out somewhere and make *sure* they weren't being backed up . . . at least for the moment. That was how Jack dealt; in moments.

"Too hot" is what they'd termed his condition.

He was moving back across the river at a nice, easy gait. Ahead, the Sexta widened out into the city's huge central plaza.

Thirty-seven contract kills on the eastern seaboard. A dozen more scattered around the middle of the country. Then there was the stint with the Frisco boys in their war with the Chinese. Even a pair of hits in Hong Kong. And now, after thirty-three years of his life spent in the rackets, they tell him he's too hot.

Retire, Jack. They'd offered him the pad in West Palm. A cut of some local action; primarily a beer distributorship. For what? To get hemorrhoids from sitting with his thumb up his ass. Play some golf and maybe shuffleboard in a few years. Like shit. Six months without a contract and he'd been ready to stick up a Seven Eleven just to get some kick back in his life. And then there was his wife, Maria. She'd taken to the life of fun and sun like a politician to bullshit. His daughter Carmen was hanging around with some green-haired freak who wore earrings. Short of murdering his loving family, Jack's options had seemed severely limited.

Then Diego Cardona showed up. Jack was down at the warehouse, masquerading as an upstanding citizen. He was on the loading dock checking a couple hundred cases of imported suds when this skinny spic with mean eyes asked to talk to him in private. That was a month ago.

The proposition was simple. Cardona had a man he wanted killed in South America. In return for the service, Jack would be paid the sum of three hundred thousand American dollars and provided with a beautiful prostitute for the duration of the operation. Jack understood cash and he understood broads. Diego explained that he would soon be in a position also to be most generous with extensive properties that "rightfully belonged" to his family. Jack shrugged. This little weasel seemed strange, but if he could produce the green and a nice little piece of ass, hell, it was all the excuse a man needed to get out from under Maria, Carmen, and the green-haired freak for a couple weeks.

5

Christopher Newman

Last night, Cardona's prostitute had appeared at the door of Jack's hotel room. She was no older than his daughter; slender, graceful, with high cheekbones and pouting lips. He had forgotten what it felt like to lay with a young piece like that; body so firm and tight. And this wasn't some whore with the meter ticking. The young girl stayed all night. She was still there when he woke up, smiling at him and taunting him to prove that what he'd shown her before was no fluke. "Too hot," they'd said. By God, he'd shown her how hot he was. Anna. He let it roll around in his mouth and off his tongue as he stepped into the shade of a bookstall and bought a map of the vicinity. No one he killed had ever meant anything to him. It was a job. If he didn't do it, some other, less talented slob would—and reap the reward. Twenty to thirty grand, generally. In this new arena, the ante had simply been upped. This fish had to be big. For three hundred grand, it made sense that whacking him would probably create some nasty ripples. He didn't need Mutt and Jeff back there, complicating things. It was time to think about clearing the way.

Henry Bueno was anchored about a mile off the Big Sur coast. A good-sized swell lifted the boat up and down, high enough to see Ginger's bright yellow marker buoy bobbing on the green sea about twenty yards off, and then down again into splendid isolation. The sparkling California sun beat on his back as he toyed with the auxiliary engine, his hands blackened with grime and his mind at peace with the beauty of another slow, lazy day. Ginger was down there somewhere, blowing bubbles and studying giant kelp. She was an oceanographer, the delicate ecostructure of the continental shelf was her passionate obsession. She'd already been up twice for fresh tanks and was well into her third hour of exploration. Henry didn't mind. In fact, he thought their interests on these frequent forays were perfectly in tune. She could pursue her vocation with utter intensity, and he was left up here on the surface, the whole world to himself. Him and the *Mañana*.

Bueno had named the boat *Mañana* to remember a time when he had actively wondered if tomorrow would ever come. A time when he could finally release the tail of the snarling tiger. Try to forget; return to the ocean he'd grown up on and loved.

6

The event that finally shook him loose was the death of his uncle. Clinton Bueno expired of a massive coronary while Henry was in São Paulo. Word reached him six days after the fact. Henry and his sister Linda had been raised on the family's coastal California farm by this iron-willed bachelor. The two of them were orphans whose mother had died in childbirth and father in the Pacific theater. Clinton had ideas of his nephew's eventually taking the reins there at the ranch. He was the last of a line that had farmed the rich central coast lowlands for seven generations. Henry, on the other hand, had no stomach for contemporary agribusiness. Mechanization, expansion, petrochemicals, labor unions. As a child of the Cold War, Henry had bitten hard into the apple of hope extended by the youthful and exhuberant Jack Kennedy. His early dreams ignored the five square miles of broccoli, cauliflower, artichokes and brussels sprouts. He was going to march off to a glorious life of helping the disadvantaged of the world in Kennedy's new Peace Corps. Times changed. He never dreamed of the debacle that was Vietnam. But even when the going got rough, young Henry clung to the ideal, asking what he could do for his country. He ended up doing *plenty* for his country, most of it brutal and ugly.

Clinton died and Henry came home. He found his sister Linda forced to shoulder the entire burden of grief. She didn't blame him for missing the funeral. Long absences were in the nature of his work.

The family attorney read Clinton's will the morning after Henry's arrival. The estate was divided equally between Linda and him. Most of the assets were nonliquid; the cattle ranch in the San Joaquin Valley, the vegetable farms in Watsonville and the Salinas Valley, the apple orchards here in Corralitos where the big house stood. There was also considerable capital invested in stocks, bonds, and precious metals, close to nine million dollars worth. The capital of Bueno Inc. was a working fund, enabling the organization to avoid bank loans and exorbitant interest rates in times of strife. Unless Henry chose to cash in his chips, the only income available to him from the estate existed in the form of a salaried job.

Linda's husband Larry Amati had worked his way up through the corporation to become executive vice president in charge of operations. Clinton Bueno had entrusted him with his day-to-day business as well as a primary heir's hand in marriage. Henry hardly knew the man, but he knew that it would be his uncle's wish to see a hundred and forty years of Bueno sweat and tears live on. Linda and Larry Amati had three boys who were all working in one phase or another of the business. The ranches were really theirs now.

Henry found himself alone in the big Victorian farmhouse overlooking Corralitos. The ghosts of his uncle and father were present in that place, and it was hard to see himself fitting into their vision of the world. He had given all he could for his country, laying his life on the line countless times. Perhaps there were other priorities. Taking time to discover them was the only way he could see to progress. Maybe mañana *had* finally come.

The boat, a high-aspect forty-three-footer, had been designed by a guy down in San Diego for open ocean racing. Sometime later, it had been outfitted for comfort. Henry bought it shortly after returning home for good and used it as a second home when he wasn't struggling to seem useful to his brother-in-law. He wasn't sure that Larry Amati didn't find him more of a nuisance than anything else. Linda, on the other hand, had explained the situation clearly enough. Her brother was half-owner of all the family's assets. They needed his support. Without it, Bueno Inc. might well end up on the auction block. Her husband could learn to live with her brother cluttering up the corporate offices. Nobody said a word when Henry went off to sleep on his boat and spent days idly sailing the ocean and bay.

Now, as he tinkered with the boat's auxiliary engine, sweat glistened on the hard muscles of his bronzed back. Six months had passed since he'd resigned from the "Company." At thirty-nine, the scars of three bullet wounds, a long knife slash across his left shoulder blade, and the gnarled knuckles of both hands attested to how close the rangy, heavy-framed Californian had come to missing his boat. The way the brass at Langley chose to view it, he was getting out at the peak of his effectiveness. Too early by a dozen years. The way Henry saw it, counting his Navy SEAL time spanning three Vietnam tours, he'd been a government intelligence agent committed to front-line duty for seventeen years. Plenty long enough.

The powers in Washington, masterminding their intelligence game, saw this gung-ho commando as a dream come true. His slightly watered-down but authentic Hispanic heritage especially appealed to them. On top of that, he was legitimately trilingual. His mother, a Frenchwoman from Lyon, had insisted that her children learn and speak both Spanish and French in the home. French had served Bueno well in Vietnam, and Spanish, more recently, in Latin America.

They'd recruited him out of Southeast Asia because of this remarkable array of ideal qualifications. Marxism now reared its ugly head on the American mainland. Bueno, posing as a French soldier of fortune, carried a passport bearing his mother's maiden name, to remove the stigma that would attach to a dirty gringo. He ostensibly hunted exotic snakes in the jungle lowlands. In truth, he moved as an elusive force, cloaked in mystery. He haunted the back alleys and jungles of Central and South America. Santiago, La Paz, Quito, Cali, Barranquilla, Cartagena, Managua, Tegucigalpa, Guatemala City, and on. Then, six months ago, he vanished.

Bueno squinted at the sun and figured that Ginger would be coming up soon. The new set of points was installed, and the auxiliary engine was retimed. He stood, all six-one, two hundred pounds of him, stretched, and moved to smear his hands with waterless cleaner.

Ginger, a big, rawboned blonde, was already on board and stripping off her neoprene wet suit when Henry emerged from the galley.

"How's the vegetation?" he asked. She was having trouble with one arm of the jacket, and he stepped over to help her out of it.

"The urchin population is really down. Did you see the otters? There must be half a dozen of them. Way out here!"

Bueno stooped to pick up her exhausted tank and rack it alongside the two others. "That's what I like about you. A girl who can get excited about slimy green weeds and rodents."

"They're not rodents, and *you* might be a little more appreciative if you'd just let me take you down there with me."

"You've seen one glop of seaweed, you've seen them all." He slid an arm around her. His fingers traced the taut skin of her bare waist and hip. She was twelve years his

9

junior, lean-muscled and almost self-conscious of her face and build.

She smiled at him, rumpled his hair, and leaned to stick her tongue in his ear. He squirmed away and scowled.

"I don't know, lady. You don't look like you've got the strength left to match any of your big ideas."

Ginger regarded him calmly, her clear blue eyes staring directly into his own.

She reached behind her back to unhook the strap of her top. "Try me," she dared him.

TWO

Piece by piece, Jack Terranova gathered the components of the .22-caliber Walther GSP match pistol from compartments secreted in his belongings. With a soft cloth soaked in gun oil, he went over each component, scrutinizing it in detail. Each was cleaned until it shone with a dull luster, not a speck of grime escaping his expert eye. The assembly process was swift by comparison, completed with a thorough check of the action.

Removing a raincoat from his hang-up, he carefully ripped the stitching from the collar and shook a series of .22 long-rifle bullets into the palm of his hand. From his shaving kit, he extracted two five-shot clips from beneath the vinyl lining. Each bullet had been scored with a deep X in its soft lead nose. One by one, he pushed them into the spring-loaded magazine mechanisms, the remaining ammunition going into his trousers pocket. With one clip shoved home ahead of the trigger guard, he chambered the first round, engaged the safety, and secured the weapon in a holster strapped to his ankle. He was ready now.

The map indicated a little town named Pance, situated about a thousand feet above the Valle de Cauca in the nearby Farallones. These mountains, observed from the city on those rare occasions when an enshrouding mist parted, were awe-inspiring in their wild ruggedness. Perfect for his little game of fox and hounds. He had already told the girl, Anna, to find them another place for that night. He would not be returning to this hotel again.

Downstairs, in the hotel garage, Terranova wedged his bulk behind the wheel of a tiny, rented Renault. Earlier, he had made sure that the nose tackle and his boyfriend were watching while he rented the damn thing and later, while he parked it here. A quick scan of the undercarriage revealed a tiny transmitter planted alongside the gas tank. Perfect. He left the garage, confident that as he drove south and west from the city the G-men would never be far behind. At an intersection a block from the hotel, he pulled to the curb, and Anna jumped in.

The smog-belching congestion of evening traffic began to abate as the little Renault climbed into the foothills rising above the valley. After turning off the main road south, their way became steep and twisted very suddenly. The underpowered car labored with it, engine growling furiously at a high rpm. All the while, a gray Jeep CJ maintained its distance a couple of turns back. Parallel to the road, a tributary to the Rio Cauca rushed down from the heights ahead, white water surging over the boulder-strewn streambed.

The little town of Pance itself wasn't much. There were a number of open-air picnic and dancing pavilions catering to valley weekenders. Several *bodegas* lined the main drag, selling cold sodas, beer, cigarettes, and *chincherones*. On that day, a Tuesday, the place was like a ghost town as the Renault threaded clear of potholes in the pavement and strained up the mountain.

Jack hadn't been sure of exactly how he intended to proceed until he began noticing the little weekend *fincas* tucked away in overgrowth on either side of the ravine. Some were obviously occupied, but most were shuttered up, with no cars in the drives and gates chained shut. One of these would be perfect. The gray Jeep following them had dropped back out of sight, and was obviously relying on the transmitter signal. Jack would select one house that was particularly secluded, and then the fun could begin.

The deep gorge narrowed considerably up here. The adjacent hillsides were thick with a jungle profusion of flowering trees, wild orchids, and roaring water. Every couple hundred yards a waterfall tumbled down over the cliffs above to join the swollen stream.

The house Terranova selected met his criteria perfectly. Set back about twenty yards from the road, it was situated all but beneath a twenty-five-foot waterfall. The roar of the water, mixed with the screeching of birds, would effectively screen out any incidental noise. After slowing to give the place a good once-over, Jack turned the car into the drive and nosed it up to the gate.

"C'mon, baby. Let's move it," he told Anna.

The girl opened the door and climbed out, following him.

"What are we doing, Señor Jack?"

"Exactly what I tell you."

They slipped into bushes alongside the house and out of sight. Anna watched in fascination as he removed a set of picks from his pocket and expertly jimmied the latch of the wide, rough-hewn wooden door.

"Get your clothes off," he ordered once they were inside.

Together, they stood in the middle of the *finca*'s single, low-ceilinged room. The place was rustically furnished. Thick dust lay on every surface. Jack hurried to one corner and grabbed the one double bed, pulling it to the middle of the room in front of a window as Anna began to comply. Outside, he heard the engine of an approaching Jeep drop to idle before quickly picking up again and moving on past.

Carl Stickley wondered what the hell the man was up to. It didn't make sense that he was taking the good-looking little broad up here to screw her when he had a perfectly acceptable hotel room in town. He doubted that Terranova was making a meet, after leading them right to the spot. The whole thing had a fishy smell to it. This guy was dangerous as hell, no matter what Langley said about passive action. Just in case, he'd told Tanner to maintain his distance as they followed him up the mountain, letting the tracking device do the work.

And then there it was, Terranova's rented Renault nosed up a drive and parked against a gate. The kid reacted without thinking, removing his foot from the accelerator to slow and peer at the house beyond.

"Keep moving!" the older agent snapped. "Jesus fucking Christ! What *did* they teach you? If the son of a bitch had any doubts that we were following him, he sure doesn't now."

"You think he's made us?"

Stickley looked thoroughly disgusted. "Yesterday," he told him, shaking his head. "Park it up about two hundred yards."

"What do you think he's up to?"

"He's dicking with our heads, sport."

"What for? What's he want?"

"I expect that's exactly what he wants us to come find out."

Tanner pulled in alongside the road, set the brake, and switched off the ignition. There was suddenly a strange sort of quiet, birds and roaring water creating a din of white noise.

"And you're going up there?"

"More or less," Stickley replied. "Not into the house, but just to check around. If they're inside, then they're welcome to whatever they can find to amuse themselves. I'm just going to run up above here and make sure this dump isn't fronting for something we can't see, further back."

"What do you want me to do?"

Stickley removed his little Beretta Model 84 from its ankle holster, chambered a round with a tug on the manual slide, and then returned it.

"Give me twenty minutes. You sit tight."

"That's it? You don't want me to back you up?"

Stickley looked him straight in the eye. "Trust me, sport." He opened the door and climbed out. Seconds later, he'd disappeared into the undergrowth.

Carl Stickley could move quickly and noiselessly through jungle terrain. God knew he'd trained so many men in the art on the Philippine island of Mindanao through the Indochina years that he himself had become a virtual master. Of all of them, only Bueno had eventually surpassed him, but that kid was born to be a jungle fighter. A natural. Most of it was concentration. Focusing the mind so sharply that a hyperalertness resulted. Every sense came into play. Stickley remembered Bueno swearing that he could even *taste* movements in the jungle air. He missed having a man with such a sixth sense as backup.

The little bungalow was below him to his right as he made his way up along the steep embankment. With each step he paused to scrutinize foliage for bent leaves and the ground underfoot for unusual disturbance—anything that might indicate human passage up this hill. If he moved in a broad arc above the house, his path would eventually terminate at the waterfall he'd seen from the road. Already, he could occasionally glimpse white water through the trees.

Stickley felt a wave of contentment wash over him, in spite of himself. With no family and only a very few close relationships, he felt as much at home here as any place on earth. Carl knew that, unlike his pal Henry, he would never leave South America until they carried him out. The deep, heavy odor of decay was perfume to him the way it mixed with the sweetness of jungle flowers. Everything was perpetually painted this vibrant green. The warmth was womblike.

The .22-calibre dumdum bullet smashed into his temple and mushroomed as it plowed through soft brain matter. For Carl Stickley, the lights went out before his senses could register comprehension, terror, or pain.

Eight yards from where the nose tackle lay convulsing in the throes of death, Jack Terranova lay flat on his belly. The critically tuned sights of his silenced Walther were no longer trained on the target's temple. One long-rifle slug had done the job, lead peeled back from the point where the X had been scored. It dragged brain matter with it as it slammed into the opposite side of the skull. The bullet's velocity was so dissipated by the internal havoc it wreaked that it no longer had the power to push through the bone it was embedded in. Instantaneous death, contained all nice and neat. One tiny crimson hole.

In his sixteen years as the East Coast's most effective and sought-after shooter, Terranova had, above all else, learned one thing. If a man could train himself in the patience of Mohammed, the mountain would most certainly come to him. Because he was not the least interested in combat or any other sort of confrontation, a combination of careful planning and stoic patience had always served him well.

Scott Tanner sat drumming his fingers on the steering wheel. His mind had wandered back to the young whore he'd met in the hotel bar after Stickley went to bed the previous night. Back at Princeton, he'd never once paid for sex. Since then, through graduate school at Georgetown, recruitment by the Company, and training, he'd been living with his girlfriend, and he figured that D.C. was crawling with so many horny broads that a hooker'd go broke there. Linda was a Congressional press aide with a pretty fair pair of lungs on her and what amounted to a near-paranoid eagerness to always keep her CIA agent satisfied. Linda wasn't all that secure. The way she saw it, competition was swarming like piranha out there. Still, she wasn't very imaginative. Sex with her had started to get stale lately. Linda was just a bit too . . . conventional.

The little number he'd picked up last night was a different story altogether. He discovered that he liked that detached, almost bored proficiency as she undertook to satisfy him. Unlike Linda, she hadn't brought anything to the act but pure, bottom-line sex. No visions of engagement rings dancing in her head. No wanting him to assure her of how much he cared for her. The freedom he experienced excited him. He'd never let himself go like that. She even left him to sleep the rest of the night alone in his own bed. Tanner had never gotten used to sharing a bed with someone else. Not the presence, nor being touched in the middle of the night. He enjoyed being sent out on the road now because he could sleep by himself. This experience of getting his end away and being left to drift pleasantly off into his own oblivion—that was something new and wonderful. He hoped she would be in the bar again tonight.

He checked his watch. Carl had been gone for twenty minutes. Shit. Now what was he supposed to do? Strange fucking bird, this guy. Thought he was Sergeant Rock or something. Back at the Company headquarters in Langley, they'd told him he was lucky to pull an assignment with a man of Stickley's caliber and experience. So far, all the man had done for him was make him feel like he was walking around in two left shoes.

Twenty-*five* minutes. What had he found up there? Probably had circled down and was watching the overweight mobster screw his brains out with the good-looking little Latin babe. God damn, she was particularly hot, that one, though the entire country appeared to be full of them. One of the guys at Langley contended that all these broads had such great asses because they were dancing all the time. Everybody. Every night. Dancing their asses off. Tanner liked the image . . . and if that was what did it, then the rest of the world ought to be dancing, too, he figured.

At thirty minutes, Scott Tanner was seriously concerned. He

let another five go by and then slid from behind the wheel of the Jeep to steal back down along the road to the house.

Jack Terranova observed the college boy's progress from the cover of high ground above the road. Just as he had been able to predict the nose tackle's cautious approach, he now watched with amusement as the kid went directly for the second bait as if he were following a map. Even as Jack gloated, he shook his head in disgust. This jerk *deserved* to die.

When the opportunity, as planned, presented itself, the hit man used the cover of the *finca* to adjust position quickly. A moment later, as he hunched down, obscured by ground foliage and a large fallen tree, the young Ivy Leaguer appeared along the verge of the drive. With a small automatic clenched tightly in one fist, he moved through the trees to the waterfall and then up alongside it, parallel to the house. What he saw going on inside stopped him cold in his tracks. Through an open window, a very naked Anna could be observed writhing in apparent ecstacy, on her knees and straddling someone out of view. Terranova watched Tanner swallow hard and press forward for a clearer view. Inside the bungalow, Anna was doing a real job of it, rolling her head around, moaning, and grabbing her breasts to rub the nipples.

Jack eased his bulk from concealment. He was now directly to the left of and six yards behind the engrossed young agent. Easy money. The nice thing about the .22 was its superb accuracy. In the correct hands, it could kill just as surely as a heavier caliber weapon, but with less kick. If necessary, Jack knew he could squeeze off a round and then rethread the needle inside a cool second. A bigger, less accurate weapon couldn't provide the same luxury. Calmly, trying to suppress a grin, he cleared his throat with a loud cough.

The surprised youngster whirled and froze, his mouth wide in terror. Jack put a single shot in his open gob, ruining a set of perfectly straight, Ivy League teeth.

That night, after his ambush of the two CIA agents, Terranova and his Anna traveled further south. They stayed at a little *pensione* in a quiet back street of the pretty town of Popayan, and they made love in a large, carved mahogany bed. With the recent action, Jack felt more alive than he had in months. He was back in the groove and moving ahead. He swept Anna along with him, crushing her to his barrel chest and driving into her again and again as she writhed beneath him. Never once did she complain as she bore the brunt of his wild enthusiasm without a whimper. When he came, it was in a frenzied, almost convulsive surge that left him so spent that he could do nothing afterward but collapse beside her.

The face lying next to him there in the gloom was serene and impassive. He reached out to touch her lips with his fingertips and then dragged his hand slowly down her neck, chest, and hard, flat belly.

"You are some piece," he murmured. "You do me right. I like that in a woman."

Her head turned and her eyes probed his. Her fingers reached to work deep into the matted hair of his chest. Planting a palm, she pushed herself to her knees and crouched beside him on all fours, dipped her tongue, and licked his belly. Hot breath moved down through his pubic hair to where what was left of his own heat lay lolling to one side. Slowly, the pouting lips sucked him into her mouth, the flickering tongue caressing and urging him. She couldn't want more, he thought. It wasn't possible. Then again, even as he lay watching her, she climbed above and straddled him, pushing his spent enthusiasm between her legs. A smile of defiance crossed her lips.

After a night at her place, up the bay in Capitola, Henry and Ginger hit the road before dawn and were back out on the water by sunrise. They'd taken advantage of a twelve-knot breeze to leave the bay and sail up the coast. There were several sizable giant kelp beds up there that Ginger wanted to compare with her own test area between Point Lobos and Big Sur to the south.

They returned to the Moss Landing yacht harbor in late afternoon. Henry worked on the foredeck now, hosing it down, while Ginger cased samples for transport to the marine lab. All up and down the dock, boat owners were busy with last-minute preparations for weekend sailing. Radios blared, rigging clanked against aluminum masts in the breeze, and voices conversed enthusiastically about weather, ocean conditions, and equipment.

The high-pressure stream from Bueno's nozzle quit abruptly as he straightened from his task and frowned. Two men were approaching up the dock, headed in his direction. There could be no mistaking who they were or where they came from. Erect in bearing, totally out of place in their summer-weight suits, but still managing to appear both confident and ominous.

Ginger had just emerged on deck and was now looking at him curiously as he slowly coiled the hose and stepped aft. The two men stopped alongside as Henry moved to meet them.

"Permission to come aboard?" the older of the two asked. He was perhaps fifty-five, with salt-and-pepper gray hair gone snowy white at the temples. His speech was softly accented with a hint of the near South.

"How you doing, Cam?" Henry asked, waving him ahead. "You're a long way from home."

"We've got to talk, Henry," the man called Cam told him. He eyed Ginger in her French-cut one-piece, not missing a curve. "In private."

Bueno shook his head. "There's nothing I'd want to talk about that couldn't be said right here. I'm a private citizen now, buddy. The sun's shining, and I don't give a rat's ass who they've got managing the Orioles."

"Carl Stickley was taken down last night."

Henry felt his body stiffen. "That's hitting below the belt."

"Can we talk now?"

Bueno turned to Ginger. "Sorry. This'll only take a sec." He led the two men below and secured the hatch.

Cam Stebbins and the second man surveyed the informal chaos that was the agent once called the Snake Hunter's new life. Bunk unmade. Ginger's tanks racked against a teak bulkhead. Dirty dishes in the tiny galley basin. Books, charts, and paperwork stacked everywhere. Henry cleared some of it aside and invited them to sit.

"The lady's an oceanographer," he explained, waving at all the paper.

"Nice-looking woman," Stebbins acknowledged. "You seem relaxed."

Henry ignored him. "What's this about Carl, and who's your friend here?" Stebbins had been his boss, running him in the Southern Hemisphere before being promoted to deputy director. They didn't necessarily like each other.

Stebbins glanced at his associate. He was a distinguished, no-nonsense type with jet-black hair and piercing blue eyes. To that point, he'd taken a back seat. Henry couldn't help noticing the cut of his suit. Hand-tailored. British styling. He spoke now for the first time since arriving.

"Ted Latham. I work the Latin American liaison post now."

Bueno's reaction was one of mild interest. If he hadn't chosen to throw over the Company for private life, this guy would be his new boss.

"Have you ever heard of a Jack Terranova, Mr. Bueno?"

Henry came up blank. "Can't say as I have. Not by that name."

"He was a contract assassin for East Coast organized crime interests. There is no reason you *should* have heard of him. His work was almost exclusively domestic, with some incidental Hong Kong activity several years ago." Latham removed a filtered cigarette from a silver case. "Smoke?" he asked. When Henry nodded, the Latin liaison thumbed the wheel of a chrome Zippo engraved with Airborne insignia. "Fifteen months ago," Latham continued, "the people Terranova worked for retired him to the Miami area. West Palm Beach. To that point, keeping tabs on him was an FBI matter. The only interest we ever had in him was in relation to the two Hong Kong murders he most likely was responsible for. They were prominent Tongs, involved in a territorial dispute in the trafficking of heroin. Then, three days ago, he flew to Cali, Colombia after being contacted by a man the FBI believe to be an agent of the Sandinistas. His name is Diego Cardona, and he is also suspected of running a cocaine operation to finance the Nicaraguan purchase of weapons from the Eastern Bloc."

Bueno now shook his head. "That name is familiar, but the guy I'm remembering wasn't any Sandinista. He was a notorious major in Anastasio's secret police."

Latham blinked and frowned. "Perhaps he is the same man and has gotten a better offer. Allegiances in that part of the world are a curious thing, as I am sure you know."

"Oh, I know," Henry grunted. "What's all this got to do with Carl Stickley?"

"We put him, and a new kid he was breaking in, on Terranova when he arrived down there. No specific orders. Just to keep an eye on him and see if they could determine what he was up to. Late last night, the owner of a house in the mountains outside Cali called the police when he discovered he'd been broken into. They found the kid, Scott Tanner, in the bushes just off the drive, then located their Jeep up the road. They found Carl this morning. Each man was shot with a single .22 dumdum in the head. Real pro stuff. Knowing the history of your relationship with Carl, we thought you'd want to know."

"Sure you did," Henry shot back. "What's the rest of it?"

Now the older man, Stebbins, stepped in, nodding. "Right. Carl left instructions that if ever he were to be taken out in the field, you were to get this." He handed Bueno a sealed, legal-size envelope.

Henry accepted the letter. Inside, his guts were churning. As his SEAL commander in Vietnam and the man who had recruited him into the company, Carl Stickley had been like a father to him. Because of his hard-nosed discipline and exhaustive training, Henry had survived where many others had perished. As a green junior officer, fresh out of the academy, he might have been dog food for this elite unit of commandos if Carl Stickley hadn't forced him to become better than all of them. Later, when Henry took two slugs in an ambush in Bolivia, it was Carl who'd humped him over thirty miles of wilderness to a doctor.

He stared out a port at Ginger as she stacked her specimen boxes dockside. It would take a good man to get the drop on Carl. He remembered his former commander laughing when he'd told him he wasn't coming back, that he was going to buy a boat and become a bum. Old Carl'd said it wouldn't take him much practice, at least the bum part.

The deputy director pointed at the envelope in Henry's hand.

"We trust that if that has any bearing on national security, you will do what is right."

Bueno nodded, slipped a finger under the flap, and tore it open. Inside was a single page of notepaper, scrawled on in Carl's hand.

YOU'RE THE ONLY ONE I CAN TRUST TO GET
THE BASTARD WHO DID ME, SPORT. HATE TO

SPOIL ALL THE FUN YOU'RE HAVING PICKIN'
BUTT, BUT A DEAL'S A DEAL.

C.

His hands trembled as he read. The sneaky shit had played
the one hand he knew his old pupil couldn't ignore. It was a
perverse, after-the-fact insurance policy. They *had* made such
a deal one drunken night.

Latham and Stebbins stood adjacent, consumed with curiosity. Henry wondered if they'd already opened the thing, if
they knew they'd just delivered a mob hitter's death warrant.

"What is it?" Latham asked.

Henry glanced at him absently, creased the note, and shook
his head. "A marker an old friend just called."

THREE

It was cool along the edge of Monterey Bay as Henry Bueno pushed the old Healey ragtop south on California One from Ginger's little place in Capitola. The late summer fog had rolled in heavy around sunset and still lurked with the approach of dawn. It hadn't been easy to peer one last time at the peace in her slumbering face and then steal off into the darkness. There was no hope of explaining to Ginger what he was going to do next, what he *had* to do. His past was something he'd kept hidden from her, simply failing to explain the scars on his torso and the moods he would sometimes slip into. She surely had her suspicions, but casual imaginings could never approach the many sinister truths—not where she and most of her wonderfully benign kind came from.

The yacht harbor was all but dead at that hour. The Healey purred as he pulled to a stop between the painted stripes of his assigned space. Two or three fishing boats were being prepared to motor out onto the open ocean and join sister craft already engaged in the commerce of snagging snapper, cod, and maybe even a few salmon for the local markets. A tough way to make a living. The skippers actually making a buck tended to journey further north, staying out for a month and more. Henry wandered down the docks until he reached the *Mañana*, moored low in her slip, rigging snicking just audibly in a light breeze. On board, he moved directly below. There was a gooseneck clamp lamp over the chart table. He switched it on, stooped to reach back below the table, and worked the combination on a small, concealed safe. From it he removed Carl's brief letter and a metal strongbox. Both these things went onto the surface of the table before he pulled up his stool and sat hunched over it.

Something was wrong. Not with what sat before him. These things were fine. The contact man of Carl's alleged killer was *all* wrong. Henry hadn't let on everything he knew about Diego Cardona to Ted Latham and Cameron Stebbins. He hadn't let on *anything* he knew about the shifts occurring in the cocaine power structure servicing North America. These had never been his area of concern. But on the other hand, he couldn't have operated where and how he had without hearing scuttlebutt of significance. The Sandinistas, as a political entity, certainly had their faults, but cocaine trafficking wasn't among them. There was most definitely a power struggle occurring at that very moment, but the players were a more sinister bunch than Nicaraguan President Danny Ortega and his pals. Certain Colombian drug lords were now engaged in a battle for more than just their economic lives. New players in the game were intent on depriving them of breath as well. Henry knew from fairly reliable sources that prominent among these new players were certain disenfranchised Nicaraguans. Economically depressed Central American areas, notably Mexico, were known to be looking the other way as new smuggling power bases were established. If at least part of the Company's diagnosis was correct, then Diego Cardona, political affiliation aside, was involved in the happy-dust trade and had traveled to Miami to engage himself a very heavy hitter named Terranova. Old Carl hadn't copped to the seriousness of whatever was going down and had paid the highest price. It was time to determine just what it was that Diego Cardona was up to. Mob shooters rarely pulled the trigger for the pure therapeutic joy of it. The good ones—and this Terranova was supposed to be *very* good—performed their services for envelopes tightly packed with green.

Where to start was always a question in this sort of situation. Carl Stickley had been killed outside Cali, Colombia after the hitter was contacted by an expatriate Nicaraguan in Miami. Cali was a notorious cocaine capital, and cocaine, in connection with Cardona, had been mentioned by name. Henry ran through the mental data banks, looking for sources of information that could be useful to him. There was one possibility that came to mind. Prominent in the Cali drug culture was a certain trafficker who had once been proclaimed to be an enemy of the American way of life by the drug enforcement apparatus. This very same villain owed Henry a favor.

Henry addressed an envelope with Ginger's name on it. He wrote out a check in the amount of ten thousand dollars, slipped it into the envelope, licked the flap, and sealed it. His lover's passion for giant kelp and its habitat could often get expensive. There were scuba tanks constantly in need of charging. Boat trips. The constant flow of grant proposals and unnumbered rejections on the return tides. Ginger's enterprise was perceived as a completely noble one, but the excuses from funding organizations were always the same. The money simply wasn't there. Bueno licked a stamp, affixed it to the corner of the letter, and prayed to God that the thing would pass unhindered through the Postal Service maze. Either way, he knew the big, beautiful blonde would never understand. Henry wondered if he himself understood.

He opened the strongbox and lifted a Walther P-5 wrapped in a soft cloth from within. It was the first time he'd touched the gun since locking it in the safe a week after buying the boat. The weight was eerily familiar in his hands. All three clips stowed alongside in the strongbox were full. Quickly, he disassembled the weapon, inspecting each component with a practiced eye. Fitting them back together was something he could have done blindfolded, even after the layoff. One clip went into the butt of the gun and two, along with it, into his jacket pocket. He fingered a four-inch noise suppressor from the bottom of the box and dropped it into the pocket as well.

There were two passports that he now removed from the safe. One was a standard American job identifying him accurately. The second bore his photo likeness but named him as Henri Riberac, French national. His occupation, described in French on the inside of the front cover, was that of an exotic snakeskin hunter, the skins of many jungle snakes being a lucrative trade item. Hunting these snakes, in possession of the proper government permits, allowed him to travel unchallenged through many regions. Within a day, Henry Bueno would become Riberac again.

As Riberac, Henry traveled light. He carried a well-stocked knapsack, a Finnish *Tikka*, over-under "turkey-gun" with barrels and actions to accept both twelve-gauge shotgun loads and .222-caliber Remington rifle bullets, and the 9mm Walther sidearm. Around his waist he strapped a zippered belt containing twelve Canadian Maple Leaf gold coins. The knapsack and rifle, stowed in an overhead locker, were left perpetually at the ready by force of habit. With the knapsack shouldered and the rifle case in hand, Bueno ventured above, secured the hatch, and carried the gear to his car. Most international flights left the area from San Francisco, but Henry was headed south to the Monterey airport. There were any number of ways to embark on a journey below the border, many of them beneath the scrutiny of any government's customs operation. Over the years, Henry Bueno, a/k/a Henri Riberac, had learned them all. Today he was hoping he might find a fully fueled Beechcraft Bonanza. The single-engine plane was a true beauty, and it had been some time since he'd had the pleasure of flying one.

Cam Stebbins was an astonishingly gullible idiot, but Ted Latham, under the circumstances, couldn't very well mind. Some of Ted's affiliations within government weren't exactly as "official" as the deputy director's were. Congress had moved to all but hogtie the U.S. intelligence community, and a certain clandestine association of concerned patriots had united to see that the integrity of American intelligence would be preserved at all cost. Cameron Stebbins was not a member of this anointed conspiracy. He was too old-school to be thoroughly reliable. On the other hand, he and Latham had a very solid relationship, and he was more than just willing to receive the junior man's reports on political activity in the South and Central American fields. He was useful to the concerned patriots because his reputation in other branches of government fairly glowed with level-headed esteem. The patriots regularly counted on Latham to channel information with the "right slant" to the deputy director.

All of this, more or less, was going through Latham's head as he wandered down the third-floor corridor of the Waldorf Astoria in New York City. The members of the anointed conspiracy were good; perhaps the best from the Company, State Department, National Security Council staff, FBI special units, and several other relevant walks of life. Because of who they were as a group, things happened when they were pulling the strings. A natural satisfaction arose from his knowledge of this.

Luis Ecchevarria answered the door to 304 after the brief, agreed-upon knock. New York had become their preferred meeting location because of the easy accessibility from both Miami and the District of Columbia. Ecchevarria was a good twenty years Latham's junior, but they had one very important thing in common. Their fathers had been classmates at West Point, creating a bond that went deeper than any outsider knew. When Anastasio Somoza's government fell in 1979, the powerful Ecchevarria family escaped to Florida, where the aging patriarch had died of a broken heart. This young, disenfranchised man now occupying a two-hundred-dollar single in the Waldorf was a captain in the Somosista wing of the politically ambiguous Contra resistance.

"What the hell's that guinea son of a bitch doing, shooting *our* people?" Latham demanded as the door clicked closed.

Luis looked as though he expected invective from this angle and moved to parry it as diplomatically as his limited skill allowed.

"Don Diego asks that you attempt to understand. This was something out of his control."

Latham shook his head. "He'd better get it *under* control."

"Yes, señor," Luis agreed wholeheartedly. "I am here to assure you of one thing. We still proceed as agreed. The killing of two CIA men was something unrelated and very much regretted."

Latham, knowing his control was limited, sighed and moved to collapse into a chair. Things had been hot around Langley the past few days. An agent getting whacked in the field was something that raised more than a few eyebrows. An agent of Carl Stickley's experience and caliber getting killed *really* started some gears turning. Cam Stebbins's committed endeavor to deliver the dead man's last wish to Henry Bueno had sent members of the anointed conspiracy heading for liquor cabinets all over D.C. This was a real monkey wrench in the works. If anyone could queer everything they'd been working on for more than a year, it was this well-oiled machine of their own miserable creation. Airports all over the country were being watched, but Latham knew damn well that Bueno was already down there somewhere, flat disappeared and moving like a jaguar with an IBM mainframe for a brain. He checked his watch. It was three in the morning, both New York and Colombian time.

"Your shipment still set for tonight?" Latham asked. There was both resignation and weariness in his voice.

Luis nodded. "Just before sundown."

"Make it work," Latham growled through gritted teeth. "And tell your boss there's real heat building under his goddamn dope interests."

At this Luis risked a slight smile. "Don Diego believes you should be satisfied with how we have held up our end of this deal. Many components have already been shipped to the staging area. We are actually a bit ahead of schedule."

Looking somewhat relieved, the Company man shot a quick glance around the room. "You got anything to drink in here? It's been a long fucking day."

Luis moved to retrieve a bottle of Dewars and two glasses from the bathroom. He poured a couple of fingers into both glasses and handed one to this son of his father's classmate. Latham took his glass and reached to click it with the kid captain's.

"No matter the setbacks," he told him. "You just assure Cardona that if he manages to keep his end of our deal and keep his nose clean, the shit will *definitely* hit the fan. Aside from you boys, there's some mighty big fellas in this country counting on it."

Any other man, staring out at the view Willie Faro now contemplated, would imagine that all was well in his tranquil kingdom. A maid watched while his children splashed in the sparkling pool. Two hounds slumbered in the shade of a lime tree. The sun poured down on the Valle de Cauca, causing all of nature to contentedly hum its praises. But Willie Faro was, at that moment, anything but content. Willie sat at the desk of his library, curtains drawn back on a pair of French doors through which he viewed the landscape, while inside, his stomach churned with frustration.

As the former king of a Colombian cocaine empire, Willie Faro was a man who thought he understood complexity. Born an aristocrat who could trace his lineage back to the Spanish viceroys of Nueva Grenada, he'd survived a wild, rebellious youth to shun family connections and build, instead, with his own wits. His successes in both the Colombian and American underworlds were so prodigious that in 1981 the United States Justice Department had named him specifically as a menace to the democratic way of life. There had been follow-up stories in *Time* and *Newsweek*. Newspaper articles. All of them described him as an immensely wealthy parasite who fed off the weaknesses of others and lived beyond the reach of American justice. He was indeed immensely wealthy. Accounts containing upwards of four hundred million dollars, in five countries, with him as the only signatory, existed beyond the reach of American justice. Still, in the past two years Willie Faro had seen his entire cocaine network collapse.

Willie Faro was a man who had learned not to lose patience. Never get mad. Get even. Fortunately, the Colombian mind understood getting even. If a man played this particular game, he understood the rules, the implications of betrayal. If he contemplated treachery, he also thought of his mother, father, wife, and children and had every reason to fear for their lives. His treachery would sign their death warrants.

Willie's main man stateside, Rocko Strathmore, had squealed under pressure from the federal prosecutor in San Francisco. Arguably the largest single distributor of cocaine to the film and record community in Los Angeles, Rocko had been indicted by a federal grand jury on tax evasion charges. The stuff they had on him was rock-solid, and Rocko was looking down the barrel at twenty years. He turned state's evidence, fingering Willie's entire American organization from Miami to New York, New Orleans to Detroit, Chicago to California. In return, the feds gave Rocko immunity from prosecution, a new name and face, and put him into the Witness Protection Program. Many of the men implicated were Willie's personal friends, handpicked and trusted. Ten of them were currently doing heavy time in federal stir. The Colombian DAS visited Willie's hacienda regularly now, and not for the purpose of accepting large cash bribes, as in the old days. The tax crimes he was implicated in were not grounds for extradition under Colombian law. Still, under increasing pressure from the American government, the Colombian police circled like vultures, scrutinizing his every move. A business grossing nearly half a billion dollars a year lay in shambles.

In an effort to appear legitimate, Willie invested aggressively in diverse enterprises. In the eyes of his own government, an inherited fortune of five million dollars was being parlayed into a fortune in excess of ten times that, all through shrewd market manipulations. Farm machinery. Clothing manufacture. Coffee. Sugar. Fertilizer. Methane gas production from organic materials. Some knew differently, but no one could prove a thing. Not as long as those close to Willie continued to love their families.

It irritated Willie that there was nothing he could do to retrieve the water now under the bridge. Rocko's back flip also bothered him, but mostly because Rocko was one of the most meticulously careful men he'd ever known. The feds had come right at him. They'd known the precise time and place to catch him with his finger in the pie. Regretfully, Willie sent two men to California with orders to find Rocko no matter how long it took. Find him and kill him. Accomplishing this still wouldn't solve the mystery of the leak. If a friend like Rocko had to die because of his weakness, Willie was determined to discover the reason for his being forced to make this terrible choice.

Rumors persisted about a movement afoot, financed by Nicaraguans, to corner a large chunk of the American drug game. The players were thought to be high-level and very well connected in diplomatic circles, with headquarters somewhere in the Miami area. From several still-active members of his fragmented organization, Willie learned of almost overnight movement into his former territories. People capable of delivering volume. He also knew that his was not the only operation affected. His two largest competitors had been attacked with similar effectiveness, and one of them now was dead after a combined DEA/DAS raid on his mountain stronghold near Medellin. Of the five tons of product confiscated in that operation, less than four hundred pounds could currently be accounted for.

Gringos were still snorting the fun-dust by the shipload. The cocaine power base, however, after being firmly entrenched in Colombia for two decades, was making a radical shift north. The Mexican government, in desperate need of capital infusion, was quietly offering safe haven to anyone who might be able to help pay the freight. The Yucatán was once again crawling with freebooters, many new to the game.

There was an architect of Willie Faro's downfall. He would be willing to stake his fortune on it. On the one hand, he liked to suppose that being out of the drug trade wasn't such an altogether bad thing. His nest was comfortably feathered. The children of this, his second marriage, were growing so fast it amazed him. He could spend more time with them, and yes, *many* of his needs were different now. But if there was such an architect, to let his transgression go unpunished would be unwise. A man who thought he could inflict damage on an enemy at will, and had indeed proven he could, would do it again. This was simple logic and human nature. Inquiries were being made in Florida and Mexico. Of particular interest were the Nicaraguan Contras known as Somosistas. Once again, there were rumors. Each was being patiently followed up. Willie Faro was a patient man.

The morning dawned bright and cool in the high-altitude atmosphere of Popayan. With sunlight forcing its way past decrepit curtains and streaming across the bed, Jack Terranova pushed himself away from the girl's firm body and swung his legs over the side. The place they were headed for, in the hills to the east, was supposed to be a day away over barely maintained dirt roads. The little Renault he'd rented wasn't exactly a terrier on an incline. According to his map, the way ahead was *all* incline.

Jack heaved to his feet and padded to the bathroom. An ice-cold shower invigorated him. Even after another wild night, he didn't feel at all stiff. Hell, two weeks ago he was feeling sorry for himself, wondering if he *was* too old. Now he could laugh scornfully at the notion. Just ask Anna if he was too old. Like shit.

When he reentered their room, he saw Anna dressing, her breasts uplifted in silhouette as she pulled a loose-fitting cotton blouse over her head and shoulders. Jack wondered if he could ever get enough of that. He caught her with an arm in passing and kissed her neck before sitting at an old table along one wall. The map was marked per Diego's instructions. East from Popayan to Purace (15 km), on to San Agustin (80km), then finally to Pitalito (30 km). They were to arrive at the airstrip at 1700 hours. The journey described ran a hundred and twenty-five kilometers over extremely mountainous terrain. Jack reached out, picked his watch up off the pitted surface of the table, and strapped it on. It was nine A.M. already. It might be wise to eat breakfast in the *pensione* dining room rather than waste time seeking out a nicer cafe. Disappointing. This was a beautiful old provincial city. He would have enjoyed dawdling in it.

Willie Faro's investigations were beginning to bear fruit. His two men in the Miami area had managed to track down one of the new players in his old game. This man, a Nicaraguan, was now supplying one of Willie's former distributors in the Cleveland area, a guy who remembered old favors. He was willing to finger his new source in exchange for Willie's introduction to an Ecuadorian source of supply. Their prize, it turned out, was not terribly fond of excruciating pain. After a bit of it, he proved more than willing to talk. His knowledge of the system he worked for was not vast, but the answers to two irksome questions came to light.

The man was a Somosista who had fled his country in 1979. He worked for a former secret police major named Cardona. This Cardona was apparently the mastermind of a huge undertaking to corner the supply of cocaine to the United States. He was headquartered somewhere in the Coral Gables area, with way stations in Mexico and the Caribbean. Details of his operation and any ultimate plans were apparently guarded very closely. The man who hated pain could not divulge much about them, but he did know that Major Cardona was the man directly responsible for the hijacking of Willie Faro's donkeys.

Once a month, back when his organization was a well-oiled machine, Faro's men would herd close to a hundred donkeys south through the mountains into Ecuador from a hacienda in the Narino province on the border. Well-fed on the Colombian end, the animals were penned and kept without food in Ecuador for several weeks before being loaded with seventy-five kilos of cocaine base and turned loose. The effect of this carefully calculated starvation caused the donkeys to perform much like homing pigeons. The hacienda in Narino, some hundred and thirty miles away, meant food. Freed in the wild, the donkeys made a beeline for it. Willie's cocaine base was delivered through terrain the government found very difficult to patrol. Occasionally, a few of the beasts were lost to bandits, border guards, or large cats. By and large, the losses fell within an acceptable range.

When things started to come apart stateside, Willie struggled to stay in business as a major source for Colombia. The last two donkey runs put an end to even this humble ambition. In each instance, two thirds of the surviving burros arrived in Narino minus their payloads. At first, Willie believed a government or guerilla force must have gotten lucky. After two in a row, he knew his security had been breached. He moved to deal with the problem, shifting the entire operation—farms, times, everything. Again, the results were the same. He was hearing word that others were having similar problems: police raids without warning, hijacked shipments. With his operation in the States destroyed and demand for his services dwindling in the face of erratic delivery capability, Faro had seen no choice but to throw in the towel. Now, one new player had provided important pieces of the troubling puzzle. He had a name. Cardona. It was time to find this man and have a little heart-to-heart with him. He would get some answers to other troubling questions.

Willie's wife, Cristina, entered the library, the interruption destroying his concentration. He scowled in greeting.

"There is the consultation with Miguel's teacher at the academy," she reminded him quietly. "You promised to attend this time." Tall, statuesque, and possessing the deeply sculpted bones of a fashion model, the woman, with her blonde hair and blue eyes, looked more European than South American. Born to an aristocratic Venezuelan family of ancient lineage, she'd married Faro a half-dozen years ago and had since borne him two children.

"When?" Willie asked.

"Half an hour. I've asked Rafael to bring around the Mercedes."

"Tell him to sound the horn. I'll be right out." It was delivered as a dismissal, and Cristina had no trouble reading it. With a nod, she turned and left. Willie buzzed for his security chief, Che Aguillera, and moments later the expatriate Argentinian appeared through a pair of big mahogany doors opposite those Cristina had departed through. Faro bade him to take a seat opposite the ornately carved desk.

"Word is in from Florida," Willie told him. "They've managed to turn a worker bee in the new supply setup. It's sure now that the bastards are from inside Somoza's old power structure."

Aguillera, a slightly-built but tightly-muscled man with longish curly hair and expressive eyes, nodded sagely. "There is a name?"

"Cardona. A former major in the secret police. There is very little known about his location or the way he operate. The best we have is the general vicinity of Coral Gables. Carlos and Pepe will need help, I think."

Before Che could offer some suggested names, a car horn sounded outside.

"Damn," Willie growled. "It seems that I must pay my respects to little Miguel's tutor at the academy. Cristina has learned more of my nocturnal escapades through one of her bitch friends, and even though she hasn't said a word, she's been making life miserable."

"Women," Che offered with a quick, sympathetic smile. "We can select the best additional men for the job on your return. I will put some thought to it."

The Beechcraft King-Aire he'd commandeered outside Tucson took Henry Bueno south to a tiny airstrip he knew outside Mexico City. A couple of bus rides brought him to the international airport and the selection of a Piper Cherokee for the next three hops down through the Yucatán, Guatemala, and into northern Costa Rica. More buses saw him to the outskirts of San Jose and into the cockpit, finally, of a ten-year-old Bonanza for the final shot along the Pan-American Highway above Panama and into Medellin, Colombia. There were a few rules one followed in such an endeavor, primary among them being the recognition of a "borrowed" aircraft's possible infirmities. Even though he was an accomplished swimmer, Bueno would rarely fly such a craft over large bodies of water. Believing an airplane's glide capabilities to be more reliable than its engine, he generally kept power demands at about sixty-five percent of the boasted capacity and tried to maintain altitude down as close to terra firma as was safe. Another axiom insisted that once he was on the ground, he avoid run-ins with the authorities. Traveling blithely about with no evidence of emigration could create real ugliness in certain sectors of the Third World. Once he arrived at his destination, Henry could pay some rubber stamp artist to give his papers that legal look.

The heat and humidity of Colombia in mid-autumn turned the lowlands into a steaming sweatbox. In the mountains, increased air movement and a slightly lower mean temperature made circumstances a lot more bearable. Bueno wore white cotton peasant garb as a rule, finding that as long as he remained unshaven and a little dirty, he could pretty much blend in. The loose-fitting garments were also more comfortable than tighter Western wear.

He moved the rest of the way south to Cali on the bus. The terrain was totally familiar to him. Henry had spent a lot of time in these mountains, part of his job being to keep track of cocaine producers and explore their connections to the revolutionary guerilla group known as M-19. The politics of these associations were typically as obscure as most such undertakings in the area. Washington preferred to label M-19 as leftist, Cuban- or Moscow-backed. Henry was not at all sure. The group's leaders would certainly take money from anyone who offered it, but Marxists they were not, in any recognized sense. Organized bandits was a better bet, responsible in large part for the vast migration into the cities of frightened farmers.

Such a city was Cali, looming ahead through the dusty windows of the bus. Its vast urban area sprawled from a mountain rim to the west and out onto the floor of the Valle de Cauca, an alluvial plain stretching between the Occidental and Central ridges of the Andes. Cali was a provincial capital whose population had swollen in the last several decades from a few hundred thousand to a million and a half. The problems of such rapid expansion in a country of limited economic means were many. Vast slums surrounded a core occupied by the aristocracy and an emerging middle class. Roads could not cope with the ever-increasing auto population. The air was tainted with smog. The streets were filled with homeless children and crime. Henry Bueno descended into this city, acutely aware of its problems. He had formerly spent much time here.

The visit to little Miguel's teacher at the exclusive academy he attended went much as Willie Faro had expected. The children were taught both French and English here, as well as

Spanish. Miguel was doing miserably in all three while at the same time displaying a wizardry for mathematics. The tutor had attempted to make Cristina and Willie understand a confusing affliction termed "dyslexia" that those in the know were now convinced Miguel suffered from. Cristina, a more patient soul, seemed to be able to absorb it. Willie found the tutor, the concept, and everything else about contemporary educational methods impenetrable. He was relieved to be back in his library and tackling the more immediate matters awaiting his attention in Miami. There were several men he could send to join Carlos and Pepe, and he studied a list of six, trying to settle on two.

Che knocked quickly and poked his head into the room.

"Don Willie. There is a man here to see you. We told him you were busy, but he is insistant. I have never seen him, but he claims to know you."

"Is he armed?" Faro asked.

"He surrendered two weapons at the gate. It is curious. He speaks with a strange accent that is not Colombian."

His interest piqued, Willie tossed his pen aside and nodded.

"Show him in, but hang around." Slumping back in his chair, he rubbed his eyes.

In another moment, the door swung wide. A man with several days of heavy growth on a strong jaw and dressed in soiled peasant garb stood before him. A man too tall and too powerfully built to be of local issue. There was untold strength in his bearing.

Faro's eyes widened in surprise. His guest hadn't changed much in seven years. It was remarkable. The snake hunter.

The time was late November, 1978. The place: Guaqui, on the border between Bolivia and Peru. Guaqui is a rail spur town on the shore of Lake Titicaca, down the mountains from La Paz. The huge lake, cradled in the Andes at over twelve thousand feet, is difficult to patrol. It serves as a conduit between the two countries—a smuggler's dream.

Back then, Willie Faro's star had been very much on the rise. Through shrewdness and unflagging attention to detail, he had built an empire spreading across seven countries on two continents. His Colombian power base was secure. From it, he was careful to oversee all aspects of his operation personally. Bolivian and Peruvian harvests. Cocaine base manufacture in Ecuador. Refinery in his own country. Export to the United States and distribution. The money machine ran day and night, pumping wealth by the truckload to Bermuda and the Cayman Islands. He retained and worked closely with lawyers and investment counselors. Every week he watched shipments of absolutely clean money wend their way to Switzerland. Willie Faro was a very busy man. And then, on this particular night in Guaqui, all his accomplishment hung balanced on the very sharp tip of a five-inch commando knife.

He had been too reckless. Having pursued a deal with a certain Indian cooperative for months, he had seen the agreement they'd reached that evening as reason to celebrate. Their meeting room, in a ramshackle waterfront hotel, was abandoned for the bar downstairs. Willie should have been warned off by the place's atmosphere. Populated by boatmen, drifters, and entrepreneurs of the shadow worlds, it was no place to let down his guard and relax.

They were sitting at a table drinking Aguardiente, toasting a profitable association. For his Indian guests, this was uncharacteristically cosmopolitan. He could read in their faces that they would have preferred to return to the comfort of their mountains. Feeling good, Willie figured what the hell. A little change of pace couldn't hurt them.

There were a half dozen whores working the place, the sort of social dregs one might expect to find in such a setting. Two of these were watching the merriment at Willie's table from the bar. The Colombian was showing his bumpkin friends a pretty good time, and they got it in their heads to wander over and see if he'd like to up the ante any. Irritated by the interruption, Faro waved them away. One ignored him and slid her arm around the eldest Indian's neck. She tickled his cheek, taunting him. Willie nodded to one of the men he had with him. The guy stepped over and tapped the offending party on the shoulder, murmuring something indistinct. The whore sneered, threw back her head, and spat in his face.

"Pig!" she snarled. "Keep your hands off me!"

The henchman, a big, nasty-tempered man named Lucho, smiled and backhanded her so hard across the face that she was knocked sprawling onto the floor. In the next instant, his head exploded like a melon as a deafening crack split the close atmosphere of the bar. As the second of Faro's security men began to react, he jerked spasmodically, his eyes glazing over. He fell onto his face with a knife protruding from his back. Willie was in the act of reaching for the pistol in his belt when he felt the sudden, cold prick of sharp steel at his throat. A hand caught him by the hair and jerked his head back.

As Faro sat and anticipated a horrible death, a sweat-stained, hard-muscled man approached him. He was dressed in dirty khaki with a gold loop in one ear and several teeth broken off at the gum line.

"You don't like girls, amigo?"

Willie tried to swallow. The eyes confronting him had a maniacal gleam in them.

"Go fuck your mother," he growled. From behind, the hand controlling the knife let it cut him just a bit. He winced.

"Perhaps you don't like my girls because you like men instead, eh, señor? Well, here is one, amigo." He prodded something with his boot, and the hand holding Faro's hair let his head forward enough to allow him to view the dead Lucho. The hard-muscled man squatted to undo the corpse's pants and jerk them down to its knees. "All ready for you, señor. If you hope to walk out of here with your life, we are all going to watch you fuck *him*."

Only the metallic grating of an antique ceiling fan broke the deadly quiet. Willie contemplated the dead Lucho, a bloody pulp above his shoulders and bare-ass naked.

"Go ahead, señor. Since you do not like my girls." The man motioned to one of the girls. Licking her lips, she approached and began to unzip his fly.

The quick, double click of a round being chambered in an automatic pistol seemed thunderous. Willie's antagonist jerked around to stare into the blackness of a far corner. With his movement restricted, Willie could barely read the man's face. It looked for just an instant like fear. Then it recovered and became bravado.

"Tell your man to put the knife down or I drop you on the spot," a quiet voice said. The accent was strange, a mixture of many places, or possibly pure Spain, Castilian without the lisp. At this moment, it was music to Willie Faro's ears.

"What do you propose, señor?" the now-cautious pimp asked. "That you can shoot me effectively from half darkness? Do you think I am a fool?"

38

"More," the voice returned coolly from concealment. "I am in darkness, but you are quite easy to see from where I stand. I can not only tell you the exact point where the bullet will enter, but also how far it will travel, where it will exit, and how deep it will embed itself in the wall behind you. As it will be traveling through the bulk of your heart, you'll just have to take my word for it."

Doubt crept back into the mean pimp's eyes. Willie had watched this phenomenon before in other men. When this look of fear returned, a decision had already been made in their bowels. Willie's own heart, which had all but ceased beating, resumed pounding furiously in his chest.

"Tell your man to drop the knife," the calm, musical voice insisted. "Now."

The pimp nodded with a noticeable swallow, and the grip on Willie's hair loosened. The scrape of footsteps receded behind him once the knife disappeared. As Willie worked to loosen his stiff neck, a figure emerged from blackness and walked into view.

Willie was struck by the way he moved. For a man of considerable size, he glided on his feet like a matador. Every muscle was relaxed and ready. He was taller than the bulky-muscled man, perhaps as many as two full meters in height. His shoulders were broad without being heavy. His clothes fit him loosely, but there was power in the body beneath. This approaching figure held the energy of a coiled bullwhip.

"I believe you and your friends should leave with me," he told Willie.

FOUR

There was something very odd in SYSTEMATICS's quality control report. Leo A. "Bill" Counihan had been wrestling with the numbers for a week and still couldn't put his finger on the problem. This failure, in itself, was odd enough. Bill Counihan had built SYSTEMATICS from a one-horse operation in the garage behind his house in Los Gatos, California into a fiscally sound and innovative Silicon Valley contender. He was famous for being a "hands-on" type of guy, overseeing every aspect of his operation. Only in the past three or four years had his business seen such fantastic expansion that he was no longer able to control *every* phase of it. Where he couldn't be, he'd inserted handpicked men and women of the highest caliber to assist him. Most of his managers had been with him from the beginning and were fully capable of keeping him abreast of exciting developments *and* potential problems.

So why didn't the damn numbers make sense? In this industry, the bottom line for defectives hovered around ten percent. Bill Counihan, though, was a perfectionist. On the other side of the Pacific, the Japanese were breathing fire, their production capabilities threatening every bottom line in the domestic industry. In the manufacture of computer hardware and other high-tech components, a product rejection ratio of one in ten was no longer thinkable. From 1982 to

1987, Bill's company had managed to realize only 2.7 rejections per hundred production units. The target for 1987–88 was 2.5. Why, then, in God's name, had the number suddenly jumped between August and November to an almost flat four? A glitch? A one-time aberration? Like hell. Not in *his* organization. After a week of studying them, Bill couldn't get the numbers to bear out anything reasonable. Even more curious were the precious metals recovery assays he'd received midweek. They *proved* that something was way out of whack.

At SYSTEMATICS, and most other such manufacturers in the industry, all rejected circuits were sent to a salvage unit where they could be stripped of gold, platinum, and other precious metal conductors. This salvaged material was sealed in canisters and sent to a recovery specialist under tight security. The specialist would smelt the metals into bullion and credit the corporation's account toward further purchases of the same materials.

This quarter's salvage report clearly indicated a downturn in total recovery numbers. Between the two reports he was now attempting to justify, Counihan saw rejections up and metals recoveries down. It was like adding two plus two and getting three. Larry Ransell down in Salvage insisted that he could back up his numbers. The influx of rejected units was recorded on videotape. An infrared scanner automatically stored an identification code taken from each unit. After a month's time, these numbers were reintroduced to production. As a backup, these numbers were also recorded during rejection at the various test stations. This process was nowhere near as reliable as the scanning in Salvage, because rejection could take place for any number of reasons, at any stage of production. Quality Control maintained their inspection stations all along the way. Generally, with a 2.7 rejection number, the largest number of failures occurred in final testing. Even with the failure rate way up, this seemed to still hold true.

Counihan's desk was piled high with printouts ordered from his various departments. He'd been up all night poring over them. So far, the ID code of every recorded rejection matched with the receiving report from Salvage. What *didn't* match was the correlation between the number of codes recorded as rejections and the actual number of units produced.

Somewhere along the line between Q.C. and Salvage, SYS-TEMATICS had a leak. A big one. Bill had to face the possiblity that rejected units—or, even worse, *faultless* pieces—were being siphoned off and somehow removed from the plant. If this were the case, SYSTEMATICS was in very deep shit. Aside from an impressive array of state-of-the-art business and personal computing hardware and software, the corporation held half a dozen lucrative government contracts. Four of these contracts were for extremely sensitive missile guidance systems.

Bill leaned back in his chair and rubbed his eyes. With the button depressed on his intercom, he spoke to his secretary in the outer office.

"Page my daughter, Grace. Have her drop whatever she's doing and get over here on the double."

The road running east from Popayan toward Purace was not paved. Jack Terranova's rented Renault growled doggedly up the steep inclines, tires crunching gravel and churning up a billowing cloud of dust. With Anna riding serenely in the seat beside him, Jack tried to take in a little of the scenery while still keeping his car on the road. Alongside, down a deep gorge, the mighty Rio Cauca had now thinned considerably. It cascaded in a great hurry of whitewater through the thick vegetation that crowded its banks. Jack had never seen country like this. The temperature had dropped below sixty degrees. Around him, on many peaks, he could see snow. One of the big mountains ahead was fifteen thousand feet high, according to his map. And the *birds*. There were real parrots in the trees. Hundreds of them. Green and yellow and blue. Jack thought he could get to like a place like this. It might be full of spics, but they weren't like the greaseballs in Miami and New York.

Thirty kilometers beyond the town of Purace, which hadn't been much, he felt his stomach growl. It was coming up on one o'clock, and they were already two thirds of their way along on the day's journey. Granted, this last leg of the way was due to be their slowest going. By the map, the road ahead was steep and hellishly twisted. Still, even at ten miles per hour, they could make Pitalito in plenty of time. He could afford an hour or so for lunch.

Beside them, the Rio Cauca had shrunken so rapidly that it

was now no more than a small stream. Around a corner, he spotted a low, shaded cantina perched above it. There were a half-dozen open-air tables. Three were occupied by Indians wrapped in heavy wool blankets, machetes dangling from their belts and bottles of beer in their fists. Jack grinned at Anna and nosed the Renault over onto the shoulder. Setting the brake, he switched off the ignition and gave the little four-banger a well-deserved rest.

A big, heavy-shouldered gringo in the company of a striking young Latin woman seemed to be enough of a break in the local routine to attract open attention. Jack and Anna were seated with all eyes on them. The handles on those machetes were glossy and well worn with use. The button man decided that this was no place to find oneself stranded after sundown with a flat tire.

One of the patrons was working on what looked for all the world like a large brown trout. Jack squinted, unable to believe his eyes. Up here, in the mountains of South goddamn America.

"Have 'em bring me one of them." He pointed, addressing the bilingual Anna. "The trout . . . and a beer."

"Trucha," Anna translated, smiling.

"Call it whatever you want," he growled good-naturedly. "Fresh fucking trout. Big ones. I'll be damned."

When the meal hit the table some fifteen minutes later, Jack sat and stared. The skin was crispy brown, the flesh beneath broiled to perfection. Alongside it, they'd dished up a supply of those fried things that looked like bananas but weren't. Them and a big pink bean. Christ, did they ever have the beans down here. He figured he must have had them all by now, every one of them pretty good. Even the banana things, *platinos*, were something he was getting used to; starchy like a spud, but almost sweet once they were fried. He shook salt on them and squeezed a little lime on the fish. Anna was eating a beefsteak with more beans.

It was finally getting close. Jack looked forward to employing his special skills once again. This was turning out to be one sweet trip all the way around. The piece of ass old Diego had promised had exceeded his most prurient expectations. The air was clean and cool down here on the goddamn *equator*. Watching the nose tackle collapse in a heap with surprise in his eyes had given him back that good feeling again. He'd been out to pasture so long, he'd nearly forgotten he was the best.

After lunch, these two traveling strangers lingered for a few minutes over cups of thick coffee before paying and climbing back into the little French wheels. Two o'clock. They were right on schedule.

Willie Faro prided himself on his cocky and even arrogant nature. He was, after all, master of his own destiny. There were few memories of past experiences that could contradict this secure self-image. One of them was the memory of the snake hunter advancing from the gloom that night long ago. Facing that, arrogance gave way to uncertainty. He pushed back from his desk and extended his hand in welcome.

Seven years. The lines around the mouth and eyes had deepened. A whitened scar running along the temple at the hairline had not been there. And there was a look of calm that hadn't been there either, as though some invisible spring, which once pushed him steadily onward like a clock, had unwound.

"Amigo," Willie said, meaning it. The man had saved his life and asked nothing in return. His appearance after so much time would mean that he now intended to somehow exploit the bond that lay between them. "Welcome to Cali and my humble home."

The man he knew as Henri Riberac reached to shake his hand.

"Please, sit. Can I offer you a drink?" Willie asked. The snake hunter's clothes were soiled with the grime of travel. He looked the slightest bit tired.

"A cold beer, if you have one," Bueno replied. The succinct, musical Spanish once again struck Faro. A tongue to mesmerize the anaconda.

Willie slapped his hands together, and a housegirl appeared.

"Dos cervezas," he commanded. Sitting and settling back into his chair, he eyed the Frenchman, or whatever he was.

"You look well," he commented. He smiled. "Whatever path you follow seems to suit you."

"Well enough," Bueno returned easily. "Word reaching me does not speak so well of your recent fortunes."

Faro could not help but betray some surprise. The man was

44

well informed indeed. "I did not suspect you of also being in the trade. Could I have been wrong?"

A slight smile twisted the corners of Henry's mouth. He shook his head. "I simply travel and have big ears. It is no secret that the old power balance has shifted."

"I suppose it is not," Willie sighed, shaking his head.

The maid entered with two chilled bottles of Poker beer and set them on a tray before them. Henry waved off the proffered glass and touched his bottle to Faro's with a nod before he drank. Willie drank with him and wiped his lips with the back of his hand before speaking again.

"I too have big ears and once followed word of the snake hunter with interest. For nearly a year now, the winds have not brought even the seeds of rumor about him. So what does a snake hunter do once he ceases to hunt snakes?"

"He goes away from where the snakes live," Henry replied. There was a twinkle of amusement in his eyes. "He tries to forget about them."

"But he cannot," Willie suggested. "Something prevents him from forgetting, and he returns?"

"There is nothing like a cold beer on a hot day to cut the dust in a man's throat," Bueno mused. "Your troubles, I have reason to suspect, could have some bearing on a matter that now interests me. There is a new player in the Yankee cocaine game. A former major in Anastasio Somoza's secret police by the name of Diego Cardona. I wonder if that name is of any interest to you?"

Bueno watched with some amusement as Faro's eyes came open wide at the mention of the major's name.

"What do you know of this man?" Willie shot back, vehemence edging his voice.

Henry shook his head. "Not as much as you would probably wish. Only some specifics from his past and rumors about his current work. He is a man with a talent for ruthlessness. He may also be responsible for the death of a friend. This is something I wish to ask him about."

"And you come to me believing I might know something useful of this man?" Willie asked.

Henry took another pull on his beer and stood to approach a large window. It looked out on lush gardens and across a manicured lawn to a swimming pool. A statuesque, sandy-haired woman in a string bikini played alongside the pool with two small children. Even from this considerable distance, he could see that the woman was unusually beautiful, with long, slender legs and a deep golden tan.

"Less than a week ago"—he spoke softly, his back to Faro and sunlight warming his face—"two U.S. agents were shot and killed near Pance. They were trailing a contract killer from the U.S. East Coast crime syndicates. My information has him here on some sort of free-lance assignment. Three weeks ago, Diego Cardona was observed making contact with this man in Miami. This same man has now checked out of the Intercontinental Hotel here and vanished."

Faro studied his visitor's profile as he spoke. "The deaths of these Americans were reported in the newspapers," he confirmed. "No mention was made of their being American agents." The naming of Cardona had shaken him. His mind raced now as he worked to process the possible significance of the snake hunter's new information. Where had he gotten it, and what role did he play?

Bueno turned to face the drug trafficker again. "Cardona has managed to convince certain intelligence bureaucrats in the States that he is part of a Sandinista effort to control the movement of cocaine in this hemisphere. It's my belief that, quite to the contrary, any self-respecting Sandinista would shoot the man on sight."

Willie smiled now. "I admire a man who gets straight to his point. You know that I, too, have motivations for gathering certain intelligence."

"Judging from the damage this man has inflicted on you, it would only stand to reason."

Faro pushed back in his chair and swung his feet up onto the desk. He eyed his guest as Riberac returned to his own seat and took another pull on his beer.

"As you must know, then, this Cardona is of great concern to me. I believe he is directly behind the damage to me that you speak of. He is firmly entrenched in the Somosista camp. It is ludicrous that he masquerades as a leftist."

Bueno nodded. "As I suspected. There's no way a man of your stature wouldn't have deployed a net by now. The reason I've come to see you is simple enough. I want the American killer. He and Cardona are up to something. Perhaps we can be useful to each other in finding them."

By this time, Willie Faro was wondering if he should

believe his ears. Who this man was still puzzled him. But he had just vastly narrowed the field of possibilities. His information ran to very privileged depths. He was looking to avenge the murder of a CIA agent. If Willie's suspicions were correct, then this snake hunter was making an unprecedented and curious proposition indeed.

"I'm a *marijuanero*, amigo. An enemy of the United States government."

His guest shook his head. "That's not my problem, Willie. This is strictly personal. Just something between me and the man who put a bullet in a good friend's brain. Who we are doesn't matter here. Not now."

The trafficker shrugged and allowed a time of silence to pass. Both men finished their beers and returned the empty bottles to the tray. Willie pulled his feet back off the desk and sat forward with his elbows in their place. This man Riberac was a strange new ally in his grudge war against the Central American interlopers. Strange but powerful, and he needed all the help he could get.

"Okay, amigo," he agreed. "Perhaps we can help each other."

Maureen Counihan was SYSTEMATICS's thirty-one-year-old executive vice president in charge of finance and marketing. A 1979 graduate of the University of Chicago MBA program, she'd joined her father's company after three years with a rival electronics firm in Palo Alto. Bill Counihan had recruited her for less nepotistic reasons than might initially be assumed. She'd proven herself a marketing wizard with her former employer, launching a software campaign in the dog-eat-dog PC field that came to be considered state-of-the-art. Instead of seeing her leap at an opportunity to join Daddy's firm, the senior Counihan had been forced to do a real hard-sell job before persuading her to switch horses. Since making the move, the headstrong young woman hadn't regretted her decision. Instead of the patriarchal domination she'd feared, her father encouraged her to make her own decisions. She was challenged to be both aggressive *and* imaginative.

In the five intervening years, the woman called "Mo" by her dad had blossomed. There were times when her father wondered if his little girl didn't understand the business better than he did. As time went by, he found himself relying heavily on her instincts and expertise. On that November afternoon when he called her to his office, he was hoping that she might be able to help him unscramble the current puzzle.

"What's up, Pop?" the redhead asked, breezing in with an air of cool confidence and efficiency. "I was just with George Anderson's design team going over the specs on the new modem for the JTX series. Have you seen the prelims? *Ugleee!* Kids in a high school drafting class could do better." She stopped short, noticing the weariness in her father's eyes and the uncharacteristic clutter on his desk. "What's going on?"

"Sit down, baby," he sighed. "We've got problems."

Step by step, the senior Counihan outlined the process of elimination he'd engaged in to come to the conclusions he now laid before her. As he spoke, her concentration intensified behind a deep-knit brow. She knew how much those government contracts meant to the financial health of SYSTEMATICS. With the Japanese busy eroding hell out of the commercial markets and the bigger conglomerates with their multimillion-dollar R and D budgets working to strangle the smaller competition, it was their government work that enabled them to be more innovative in the commercial field.

"Son of a bitch!" she snarled, clenching her fists. "Three months, you say?"

"At least," he replied.

"We don't have any choice," she said.

"How's that?"

"Anyone who's ever been caught in an attempted cover-up will tell you they aren't worth the effort, Dad. We've got to call in the feds. It may be uncomfortable in the short run, but I think it'd be better to come clean right away."

"Do what?" he asked, incredulous. "They'll cancel us out. Going to the FBI with all this would be tantamount to admitting we've blown it."

Maureen shook her head emphatically. "Not necessarily. Not if we made it clear from the outset that we're willing to eat the expense of reworking the designs, making any pirated equipment obsolete. Anyone can have their security breached. We've complied with every letter of the prerequisite they handed us."

"Jesus," he groaned hollowly. "First the FBI and then suffering through those jackass generals again."

"Let me handle it," she offered. "I'll act as your personal liaison in the matter."

"That's too much," he objected, waving her off. "I should handle it."

"I *want* it," she insisted. "I want to find the bastards who are doing this to us. You give it to me, and I'll nail their butts to the wall. Besides, you've got plenty to worry about just trying to run this place."

"And you don't?" he asked. "What about the modem design? How about the new financial statement, and the marketing survey?"

She grinned a triumphant grin. "The survey data is in and being processed as we speak. The financial report went to the printer this morning. I just told Georgie and his prima donna designers that they've got twenty-four hours to get me something acceptable or I'm *giving* it to a high school design class."

Bill Counihan threw his pencil onto the pile of printouts before him and capitulated. "Okay, Mo. Call in the goddamn Man from U.N.C.L.E. if you want to. You save our asses and I'm gonna seriously think about retiring and turning over the entire ball of wax."

"Don't offer the crown quite yet," she cautioned. Jumping quickly onto her feet, she leaned over to scoop the pile of paper from his desk. "I'll be in touch. Right now, there's work to do."

"What exactly are these sons of bitches trying to pull, Ted?" Cameron Stebbins asked. The two men were seated across from each other in the deputy director's comfortable office at CIA headquarters in Langley, Virginia. Latham relaxed with a Winston in his right hand and one ankle over the other knee.

"There's a lot of information still trickling in, sir," the junior man replied. "The best guess we can make is based on information gathered by Contras who have infiltrated. It looks like the Sandinistas have made some sort of back-scratching deal with the Reds. With the high-tech embargo being enforced against the Soviets, these guys figure they can curry favor by supplying the stuff bootleg. We haven't been able to pin down any specific sources yet or any of the ways they're funneling the stuff out of the country.''

"So we have no idea of how bad it might be hurting us?'' Stebbins asked. "Specifics?''

"Not really,'' Latham admitted. "This is pretty raw intelligence. Recently gathered. Frankly, I think it's damn lucky we were able to find it in the early stages. There's no evidence that anything's actually been delivered yet. The rumors our people are getting have the lefties stockpiling the stuff down there somewhere. All we know for sure is that they're supposed to be missile guidance components.''

"Christ!'' Stebbins snapped. "It stinks but makes sense, I guess. You want helicopter gunships from the Soviet Union, you'd better have something significant to buy them with.''

Latham blew smoke and nodded. "We're following up everything we hear down there now. Monitoring traffic and communications overseas and to their embassies in the region. We've got some pretty reliable ears down in the area.''

"Good work,'' the deputy Director said. "Let's keep this thing close to the vest for the moment. The Bureau gets wind of something like this, they'll crawl all over it and scare the players off. I want the *big* fish in this net.''

Fifteen minutes later, Ted Latham sat in his own office, reviewing the developments to date. Stebbins was the perfect shill for their little game. If only he'd been able to dissuade him from making the trip west with Carl Stickley's letter in hand.That one had come out of left field, and there'd been very little he could do about it. Having Henry Bueno back in the area was a big negative. Bueno scared the shit out of Ted Latham. He could only hope that the entire sideshow this crazy fucker Cardona was currently engineering was so far off the mark that Bueno would never stumble over the real covert operation. Diego Cardona was a dangerously greedy bastard. This cocaine game they were allowing him to play was going to backfire in their faces if they didn't nip it in the bud. He hated to admit it, but right now they needed his skinny little greaseball ass. At least Stebbins and the other higher-ups had bought the garbage he'd fed them about how the major was now playing for the other team.

* * *

Jack Terranova and Anna arrived at their destination outside Pitalito with fifteen minutes to spare. The hard-packed dirt of the mountain-bound runway lay deserted, a light breeze barely filling the windsock at the far end. Next to a low, ramshackle outbuilding, an old PBY amphibious aircraft stood in serious disrepair. Its cowlings lay half full of water on the ground, the exposed engines rusting in the weather. Two smaller aircrafts were parked a dozen yards beyond it. One, a Piper Cherokee, had been stripped of its fancy factory detailing and painted a dull, primer gray. Other than that, it appeared to be nearly new and in excellent working order.

As the button man parked the Renault, a grease-stained man in tattered coveralls emerged from the wooden shed and ambled toward them. A cigar so short it threatened to burn his lips was clenched between stained teeth. The sight of such a pretty girl up here in the middle of nowhere was obviously more intriguing than that of an overweight, middle-aged gringo.

"Buenos tardes, señorita," he cooed, attempting a smile. *"Como esta? Bien?"* The cheap cologne on him was overpowering.

Anna did a good job of appearing disgusted as she took a step back and let Jack occupy the high ground.

"We're meetin' a friend in ten minutes. *Comprende?*"

The man eyed him. "You are the gringo meeting Don Diego," he declared matter-of-factly in pretty fair English.

"That's right. You got any java in that chicken coop?"

"Java?"

"Yeah. Coffee. *Cafe*, or whatever the fuck you want to call it."

"Cafe negro," the guy told him. "Java." He was trying it again and letting it roll off his tongue. "Java." Seeming to like the sound of it, he led the way to the interior of his shed.

The place was full of greasy engine parts and the nose-searing odor of gasoline. No wonder; the man in the monkeysuit had a dozen trays of gas sitting out and parts soaking in them. Terranova winced and held his breath as their host fired a match and held it to the stub of his cigar. Nothing blew. Jack thought it might be due to all the daylight visible through the exterior siding. Ventilation.

The grease monkey's java was as rank as the rest of his operation. As he and Anna tasted it, Jack took in the workbenches along the walls, the chain hoist, stacks of fuel drums, piles of greasy rags and worthless parts. Back home, this would have been a junior fire marshal's wet dream.

After drinking the guy's coffee, Jack led Anna back outside. The sun was shining brightly down into that tiny cradle of a valley, but with less intensity than it did in Cali. He was comfortable in the light jacket he'd brought along. Together, they wandered over to the rotting PBY and stood staring at it. Her curiosity getting the better of her, Anna stepped up to stand on tiptoe and peer inside. The view of her before him, stretched out like that with her perfect ass straining against the light fabric of her slacks, had the big man trying to ignore the rising heat in his loins. With this effort, the family he'd forsaken came to mind.

He'd told them he was going away for a couple of weeks. At the time, he'd honestly believed he was. Diego's promise of young girls, heavy money, and a piece of future Caribbean action had seemed like a fantastic pipe dream then. He'd gone because he was itching for something, *anything*, to do. Now his perspective had changed. Anna alone was all it might have taken. The way she waited for him, smiling her little challenges every morning. He couldn't even remember what it was like the last time he made love with Maria. Maria with her brassy blond dye job and phony crimson fingernails. She was *always* as cold as an iced mackerel in the sack. Always all the same demands and complaints. For years he'd convinced himself that there simply wasn't any escape. He returned home at night because that's just the way it was and the way every other poor fuck had it. Not anymore. No more of Maria and no more trying to stomach the idea of his daughter spreading to take the sausage from some green-haired freak.

As far as he was concerned, Diego could ask him to do almost anything from here on out. Tight young pussy. Clean mountain air. Fresh fucking trout. There was no way in the world he could turn his back on action like this.

From far off, he heard the drone of an airplane. Straining, he listened while the noise shifted on the breeze. As it got closer, the wind no longer affected it. There, way off, to the north, he found a speck reflecting in the sun. Anna backed away from the rusted PBY to watch with him as it descended from the sky. It circled the valley once and then again before swooping to touch down in a cloud of rusty red dust.

Diego sure had some expensive taste in transportation. The plane taxiing toward them was some sort of twin-engine turboprop job—the same kind of ride his former employers used to make short hops back in the States. A side door came open as the thing reached their end of the runway. A man in fatigues poked his head out and motioned to the pair. With the girl tucked protectively under one arm, Terranova moved forward.

Inside the plane, Diego Cardona sat with two men in street clothes whom Terranova didn't recognize. In addition to the guy at the door, there were two more soldiers in fatigues and armed with automatic weapons.

"Greetings, señor," Diego said, smiling. "Sit, please." He indicated a seat next to himself. "And you, señorita."

Anna sat next to one of the young civilian men.

"We will be taking off immediately," Diego advised them. "You will want to buckle your seat belts."

Immediately upon liftoff the pilot took the bird into a gut-twisting climb up over a ridge running perpendicular to the runway about half a mile distant. Going over it they were caught by an updraft that flung the ship an additional five hundred feet in altitude. Across from him, one of Diego's associates grimaced. The pilot continued the climb. From the side of the plane that the sun was on, Jack determined their direction to be southward. Toward Peru or Ecuador, most likely. They were quickly running out of Colombia.

"It is time to discuss your mission," Diego told the shooter. "I would like to present two of my associates. Luis Echevarria and Ramon Lopez."

Terranova nodded to the pair, waiting for them to offer to shake hands. When they failed to do so, he studied them in contrast to their boss. While Diego, short, wiry, and ferretlike, was probably in his early fifties, these two were barely more than kids. Prideful, stuck-up kids, at that. Luis had a baby face and carried himself with mock military bearing. Full of himself. The other one, Ramon, couldn't have been more than twenty-two or -three. He was soft and studious-looking, with thick-lensed glasses shielding bad eyes.

Luis removed a briefcase from beneath his seat, placed it on his flight tray, and thumbed the latches. From within, he withdrew an envelope and handed it to Cardona.

"The interior ministers of the Contadora countries meet

tomorrow in Quito," he told Terranova. "They are holding a three-day conference on the control of drug production in South and Central America." As he spoke, he undid a string binding the envelope flap and extracted several items. The first to be shown was a photograph.

"Jorge Garcia-Alvarez. Colombian minister of the interior and his country's emmissary to the conference." He passed the photo to his hitter. "It is our wish that the honorable Señor Garcia-Alvarez not leave Ecuador alive."

Terranova sat staring at the face. The game was political assassination, a new wrinkle in his illustrious career.

"Señor Garcia—" Diego began. He was interrupted as the big gringo held up his hand.

"Nothing more," he insisted, shaking his head. "I don't want to know any more. Who and what are your problem. I do a job, all I need to know is what he looks like and where I can find him."

Cardona's two underlings glanced toward their boss. He nodded.

"A practical and careful man," he said with a slight smile. "Very well, then. Here is his itinerary. Needless to say, the conference will be closely guarded. We have provided you with a map of the city. On it you will find indicated the places where we consider him to be the most vulnerable in his movements."

"Keep it," the assassin grunted. "Just the face and this." He tapped the itinerary. "I work the rest out for myself. Now, there is the small matter of payment. I assume you've got the first installment?" He lifted his trouser cuff, stooped, and stuffed the papers into his sock. "By the way, you did real fine *there, compadre.*" He jerked a thumb toward Anna.

Diego nodded and smiled expansively. "The señorita is yours, señor. The first gesture of my good faith." Luis handed him a second envelope. He passed it over to the mobster. "Letters of credit payable to bearer, drawn on the National Bank of Grand Cayman. One third of the three hundred thousand, as agreed. We have played honorably to this point, no?"

"You got a girl for Luis, too?" Jack asked.

Diego looked confused rather than supremely confident for the first time. "I am afraid I do not understand."

It was Terranova's turn to work the indulgent grin. "Not

too difficult to figure, *compadre*. A hundred grand ain't three, and once I'm finished down there I'm a sitting duck unless I got me some sort of insurance, right?''

Luis shifted uncomfortably, exchanging nervous glances with his associates. Diego shook his head sadly.

"It is a shame that there can be so little trust in the world. All this is unnecessary. We are men of honor. The plane will be exactly where I say it will be to pick you up.''

Jack took his turn at shaking his head. ''You got a job you want done. Pretty badly, I'd say, from the bread you're willing to pay. Well, I've never undertaken this sort of job without certain guarantees. I generally design those guarantees myself. You want this done right, the game is simple enough to play. Looie there comes along, I do the dude, and we leave together. Nothing could be neater, right?''

Cardona was furious but chose to sit on it. The assassination of the Colombian minister was integral to the master scheme he'd put together. If trouble arose, he thought it better to deal with this overconfident lummox at some later date.

"We have no arrangements for this," he murmured. "There is only one hotel room. One pickup.''

"If that's the way it is, Looie can sleep in our room,'' Terranova told him. "I've never minded other men watching me fuck. Maybe he'll pick up a tip or two.''

"You are a difficult man, amigo.''

"Cautious, *compadre*,'' Jack corrected. "That's why I'm still alive. You ought to be able to appreciate that.''

FIVE

Federal Bureau of Investigation Special Agent Roscoe Charles eyed the cool redhead across the desk from him. It was a neat, uncluttered, high-tech desk. Gray, black, and white Formica. The office was as spartan as its occupant seemed to be. Industrial carpet underfoot, low nap and charcoal gray. Molded swivel armchairs, grey upolstery. The stark potted palms were in black ceramic pots. The walls were brilliant white. There was nothing soft or feminine about this environment, and because his subject had some attractive physical tools, Agent Charles was relieved to find her packaged this way. The business of ferreting out high-tech espionage and treason was tough enough without some corporate siren trying to soft-pedal her problems to him.

Maureen Counihan indicated the pile of printouts between them. "The numbers just won't add up, Mr. Charles. My father brought the matter to my attention yesterday afternoon, and I spent all night going over everything. This morning I interviewed our Mr. Ransell in Salvage and our Quality Control chief Greg Wing. Somewhere between their two departments, the Alamo DX production line has sprung a leak. In the past three months, I estimate we've lost as many as three hundred possibly operational curcuit boards through that leak."

"Possibly operational?" Charles asked.

"We have no way of knowing," she told him. "On paper,

Q.C. flunked them, but some of them never made it to final testing, where the only hard performance data is recorded. Of the units reported as being substandard by final testing, all of them were dismantled by Salvage. We have absolute correlation there. What we cannot seem to justify is a discrepancy between the number of units produced and those either shipped or junked. With a general failure rate of 2.6 per hundred, it's a good bet that *any* unit coming out of production will be functional.''

Roscoe Charles nodded pensively. He spread his hands and bounced the fingertips of one off those of the other.

"I appreciate your being so candid, Miss Counihan. The agency realizes full well just what you stand to lose by such a disclosure. However, this type of cooperation can go a long way toward preventing any further damage. The Defense Department will, of course, have to make their own determination under such circumstances, but I assure you that our recommendations are weighed heavily in any such action."

"I'm a businesswoman," Maureen told the agent flatly. "Someone has gone a long way to put my company in the deepest sort of jeopardy. I am not about to help him or her any further along by being a fool. I'm interested in only two things here. I want to purge the organization of this infestation and minimize any consequent damage. If the FBI can help me in either endeavor, then we're on the same side, aren't we?"

The special agent nodded thoughtfully. "I'd like copies of those printouts and a list of your personnel. At this point, I'm sure you understand the need to keep this matter entirely confidential. I would like to talk to the two department heads you mentioned at the earliest convenience. In the next day or two, we'll want to plant a man on your production line. Meanwhile, you should proceed with business as usual."

After the FBI man left, Maureen Counihan made a full report of their meeting to her father before buzzing her secretary and telling her she could be reached at home the rest of the afternoon. With all paperwork concerning the leak locked in her desk, she shouldered her bag. Her overburdened mind was anticipating a quick dip in her backyard pool and then the oblivion of much-needed sleep.

*　　*　　*

Christopher Newman

In attempting to locate a professional gunman who had completely vanished into the wilds of South America, Henry Bueno knew he had his work cut out for him. Before he could search with any effectiveness he knew he had to get some badly needed rest. Willie offered his hospitality, and Henry accepted. As his clothes were being cleaned, he took a quick dip in the pool and then caught a few hours shut-eye, awakening at sundown. Faro, the aristocrat turned dope trafficker, had himself a nice little setup nestled against the foothills of the Farallones. The actual hacienda compound, surrounded by an eight-foot wall, was about twenty acres in size. Beyond the wall, the property extended across rolling topography for perhaps a thousand acres. The house itself was huge; adobe brick rambled on for thousands of square feet, embracing beautiful little courtyards and opening out onto vast verandas. Henry's room was comfortably appointed with a carved double bed, heavy armchairs, a table, bath, and color television with VCR.

Henry was stretching after his nap when a maid knocked at the door, returned his clothing in a neatly folded pile, and announced that the evening meal would be served in a half hour's time. A quick shower and clean clothes had him feeling like a new man. He emerged to find Willie in the cavernous living room with a Scotch and water in his hand.

"Join me, please," Faro urged him. "You rested well, I hope."

"Real well, thanks. You know what I want more than anything else right now? Another one of those cold beers."

His host opened a cabinet door, revealing a tiny refrigerator. He removed a frosty Poker and pried off the cap. As Henry was accepting it, the woman he'd seen with the children by the pool entered the room.

"Ah, you have not met my wife," Willie announced. "Cristina, our guest, Monsieur Henri Riberac."

Clad in a loose-fitting but elegantly cut cotton dress that highlighted her stunning physique, the deeply tanned blonde descended the two steps into the room and approached with her hand extended. Bueno took it gently.

"A pleasure," he told her.

"No," she corrected. "The pleasure is mine. When I was still just a bride, you saved my husband's life. Since that time, you have become something of a legend in this house."

58

Henry thought she was one of the most beautiful women he'd ever laid eyes on. Her bearing was aristocratic, and the accent was out of place in this region. If he had to put money on it, he'd guess Caracas or somewhere very near it in Venezuela. As they exchanged greetings, Willie was busy mixing a drink for her, and they now toasted each other. Henry couldn't help but meet the eyes peering at him over the rim of Cristina Faro's glass. Nor could he miss the flash of open fascination in them.

After excusing himself early in the evening and getting a solid night's sleep, Bueno set out the following morning to discover Jack Terranova's last movements in Cali. The details were sketchy. Carl Stickley had been trailing the guy as he sauntered out on little forays from his nest at the Hotel Intercontinental. Accompanied by Faro's driver in one of the hacienda Jeeps, he paid a visit to the hotel and wandered around with pesos in his pockets and questions on his lips. There had been a girl, it seemed. Seventeen or eighteen, tops. A real looker, according to the elevator operator. Not local or even Colombian, according to one of the bellmen who had spoken with her. The accent was all wrong. Flatter and quicker, like one of the tongues from up north. It made sense. Cardona was Nicaraguan, and the accent described could easily be from the same region.

No one using Terranova's name had rented a car, but a man fitting his description—a big, tough-looking gringo who spoke no Spanish—had hired a small brown Renault and parked it in the basement lot. The car was one of those midget jobs that looked like a tiny station wagon. Bueno asked at the hotel for the name of any rental agency they might generally recommend to tourists. He was now receiving his latest information from a pleasant female clerk.

"The same man did not return the car," she told him. Her eyes traveled down to the pocket the last fifty-peso note had emerged from. Henry slid another out and onto the counter. "He was a man not authorized to drive the car at all," she continued. "When I told him this, he say I am lucky to see it returned at all."

"What did he look like?" Henry pressed.

"Dirty," she said flatly. "Stinking like cheap cologne and

cigars. Grease in the cracks in his hands and under his finger-nails. He left on foot.''

"Has this car been cleaned yet?" he asked.

She shook her head. "I should not think so. Enrique would know. He is around the back. It was . . ." She checked her clipboard. "Number seventeen."

Bueno found Enrique with a garden hose in his hand, splashing water at a Toyota Land Cruiser. He was just a kid, maybe sixteen, working shirtless in the blazing midday sun. His lean body glistened with sweat, and he was tanned so black that his ready smile fairly sprang from his mouth and eyes as he sighted the fifty this stranger extended toward him. No, he hadn't gotten to number seventeen yet, and sure, Henry could look all he wanted for that kind of money. A key wasn't necessary. It was open.

As Bueno wandered along the line of parked cars, looking for seventeen, he wondered how they'd managed to get a man to work in the dead middle of siesta. The sun was blazing down on the Valle de Cauca with the intensity of a blowtorch. The car rental business must really be booming.

The Renault in question was coated with dust and grime, its condition suggesting a long trip over unimproved roads. Henry stooped and ran a finger over a tire and then up inside the wheel well, finding red dust and a little dried mud of the same color. A clue of sorts, but not particularly valuable. This sort of ferrous-rich soil abounded throughout the area. Every year when the rains came, the rivers and streams ran orange with the silt of erosion. He pushed himself to his feet and tried the handle of the driver's side door.

The counter woman hadn't exaggerated her evaluation of the most recent occupant's cologne. The interior still reeked of some particularly putrid brand. There was also a slick of perfumed hair oil on the headrest. Cigar ashes covered the floor and filled the ashtray. There were two peso coins and an empty matchbox in the map pocket on the left door.

Bueno slowly worked his way back, meticulously going over the entire interior. The rear passenger area was compara-tively clean. He climbed out the back door and circled around to the rear of the vehicle to pop the back hatch. There, on the tiny luggage deck, he noticed a small pool of clean, amber-colored fluid. It felt like oil. Relatively odorless; a light grade. Something tickled his memory: he had once helped to

repair a damaged DC-3 in the Honduran jungle. A tube had
ruptured, and he held it while the pilot worked to make a
patch. Hydraulic line. That was it. The dripping hydraulic
fluid had gotten on his hands. The stuff he now rubbed
between thumb and forefinger was of a remarkably similar
color and consistency.

Henry bent in and scrutinized the area. Going over it inch
by inch, he spotted a tiny scrap of crumpled paper between
the deck and the spare tire well beneath. It could be insignifi-
cant, but who knew? Lifting the deck to expose the spare tire,
he snagged the wad of paper as it tried to tumble further into
the compartment. After making the effort to flatten it without
damage, he could tell that the scrap had been torn from a
book or catalog. Along one edge was scrawled a series of
numbers, and the paper was grease-smudged. The girl inside
had mentioned that the man returning the car had heavy black
grease in the creases of his hands and beneath his nails. Seven
numbers. A phone?

Henry returned to the Jeep, climbed in beside Willie's
driver, and directed him to a public booth. After dialing the
seven numbers from the scrap of paper, he heard a connection
made, and a phone begin to ring.

"Cali Aeronautica," a woman's voice purred into his ear.
"Buenos tardes."

Bingo. *"Buenos tardes,"* he returned. "Does your firm
handle the repair and replacement of aircraft hydraulics?"

"Yes, señor. What is it I can help you with?"

He told her he would rather come in person than attempt to
explain over the phone and asked where they were located.
When she gave him the address, he scribbled it down, thanked
her, and headed for the Jeep.

"You know where this is?" he asked the driver.

The man scrutinized the scribbled information and nodded.
"International airport."

"Let's go," Henry told him.

The twin-engined turboprop dropped in lazy circles toward
a rural airstrip down the mountain from Quito, Ecuador.
Located just a stone's throw from the equator, the city still
sustains cool, almost European spring temperatures year round
because of its extreme altitude. On a perpetually green mountainside extending upwards into the clouds, the city's three

quarter of a million inhabitants move in apparent ignorance of the space age. It is a romantic place with Old World charm and New World citizens. To an impartial observer who walked its streets at sunset and watched lovers stroll arm in arm past gardens and ancient colonial architecture, it would seem a strange place to import murder.

The young Nicaraguan named Luis was obviously nervous about staying in the same room as the professional American killer. Shortly after situating in the Hotel Intercontinental, the two men eyed each other with unbridled contempt. Luis was a patriot who would do anything for his lost homeland. He had traveled on many covert missions at Colonel Cardona's request, to New York to meet with the CIA man and to California to relay messages to Cardona's people in Silicon Valley. This was the most unpleasant undertaking he had yet faced in service of his country and his family name.

Luis was a genuinely good-looking kid, not particularly Hispanic in appearance, with bright blue eyes and sandy hair. Terranova loathed his aristocrat's brand of detachment and arrogance. Luis couldn't help these things. He'd been forsaken here, left to his own devices, and the devices he had for dealing with a crude common killer were few.

"Why don't you take a walk, pal?" the hitter suggested. He sat in his chair with one arm around the waist of the whore standing at his side. "Ask the desk about the best place to get some chow around here. Check out the neighborhood."

Luis resented being commanded by such a man almost enough to lash back. The words started forming on his lips before he thought better and controlled them.

"How long?" he asked.

"Make it an hour. And ask the desk to get a cot up here."

Anna rubbed her pelvis up against the big man's chest, distracting him. His hand slipped from her waist down to cup one cheek of her ass. As she squirmed some more, the American glanced over in irritation. The young Nicaraguan hadn't moved.

"Blow!" Jack snarled.

With Luis gone from the room, Terranova grinned into the beautiful girl's eyes. She leaned into him then, working a

62

hand inside his shirt to play with the matted hair on his massive chest.

"After the big payday, you're coming with me," he told her. "You like that idea?"

She was already on her way to her knees, one hand on his belt and the other tugging at his fly. "To be your woman?" she asked. Her fingers worked past his shorts and made contact with his heat. It throbbed against her hand.

"That's the idea," he mumbled, his focus changing. With thumb and two fingers he pulled her chin up and bent to push his tongue deep into her mouth.

Anna broke off the kiss, pushed back, and smiled wickedly with bright, shining eyes. Never releasing her hold on him, she leaned forward with tongue flickering.

"You will not regret having chosen me," she said softly. "You are stronger than any of them. A woman wants a strong man. In return for your strength, I will give you great pleasure."

As she spoke, he could feel the heat of her breath on him. As wetness suddenly engulfed him he grabbed a fistful of that lustrous black hair and held her there.

When Luis returned, Terranova was lying on the bed smoking. Anna, seated at the writing desk next to him, painted her nails.

"I hope you found us a restaurant," the big gringo said. "I haven't eaten since this afternoon."

Luis had just spent the better part of an hour resenting this fat American and being treated like his lackey. He stood in the middle of the room now, facing the man in open anger.

"No more, señor," he snarled hotly. "I will not tolerate this from you. I am *aristocratico*, the son of a Nicaraguan generalissimo. My family traces its roots back fifteen generations to the nobility of Cantabrica. I fight now for what is mine by right. You will not belittle either me or my family through me!" His eyes flashed, and veins bulged in his flushed crimson face.

On the bed, Terranova snorted derisively. "You think I give a fuck, junior? I'm the son of a butcher from Bensonhurst. You think that makes you better than me? *Might* makes right, you little shit. I can squash you like a gnat on the windshield of a speeding car." He stubbed out the cigarette in an ashtray and propped himself up on one elbow, pointing a finger. "A pack of commies squashed your daddy the same way, pal. You got the nuts to take it all back, then it's yours, hotshot. You wanna give me plane fare back to Miami and dust this minister dude yourself? Fine by me. Like I said, *if* you got the balls and the smarts. I doubt you got either."

Luis stood riveted, his jaw bulging. Anna, amused by this exchange, blew on her nails and stood. She approached the rooted Luis with mischief in her eyes. Standing directly in front of him and staring straight into his eyes, she reached out and felt his crotch. Luis colored, drawing back.

"I do not know about his brain," Anna announced, giggling over her shoulder. "He definitely does *not* have the *cojones*."

The woman working the counter at Cali Aeronautica had a good memory for recent transactions. Fifty pesos was necessary to stimulate it. There had been only one customer with a need for hydraulic equipment the previous day. A man from a tiny airport in Pitalito, a mountain town to the south. He had called ahead, inquiring about a reconditioned hydraulic fluid pump for a PBY. They were able to supply him with such a unit. He arrived with the defective part as core exchange around noon, requesting that they ship the replacement part. She remembered specifically that he hadn't wanted to take the thing with him because the car he drove was borrowed from a friend locally and had to be returned. She also remembered that he was crude in appearance, had heavily greased hair, and smelled of cologne and cigars.

Returning in the Jeep to Willie's hacienda, Henry had the feeling that he'd taken the first real step toward discovering Jack Terranova's whereabouts. He was unfamiliar with Pitalito and wondered if his host might know anything about the place. His map told him it was in the mountains to the south and east of Popayan. Not too distant. In one of Faro's high-powered vehicles he could make it there in a matter of hours.

Over a late lunch he filled Willie in on developments while Cristina listened silently. Faro received the information with furrowed brow, nodding at certain junctures. Pitalito, unknown to Henry, seemed to strike a familiar note.

"Very popular with certain interests because of its isolation," Willie told him. "The government attempts to keep tabs on such places, but it is difficult. In patrolling an area such as Pitalito, customs men, removed from the direct scrutiny of their superiors, have demonstrated a keen interest in bribe money."

"Would there be any problem with going in for a look?" Bueno asked.

"It depends," Faro told him. "If there is no current activity, the place is like a ghost town. The man who runs the airport is a mechanic there. I would only let him touch a plane I was to fly in out of total desperation. Fortunately, I have never been that desperate." He smiled.

Bueno ate soup as he thought. "I'd like to get up there tonight, if I could," he said at length. "My money says that Terranova drove there yesterday. I'm also betting that this mechanic who runs the place is the guy who returned his car this morning. Our shooter was meeting someone up there, to be flown out. The question remains, to where? Maybe that mechanic can tell us something."

"I would not recommend such a trip after dark," Willie warned, shaking his head. "The mountains are dangerous. If you were to have a flat tire or mechanical failure, you would be at the mercy of the bandits, and there are many."

Henry smiled. "I appreciate your concern, but I have been the hunter of many things aside from snakes. I find comfort in darkness. It allows more freedom than the light of day. If you are worried about your driver, I can make the journey alone. All I ask of you is a vehicle suited to those roads."

Willie had started to grin, too.

"A trip into the mountains would do me good. It has been a long time since I have embraced such danger. I begin to grow soft, thinking like a grandmother. We can take the Ford Ranger pickup. It has four-wheel drive and a powerful V-8 engine."

Henry attempted to wave him off. "It wouldn't be any problem to go alone."

From across the table, Cristina entered the conversation for the first time. Her eyes sparkled as she addressed their guest. "Please. He is like a child, Señor Riberac. If he has set his mind and could not go with you, he would pout for a week. It would be impossible for me to live with him."

"How can you face being responsible for destroying the

tranquility of this home?'' Willie asked. ''No one should be forced to put up with my pouting for a week.''

Bueno, figuring that two men together on a dark mountain road might be better than one, accepted Willie's offer.

By late afternoon, Henry and Willie were speeding along the main road to Popayan. As an extra precaution, Faro had secreted a Czech-made AK-47 automatic rifle behind the front seat, in addition to Bueno's over-under turkey gun. Both carried sidearms.

''You seem to have a fairly understanding woman there,'' Henry commented.

''A *smart* woman,'' Faro countered. ''We get along now because we understand each other. For many years it was not that way. We spent most of our time fighting. She was not willing to accept me as I must appear to the men around me.''

Bueno knew that machismo was a difficult sword to wield artfully. Cristina Faro seemed a woman with too strong a sense of herself to put up with Willie's brand of image reinforcement. He thought that in her, Willie might have met his match.

They proceeded through Popayan and on toward Purace as the shadows lengthened and night began to fall. The road was not bad as unimproved roads go. It was the dry season, and the surface had been recently graded.

''After that night so many years ago, I have heard rumors of one I assume was you,'' Willie told Bueno thoughtfully. He was also concentrating on the twisting road ahead. ''A loner who walked with death. When he appeared, the lives of men changed, as mine did. That night, I was dead, and now I am alive. I have often wondered who this man really was.''

Like Faro, Henry was concentrating on the road. Without taking his eyes from it, he spoke.

''Does it matter, Willie? As you say, they are rumors.''

Faro sighed and nodded. ''Forgive me.''

Henry turned to peer out his side window at the crimson glow of remaining light and the long, stark shadows. It was a time of day he truly loved. There was clarity in it. His eyes could drink in the sharp focus of things. Nothing shimmered as in the midday sun. There were no mirages at dusk.

The Ford four-wheeler ate up the dirt roads, and the two travelers reached Purace by nightfall. They paused for a couple of cold sodas from a roadside *bodega*. Further along, San Agustin offered an opportunity to stop and stretch a little after ten o'clock. Willie bought a bag of *chincherones,* and Henry crunched down on a hunk of the crude stuff with relish. The fatty, fried hogskin made his stomach growl. The absence of fat on his well-honed physique belied an undying fondness for food. Lunch was the last meal he'd eaten, and he was hungry. He'd once taught himself to ignore the thought of food whenever it wasn't readily available. In this, a transition from his recent life of creature comfort, the juices of digestion were busy trying to eat holes in his stomach lining.

"Will you indulge me? One more question?" Willie asked as they got underway.

Henry shrugged. "Shoot."

"Two days after I saw you last, I sent two of my men to Guaqui. They were to find the man who held me under threat of death and killed two of my friends. They were late by thirty-six hours. You?"

Bueno smiled, shaking his head. "I also hear rumors," he said. "They are about a Frenchman who hunts snakes. Some are so fantastic that I tell myself I must meet this man some day."

Maureen Counihan lay on the molded foam raft, floating with her hands dangling in the cool, chlorinated water. Late in the California afternoon, the sun angled at her from just above the mountain ridge to the west. Even with winter approaching, the weather was holding warm, and she could still indulge in these beloved sessions in her backyard pool. Eyes closed beneath dark sunglasses, she appeared to be asleep. Her breasts heaved gently up and down in a steady, rhythmic breathing, her lips slightly parted. At thirty-one, her body was easily on the plus side of good. There was no embarrassment in wearing her skimpy string bikini. Unlike a lot of redheads, she was fortunate enough to tan instead of freckle and burn.

Mo drifted, thinking and sorting through the events of the past two days. She was reflecting on how complicated her life had become. At twenty-five, fresh out of B-school, she'd thought she had the weight of the world on her shoulders. What a joke. The world weighed nothing then. It was a lot heavier now.

The FBI man with the stuffed-shirt name, Roscoe Charles, turned out to be less of a nightmare than she'd anticipated. Real standup, actually. East Coast prep to a fault; these guys were born in Topsiders and little alligator shirts. Charles at least seemed able to think on his feet. He was a lot better than one of those gung-ho military types.

SYSTEMATICS was in big trouble. She knew that. The home and business computer hardware market had gone dangerously soft in the past two quarters. There was little doubt that giants like IBM and AT&T would survive. Even some of the bigger independents, like Hewlett Packard and Apple, still had enough tricks in the bag and money in the bank to keep them afloat. SYSTEMATICS was a borderline case. As the marketing and financial whiz of the organization, Mo had to admit this. During the years when the barons of the Silicon Valley were busy butchering the fatted calf, her dad had done extremely well on table scraps. He'd even stolen a fillet or two. Now the company was in danger. Cash flow was already down, even though the actual reserves were substantial. Research and Development was still being adequately funded, but that kind of money wouldn't remain available forever with Sales and Marketing turning in the disappointing sort of numbers they'd reported last quarter. Sales and Marketing were *her* babies. Try as she might to pull another rabbit out of the old hat, she'd found very little to encourage her. Some mystery bastards were reaming her golden goose from the hind end while she labored up front, struggling to breathe life into it. The idea made her spitting mad. Nobody did this to her. Not without paying in spades. If the FBI wanted to catch these thieving interlopers, they were going to have to be quicker and smarter than she was. Otherwise, *she* was going to make personally sure that the sons of bitches paid.

SIX

It was dark in the park called El Eljido. Leaning against the trunk of a tree in deep shadow, Jack Terranova held a lit Lucky in a cupped right hand. He smoked slowly and thoughtfully. Directly across the boulevard, the stately Hotel Colon glowed like a gem set against a backdrop of midnight-blue velvet. A grouping of Cadillac and Mercedes limousines with tiny fender flags sat parked just beyond the main entrance. Uniformed chauffeurs lounged alongside, some engaged in conversation. Guarding the entrance were a pair of Ecuadorean military Jeeps bearing a number of officers of middle rank. They were positioned as a sort of command post, supervising the heavily armed foot patrols surrounding the entire hotel complex. Their men carried submachine guns and Valmet assault rifles. In addition to this most obvious security, Terranova observed the movements of another dozen plainclothes types. These carried Uzi 9mm machine pistols and moved with the expert ease of men trained to anticipate and react instinctively. The shooter was impressed. For a jerkwater Third World republic, security here was surprisingly well-coordinated. To try to bust right in there to dust Garcia-Alvarez was an act for fanatics. Jack Terranova was anything but.

With the compact field glasses he carried now eased to his eyes, he studied the Colombian minister's car and driver. It was a stretch Caddy Seville. Late model. From the way the light reflected off the glass, he estimated a thickness of at least half an inch. With an obviously beefed suspension, the whole buggy sagged perceptibly. Armored. The driver was a burly, thickset character with a heavy black beard and mirrored sunglasses. The bulge to the left in his double-breasted jacket wasn't his Norelco cordless shaver. A man practiced at his art, Terranova deftly slid a compact 35mm camera from his shoulder bag and fitted it with a telescopic zoom lens. The black-and-white film in the camera was rated at 1000 ASA. He was currently pushing it to twice that. The shots wouldn't win any awards, but they'd get him plenty to work with.

Steadying the rig against the tree, he shot while exhaling steadily, the shutter speed set at 1/15th second. The work required considerable patience. It was a full hour before the driver of the Colombian car had presented all four sides of his face to full view of the lens.

Shrouded now in moonless darkness, the road between San Agustin and Pitalito clung tenaciously to the mountainside it traversed. Willie's Ranger attacked the terrain like a terrier scrambling over a boulder. From behind the wheel he stared intently at the road, spinning the wheel to and fro. He was seemingly unmoved by jarring ruts and skidding tires as his headlights clawed at the gloom. He and Henry rode in silence now, eyes trained ahead into the hole torn by the headlamps.

The obstruction in the road appeared so suddenly around a sharp bend that Willie, had he not been concentrating so fiercely, would never have had time to brake without plowing into it. An overturned cart, apparently abandoned. No more than a second elapsed before the astute *marijuanero* jammed the truck into reverse and stomped the accelerator to the floor. Without a word passing between them, Henry tossed his P-5 on the dash within easy reach and groped between his knees for the *Tikka* M07 shotgun-rifle. They were moving backward around the turn at a good clip when the windshield disintegrated in their faces.

Both of them were already slumped down when the hail of lead hit. Jerking the wheel hard, Willie got the truck crossways in the road, tailgate planted against the landward cliff. Bueno was already tumbling out the passenger door and onto the hard-packed surface of the road. Willie landed almost on top of him.

"Four guns," Henry grunted. He was busy checking the .22 caliber Remington clip and twelve-gauge loads from his prone position. "Two behind the cart and two below the road line. They're sure to try flanking us now. I'm going down and around to cut it off. Think you could keep them busy?"

Willie grinned. "That will depend on how fast you are."

"Bandits are basically cowards," Henry told him. "If we want to draw them out, you'll have to make yourself look like easy pickings. Keep it switched to semiauto. Only one shot at a time. When the pair in the bushes down there make their flanking move, I'll give them a little surprise." In demonstration, he hefted his pistol and produced a four-inch metal cylinder from his jacket pocket. With accustomed ease, he fitted the thing to the muzzle of the gun and spun it into place.

Ahead in the road, they heard a voice shouting, ordering them to surrender. Henry jerked back the action on the Walther, chambering a round, and patted Willie on the shoulder. In another moment, he had vanished into the night.

It was not heavily wooded up at this altitude, the rugged mountains dotted instead with stands of scrub timber and covered elsewhere with bright green grass. For Willie, alone with this landscape plunged into pitch-blackness, the silence engulfing it was deafening. He leaned against the front tire of the truck and strained to hear all the sounds, sorting through them. From the mountainside rising steeply away from him on his left, he could make out nothing. There were occasional movement sounds of the scraping sort coming at him along the road dead ahead. Down the embankment to his right, Riberac was making no noise at all.

Willie dropped from his crouch onto his belly and slowly worked his way across the shoulder of the road. He slid over the edge of the embankment to give himself a better view of the obstruction in the road ahead. Huddled there, squinting into the gloom, he shivered. Total isolation gripped him, laced with a healthy dose of fear. It was occurring to him that Henri might have set the whole thing up. He was naked and alone.

After taking a few deep breaths, Faro forced himself to regulate his respiration. The thought of the Frenchman's possible treachery was pushed from his mind. If anything, he told himself, he was an excellent judge of character, though perhaps not of the Boy Scout variety. Riberac, or whoever he was, embodied integrity in the broader sense. He had saved his life once and put himself at considerable risk to do so. Right now, Henri was doing precisely what he said he would do. That meant that Willie had better keep up his end of the deal. Diversion. With sights trained on nothing in particular in the road ahead, he squeezed off a round. The crack of an explosion rang in his ear. His muzzle flash gave his position away. For his trouble, he was pinned to the earth by a withering barrage of automatic weapons fire. AKs, by the sound of it.

To his right and below, Willie heard the slight rustle of movement as the shooting died out. If he hadn't been listening as hard as he was, the telltale *pfffft!* of Riberac's silencer would have escaped him. With a smile, he leveled the barrel of his rifle along the surface of the road and cranked off two more quick shots.

When Bueno disappeared from Faro's view, he worked quickly downhill to a depth below the probable path of any flanking attempt. With an ear tuned to the scuttling of dislodged pebbles and crunch of dead flora, he crept in silence, parallel to the road above. Ten yards ahead he spotted more than he'd hoped for. A large outcropping of granite perhaps eight feet in height. Angling toward it, he slid into the shadow and pressed an ear to the ground.

The shuffle of footsteps, very close by. He raised his head, and the faint sound of heavy breathing reached his ears. Above and ahead to the left, two people. They were going to pass directly across the upper surface of his rock. He pressed in close to its coolness and inched his way ahead. He would let them pass above his outstretched gun hand.

Up on the road he heard the single report of Willie's AK-47, followed by a hail of bullets from the other team. The pair above him got careless in their haste to move under cover of the noisy gunfight. Henry sprang up the intervening half-dozen feet and moved into position behind his oblivious adversaries. The first one went down amid the dying chatter of weapons fire above. The second, unaware, continued on. Twenty, twenty-five feet away as Henry sighted at the base of his skull, drew breath, let half out, and squeezed gently on the trigger. Before the man hit the ground, Bueno turned and was off again.

Approaching a position below the overturned cart in the road, Bueno slid the sling of the *Tikka* up across his chest and over his head. He preferred the light caliber of the rifle for this sort of work. With the muzzle break, low recoil, and special infrared sensitive scope attached, it was deadly accurate in midrange sniping situations. With a twelve-gauge shotgun barrel riding above it, he was equipped for anything that could happen. His opponents had an advantage of firepower. He had the elements of surprise and versatility.

He heard Willie back at the truck, intermittently firing into the ambush position. Every bullet was answered a dozenfold. Macho bullcrap. Bueno hoped they were enjoying themselves. Their pleasure was going to be short-lived. He crawled stealthily to the level of the roadbed and raised his head slightly to survey the situation. By this time, the two men manning the barricade must have been wondering what could be delaying their confederates in their flanking maneuver. Still, they appeared content to play a waiting game with what was apparently all the ammunition in the world. It was while watching their antics that Henry first noticed the Jeep.

It was parked thirty yards further down the road, tucked back into the shadows of the cliff above. It's most notable feature was the cherry-red glow of a cigarette or cigar. It brightened as the smoker inhaled and then went dull again. Interesting. A noncombatant sitting in remote comfort and watching the show. His attitude gave him all the earmarks of a kingpin—possibly even the architect of this little ambush. Henry knew that no matter what went down from here, he would want to keep this one alive. Kingpins hereabouts would have access to information that might prove valuable in the search for Terranova. He also knew, from studying a map of the locale, that this road dead-ended at Pitalito. If this guy were encouraged to jet off out of harm's way, he would be effectively trapped just a stone's throw away. Cigar smoke reached Henry's nostrils, cutting through the blanket of cordite in the air. One of these other desperadoes could be helpful in locating this character once he'd been encouraged to cut and run.

Bueno took careful aim, training the muzzle of the rifle just to the left of the cigar glow. The ensuing shot gave his position away but had the desired primary effect. The two guys on the barricade whirled as Henry brought the *Tikka* around. One took a single slug in the heart, while his partner was spared instant death with a round cranked into his upper right arm. Up the road, the Jeep roared suddenly to life, jerked spasmodically into reverse, and turned to beat a skidding retreat. In the dirt before him, Henry watched the surviving desperado writhe in anguish.

"Willie!" he hollered. "Bring the truck up."

He stepped across, loosening his belt for application as a tourniquet.

"You're going to live, amigo," he told the man calmly as he stooped to look at the arm. The slug had gone clean through without hitting bone. Lucky.

Moments later, Faro pulled up in front of the overturned cart, hopped out of the truck, and surveyed the carnage.

"There are two more down the hill," Henry said quietly. "Breakfast for the buzzards."

Willie frowned at the wounded man and reached for his pistol. Bueno held out a restraining hand.

"There was a fifth. In a Jeep parked up the road. He was smoking a cigar like a guy in the balcony of a Sunday matinee. I ran him off, but there's not far he can go."

Faro abandoned the impulse to turn the downed man into dog meat. "So let us see what our friend here can tell us."

Henry agreed. "With the pain he's in, he'll tell us about his boss and anything else we might think to ask about."

SYSTEMATICS Research and Development chief Phil Maldonado was just back from a Mexican vacation. When Maureen called that afternoon to ask if he would have dinner with her, there was a weariness in her voice directly related to some sort of problem she wanted to discuss. He was used to such discussions, being a bit more than just the woman's colleague and confidant. Unbeknownst to her dad and the rest of the SYSTEMATICS hierachy, Phil was screwing her on a pretty regular basis. It was an arrangement several years old now, mutually agreeable and based on the fact that neither of them was interested in commitment. Both were workaholics, and each liked the occasional elegant evening out as well as the company.

He listened attentively through dinner at an upscale little French place on the main drag in Saratoga village. Maureen seemed withdrawn and troubled at first. Gradually, with a little Bordeaux and his witty asides, she began to unwind. By the entree she finally spilled it, all the way to her enlisting the aid of the FBI.

Maldonado's strikingly handsome, chiseled features clouded with concern.

"What about our government contracts?" he asked.

"The agent was encouraging," she replied. "He couldn't promise anything, but we're already a key element in the Alamo system, and with some reengineering, a security breach could be sealed. That's our story, anyway. You and I know it's really up to the fucking generals. We know how easily *they* spook."

He nodded thoughtfully. "I suppose the best defense would lie in hopping right to it, huh? Get the research rolling; have something to present. If we can convince them that the consequences of re-awarding the contracts would be more disruptive than accepting our solution, they just might go for it."

"No telling what they'll do," she mumbled, sighing. "On the other hand, I think it's our only shot."

Maldonado smiled reassuringly and reached out to stroke her hand. "You know I'll do everything I can to help."

"You're sure you can make the time?"

"No problem. The WORDWARE programs were in the bag before I left. The research runs itself these days. If you want, I could put a couple of people on the Alamo thing full-time for a while."

Gratitude was plain in the redhead's eyes. "I'd really appreciate it. This whole thing has me more than a little on edge. I'm going to get this bastard. Trust me. When I do, I'm going to nail his balls over the front door."

The engineer winced at the thought. The look on his face set her laughing. She leaned forward and whispered conspiratorially.

"Don't worry, big fella. Yours are safe. I've got plans for *your* balls."

"Is that a proposition?" he asked.

She nodded. "You get the check, and I'm as good as yours."

Their wounded captive was at first determined not to rat out his employer. Willie set a boot gingerly on the bleeding bullet hole in his right arm while Henry posed his questions.

"What is the man in the Jeep's name? Where can he be found? Where did these guns and the ammunition come from?"

The third question was perhaps more pertinent than the first two because of the implications the scattered ordinance conveyed. Such weaponry went for thousands of dollars on the international black market, if it was available. Soviet guns meant a source with its own access to the Russian military aid pipeline. The presence of AK-47s on a remote Andean road in the Colombian boondocks suggested some ugly possibilities.

The man whimpered, staring up at his antagonist with fear-filled eyes. He shook his head. Faro's boot pressed down on the arm again, twisting viciously. Henry found himself reaching out to back him off. The bandit's agonized screams echoed through the gorge. When they subsided, the questions were put to him again.

Before long, they were in receipt of the information they sought. The local kingpin's name was Felix Colon. He was an entrepreneur who operated and also served as mechanic to the airstrip at Pitalito. Because of favors done for certain parties who demanded discretion, he was quite well-to-do by local standards. Recently, he had received rifles and bullets in payment for keeping his mouth shut about the embarkation of an American in an expensive twin-engined plane. The wounded man knew these things because Colon was married to his sister and bragged exceedingly much. He also contended that he had joined Colon's expedition that night because his corn crop had failed and his children were hungry. They were looking to ambush one of the *marijuaneros* who used the airstrip at night without leaving the customary gratuity. Bueno inwardly questioned their "shoot first, ask questions later" approach.

The wounded man had lost a lot of blood. While Willie hooked a tow chain to the cart and dragged it to the side of the road, Henry checked the tourniquet he'd fashioned from his belt, loosening it briefly to let blood flow and then retightening it.

"Why does he deserve to live more than the others?" Faro asked on his return.

Bueno gazed up at him. "Because it is finished, and we know what we need."

"Are you expecting to find him a doctor in Pitalito?"

"Not much chance of that," Henry replied. "But the

Indians have their own medicine. The bullet went clean through. He will remember his indiscretion for a while, but he won't die from it—unless Felix Colon gets his hands on him."

Faro thought about this and shrugged. "Then, if we are to play such humanitarians this night, we may have to neutralize such a threat, eh?"

"Help me get him into the bed," Henry suggested. "I'll ride there in back with him. This thing should be loosened every so often to keep the circulation going."

Throughout the last nine-kilometer drive into the tiny mountain town, Bueno considered this local operator, Felix Colon. He would have access to information concerning movements in and out of the area, traffickers carrying large sums of cash. It stood to reason that a man in a position of such importance might get greedy. But Felix was a coward, content to sit back and smoke while a pack of his poor piss ant friends did the dirty work.

Pitalito well after midnight. They rolled quietly into the middle of town, keeping an eye out for a light blue Jeep Renegade. The wounded man had described the location of Colon's home and then his own. They stopped there first and carried him to his front door. His wife turned white at the sight of the wound in his arm. Willie moved quickly to slide a hand over her mouth as she started to scream. He whispered fiercely into her ear, and she regained control.

"There is an old man or woman who has the touch?" Bueno asked gently.

She nodded, eyes wide with fear.

"Go. Bring them. He is not as bad as he looks. What he needs most is rest."

Willie withdrew his hand from her mouth and pushed her on her way. Turning to Bueno, he spoke through gritted teeth.

"We are wasting time here."

Bueno's eyes were hard. "Saving a man's life is never a waste of time, Willie," he said. "We will get to Colon. I assure you."

Luis Ecchevarria and Anna were sullenly occupying opposite corners of the room when Jack Terranova returned to the Hotel Intercontinental. He chuckled as he entered, aiming a

leer at the young man as he walked in front of him to sloppily
tongue-kiss his woman. Her nipples protruded, straining the
thin cotton of her blouse. The thumb and forefinger of his left
hand kneaded one absentmindedly as he scanned the place
with a frown. The closet was too small, and he would have to
carry water there. Only the bathroom would do for his purposes.

"If either of you two have to use the *baño*, do it now," he
said gruffly. "I've got work to do, and I'm gonna be in there
a while."

Moments later he had locked himself inside the spacious
bath and was busy taping two towels over the small frosted
window. From his bag he withdrew a penlight and fixed a
small piece of red cellophane over the bulb. He ran water into
a pair of small plastic trays, then he shook fixer and developer into them from two vials. As the chemicals were dissolving
into solution he doused the lights, placed the reddened penlight
so he could see what he was doing, and carefully opened his
camera. The film went onto the spool of a stainless steel
developing tank into which was poured enough developer to
process the negatives.

When the entire thirty-six exposures were processed and
fixed, he turned the overhead light back on and held the film
up to it. On examination of the results, most of the images
appeared to be acceptable. Jack's plan A could go forward.
He felt the excitement in the pit of his stomach.

The primary plan was always the neatest one. Secondary
schemes often got messy. His enthusiasm now at peak level,
he set about assembling an ingenious enlarger that was little
more than a simple wire stand. On the flat surface of its base,
a piece of photosensitive paper was placed. Halfway up the
wire shaft was a loop. On this he laid a one-and-a-quarter-
inch magnifying lens. Several inches up from it was another
loop, upon which he laid the negative. With the penlight held
poised above the negative, he switched it off and removed the
red cellophane. The button on the penlight was hit for just an
instant, and then the red gel was replaced. He removed the
exposed paper gingerly from the base and dropped it into the
developer. Slowly, in the red glow of his light, the image of
the Colombian's bodyguard/chauffeur took shape. It was a
good, clear shot in profile.

For the next three hours, the hitter repeated the process until
all thirty-six exposures had been enlarged. Seventeen were

throwaways. A dozen more were only marginally useful. The rest, seven of them, were excellent likenesses of the man: clear, sharp, a little grainy, but very serviceable.

Phil Maldonado possessed a hard, athletic body with wide, square shoulders and a spare, muscular frame. He knew all the right moves and employed them expertly. As he labored, sweating and writhing above her, Maureen sensed his detachment. It was always like that; he simply went away, as though he were performing for himself in a void.

It frustrated her to know she lied in return. Lied in her trumped-up responses to his athletic lovemaking. The first time, it had been exciting. His detachment left her alone to slip into her own thoughts. She had a reputation for being a cold bitch. Maybe that was why she enjoyed the noninvolvement . . . at first. After their initial encounter, she'd told herself that this was just the sort of man a cold bitch needed. Unfortunately, she was nowhere near as cold a bitch as she wanted the world to imagine.

Maldonado rolled off her, panting, to claim his half of the bed. He grunted the obligatory words of casual affection and brushed his lips across her forehead. She lay staring sightlessly toward the ceiling. Maybe it was all the recent developments at the plant that had her so on edge. The surges of fury that swept over her were confusing. She was suffocating. Unable to lie still, she slipped from the sheets and padded barefoot from the room. Outside on the patio beside the pool, she looked up at a fog-shrouded first-quarter moon. The water barely reflected it, shimmering gray. She rose up on her toes and dived in.

The cool enveloped her, and Maureen felt a release of tension. With several strong strokes she broke the surface and took a deep lungful of the misty night air. The fog was stealing what little November heat still remained trapped in the valley. Its chill made her skin tighten with goosebumps. She was aware of every square inch of herself. She wanted a man who could do that to her.

Ted Latham and FBI Special Agent Conrad Burke sat across a coffee shop table from each other in Frederick, Maryland. Burke hailed from Salt Lake, was a devout Mormon, and had come to Ted's tight circle of patriot bureaucrats by way of another committed Company man. Shooting like a skyrocket up through the Bureau ranks, he'd had opportunities to prove his worth to the group on a number of occasions. He currently worked in the office of the director and had access to very hot intelligence even before it crossed the big man's desk. Just such an item was now on the table, hot enough to justify a clandestine meeting forty miles from the District and its prying eyes.

"I saw the word Alamo on the file cover and felt the old pulse kick in," Burke told the CIA Latin liaison. "The goddamn company we thought would be perfect because it was such small potatoes has gone and stumbled on us. Instead of trying to cover up like we'd expect them to, they *requested* that the Bureau step in."

Latham winced at the wretched taste of his coffee and set the big cup back in its saucer. He'd had too much today already.

"Who'd you people send in?" he asked.

"Trouble," Burke assured him. "We keep a pretty close eye on what goes on around Silicon Valley because of the espionage potential. Guy who runs the show out there is a straight shooter named Roscoe Charles. Princeton, and then a law ticket from Boalt Hall. Mister bicoastal."

Latham slouched down in his seat and frowned.

"How much do they know?"

"Too much. Not the precise nature of the loss at this point, but they're holding enough information to narrow it down in a matter of maybe a week."

Latham drummed his fingers. "That's just about all we need. With a week we can have all components cleared of the area, and our little greaser buddy can get his boy the hell out of there. Two weeks and we spring the whole game on the NSC and the president. What's the director likely to do once he sees this thing?"

Burke, a big-framed guy with close-cropped blond hair and a broad, uninspired face, shrugged. "This guy sees red everywhere he turns. First thing he'll do is order surveillance of every Sov at the Frisco consulate. Then, unless Ross Charles can dissuade him, he'll send in the clowns and turn SYSTEMATICS inside out. The noise from it is something the press is likely to get wind of. That bunch could make so much of it that you might not have any thunder left to take in and shake up the Oval Office.''

"Not necessarily," Latham countered. "They could play it right into our hands. Alamo components are reported pilfered, moved to an unknown destination. That makes everyone, from Defense on up, just antsy as hell. Two weeks from now, *we* lead 'em right *to* the stuff. They'll go for our little Rooskie–Sandinista collaboration angle hook, line, and sinker.''

The viselike fingers of a clenching hand were stealing the oxygen from Felix Colon's brain. He awoke in a flailing frenzy, struggling to focus. Before him, he saw two eyes bearing down, boring into him, burning him. His own fragile life, hanging by the merest of threads, was reflected in them. Suddenly, the hands released their grip. The metallic crack of a round being chambered split the quiet of the room. The silenced muzzle of a 9mm automatic prodded his jawline just below the ear.

"*Buenos noches*, Felix," a voice purred. "We enjoyed the little reception committee you had out on the road tonight. Nice guns. I know you didn't get those guns locally, Felix. A Nicaraguan named Diego gave you those after he picked up an American from your strip. The plane, Felix. Registration. Direction it was heading. How Diego made contact with you.''

Colon's eyes bulged. The room smelled of his cologne and the residue of a thousand smoked cigars. His wife was no longer beside him in the bed.

"My hand is sweaty, Felix. This trigger is very sensitive. The gun could go off at any moment. You should start coming up with answers.''

"They made like they were flying north," the mechanic blurted. He tried to glance sideways and downward at the gun. "But I can hear an engine for many miles. They turned south. Twin-engined Cessna with American registration. Blue and white. N706 . . . I cannot remember, I swear. The man flew into my strip three weeks ago. I never see him before in my life. He tell me I be paid well for one simple favor. When the gringo he arrive, I give him coffee. That is all of it, I swear.''

Henry backed his gun off. "Three of your town folk are

dead, Felix. Why? So you could prove that you are a big man with your new guns?''

Before Felix could formulate a response, a second man appeared. This one he recognized as one of the biggest traffickers in the country, Willie Faro.

''You are both a coward and a pig,'' Faro told him. Without ceremony, he produced his own pistol, a Beretta Model 84. Lowering it, he took aim at Colon's left knee and fired. Felix screamed a bloodcurdling scream, writhing in agony. Faro ignored the outcry from the twisting form as he drew a bead on the other knee. The second sharp crack was partially muffled by cartilage and bone. The way Willie saw it, the farmer with the failed corn crop would be safe from this animal now. If Felix Colon survived blood loss and possible gangrene, he would never walk again.

SEVEN

Jack Terranova had little time to waste. He rolled away from the slumbering Anna and padded barefoot across the cool tile floor of the room. Closing himself in the bath, he studied his face in the mirror and shaved. With each stroke, he compared his face mentally to the one in those photographs. His binoculars had revealed a remarkable similarity between the chauffeur's features and his own. Heavy bones. Thick nose. Low hairline. Strong brow. From the way the man carried himself, it was obvious that he functioned as more than a mere driver. He had an air of efficiency that Jack called "killing cool." In assessing his adversary, Jack took great pains to evaluate this quality. Casual assumptions could be costly. This guy was good at what he did. You didn't get where he was without proving yourself. This could also be a plus. Other men, even associates, tended to give a man of such stature wide berth. It was a good bet that once this man was removed and replaced, his well-disguised substitute would not be scrutinized too closely. It was a lucky stroke that the target insisted on wearing heavy sunglasses, even at night. You could tell a lot about a man from his eyes. Jack was going to undertake some very intimate aspects of the man's work. Risky enough *with* the shades. In fact, if the target didn't wear them, he would be resorting to plan B or C at this very moment.

Finished with his shave, he gritted his teeth and slipped under the stream of a cold shower. At this altitude, the cold water was like ice. The shock to his system was intense and the effect immediate. When he emerged, all vestiges of sleep and sex were gone.

A tailor must be found and put to work immediately. The only way to find one, without leaving a trail for possible inquiry, was to walk the streets. He told Anna that he was going to be out for some hours and glowered at Luis in his cot for effect. In the hotel restaurant, he got himself a cup of coffee and some fried eggs, wolfed them down, and hit the early-morning bustle of Quito. The air was brisk. A light mist lingered as he pushed his way down the sidewalks. At seven A.M., many shops were already open, and deliveries were being made.

The quality of the apparel in the window of the first shop he found didn't meet the standards of a well-heeled diplomat's henchman. The *modista* within glanced up from her sewing machine, smiled, and waved. He moved on.

Jack was impressed with the character of the city. He didn't know why it surprised him to find a place in South America so distinctly Old World. Maybe it was the stark contrast between Quito and the cities of the Caribbean rim. Concrete and glass surrounded by sprawling slums, they were that dismal Hispanic combination of New and Third Worlds. This was very different. Tight, twisting streets. Opulent old buildings. Churches like you might find in Barcelona. Donkey carts mixed in with the cars. The whole city had an atmosphere of relaxed, unhurried dignity. Sure, there were probably terrible slums sprawling off to the horizon somewhere close by, but he couldn't see them.

The shop he chose was elegant in an understated way. Bolts of Scottish woolens that must have cost a fortune were displayed in the front window. A nice street with nothing crassly commercial or touristy on it. There were a number of pre–Columbian artifact galleries. A jewelry store. A couple of high-end ladies' boutiques. Jack entered the comfortable interior, flipped the "open" sign over, and deftly drew the shade. A curtained doorway led to a room in the rear. Underfoot, a plush, heavy wool carpet muffled his steps. The furnishings were of rich old mahogany, the arrangement suggesting a salon. Perfect. He stepped to the curtain and pushed through.

The man at the sewing machine looked up into the barrel of a silenced .22-caliber automatic pistol. Slight, compact, and with wisps of snow-white hair combed across a nearly bald head, his eyes bulged, and he simply stared.

"Speak English?" Terranova asked.

Gulping, the man nodded. "*Poquito*. A little."

Jack handed him the three best photographs of the Colombian driver. "I need a suit like that. This morning."

"Impossible, señor."

"Nothing's impossible, pal. Especially when you've got a gun to your head. I'm not asking. I'm telling you."

The little man's eyes darted quickly aside and then back to the muzzle of the gun. There didn't appear to be much room for argument.

"Black," the hit man said. "Exactly like this. A little extra room under the left arm. If you get started five minutes ago and work like you've never worked in your life, you just might live to tell your friends about the crazy gringo who wanted a suit in a hurry. Now!"

The man jumped in his chair, tipping it over backward. Fumbling in agitation, he pawed through a stack of cloth, extracting a bolt of medium-weight, black worsted wool.

"Such a suit on short order will be expensive, señor. I have customers. Orders."

"You just took the morning off, pal. Unforseen personal business. Don't worry about the money. You'll be taken care of."

Terranova holstered the pistol once he was confident the man understood the situation. He removed his jacket and handed it over, directing that it be torn apart to make the pattern. That done, he presented his thick, muscular torso to the tailor in his shirtsleeves. After escorting him to a short dais, the little man began to take measurements. The bolt of cloth was run out on a large work table, and scissors came out. He used his tape and made little marks with chalk, often appearing to work by eye. The shears quickly lopped the fabric into irregular-shaped pieces. There was no doubt the man knew his trade.

The morning wore on as the tailor cut, basted, fitted, pressed, fitted, sewed, fitted. Half a dozen times, frustrated banging on the outer door floated through to the back of the shop. The telephone rang incessantly. When the suit reached that stage, Terranova told the guy to skip the interior finish, pockets, and lining.

"How can you, señor?" came the protest. "Such a beautiful suit. It is . . . insanity."

"Screw it, pal. I say skip it, you skip it." It was approaching noon, and the little man had been working feverishly for five hours. The way Jack figured it, the time allotted for this particular phase was just about up. The suit still had to be cleaned and pressed before that evening. "Just finish the cuffs and give me the goddamn thing," he growled. "I'm wasting time here."

Ten minutes later, it was ready.

"Nice work," Jack complimented. He was staring hard at the lines of the jacket in the mirror. From the neck down he was the spitting image of the Colombian's goon. 12:05. Right on schedule. He stepped from the dais and changed while the tailor stood anxiously by.

"I must have at least six thousand sucres for such work, señor," he said, wringing his hands. "The wool alone cost me more than fifteen hundred."

Dressed, Jack smiled at the man and reached into his jacket. The silenced automatic came out of its holster. He aimed between the man's panicked eyes and pulled the trigger. A neat, quarter-inch dab of crimson appeared suddenly on his forehead. As the little body began folding toward the floor like an abandoned marionette, it started to convulse.

Terranova returned the pistol to its roost and quickly scanned the carpet underfoot. Locating the casing, he stooped to pick it up. After turning off the lights, he pushed through the curtain to the front salon without a backward glance. Out on the street, someone paused before the door and knocked. Jack moved back into shadow, his hand on the butt of his gun, waiting. The knocking ceased, and in a moment, footsteps receded down the cobbles. He gave it a few minutes, then stepped to the door and lifted the shade enough to peer out. It was siesta now, and the street was quiet. The shades on adjacent doors were also pulled. He unlocked the door, turned the knob, and slid out onto the sidewalk.

*   *   *

FBI Special Agent Roscoe Charles, now hard at work trying to solve the SYSTEMATICS guidance component piracy, was awaiting Maureen Counihan in her office when she arrived for work.

"Have a minute?" he asked as she checked with her secretary for messages.

"Come on in," she told him. "You had coffee yet?"

He shook his head. "Not nearly enough."

"Rhonda, will you get us coffee, please? How do you take yours, Mr. Charles?"

"Black's fine."

They passed into her monochromatic sanctum. Charles eased into one of the gray armchairs as Maureen stowed her briefcase beside the desk, checked the soil moisture of the potted palm with a finger, and got situated across from him.

"So," she started, smiling and pushing a wisp of hair back from her forehead. "What sort of bad tidings do you bear so early on this bright and beautiful morning? Don't tell me. We're employing the entire Weather Underground."

"All but extinct," he assured her. "I was up half the night running your personnel. Nothing in our files. Nothing in the police files. You did all the required homework when you hired them."

"I suppose that's something of a relief."

"It's a fact that can't hurt you in the final analysis," he agreed. "But meanwhile, it makes my job a whole lot trickier. I've decided on *two* men. One is our own, and the other is a half–Vietnamese guy we're borrowing from the county sheriff's special industrial espionage unit. Both are crackerjack undercover men. They know this business. The Vietnamese man, Dai, is an electrical engineer from Cal. Our man, Davis, is specially trained in ferreting out saboteurs. He knows his way around a printed circuit and can handle a soldering iron."

"Any thoughts on where we might put them?"

"A couple. Ideally, I'd like Ronnie Dai in Inspection. He's got the background. Pete Davis would have a lot of freedom to move around if you could place him in Salvage. If that can't be worked, then something like Material Expedition or Maintenance."

Maureen considered the propositions. "An electrical engineer in Inspection probably won't be a problem if he's industry-

familiar. We have a lot of Vietnamese and Laotians working
on the production floor. They're a pretty close-knit community. Would that be trouble?''

"There's always the possibility," Charles told her. "But
Dai's family came here by way of Paris in 1965. His father is
a professor of economics at the University of Arizona. He's
never spent time in the boat-people communities.''

"Okay," she mused, considering the pluses and minuses.
"If he knows the language, it could be a real advantage.
They're also a close-*mouthed* bunch.''

"That's why we went out and got him. How about Davis?''

"That's tougher. Salvage would be ideal, but it's a pretty
small unit and considered something of a plum. Easier duty
than assembly-line work. With the push on to reduce defects,
we should be shrinking it, not expanding.''

The FBI man thought it over. "Would you rather go with
something like Maintenance?''

Maureen was thinking, too. "Let me talk to Dad. Maybe
there's someone in Salvage he could kick upstairs, to create a
vacancy.''

"That would be excellent. Obviously, we'd like to get
started as soon as possible. What would a good time frame
look like for you?''

Mo mulled it over. "A new inspector would be timely,"
she said. "With defects up, at least on paper, it would be a
perfect excuse to bring in some outside expertise. Might even
put a scare into the guilty party. I think we could get together
some sort of memo and put Mr. Dai to work almost immediately. My father would want to meet him. Could that be
arranged?''

Plans were made to bring Ron Dai to the plant the next
morning. He would go through the standard Personnel routine
and receive a tour of the facility and preliminary introductions. Maureen would get out a general announcement memo
about the disappointing defect figures, wording it to avoid
arousing any inside suspicion over motive. At the same time,
she would see if they could create room for a new man in
Salvage. After bidding the agent a good morning, Maureen
informed her secretary that she would be in conference with
her father and didn't wish to be disturbed. Gathering up her
notes on the FBI's strategy, she stuffed them into a folder and
carried them next door.

*   *   *

Cameron Stebbins knew he was getting old. In many respects, his had been a disappointing grab for the brass ring. He'd once envisioned himself heading up the Company, or perhaps the NSC. Neither of those dreams had been realized. He was just an old duffer very near the top now, and he would retire that way. The old dreams were laid to rest, but now there were new ones. Dreams of the last hurrah sort, something he could get a line on and employ to make his mark. Something to keep at bay the visions of his desk being filled by some young buck with fire in his eyes, good old Stebbins forgotten, a memory swept under the rug.

This recent revelation of Ted Latham's had all the earmarks of just such an item. The administration spent a lot of time crying wolf about Rooskies sneaking into the hemisphere. Down Nicaragua way, they'd had a hard time coming up with the goods. This could be just the ticket—the same sort of hard evidence as old Mad Jack Kennedy could finger during the Cuban Missile Crisis. He was going to have to play it cagey. "Jumpin' Johnny" Johnson over at the NSC would try to weave it into a laurel wreath if he gave *him* an early shot at it. No, this one was staying close to the vest until Latham delivered the hard goods. He seemed to have a pretty good liaison working with some high-up Contras, finger right on the pulse. In his years with the Company, Stebbins had gleaned enough to know that you had to bide your time if you were looking to hit the big casino. The nervous Nellies in this business were the ones who ended up blowing the big ones. Look at the Allende disaster and the Contra training manual scandal. Bad supervision and hastily-made decisions resulted in negative press.

Cam Stebbins had an old buddy from Annapolis who was wearing the hat of a joint chief these days. Admiral Pete McNichol could keep a secret. He could also have a team of SEALs ready to go in and confirm once Latham got a lock on his intelligence. That way, the Company could end up handing the Oval Office a feather for its cap without having to share the glory with the Security Council cowboys, the FBI, or anyone else. Cam Stebbins to the rescue.

The sun broke free of the horizon, dazzling a cool, misty Colombian morning. Everywhere, dew shimmered in millions of tiny, prismatic rainbows. Henry Bueno sat in a chair at the edge of Willie's vast veranda, sipping pineapple juice and staring out at the awe-inspiring sight of the Farallones de Cali. They broke abruptly skyward from the valley floor, rising almost five thousand vertical feet in just a few miles. Jagged-topped, they stood as a wall to the west, the brilliant morning sun bouncing off them.

Even though it confirmed a collaboration between Jack Terranova and the shadowy Diego Cardona, the previous night's foray into the mountains of the south had been, for all practical purposes, a dead end. These guys were definitely working together, and Carl Stickley had lost his life wedging himself between them. Whatever it was had to be big to warrant knocking off a pair of CIA agents, but where they were and what they were up to remained a mystery. Henry knew that until they made some sort of move, the trail would remain cold.

He and Willie had discussed this during their trip back to the hacienda. Faro extended an invitation to stay on as his guest until something gave. It made as much sense as anything, at least for the time being. As frustrating as it might become, he had no choice but to sit and wait. They had also had words about Willie going for the second of Colon's knees. Henry found that excessive.

Now, he eyed the sparkling water of the pool and pushed himself up from his chair. It was hard to believe that four days ago he'd been sailing on the open ocean off Big Sur. A world away. A life away. He ambled across the lawn and unfastened the latch to the low gate. Stepping to the diving board, he measured off the distance to the end, ran, sprang, and jackknifed cleanly into the water. The chlorinated coolness enveloped him as he pulled hard for the surface with long, sure strokes. Exercise was an integral part of the waiting process. The inactivity of down time could dull the senses, atrophy the muscles. He was fortunate to have the pool at his disposal. It was plenty large enough to afford him a good workout, and without it, he'd be forced to run. He hated running. After starting out with the breaststroke he soon changed to the crawl, and swam a hundred lengths.

"Good morning."

The light, musical voice of Cristina Faro floated over the

water to him as he completed his last circuit and clung panting to the side of the pool. He turned toward her.

"You swim like a seal. I don't believe I've ever seen anyone who looked so at home in the water."

"I *was* a seal once," he replied with a good-natured smile. "In another life."

The woman was wearing a light cotton wrap, which she quickly stripped off to reveal a long, well-turned physique. It was poured into an equally stunning one-piece suit. She stepped to the edge of the pool, came up onto her toes, and dived in, breaking the surface a moment later with an expulsion of breath. Hair plastered to her head and hanging in her eyes, she cleared her vision with an elegant backward dip of the head and smiled.

"I understand you will be staying with us awhile," she said.

He shrugged. "Perhaps. We wait and see what happens. The story of my life."

"I am sure it is only one such story," she contended. "I wish to extend my own welcome. You once saved my husband's life. This means more to me than even the struggle now to preserve his honor. Our house is yours, señor."

"Your hospitality is exceptional," he said.

She waved it off. "It is nothing. I am glad to finally meet the Frenchman who hunts snakes. After listening to Willie tell of you, I am delighted to discover you are *more* substantial than the myth. Such a thing rarely happens in life."

"Flattery will get you everywhere," he told her. Turning, he gripped the edge of the pool and hauled himself out. With water streaming from his body onto the surrounding cobble, he stooped to retrieve his towel.

She watched him. The muscles of his powerful frame propelled him onto the patio in one fluid motion. There were scars on his bronzed back and left shoulder. Brushes with death. It had been many years since a man had so piqued her fascination. She flipped onto her back now and started across the pool with long, sure strokes.

The double-breasted suit, now pressed and cleaned, fit impeccably. Jack Terranova stood in the middle of the room, admiring the tailor's handiwork in the large wall mirror. That afternoon he shopped for sunglasses, finding a pair almost identical to those the chauffeur wore. He had his hair trimmed, and, with the help of a bottled preparation, the flecks of gray were no longer visible.

Jack's travel kit contained theatrical makeup, and in addition he'd purchased a black wig, cheesecloth, and spirit gum. The beard the driver wore was styled below the cheekbones, scooped to accentuate his sideburns. With a pair of barber's scissors, he trimmed bits of the wig. He applied spirit gum to the cheesecloth, now cut in the shape of the desired beard, and glued the hair bits to it as uniformly as his steady hands could manage. It took over an hour to create the facial hairpiece. With the job done, he applied an even coating of the spirit gum to his own face and waited for it to get tacky before pressing his creation into place. It looked good. He handed the best two photographs to Anna, slipped on the new shades, and stood face-to-face with her for a critical inspection.

Luis also moved to regard the hired killer's new look as the girl exclaimed her approval. "Remarkable," he said softly. "They are the same man."

"Close enough," Jack growled. "I'm doing you people a favor, pal. You guys expect me to come down here and blow this government honcho off so you can finger some shithead and that's that. Wrong. You pull that sort of shit and all hell breaks loose. I don't know who you want to finger for the job afterward, but this way is cleanest. A guy on the *inside* turns on his boss, shoots him, and disappears. You've got the added element of confusion. Speculation over how much it took to buy him off. All that shit. In a couple hours, *I'm* gonna be that man on the inside. Tomorrow, they find the driver in this hotel room, an apparent suicide bullet in his brainpan. He'll leave a note about how he had some second thoughts, and the *note* fingers just who you want to implicate."

"The biggest cocaine trafficker in Colombia," Luis told him. "A man your Justice Department calls an enemy of the United States. His name is Guillermo Faro." The youngster's eyes gleamed brightly as he spoke. "This man has had reversals. We want it seen that he found his own government's antidrug crusade to blame."

"I could give a fuck," Terranova snarled. "Your business is yours, and I don't want to know fuck-all about it."

*   *   *

The itinerary Diego Cardona had provided told Jack that on the morning of the third conference day, the collected Contadora ministers would attend a breakfast at the presidential palace. Early by American standards, it was being hosted by the first lady and was scheduled for seven o'clock.

In his shopping, the hit man had made one other purchase. Now, with Luis and Anna before him in the hotel room, he opened a parcel and lay an expensive, revealing evening gown out on the bed. When the girl saw it, her eyes sparkled.

"Like it?" he asked.

"Very much. It is beautiful."

"Try it on," he encouraged her. Lifting it, he held it out.

With a mocking glance at Luis, she stripped out of her clothes, stood naked before them, and slid into the new garment. Luis, trying to take it all in with a proper measure of nonchalance, came up way short.

Anna turned her back to Jack, bent her head, and lifted her hair. He zipped her and fixed the tiny eyelet clasp. Her shoulders and arms were bare. He ran his hands over the firm, smooth texture of her skin, gently gripping and turning her around. The bodice was cut to give the impression that the slightest upward movement would send her breasts tumbling free of the fabric containing them. The red satin clung to her waist, thighs, and buttocks without a square centimeter to spare.

"Makes your nuts ache, don't it, Looie, old buddy? You look like a million and change, sweet tits."

Anna, flattered, smiled mischievously.

"It is beautiful, Señor Jack."

"Let's hope a certain Colombian gorilla thinks so."

"I do not understand." Anna's eyes clouded in sudden confusion.

"Don't worry," he comforted her, patting the bare shoulders again. "You're just gonna do Daddy a little favor in this rig. The man in the picture. All I want you to do is walk up to him, blow him a kiss, and hand him the phone and room number here. Seeing you in *this* getup, he'll call. When he does, I want you to say you think he's a handsome stud and you're dying to get together with him. Insist on meeting in this room. Don't worry. I'll take it from there."

The hit man's plan began to dawn on Anna. She smiled conspiratorially. "I can keep the dress?" she asked with a hint of hope in her voice. Twirling, she admired the figure she cut in the mirror.

"Why not?" he asked, turning to leer at Luis. "Don't you think she oughta keep it, Looie? You bet you do. Meanwhile, why don't you go lock yourself in the *baño,* jerk off or whatever. I gotta discuss somethin' with the little lady."

Terranova sat in the gloom as Anna rose from the bed and padded barefoot to the bathroom door. Knocking softly, she demanded entrance from Luis. Head down, painfully aware of her nakedness, he slid by. Jack grinned at the kid and offered him a cigarette. Luis refused and sat, scowling, knees close together. The water in the shower came on as Jack lit a smoke and sat back to enjoy it. He studied Luis in silence, wondering what Diego could possibly be thinking, surrounding himself with wimps like this guy. When the water finally stopped, Anna emerged, toweling herself. Pointedly, she dropped the towel at Luis's feet, glided forward to stand before her man, and met his eyes.

"God, you're one hot piece," he murmured.

"You are pleased, yes?" she asked.

"You'd go to hell for me, wouldn't you, baby?"

She just stood there, staring defiantly, pride flashing in those dark brown eyes.

"That's a good baby," he cooed. "Where we're headed from here, it's us against the world."

Anna slid to her knees and lay her head in his lap. They remained that way, him stroking her hair until he'd finished his cigarette. "Okay, baby," he told her, running a hand down her naked back. "Put the dress back on. It's show time."

Ron Dai and Peter Davis were scheduled to arrive two hours apart in order to have the SYSTEMATICS offers of employment, both made on the same day, seem no more than coincidental. Maureen Counihan showed the sheriff's department man into her office at nine-thirty sharp. For a woman who wasn't necessarily attracted to Oriental men, she found herself preoccupied with how gorgeous this guy was. He wasn't tall, maybe five-ten, and he appeared to be part-Caucasian from the softness of his exotic facial features. His skin was a smooth walnut, and when they shook hands, a pair of terrifically sexy laugh lines punctuated his smile.

"Miss Counihan," he started in, getting directly to the job at hand. "Agent Charles has briefed me in depth on the situation, but anything you might be able to add would be extremely helpful."

"Thanks for giving me the opportunity," she replied. "It's appreciated. Please sit down. Coffee?"

"No, thank you. I'm afraid my caffeine tolerance is pretty low. You're quite a legend in Valley circles, you know. I'm sorry to have to meet you under these circumstances. These must be trying times for both you and your father."

She sighed and leaned back in her chair. In the bullshit world of business, you learned to appreciate candor.

"Could be worse," she allowed. "The FBI appears willing to bend over backward and give us every benefit of the doubt. Agent Charles seems quite capable."

Dai nodded. "Ross Charles is one of the best. I've worked with him a number of times now. He understands the delicate nature of this sort of thing. Believe me, Miss Counihan, his interest is not in running a company like SYSTEMATICS out of town on a rail. We want to catch and prosecute criminals. That's the all of it."

"Call me Maureen, please," she requested.

He smiled. "Okay. Maureen. I want you to feel free to contact me any time something comes up. Day or night. If you think it's the least bit significant, don't wait." He reached into the breast pocket of his jacket, extracted a pen and a business card, and wrote a number. "This is my home," he told her, handing it over. "There's a machine on it. Leave a message if I'm not in."

Maureen quickly transcribed the number on the card into her week-at-a-glance book before dropping it into the shredder beside her desk.

Dai was impressed. "You give me confidence," he commented.

"I'm plenty embarrassed already by what's going on here, Mr. Dai. I certainly don't need to compound the existing problems."

"Ron," he insisted. "Want to start with a tour of the facility?"

*   *   *

An hour and a half later, Maureen left the engineer in the hands of the personnel director, busily filling out health insurance and tax forms. All around the place, as they toured the production line, research labs, and marketing offices, the air was charged with the electricity of the lightning-bolt memo she'd cast down from the heavens the previous afternoon. SYSTEMATICS's "Brooding Bitch" was on the warpath over the latest quarter's defect figures. Questions were going to be asked. Tough questions. Once she got some answers, heads were going to roll. They were bringing in a quality control engineering expert. He was getting a free hand to pick the place apart.

The FBI agent, Peter Davis, was another matter altogether. Close to Maureen's age, he carried himself with a swagger and smug confidence. He clearly saw himself as a rising star in the federal sky. San Jose was a backwater. SYSTEMATICS was small fish. But *treason* was something else again. No matter where it reared its ugly head, Pete Davis was going to root it out and squash it like a bug. Maureen read all of this and more in him before he even opened his mouth.

"Special Agent Peter Davis," he announced, pumping her hand. "Call me Pete. I'll call you Maureen, and we'll dispense with the bullshit. Right? Right."

From behind the big desk, Maureen frowned. "Please sit down, Mr. Davis. Agent Charles informs me that we have no time to lose. I take it that he has thoroughly briefed you on the problem and on your capacity here."

"He has," Davis said slowly. "But I thought that we might be able to grab some lunch and discuss it at greater length."

She nodded. "I see. His idea or yours?"

"Oh, uh . . . mine." He tried a disarming grin. "We're allowed a fair amount of latitude in the field, you know. Take the ball and run with it. The Agency encourages innovation and self-reliance."

"Do they encourage thinking?" she asked. "How would it look for the executive vice president to be seen having lunch with the new low man on the Salvage totem pole?"

"That's one of the things I wanted to cover," he countered quickly. "I believe that I might be employed to vastly greater—"

"Whoa." She held up a hand. "We have established a game plan, Mr. Davis. So far as I know, it hasn't changed. We made room at the position Agent Charles thought best suited to the pursuit of this investigation. I haven't been apprised of any change in that plan."

Davis was not prepared for the forcefulness of her approach. He paused to probe that hard, unflinching glare. "Hey," he offered patronizingly, "no problem. Just suggesting we explore some alternative possibilities. If you want to go straight down the line, though, okay by me. Boy, I can see how you've gotten the rep for being such a hard nose."

Her hackles rose as she leaned forward across her blotter.

"And just what is *that* supposed to mean?"

"Nothing." He shrugged and smiled again, too quickly. "I admire a woman who knows what she wants and goes out to get it."

Maureen swallowed hard. She wasn't going to let her irritation show more than it already had. With concentration focused on her breathing, she pushed back in her chair and stood.

"I've prepared to have your section chief, Larry Ransell, show you around the plant. He'll drop you at Personnel. There is at least an hour of paperwork to be done before we can officially turn you loose. I trust you will keep me informed of any progress or problems. We want to cooperate as closely with the FBI as we can."

"That's it?" he asked.

"That's it, Agent Davis. My secretary will show you to Mr. Ransell's office." To further punctuate the termination of the interview, she glanced at her watch and scooped her handbag off the cabinet behind her desk. Following him into the outer office, she stopped in front of the reception desk.

"Rhonda, this is Peter Davis. He's the son of one of Dad's old business associates and will be working for us in the Salvage Department. Would you please show him to Mr. Ransell's office?"

She turned to the FBI man, extending a hand. "Welcome to SYSTEMATICS, Mr. Davis. Regards to your father. I hope you enjoy working here." Without pause, she turned to move ahead of him and out into the hall.

Ron Dai was just finishing up with the photographs for his clearance badge when Maureen entered the Personnel office.

"Almost twelve-thirty, Ron," she announced with a smile. "My father is away on business in Houston and regrets not being able to take you under his wing personally. Buy you lunch?"

"The first one's free?" he asked, grinning.

"Something like that," she agreed. God, he had a fabulous smile.

EIGHT

The thickset chauffeur leaned casually against the front fender of his employer's stretch Seville. He was smoking, eyes flicking back and forth over the scene around him. Army and plainclothes security units moved about the perimeter of the hotel, ever vigilant. Inside this storm of activity, the Colombian henchman projected an almost bored attitude.

The night was cool, with a light breeze coming from the west. An hour earlier, it had rained for ten minutes, leaving the air with a fresh, earthy smell. The Hotel Colon stood ablaze with light, the atmosphere festive. Tonight was the occasion of the Ecuadorean interior minister's ball. The entire local diplomatic corps and dignitaries from the Quito government were arriving to join in the merriment. There was nothing like a party to take the men's minds off the sobering mission they were meeting here to promote. For the moment, the crisis of hemispheric drug trafficking would be forgotten.

The Colombian chauffeur watched as the Soviet ambassador and his wife climbed out of their armored Zil and up the front steps. A burly man with puffy features and a shock of white hair, he had a scandalously young wife—and pretty. The more power to the Bolshevik bastard.

A moment later, the chauffeur's sharp eyes picked up a young woman on the street. All rumination over the Russian's wife vaporized. This one was on foot, lingering there, watching as the beautiful people arrived laughing and shimmering in their evening finery. She observed from the sidewalk, outshining them all. The soldiers paused in their patrolling to stare openly. The dress she wore left nothing to the imagination. He found himself gazing hungrily at her, feeling that unmistakable stirring in his crotch. God, what he'd give to be able to hump a piece like that tonight.

And then she was staring directly at him, a slow smile turning the corners of her mouth. At him. For him. He was sure of it. There could be no mistake. Then, just as he was trying to absorb his possible good fortune, she began to walk toward him. No one moved to stop her.

"*Buenos noches,*" she purred. Her eyes took him in, up and down, a challenge smoldering in them.

He wanted to pinch himself to make sure this was really happening.

"*Buenos noches,*" he returned. It was drawn from the depths of all his imagined charm. My God, she reeked with sex. Every curve. Those magnificent breasts.

With a toss of her thick black mane, she regarded him with open satisfaction. "Yes," she said, nodding. "I noticed you earlier today." With the sweep of an elegant, long-fingered hand, she reached into the dress between her breasts, extracted a piece of paper, and held it out to him.

He unfolded the paper. On it were scrawled phone and hotel room numbers. Her fingers came up to press lightly against his chest.

"I hope you can come," she said. Her eyes bore wistfully into his. Then she turned on her spike heels and walked away.

The tight, controlled sway of a perfectly proportioned ass. The way she carried her shoulders. He stared down at the piece of paper, dumbfounded. A hooker? he wondered. But *what* a hooker. All along the street, soldiers hooted to him. They gestured obscenely with their hands and laughed. Inside, he wasn't laughing. The stirring in his crotch had become much more. He had not been with a woman since leaving Bogota—and perhaps never a woman such as this. She was the sort of female who came in dreams, causing one to awaken in the middle of the night, clutching frantically at the sheets. Such an image was now accessible in the flesh. She'd come to *him*, saying she'd seen him earlier.

An hour passed before he could stand it no longer. So what if she was a whore? She could want every peso in his wallet, and he'd gladly surrender them all. The minister would be at the party for several more hours. There was a telephone in the lobby.

Maureen Counihan and Ron Dai dined in an oak-paneled, fern-laden spot on the main drag in Los Gatos, their conversation ranging from the specifics of SYSTEMATICS's immediate problem to the general problems of industrial security and how to enforce it in their business. Dai was soft-spoken and unassuming. She got the feeling that this man from the sheriff's unit was more in tune with the valley and its unique circumstances than even Agent Charles. There were hundreds of small electronics firms littered across it. Dozens of them did sensitive government work. The situation was touchy enough to warrant a State Department ban on travel here for any Soviet citizen. And there were dozens of factors that could precipitate espionage. Drug abuse was rampant among the work force. Pressures could be brought to bear. Then there was the cutthroat competition of rivals trying to land the same contracts. There were the obvious interests of "friendly" foreign powers.

"How do you get into your line of work?" Maureen asked. "Can you just walk in and sign up?"

The place was full of noisy young professionals, most of them vying for some prize they imagined just beyond their reach. Dai was definitely different from them, absolutely confident, yet relaxed.

"Not exactly," he answered, a slight smile forming again. "Originally, I was pursued by the CIA because of my background and linguistic skills. It wasn't too thrilling, the idea of becoming a spook, so I turned them down. One of the people who interviewed me eventually turned up here. He was working with local law enforcement, setting up what is now the Sheriff's Special Task Force. We met in a hallway while I was working for Hewlett Packard."

Maureen noticed some guy who looked vaguely familiar leaning against the bar and openly ogling her. She shifted in her chair to cut off his line of view, imagining that she'd probably smiled at him once in passing and given him big ideas.

"And this time, becoming a spook wasn't so unappealing, huh?"

"I like to think that the lines are a little more clearly drawn here," he replied. "They were having a lot of trouble in the boat people community. Drug abuse, mostly. People were working sixteen-hour double shifts, trying to get rich overnight. Secrets were disappearing. It was mostly intramural warring between companies trying to get the jump on one another."

Their waiter appeared, serving after-lunch coffee to Maureen and a club soda to her guest.

"Do you think our problem could be drugs?" she asked.

Dai shook his head. "Too early to speculate. It's certainly possible and generally the first place I look."

With a wistful sigh, she slouched a bit in her chair. The weight of this thing was starting to get to her.

"That would be almost too easy, I guess. Wishful thinking."

"It's never easy," he assured her. "But I know what you must be going through. You find yourself grasping at straws, hoping it's something like that. Anything else, you don't *want* to think about."

"But I *do* think about it."

With that smile of his again, he withdrew a pack of cigarettes from his jacket pocket.

"You have to," he supposed. "Mind if I smoke?" When she shook her head, he fished a Camel filter from the pack and lit it. Blowing the smoke to the side, away from where she sat, he looked thoughtful. "I've always been intrigued by what I read about your father. A pioneer. Innovative. Fiercely independent. Integrity is a word you see used a lot."

"He has it," Maureen asserted proudly.

"Nobody in enforcement wants to see a guy like your dad and a company like SYSTEMATICS smeared. They're the lifeblood of this valley. It's an industry thriving on diversity. We'll work our asses off to pull yours out of the fire. I can promise that."

Maureen sat suddenly forward, her brow knit in intense earnestness. "I want to help."

He smiled again. "You'll get your chance."

She thought about it, taking her time as she formulated her next question. "Strictly off the record," she began slowly. "This Davis. What's your read on him?"

Dai's eyes clouded for an instant before he shrugged. For the first time that afternoon, he appeared evasive.

"From what they tell me, he's had some success in the field. East Coast. Cambridge and the Outer Ring."

"You aren't really answering my question," she pressed.

It was the detective's turn to sigh as he nodded. "The relentless Miss Counihan we've heard so much about. Okay. Everyone has his own operating style. I find his a little headstrong. He hotdogs it. But don't be too quick to count him out. He may rub you the wrong way, but who knows? He also might get results."

The Colombian driver fought to control his impatience. The woman retained the thick, almost palpable excitement of anticipation when he spoke to her on the phone. She stayed at the Hotel Intercontinental. A woman of means. One who wanted him more than any other man in Ecuador that night. He told her the interior minister he worked for would be returning to the Colombian embassy sometime after midnight. She hoped that he might slip out to rendezvous with her once his duties had been dispensed with. Regardless of the hour. She would leave word with the desk that he was expected.

His fantasies now were close to maddening. He could not push the image of that body from his mind. As time wore on, he found himself cursing his boss. When the man finally appeared on the steps of the hotel with his jewel-bedecked wife hanging a little precariously on his arm, the chauffeur fairly leapt into frenzied action. The minister was forced to ask him to take it a little slower as they raced through the all-but-deserted streets toward the embassy.

With the car parked in the garage, he informed the night guard that he was going to stretch his legs and sauntered off into the night. Once he'd turned the first corner, out of sight, he hurried to the nearest boulevard and hailed a taxi. Within minutes he'd entered the lobby of the Intercontinental and was approaching the main desk.

The woman occupied a room on the third floor. He rode up in the elevator, working to straighten his tie and adjust his jacket. His eagerness had become like the flames of a fire licking at his balls. A throbbing erection had barely subsided in the three and a half hours since she'd first approached him. Now it strained against the fabric of his fly with redoubled intensity. It was truly his lucky day. And already, his imagination planned how he would satisfy her in such a way that she might desire him again and again.

A low, musical voice bid him enter as he knocked. Turning the knob, he pushed into a darkened room. The only light came from a flickering candle next to the bed. And on the bed she lay stretched seductively, smiling at him. He closed the door behind him, licking his lips. She did not say a word but raised a hand and beckoned him to her. As he stepped forward, the jarring iciness of gunmetal touched his temple. From the corner of his vision, a figure loomed. In confusion, he thought there must be a mirror on that wall. He was looking at himself. It was still dawning on him that this, his own image, was holding a gun to his head, when the lights went out.

When the corpse of the hulking chauffeur hit the carpet, Jack Terranova moved into action. He flipped on the lights and wiped the butt of the gun clean. After removing the silencer, he put the weapon in the dead man's left hand. The photographs revealed him smoking with his left and opening the car door with that hand as well.

Inside the man's jacket he found an Uzi 9mm machine pistol. It was just the sort of thing that could make a real mess inside the confines of a car. Professionally, Jack abhorred messes, but for authenticity's sake, he would put pride and personal taste aside. It would have to look authentic. He checked the oversize, thirty-two-round magazine and slipped it into his pocket. Stooping, he caught the dead man under the arms and hoisted him into a chair. Again, because of the small caliber and dumdum nature of the bullet that killed him, the mess was contained, all nice and neat. Death had been instantaneous, with just a single trickle of blood barely an inch long dripping from his temple. Jack's gun fell from the corpse's hand and clattered to the floor. It was now effectively covered with his victim's fingerprints.

Anna had meanwhile risen from the bed, slipped the evening gown over her head, and pulled on a simple cotton shift. Luis, wide-eyed at the sequence of events, tried to avert his eyes and couldn't quite force himself to do it. As Jack worked at arranging the corpse in an attitude of self-inflicted death,

Anna bent to change her shoes and fold the beloved dress carefully before packing it.

Earlier, Jack had sent the young Nicaraguan to the lobby to compose on a hotel typewriter whatever confession Diego wanted.

"Where's the note?" he now growled.

Luis stirred from his daze, fumbled in his shirt pocket, and produced a sheet of Intercontinental stationery. Terranova took it from him, laid it flat on top of the dresser, and wiped both sides with his handkerchief. Picking it up gingerly, clamped in the cloth, he carried it to the corpse and set about getting some fresh new prints on it. Task accomplished, he returned it to the dresser and left it in plain view.

Next came the machine pistol. Unwilling to leave anything to chance, the hit man broke it down quickly on an open newspaper, cleaning and oiling each piece. Once it was reassembled, he removed the clip from his pocket and slapped it home.

"Make one last check of the room," he commanded Anna and Luis. "Under the bed. Behind the furniture. Double-check the trash in the bath."

They scurried around, scrutinizing every nook and cranny. Jack stood to one side, contemplating his handiwork. The hotel would report rental of the room to a pair of men and a woman. It made sense that the assassin might have had co-conspirators. How these people might fit in would remain a mystery long after the discovery of the driver's body. A lot of time and effort would be expended trying to discover who these mystery confederates were. Meanwhile, the note spelled out the dead man's involvement and fingered some Colombian drug runner. Who and why was of no interest to Jack. Once satisfied, he hung a Do Not Disturb sign on the door and led Anna and Luis out of the hotel through a service access.

The Ecuadorean first lady was heavily involved in a recent international crusade to combat drug abuse. This morning she was hosting a breakfast in that interest. Forty-five minutes before this event was to commence, Jack Terranova strolled up to the gate of the Colombian embassy compound, grinned conspiratorially to the soldier on guard, and wandered around back to the garage. The keys to the Caddy stretch had been in the dead man's pocket. He inserted one into the door, opened it, and slid in behind the wheel. The big car turned right over, its engine purring like a kitten. He backed down a long side drive, then swung around in the parking area to the left of the ambassador's residence and nosed around the half-circle drive to the front door.

Once he left the embassy, Anna and Luis would follow at a distance in a rented Simca. After the hit went down, they would fly out of the same airfield they'd flown into. Diego was apprised of their timetable, and at that very moment the plane should already be on the ground and waiting. The pilot had orders to leave if they didn't show up by seven-forty-five. After a political hit like this, every quick exit from Quito would surely be shut down in a hurry. Their plan was to get out under the wire.

Outside of the car, he popped the trunk and removed a chamois from the cleaning kit. Keeping an eye on the front entrance of the building, he set about polishing the already-spotless surface of the left front fender. It allowed him to keep his head down, lessening the chances of discovery. It was overcast, almost cold. He turned the collar of the jacket up against it, regretting having killed the little tailor before he could put in the lining. Above him, at the top of the steps, the door to the residence opened.

The Colombian ambassador stood aside, shook hands with the interior minister, and kissed his beautiful young wife on the cheek. She was a good-looking piece, maybe thirty-eight or forty, with great skin, high cheekbones, and a slim body. Against the cold she'd wrapped herself in a fashionably cut, jet-black lambskin jacket. It would be a pity to put holes in a job like that. When Maria had bought one like it in Milan a year ago, it had set Jack back eighteen hundred bucks.

He stepped quickly around to the trunk, tossed the chamois in, and slammed the lid. Continuing directly to the back door on the building side, he pulled it open and stood aside at casual but respectful attention. The minister and his wife barely glanced at him as they climbed in.

At the gate he nosed the limo left into traffic, toward the presidential palace. On the way over, in the rented car, he'd driven up and down the nearby streets, searching for a quick dodge isolated enough to do the job. He wanted something that would avoid any more attention than would otherwise be focused on a gleaming, twenty-eight-foot American car. Now, a quarter mile up the boulevard, he veered sharply into a small residential lane, reversed abruptly behind a streetside building, and yanked the machine pistol out from inside his jacket.

The reflecting glasses obscured his eyes from the querying looks of his passengers. He brought the weapon up onto the back of the seat and opened fire. It was all over in a matter of seconds. The bullet-ridden bodies of the minister and his wife slumped against each other in the middle of the seat. Blood splattered everywhere—ceiling, windows, seats, floor, and doors. Quickly switching to semiauto, Jack put an insurance round into the middle of each of his victim's foreheads, pulled the door release on the driver's side, and raced to the idling Simca, parked a few yards away.

Cristina Faro wanted to be the proper hostess to their houseguest and to show him off to her surely envious friends. The evening after Bueno and Willie ran into a temporary dead end in Pitalito, the lady of the house was preparing a small dinner party. Henry could tell that something was afoot by the way the staff scurried about the place. They moved as though spotlessness were a newly discovered religious precept, guaranteeing entrance to heaven. He and Willie were spending the afternoon in the shade of a little walled garden off the library. One of Willie's men had just that morning returned from Miami. He'd been making further inquiries concerning the Somosista Contra base of operations in the States.

According to this lieutenant's best information, Diego Cardona had departed from Florida two weeks ago. The Somosista patriots were maintaining what amounted to a government-in-exile in Coral Gables. Their enterprise occupied half-a-dozen estates from which they mounted fundraising campaigns and pushed their lobbying efforts. He reported on several other interesting rumors that supported the contention that these people were cornering larger and larger shares of the cocaine market. Evidence suggested that they now controlled a funnel running north through Central America and the Yucatán in Mexico into both the Louisiana and Florida areas. They appeared to be consolidating their own distribution system in the wake of recent Colombian reversals. All this had to be more than coincidence. Up in Miami, the resident Colombians were now talking war. It looked like it was going to be a tough fight. The Nicaraguans were both well-organized and well-financed. Profits generated by new drug activities were being used to purchase ordinance in large quantities, ostensibly to help in fighting the Nicaraguan civil war.

"These bastards are *never* going to back off," Willie snarled, shaking his head.

"If you thought they might, you underestimated them," Henry countered. "Somoza believed he could fuck the people of his country by divine right. The people around him liked the implications of that. It meant that if they hitched their wagons to the general's star, *they* had the right as well."

Willie pushed himself up from his lounge chair and paced back and forth. "What amazes me is how bold they are," he said. "Taking me down is one thing, but if you're right, they're even killing CIA agents. Can they believe they will get away with such audacity?"

"It comes with pride," Henry said calmly. "Pride and the resulting delusions of grandeur."

Willie sighed. "Perhaps a trip to Miami is in order. If we cannot work forward, then maybe we can get some answers by working backward."

"The thought has occurred to me," Bueno agreed. "Cardona originally contacted Terranova in Florida. He can't be working without any sort of net. The economics of hiring such a man and transporting him down here under cover are too staggering. We may have to light a few fires in order to smoke these fuckers out."

"Arrangements would have to be made," Willie told him. "I am not exactly welcome in the States. It would take a few days."

"As soon as possible," Henry said. "By the way, what the hell's going on around here? This place is a madhouse."

"It's Cristina," Willie chuckled. "She wants to play hostess. There are a number of friends coming to dinner tonight. Don't be surprised if these women try to shove some eligible female down your throat. Matriarchal conspiracy and all that. They do it every time they can get their hands on a loose one like you. If you're introduced to some pretty thing who stares at you worshipfully with big cow eyes, my advise would be to run the other way as fast as you can. We have *patriarchal* institutions in the city designed to short-circuit these little campaigns our women engage in.''

''I seem to recall one in particular,'' Henry reminisced. ''Many years ago. You drove into the place . . . to the door of your room. All very discreet.''

''It is still there.'' Willie was grinning. ''Perhaps later tonight.''

Cristina Faro's dinner party was an elaborate, festive affair. And sure enough, the half-dozen fashionable, well-heeled wives in attendance just happened to bring along an eligible little sister, allegedly to fill out the male–female balance at the table. It became obvious from the way they continually steered her toward Bueno that she was there for much more than balance. The curious thing to Henry was that she possessed genuine beauty—the type of young woman who should have men by the score trying to court her. But not in this world. A political alliance was much more important than any notion of base infatuation. Henry was perceived as an alluring political possibility because he had once saved Don Willie's life. Don Willie was *the* fat cat in these parts. A woman could do no better than to marry a man to whom Willie Faro owed a debt of gratitude.

Her name was Patricia. Henry was polite to her. Solicitous, but careful to avoid any appearance of aggressiveness. It was like the ritualized dance of the mongoose and the cobra. He'd been through it before and was much better than just good at it. No strings was the name of the game. He *couldn't* have them. Not down here, and maybe not anywhere.

It was two in the morning before the party finally broke up. Willie rolled his eyes at Henry as the last of the guests finally made their way along the main drive of the compound to the gate.

''High pressure, man,'' he commented, grinning. ''You were a star.''

''I've been there before,'' Bueno assured him. ''Real pretty girl. Too bad.''

''Yeah,'' Willie mused, looking at it philosophically. ''Feel like going into town and hitting a few clubs?''

''Now?''

''Sure. Why not? The action never really gets started until

about now. We could have a few drinks, listen to some music.''

"Hit the joint with the drive-in rooms?" Henry asked. "Not tonight, amigo. Tell you the truth, all that sidestepping's got me beat. I doubt if I'd be much fun.''

Willie spread his hands, a twinkle in his eyes. "Suit yourself. I think I'll take a little drive." He began to turn away when a last bit of their business occurred to him. "Oh, I've sent word to a cousin in Miami. He'll probably be able to run us in, day after tomorrow. He's asking around right now, getting some details from a real estate agent friend about the places my people fingered in Coral Gables. It's sometimes nice if you can get your hands on a couple of floor plans.''

"I can't shake the feeling that any arrangement between them and a shooter like Terranova is truly unholy," Henry told him. "Most of you guys are out of business and no immediate threat. Damn, I wish I knew what they were up to.''

"We probably won't know until it happens," Willie said. "But I get the feeling that all this new activity is somehow tied to the problems my friends and I have had.''

As Henry prepared to retire in his room, he heard the muffled roar of an engine moving past and down the drive. Peering out through the curtain, he watched as Willie and his security man, Aguillera, rolled toward the gate in the Ford four-by-four. He probably wouldn't be back until well after sunup. When he returned, his wife would pretend he'd been home all night. It was the way they played it down here. Henry smiled, shaking his head. It was late, but he stretched, dropped to the floor for a quick hundred push-ups, and then stretched some more. A pre-bed shower came next and felt good. The alcohol had been flowing that night, and he had been feeling a little green around the gills before he got the blood pumping. Standing under a stream of hot water, he unwound from the pressures of being social in a fishbowl. The eyes of every one of those goddamn women had been on him, gauging his reaction to the bait they dangled. It was a shame their sexual politics had to be so predictable. In another setting, he could have found the girl quite desirable. Sometimes he wondered if his uncle hadn't been right in wanting him to become an accountant.

A soft knock came at the door as he reentered the bed-chamber. He moved to open it, a towel wrapped around his waist and rubber thongs on his feet. Bad move. Cristina Faro was standing there in a dressing gown. She smiled sheepishly.

"I was hoping you would still be up," she said. "My husband has left for the city."

"I saw him go." He stood there holding the door, watching her eyes.

"May I come in?"

"Do you really think that's a good idea?"

She flushed slightly and shook her head. When she spoke, it was with the voice of surrender and defeat. "Does it matter if it is a good idea or not?"

"I'm not sure I'm reading you," he said. A lie. He was sure.

"You must be," she replied. "Where is Willie off to? He has three mistresses and five bastard children he supports in Cali. Because I look the other way and keep my mouth shut, do you think it hurts any less?" Her jaw quivered as she spoke, eyes flashing defiantly.

Bueno shook his head, puzzled. "I think I can understand your anger. But what does this, what you're doing now, have to do with it?"

"Even a woman who is a wife and mother has desires," she said angrily. "Because of my station, I am expected to deny my feelings while my husband openly indulges his."

With purpose in her eyes, she pushed past him and into the room. At the bed, she pulled the dressing gown over her head and threw it to the floor. Confronting him, her voice changed. She was beseeching him now.

"I want to be treated like a woman, not an object. Am I an object to you as well? Was I one that first moment our eyes met?"

Henry shook his head, eyes taking in that amazing body. It was the stuff of dreams. Willie must be insane, leaving her to chase *anything* else in Cali.

"No," he replied hoarsely. "But this is crazy."

"You do not want me?"

"I wouldn't want to meet the man who didn't," he said. There was that uncontrollable stirring in his loins, and the beginnings of a rapidly rising erection pushed the towel out away from his thighs.

Cristina stepped proudly toward him, fully aware of what she was doing to him. He opened his mouth to utter some further protest when she put a finger to his lips, her eyes holding his. Her other hand lifted the towel and slid beneath to stroke him with determined firmness.

Henry felt the towel fall away and her nipples brush against his chest. The finger across his lips moved aside as she leaned in to press her mouth to them. He was no longer able to hold himself back. His tongue moved to meet hers. His hands encircled her waist, fingers spread and caressing as they drifted down to cup the cheeks of her beautiful tanned ass and pull her hard against him.

"You're a jerk," a little voice chided. And he didn't doubt it, but he wasn't about to stop now, with the thing already this far out of hand.

NINE

"What the fuck's this clown up to, Ted?" Rodney O'Doyle demanded with some heat. The Drug Enforcement agent leaned across the tiny table between him and Latham. They were occupying a secluded corner of an all-but-abandoned bar in the Cafe America. It was near closing time, in the wee hours of the morning.

Latham held up his hands and shook his head. "We all agreed that we needed a *doer* from inside their organization. Cardona was judged best by more than just my evaluation. Don't go trying to shove a stick up my ass about him now."

"The son of a bitch is turning himself into a fucking underworld superpower with our blessing!" O'Doyle hissed. "The big boys upstairs are getting real tired of the smoke I'm blowing up *their* asses about this guy. They've got a file as fat as your head on him." He was a big, burly man, and his florid face was flushed with anger.

"Two weeks, a month tops," the CIA man pleaded. "Then you can crawl down his throat or any other orifice you choose. Just not yet. You unload on him now and you fuck up everything we've worked for."

O'Doyle shook his head in frustration. "Fine, hotshot. But only if you can answer me one question. What the hell's he doing with a heavy hitter like Jack Terranova down there?

113

Jesus Christ, a guy like that'd take out the Blessed Virgin for the right price.''

Ted Latham took a quick gulp of his tequila gimlet and tugged at his tie. ''We're running with him on one operation,'' he said defensively. ''It's going slick as Vaseline on a baby's ass. The other shit he's into we try to keep track of, but we don't have the manpower to baby-sit him twenty-four hours a day. He moves around plenty. The way I figure it, no matter what he's into, once the shit hits the fan down there, his fat's in the fryer along with the rest of the greaseballs.''

''You ever listen to yourself?'' O'Doyle asked in exasperation. ''I hear from one of our boys stationed down in Cali that fucking Henry Bueno's back in the field. You want to know something? The idea of having Henry Bueno sniffing around anything I even *know* about scares the livin' shit outta me. The dude is a square shooter. Cardona's into somethin' scum-ridden with this Terranova character, and if Bueno catches wind, we're gonna lose ourselves a keystone greaseball and have nothin' to show for all the time we spent playing patty-cake with his scum-ridden ass.''

''Two weeks,'' Latham insisted. ''You're worrying too much. The word we have on this whole cocaine thing is that the Colombians are plenty burned up about the way they've been fucked over. They're talking war down in Miami *and* in their own country. They seem to know all they need to about the mechanics of revenge. I trust they'll get something in hand pretty quick. Ask your DEA buddy down in Cali what he's heard. He'll back me up on this.''

''What do I do for a living?'' O'Doyle shot back. ''You're sitting here telling me about the Colombians? You CIA assholes think you're the only ones who could tell shit from Shinola. Fuck *you*, buddy. Get your boy under control, or I find myself some new playmates. It's better than looking for a new job.'' He slugged back the remainder of the Black Bush in his glass, stood abruptly, and stalked out without a backward glance.

Sun streamed brilliantly through slightly parted curtains and onto the bed. Bueno stirred. Noises in the distance had awakened him. Now, again, the distinctive snap of a rifle shot. Two, maybe three hundred yards. Accompanying it came the rumble of Jeep engines. Quite a number of them. Another rifle report, this one of a different caliber and much closer. Someone was returning fire.

Cristina was gone. Her pillow was slightly indented, with several strands of ash-blond hair across it. Men were by and large fools, he reflected, himself and Willie included.

The cacophony of Jeep engines advanced on the compound. Henry slipped from the bed and peered, squinting, out across the courtyard toward the gate. As his eyes adjusted, he saw the military green canvas tops of a caravan, moving quickly. Just as quickly, Willie's staff scurried to take up position in defense of the perimeter just inside the compound wall. They carried automatic rifles. What the hell was going on?

Henry dressed hurriedly in his loose-fitting cotton peasant whites, grabbed the *Tikka* rifle, checked the load, and slid his still-silenced pistol into the top of his boot. Outside, the morning was being ripped with bursts of automatic weapons fire. On leaving his room, he encountered a maid racing by in the hall.

"What's happening?" he demanded.

"The army," she blurted breathlessly, eyes wide in fright. "They killed one of the guards at the gate. Just shot him down."

Outside, he could hear the battle moving into full swing, with dozens of weapons engaged in the exchange. Willie had at least twenty men employed to secure the hacienda, and each of them was armed to the teeth. If the army wanted in, they had to know what they were up against and that it wouldn't be easy. Still, they could get in if they wanted to, and the situation was only going to deteriorate from here. Bueno's concerns moved to Cristina and the kids. Willie was probably still in the city.

Keeping his head low, he ran toward the family end of the house. Already, by the sound of it, the defensive perimeter was being pushed back. The house was being hit, an occasional slug zinging through a window, shattering glass and sending shards spraying. He found Cristina and the two children huddled behind the bed in the master suite.

"You've got to get out of here," he told her. She had a blank look in her eyes, and beads of cold sweat stood out on

115

her forehead. Without hesitation, he reached out and slapped her hard across the face. "Now!"

A look of surprise seized her face, then the world came back into focus as terror evaporated.

"What's the best way out?" he demanded. "Quickly."

"Th—the courtyard. Off the library. There is a gate, and then a stream running past the garden."

"Let's go." He scooped up the little girl, Rosa, and swung her onto his back. "Hold on tight, now," he instructed. "Okay?"

Tiny, even for her five years, she nodded now with tears in her eyes. To Henry she seemed impossibly light and frail. This was madness. He turned to the seven-year-old boy, Miguel.

"It's not bad to be afraid," he told him. "All of us are afraid, but you are going to have to help your mother and me by being strong. Do you think you can do that?"

Miguel stared wide-eyed between this visitor and his mother. He swallowed hard and nodded. Bueno smiled reassuringly and rumpled his hair. Stooping until he was almost on all fours, he led them from the room. By the sound, army troops were pressing in on the house from the east now. As they crossed the living room and entered the library, a whoosh of concussed air hurled them to the floor as the far wall and several tons of ceramic roof tile collapsed behind them.

"Shoulder rocket," he grunted, pushing himself back onto his feet. "You all right?"

Cristina nodded, pulling herself together. She held Miguel by the hand. "But why?" she asked. "I do not understand."

"Beats me," he replied, shaking his head. "Your husband isn't in the most stable line of work. Whatever it is, you can bet he's made someone pretty upset."

The noise of the fighting was deafening when they emerged from the library into the sunny little side garden. Motioning for them to stay put, Henry slipped to the gate, cracked it an inch, and peered out. The main vegetable and flower gardens lay quiet in bright sunlight. The pool, sparkling aqua, was undisturbed. Half-a-dozen yards lay between them and the shallow stream meandering through the estate. Its banks were thick with heavy bamboo.

To move downstream would be suicide. Above them, the water rolled more quickly over a series of drops in the topography. The ground undulated a bit there, affording possible cover. The first several hundred meters were going to be the tricky part.

Bueno withdrew the 9mm from his boot and held it out to Cristina. "You ever use one of these before?"

"Che taught me," she told him, nodding. "For protection while out in the car at night."

"Good. Take it. You see somebody in a uniform—anybody—shoot him. Think much about it, and it may be the last thing you do. We're going upstream." He pointed ahead. "Once we get into those foothills there, we can hide you out of sight while I circle back and try to figure out what the hell's happening. You ready?"

When she assured him she was, he pushed the gate open, grabbed Rosa's wrists with one hand, gripped the rifle with the other, and ran pell-mell for the creek. As he hit the water, Henry glanced over his shoulder to make sure Cristina was still with him. Together they began to scramble upstream.

A voice shouted a hundred yards off to the left, well beyond the house. Several soldiers engaged in a flanking maneuver had spotted them. A bullet zinged into the dirt just feet ahead. Bueno slid low into the water and swung the rifle up, sighting instinctively on the sound. As soon as the man came into his sights, he squeezed the trigger. The uniformed figure clutched at his chest and collapsed in surprise.

"C'mon," he grunted. He circled Miguel with an arm and humped both kids simultaneously up the hill.

As voices below clamored with excited confusion over the killing of their comrade, the fugitives reached the thick cover of bamboo. Bueno set Miguel down and urged him to scramble ahead with his mother as he crouched to check the pursuit.

Three men were hurrying in their direction, running low to take advantage of whatever cover the terrain would afford. Henry caught the glint of an officer's insignia in the sun, drew bead on the man wearing it, and dropped him. In doing so, he gave away his own position—a necessary evil.

"Upstream!" he ordered Cristina. "Stay as close to the bamboo as you can."

117

Suddenly, the air was filled with the far-off reverberation of an approaching helicopter gunship.

"Holy Jesus," Henry moaned, shaking his head. "Let's go. We've got to get to better cover, fast."

As they raced up the streambed, hugging the foliage, Bueno continually checked their rear. He watched as the two remaining men pressed on in pursuit. Then, from around the side of the house, a Jeep roared into view, churning on toward the pair of footsoldiers. It pulled up short in a cloud of dust. They pointed frantically ahead. The passenger in the front seat of the Jeep had a radio. The helicopter. Its thunder was almost deafening now while it somehow remained out of view.

"What is happening?" Cristina yelled above the furor.

"Your husband has really pissed someone off," Henry shouted back.

As he spoke these words, a wide, squat helicopter, hovering like some sort of obscene, lethal dragonfly, appeared above the roofline of the house. Breathing fire, it unleashed a fury of 20mm cannon shells, raking the compound. Several rockets followed. They tore into the residence itself, the explosions shaking the earth beneath their feet.

"Oh, my God!" the woman cried.

"Forget it," Henry barked, shaking his head. "It's history now. We've got our own big trouble right here."

The stream moved through a narrow gorge as it cut a low, rolling ridge in half. As they pushed up it, the bamboo gave way to larger, heavier timber. Bueno took in the terrain ahead and allowed himself the first glimmer of hope. Boulder-strewn and varied as it began to form the foothills of the Farallones, the stream geography would give him a fighting chance if he could get the Faros to safety and tackle the opposition unencumbered.

He gestured on ahead and touched Cristina reassuringly on the arm. "We're going to get you and the kids into those trees up ahead there," he told her. "I want you to hide while I try to circle back and work on the pursuit."

She looked him in the eye and swallowed hard, evidently making the decision to give it her all. With Miguel by one hand and Henry behind, carrying Rosa, she led the way up the ravine toward the trees. At the base of a small knoll, Henry stopped long enough to put the little girl into Cristina's arms.

"I'll be back," he promised. Hefting the turkey gun, he sent them scurrying into the dense undergrowth.

Downhill, the Jeep and two footsoldiers were advancing cautiously. Bueno took to the water, crouching low in it, with his weapon held high. Downstream about twenty yards, a boulder outcropping would afford reasonable cover for perhaps thirty or forty seconds. He timed it so that the man driving the Jeep was in profile before he raced to the rocks, falling flat on his belly and squeezing off a round as soon as he'd steadied himself. As the driver slumped over the wheel, the Jeep veered crazily. It hit a boulder and flipped as the man with the radio leapt frantically free. The footsoldiers, spotting his position, were hugging the dirt and laying down a withering fire. Henry scurried for better cover. The officer from the Jeep scrambled to recover his dropped radio. Moments later, while Bueno huddled on the bank of the stream in a clump of heavy brush, the helicopter swung around from the house to turn its attention in his direction.

The hunted man waited. It was a long time since he'd done combat with a chopper. Southeast Asia. It was the end of the American involvement, and the North Viets were already operating a number of captured American Sikorskys. They were similar to this bird. He knew the vulnerable points from his advanced training and was aware that, with current fuel-cell technology, the only way to bring a baby like that down was to get either the pilot or the tail rotor assembly.

The chopper made a pass over his position as the pilot scanned the terrain. A mere thirty feet away from Henry, a rocket darted into his former position, reducing it to rubble. As back-up, he switched to the twelve-gauge firing position on the *Tikka* rifle and chambered a triple-aught magnum buckshot load. In reality, he knew that the Jeep was his only real hope. Mounted behind and between the front seats it carried a .50-caliber machine gun. Enough firepower to do the job, if he got lucky. The chopper swung into its turn for another run. He eased the *Tikka* to his shoulder and drew a bead on the man with the radio next to the twisted but upright Jeep. With a deafening blast and a crushing jolt against his shoulder, the shotgun brought the target down. Henry abandoned all caution and sprinted for the Jeep. The fifty came around easily in his grip. He cleared the bolt, aimed skyward, and prayed. Completely exposed as the Sikorsky bore down on him, Henry expected a cannon shell to annihilate him at any instant. Then, instead of continuing ahead, the chopper turned and dove for a second run at the stream. The pilot was obviously unaware that his ground contact was now dead. He moved obliviously down the ridge, pouring fire into the rocks close to where the quarry had just been. Bueno realized he'd been holding his breath and now let it escape.

"You goofed, friend," he muttered, lining the tail rotor up in his sights.

The jarring recoil of the gun sent shock waves up his wrists and arms to his shoulders. Phosphorescent tracers arched like bees swarming from a hive. A flurry of heavy, copper-jacketed slugs tore into the aft end of the helicopter, causing it to lose its hold on the heavens. Minutely at first, and then more radically, it swayed from side to side like a shark lashing its tail.

"I'll be fucked," Henry chuckled, congratulating himself. "Nice shooting, buddy."

He lost no time in dashing back to concealment, grabbing his rifle, and heading for high ground. The helicopter was careening wildly now in its death throes. The pilot fought frantically in a losing effort to control his descent. Henry shook his head as the chopper caught a rotor on a side slide, flipped in the air, and thrashed to the ground. The fireball from the explosion was tremendous, sending Henry sprawling. Regaining his feet, he turned his attention to Cristina and the kids. They'd just bought some time, and they'd better use it.

The first news of the Colombian Government's reprisal attack on a dope dealer's stronghold filtered in as the sun climbed in the morning sky. As yet, details were scant, but a satisfied Diego Cardona smiled, one ear cocked to the radio. He nodded to his young attaché, Ramon Lopez, indicating he had heard enough. Barely able to contain his excitement, the younger man reached to turn off the set.

"Careful planning," Major Cardona told him. "Remember that always. There is no such thing as too much patience or too much precision."

The pair sat eating breakfast on the veranda of a beach

estate on the Columbian Island of San Andres. This was the nerve center of their effort to recapture the homeland from the Sandinistas. A young mestizo housegirl approached their table with juice. Beneath the shade of a patio umbrella, Diego removed a cigar from his shirt pocket. He clipped the end and wet it with his tongue, as Ramon hurried to light it.

"My friend," Cardona addressed the young man as he extended his Zippo, "I wish you to depart immediately for Colombia. I want confirmation of Willie Faro's destruction and an accounting of the devastation done to his property. With his passing, the Colombian traffickers will be in a panic. Surely there will be accusations, other reprisals, and utter chaos."

The young man agreed readily. Since this operation had moved into full swing, he had found Don Diego willing to heap greater responsibilities upon him. Regardless of his youth, Ramon was seen as the product of his upbringing. He was a thoroughbred born of warrior men and beautiful women. Diego Cardona believed in seasoning such green timber by exposing it to heat. Ramon and others of the next generation would carry on the proud tradition of the Conquistadors. Those who survived the glory of battle.

"Pitalito?" he asked.

"You can have the grease monkey, Colon, give you a ride north in his Jeep," Diego told him. "And Ramon . . . bring me Faro's *cojones*, eh?"

Ramon colored slightly and grinned sheepishly.

A light knock came at the door. Light streamed through a crack between heavy curtains, and Willie Faro knew that morning had long since broken. Yawning, he worked to push sleep away. He pulled the sheet back from the naked form slumbering beside him and slapped the tight, smooth rump.

"Up," he snapped. "Or would you rather sleep the entire day away?"

The young girl reacted to the sharp sting of his hand, jerking awake with a start. Easy come, easy go. Willie had seen the nubile youngster dancing with abandon in the second disco they'd hit. Tall, no more than seventeen, great body. An invitation to join them at their table was followed by drinks, dinner, and several trips to the *baño* with his special stash to light up her eyes. She'd come to this place willingly. Clumsy in bed, but eager to please. He liked the way that being the focus of such youthful worship made him feel powerful. They'd snorted more blast while they fucked, drinking brandy to keep on an even keel. At last he'd grown weary of her frenetic thrashings, frustrated with his own inability to ejaculate. He flipped her over, pinned her to the bed, and took her from behind, hand over her mouth to muffle the cries of pain. Panting and sweating in these close quarters, he'd finally come. There was no pleasure in it. There rarely was anymore.

And now, in the light of day, his head throbbed from the alcohol, and his penis burned with the raw hurt of such marathon humping.

"Time to go," he told the girl. "Get dressed."

She looked at him, disappointment plain in her eyes. She had hoped that there might be something more. Her imagination did not have the capacity to conjure what this might be, but it was clear he had money and power. Now, as he stood, he removed a roll of notes from his pants. Peeling off ten thousand pesos, he threw them at her on the bed.

"Come on," he repeated. "Go." With his back to her, he slid into his trousers, zipped the fly, and buckled the belt. After crouching to tie his shoes, he opened the door. Brilliant sunlight flooded the room, illuminating the stained wallpaper and casting little shadows where humidity had curled it at the edges. The floor was bare concrete, grimy with stains. On the bed, the girl shielded her eyes from the light. As Willie closed the door behind him, she began to sob.

Che Aguillera waited by the truck. He looked to be in considerably better shape than his boss. At least he'd shaved and showered. On these nights when Willie caroused, Che stayed with him until he scored and dragged his victim off to one of many divey haunts. Once Willie was tucked in, the Argentinian would drive to the home of a certain woman and spend the night. Try as he might, Faro had never been able to persuade his number-one man to reveal this lady's identity. It was all part of the little game they played.

"Why are you looking so satisfied?" Willie growled.

"I'm not," Che replied, shrugging. "You just insist on measuring other people's dispositions by comparison with your own. It would appear you've hit a new low today."

"Screw you. I wasn't aware I paid you to philosophize."

"You don't," Che said amiably. "But you asked."

They drove back out of the city and toward the hacienda in silence. The morning rush hour had yet to move into full swing, and progress was easy. According to Willie's watch, it was just before eight. Cristina would be up. He would dodge her withering glances and head off for some additional sleep. He was working on about an hour and a half's worth right now and felt dead on his feet.

As they cleared the city, the morning calm was shattered by the thundering racket of an army helicopter overhead. One of the new jobs, looking like death on wings. It looped around at low altitude and swept down on the foothills behind his estate. A sound like the ripping of fabric was followed by a distant dust cloud.

It wasn't until they turned off the main road and onto the long, winding gravel road leading to the hacienda that Willie realized something was very wrong. Suddenly, through a break in the trees, the helicopter they'd observed now loomed in the near distance. It was apparently out of control, its tail lashing wildly in the air. A moment later it disappeared, and the earth shook. The sky was filled with a fabulous fireball.

"What the . . ." he mumbled.

Che spotted them first. Jeeps in the road ahead, outside the main gate. There were troops everywhere.

"Get us out of here!" Willie yelled. He reached under the seat for the automatic pistol he kept there.

Aguillera swung the pickup around in the drive. He gunned it through the brush and back toward the main highway. The way was quickly blocked by a pair of Jeeps emerging from cover and coming head-on. One with an open top carried a rocket launcher. The man behind it opened fire. Willie and Che never had a prayer. The entire cab of the truck disintegrated. Death came so quickly that their lives had no chance to flash before their eyes.

Once the pursuit was disrupted by the crash of the helicopter, the remaining footsoldier, recognizing a reversal when he saw one, took flight. He ran helter-skelter for the compound. Henry was not about to sit around and wait for him to round up reinforcements. He found Cristina and the two kids huddled in the trees.

"Hurry," he told her. "Up the ridge. Fast."

"You shot down a helicopter," she murmured wonderingly.

"Yeah." He swung the little girl, Rosa, up onto his shoulders. "I got lucky. Where's the nearest place I can steal a car?"

Cristina thought a moment. "There is the country club. Beyond this hill. The polo ponies are kept in stables close to this stream. Several cars are usually parked nearby."

He nodded. "Okay. You might as well steal a Mercedes if you're going to steal a car in Colombia. They stick out like a sore thumb, but they're also faster than anything else around." With that, he set off.

Cristina wasn't exactly dressed for hiking over boulder-strewn terrain, and yet she'd taken little Miguel in hand and carried her end of the load. Henry knew she had to be hurting, wearing nothing but bedroom slippers on her feet. But she slipped and fell without complaining. Willie had chosen much better than he seemed to realize, but then Henry had already been quite graphically convinced of *that* some hours earlier.

Willie. Bueno wondered where he was and what might have become of him. Something serious had provoked the government of Colombia into this very violent reprisal. It had to be *heinous* to bring down such wrath on a man so well connected. His family held positions of respect and power in both government and the national economy. Black sheep or no, one of a country's fortunate sons was not butchered without real cause.

Answers would undoubtedly come with time. Meanwhile, Cristina and her children weren't safe here. As soon as it was discovered that they'd escaped the carnage at the hacienda, a search would be initiated to find them. Nowhere would be safe until they were out of the country. She was Venezuelan by birth. There was family in Caracas. He had to get them there. The hunt for Carl Stickley's murderer was getting a lot more complex than anticipated. Nevertheless, first things had to be taken care of first. He had a couple of toddlers on his hands. Buenaventura was the answer.

West of the Valle de Cauca, across the Pacific ridge of the Andes, lay the steaming jungle port. Anything but a good venture, it was considered by many to be the asshole of the Western Hemisphere. Rife with poverty and teeming with all manner of cutthroat desperadoes, it functioned as a port for the giant lowland pulp lumbering tracts. It was situated at sea level in the equatorial doldrums, unmercifully hot, mosquito-infested, and filthy. Bueno had been there at least a dozen times, and each time he had sworn he would never return. Now he contemplated returning yet again, with a beautiful woman and two small children in tow.

A run for the coast was going to take a bit of luck. It was only fifty or so miles, but if the army was still hunting Willie or looking for his escaped wife, there would be roadblocks. The sooner he got a car, the better.

Cristina, it turned out, had ridden to the country club many times on horseback. Less concerned with discovery now, Henry gave her the lead. It was another forty minutes before they crested the ridge overlooking a lush golf course, sprawling clubhouse, and the stables adjacent to them. Henry led the Faro family into a wooded depression beside the access road, traded Cristina his rifle for the pistol, and told her to wait.

At midday, with siesta officially underway in the city, the country club was a hive of activity. Dozens of expensive European cars jammed the main lot. There was also a pair of uniformed attendants, and the whole setup looked too risky. The stable lot was a more informal situation, with no attendants and a location off the beaten path.

Bueno crept cautiously around the central buildings, giving them wide berth. In his hasty retreat from the Faro hacienda, he hadn't had time to check his appearance. He wasn't shaved and knew he must look bad after two hours of mucking through a streambed. It was too hot for members to be out playing golf. Most were likely to be drinking and eating. He could hear the noise of laughter and splashing in the pool. Sticking to the thick wooded verge of the road, he skirted a fairway and gained the lot outside the stables without incident. Between buildings, he could see two mounts being put through their paces out on the polo pitch. A quick survey of the stables themselves revealed an attendant napping with a manure shovel at his feet.

There were three cars to choose from: a Jaguar XJS, a Mercedes 450 SEL, and a fully loaded Chevrolet Silverado pickup. The Benz was a serious temptation, but he passed on it. The Jag and its siblings were notoriously unreliable in this climate. He eyed the Chevy truck. With four-wheel drive and a big V-8, it would be both versatile and fast. It also wouldn't stick out quite as much, even though it was expensive by *any* standard in a country that imposed a one hundred percent import tax on motor vehicles. Then again, Colombia did manufacture *Ford* trucks in-country, making other vehicles of similar appearance a bit more commonplace. Until he actually had it started, he wouldn't know how much gas it contained. One could only hope. Crouching low to the ground, he scurried to the driver side door, looked quickly in both directions, and removed his boot to extract the lock picks secreted in the lining. Henry took a deep breath and exhaled slowly.

Lock picking is an art not fully appreciated by those who watch a lot of television. On the tube, every hack with a gun and a private dick's photostat can get a lock open inside of fifteen seconds. Pure crap. An experienced locksmith who puts in a couple hours practice a week can perhaps work his way through a relatively complex set of tumblers in under five minutes. Bueno, once schooled by the best and reasonably proficient, was completely out of practice. He fumbled and sweated as he worked. Crouched alongside the truck in a small open lot, he was completely exposed should anyone approach. The minutes ticked by. The twelve it took to open the door seemed more like eternity . . . and there was still the ignition to deal with. Once he could slide into the scorching interior and lay on his back below the window line, he set to work on it. The tumblers were the same as those in the door lock, making this second operation easier than the first. When the steering wheel locking mechanism finally clicked free and he could twist the ignition into the "accessory" position, the gas gauge needle began to creep upward. It came to rest at three quarters of a tank.

Lifting his head, Henry peered around the stable area. All was still quiet outside. He sat up quickly, kicked over the engine, and was delighted by the quick response and reassuring growl of enormous horsepower under the hood. This engine wasn't just *any* V-8, and he wasn't about to argue over the amount of gas it would consume.

Big, oversized tires spat gravel in all directions as he reversed, roosted onto the access road, and hurtled toward the place where Cristina awaited him. She and the kids ran out of concealment as he flung the passenger door open. He caught little Rosa as she was pushed in, waited a moment, and was out of there before Cristina could get the door closed again.

One twelve-gauge blast from the *Tikka* rifle cut down the telephone line where the access road to the club met the main highway. News of the theft might travel a bit more slowly now. They had no choice but to enter the outskirts of Cali in order to gain the coast road, and Henry wanted the best possible chance of making it.

Cristina huddled beside him on the seat, all but spent, with her children clutched to her. She stared blankly ahead as Henry drove. Once they'd put some distance behind them on the highway, he fiddled with the radio in an effort to find out what the hell had happened that morning. It was some moments before he could locate the appropriate special bulletin. The announcer reported that an early-morning raid by the army had destroyed the home of suspected cocaine trafficker Guillermo Faro. The action was allegedly a reprisal for Faro's part in the assassination of interior minister Jorge Garcia-Alvarez in Quito yesterday morning. The Colombian DAS was said to be in possession of a confession penned by the minister's chauffeur/bodyguard. He was said to have committed suicide after carrying out this gangland-style execution. Faro had been apprehended while approaching the house and killed while attempting to escape. His wife and children were also reported dead.

"Holy shit," Henry mumbled hollowly. "God, I'm sorry." He looked at Cristina. Tears were streaming down her cheeks, her face white with shock. He really felt for her. This was no way to get that kind of news. She may have hated Willie for the way he treated her, but he *was* the father of her children.

Forcing himself to concentrate on the road ahead, Henry tried to put the pieces together. It wasn't all that hard. Most of them were staring him in the face. First they'd killed Carl, and now they'd killed Willie Faro as well. Terranova *and* Cardona. There was no distinguishing between employer and employee when you played this game.

Henry thought of his boat and the deep blue sea off the rugged California coast. They weren't making any of this easy.

TEN

"You read this thing?" Cameron Stebbins asked Ted Latham wearily. "The city of Miami is full of these people, and they're little better than animals."

Ted Latham stared at the report lying face-up on the deputy director's desk. It contained all the hastily compiled intelligence the Company could gather on the latest Colombian dope situation. The region was admittedly unstable, but interior minister assassination ranked right up there with the siege laid on the Colombian Supreme Court in Bogota a couple of years back. A big trafficker in Cali had been fingered as being behind the whole thing. The Colombian army was reported to have leveled his opulent hacienda and killed his family in the process.

"Yes, sir, I've glanced over it, all right," he replied. "It *is* my area."

"So what's going on down there, Ted? Why Cali, of all the godforsaken places? First we lose a man like Carl Stickley not to mention that kid. Now this. What are we missing? You got any feelings?"

Latham had plenty of feelings, most of them tinged with a healthy dose of paranoia. The man into whose hands he'd placed his entire Central American game plan had gone and imported the East Coast's most notorious mob gunsel down to Cali. A couple days later an old hand like Stickley is stretched

129

out on a morgue slab. Major Cardona, unknown to him initially, had his finger in a lot of drug pies. He was suspected of trying to cut some pretty big Colombians out of the picture. If this was a setup of his, aimed at eliminating a thorn in his side, then he'd really gone bananas with greed. Already, Ted had a few of the players—like O'Doyle—breathing down his neck about him. They needed him, but they *didn't* need him fucking up on this level.

"It's got me, sir," he said sincerely. "Coincidence, maybe? I don't know. We can always look at it as a blessing in disguise. The heat's going to be on everyone involved in the cocaine trade down there now. This minister was their president's cousin. The DEA's probably throwing a party over at HQ."

Stebbins shook his head, fingering the edges of the report.

"Something stinks about this," he grumbled. "Something stinks, and with Stickley dead and Bueno working incommunicado, I can't even get a decent read on the damn situation. The director is going to be asking me questions because the White House will have asked him first. It's your goddamn sector, and you've given me a dry well."

"I'll poke around and see if any of my conduits can clarify things," Latham promised him. "I doubt it's as bad as you fear."

As he circled high above the Andean valley cradling Pitalito, Ramon Lopez contemplated his task. He would catch a ride from Felix Colon and spend the night in Popayan. He could then approach the Faro estate under cover of predawn darkness. There, he hoped he would simply have to pick through the rubble. With the bodyguard's confession putting the finger on Guillermo Faro, the Colombian government would surely have taken direct action. Such an assassination, in the midst of a Contadora drug conference, merited the harshest sort of response.

The atmosphere on the ground was tranquil once he deplaned. Ramon noticed that the old PBY aircraft he'd observed on his last trip was still standing with its cowlings in the dirt, engines exposed to the weather.

"*Hola!*" he shouted, approaching the mechanic's shed. When there was no response, he tried the greeting again. Reaching the door, he pushed in and peered around. The place was deserted. A tin pot of coffee, perched on a make-shift burner, had a thin scum of mold growing on top of the muddy liquid inside. There was dust on the nearby work-benches, no sign of recent activity, and no sign of Colon's beat-up Jeep. Resigned to hoofing it down the hill to the little village, Ramon shook his head in disgust. He wore brand-new snakeskin loafers. Six hundred and seventy-five dollars American.

Pitalito lay sleeping in the late afternoon sun. Ramon wandered wearily down the main street. His feet hurt, and he was generally irritated. Collaring the first Indian he encountered who wasn't asleep, he demanded to know the whereabouts of Felix Colon. The man looked at him with frightened eyes, taking in the strange cut of his clothes and his accent. He pointed the way to a house near the end of the street.

"He is with the old woman," the man said.

"What old woman?"

"The one with the touch," the Indian told him.

The young Lopez was puzzled. He hurried down the rutted way, kicking up dust.

The place where the old woman lived was a low-ceilinged hovel. Through the gloom inside, he could make out the inert form of a man on a cot. A gnarled old woman of indeterminate age bent over him. Ramon entered, a frown creasing his brow as he made out the contorted features of the mechanic.

"What is it?" he asked. "What is the matter with him?"

The old woman appraised the cut of his city clothes suspiciously before responding. "He is shot in both legs."

"Holy mother," Ramon gasped.

She had drawn back the filthy sheet and was pointing to the man's legs. The skin from thigh to foot was blackened and festering. Gangrene. There were poultices on both knees. The odor of rotting flesh sent the young man reeling back; his hands shot to his mouth in an effort to control the urge to vomit.

"Who did this?" he croaked.

The old woman shrugged. "Two men. Unknown to this village. A bullet in each knee. Another was shot in the arm. He lives. This one will not last the night."

Ramon's mouth opened and closed.

"Who is this other? The one who was also shot?"

The old one gave him a name and directed him several

streets to the south. Ramon thanked her and hurried to leave that stinking place where death lingered heavy in the air. On the other side of the village, he found a pale man recuperating from a gunshot wound in the arm. He sat in the afternoon sun, heavily bandaged and obviously weak. Beside him, his wife and a small child crouched while the woman shucked beans. The man looked up, eyes fearful as he watched the approaching stranger. The Nicaraguan held up a hand, hoping to indicate that he meant them no harm.

"I have only come for information about the dying man at the old woman's," he announced. "I must know who did this to you and who would do such a thing to Felix Colon."

The man eyed him cautiously. "Who is asking this?"

"My employer does much business with Señor Colon. It is he who would want to know the circumstances of this outrage."

The wounded man shrugged with sadness in his eyes. "It is perhaps not such an outrage," he said softly. He went on to relate how they'd lain in ambush, hoping to pick off an unsuspecting trafficker, and how the ambush had backfired.

"There were two of them," he concluded. "Felix told the old woman that one was a *marijuanero* from the lowlands. The Valle de Cauca. The other was a stranger to him, with a strange voice. Not Colombian, I think. He had great power in his eyes."

Ramon considered this information. A *marijuanero* from the vicinity of Cali? Could Willie Faro have discovered something about the American gunman and their plan? These thoughts troubled him. If Faro knew, then how deep could such knowledge run? And who was this other man?

The recuperating man knew that Felix Colon's Jeep was parked behind the old woman's hut but did not know how much gasoline the tank contained.

With Henry Bueno at the wheel, the Chevy Silverado pickup devoured the fifty miles between recent chaos and a fighting chance. Fortunately, the roads around Cali were lightly trafficked during the afternoon siesta. With Cristina beside him, absorbed in her own confusion, Bueno kept his attention on the road and the journey ahead. At every turn he anticipated trouble. He studied the terrain, formulated contingency plans. Such an exercise was routine for him, ingrained by force of habit over many years. It allowed his mind to function peripherally in other realms. At the moment, those realms were the theoretical. He was still putting pieces together, some fitting and others obviously out of place. It was clear from the outset that Carl Stickley had been onto something much bigger than he knew. If the information Willie had managed to gather was correct, Diego Cardona was mounting a massive campaign aimed at cornering the entire U.S. cocaine market. Audacious though it might seem, the plan appeared to have some wheels. Avarice could be a powerful engine.

On the immediate front, Henry knew he had bigger problems. He was driving into a cesspool like Buenaventura with a woman and two children in a stolen, thirty-thousand-dollar truck. Somewhere outside the city, they were going to have to ditch the truck and make their way on foot. He supposed that it might be time to talk it over with Cristina.

"How are you feeling?" he asked.

"How do you think I feel?"

He apologized. "Sorry. I hate to bring it up, but we're going to have to abandon this crate before we reach the coast. It's going to mean some walking. How are your feet?"

"I can walk," she said stoically.

"I'm sure you can," he countered. "But how far?"

Irritation flashed in her eyes. "As far as I must, I suppose."

"Okay," he relented. "I'm going to try to get as close as I can and still be on the safe side. I know the dangers of this place. It would be better to wait until dark before we enter the city. Our luck has held up too well until now. It's bound to change if we push it."

Cristina glanced at her children, the two of them curled up against each other and sleeping fitfully. She nodded abruptly in agreement. "Yes. We should take no unnecessary chances."

Henry drove a bit further in silence. This was difficult. He'd never been much of a talker, but something had to be said.

"Listen," he said softly. "I know it can't help you, but I feel pretty bad about all of this, too. Willie and I were on the trail of two men who are probably responsible for what happened this morning. I also have other reasons that guarantee I'll either get them or die trying."

She looked to him, a heavy sadness etched in her face and tears beginning to stream freely down her cheeks.

"Why?" she asked. "I have never seen anything so horrible."

"The price of life in the fast lane can get high," he replied. "I think Willie knew that. I suppose he fed on that knowledge. It's what made him so alive. Living for the charge and the challenge. The possibility that something like this might happen was always there. Believe me, I know better than most."

"And do you do it for this 'charge' as well?"

The question hit Henry hard. He thought a moment.

"I don't honest to God know anymore," he told her, shaking his head. "I thought I could get out any time I wanted. I even quit, six months ago. And here I am again. Why you start and the reasons for continuing are often very different."

"Who are you?" she asked earnestly. "Truly."

He shook his head, the sadness now creeping into his own eyes as well. "A snake hunter who thought he no longer had to hunt snakes," he said. "A fool, perhaps."

Three miles above Buenaventura, Bueno found an ideally dense clump of jungle foliage and steered the pickup into the midst of it. While Cristina gathered up her children, he cut a large frond with his knife and set about obliterating any traces of their passage. Several branches were now bent or broken and had to be removed. Otherwise, they would begin to yellow in a matter of hours in this heat. When he'd completed the job, there was no trace of the truck visible from the road.

It was late afternoon now, but still several hours until sunset. There was a cantina somewhere nearby, according to Henry's recollection. He'd laid over there several years back when the Jeep he was driving hit a pig, crushing the radiator. The pig, it happened, belonged to the old woman who ran the place. He'd overpaid her for it without argument, and she took to him. An afternoon was spent telling lies in the heat, he drinking beer and she orange Fanta. When he was able to hitch a ride down the mountain in search of assistance, she sent her grandson to sit in the Jeep and prevent vandalism.

Bueno carried Rosa on his shoulders again and set out, eventually leading his weary troupe to the old woman's roadside hovel. It wasn't much, built of creosote-soaked logs and set back in the deep shade of two giant mahoganies. A couple of the dozen cafe tables were occupied by groups of grizzled, weatherbeaten black men playing dominoes. A skinny, rust-colored hound of indeterminate origin loped out onto the shoulder of the road to bark at their approach. As soon as Bueno bent to pat his head, he began wagging his tail and advanced to lick his hand.

The domino players glanced up from their games to take in this disheveled family. The man wore the rumpled cotton dress of a peasant and carried a scoped rifle of curious construction. The woman, though red-eyed and weary, was quite beautiful. They watched as the proprietess emerged from the interior of the place to greet them. A quick grin of recognition spread across her deeply lined and toothless face.

"Buenos tardes, señor,'' she greeted Henry. "It has been a long time. Have you killed another of my pigs?''

He laughed. "No, Mother. But we *are* hungry. This woman and her children have had a tiring day. I would be most grateful if you could provide them with food and rest.''

She surveyed the beautiful Cristina and her two children. People around Buenaventura had long since learned not to ask many questions. When Henry peeled two thousand pesos off the roll he carried, she smiled and nodded.

"It is much cooler inside," she said to Cristina. "Come.''

They were led to a small room behind the *bodega*. There was a large cot and not much else, but the place was clean. Cristina sat wearily and pulled her children to her.

"I will bring them food here,'' the woman told Henry.

He nodded his appreciation. "They need rest. I will eat outside. Perhaps you will join me and we will tell some lies, eh? It has been too long.'' He turned to Cristina. "See if you can get some sleep. We have several hours before we move.''

She attempted to smile, grateful for the chance to be alone with the kids and her grief.

"I'll be right outside,'' he assured her.

With the old woman in his wake, Bueno wandered back into the shade of the cantina and pulled up a chair. She brought him a beer and set it on the table without his asking. He sipped the cool, refreshing liquid with his eyes squeezed shut and then allowed himself to slouch and relax for the first time since early morning.

"It is important that no one know they are here," he told

135

the woman in a low voice. "Their lives may depend on it. If soldiers or the police come, you have not seen them."

She looked long and hard into his eyes, the twinkle of conspiracy developing in her own. "A woman and two small children could have done little wrong," she pronounced at length. "They will be safe here."

"Good," he told her, sighing. "You appear to be thirsty. When you have fed them, please join me."

Ramon Lopez spent that night in Popayan after driving the dying mechanic's dilapidated Jeep there. It was a night full of questions, and he had difficulty sleeping. There was little wonder as to how Diego would react to a possible breach in his carefully plotted scheme. His worries would be similar to those Ramon was experiencing as he tossed in his hotel bed. Could there be a traitor in the midst of the Somosista campaign to regain the Nicaraguan homeland?

Outside his hotel room, on the streets of this southern Colombian city, word of the assassinated interior minister buzzed like an electric current. The attack on Guillermo Faro's hacienda was also reported in detail on the radio. The wounded man in Pitalito had described *two* men, one of Faro's appearance and another, bigger and much more dangerous. This second, unidentified one was the element that gave Ramon serious concern for his own exposure. If there was a traitor within the Cardona faction of the Somosista movement, surely they knew of his presence in Colombia at that moment.

His heart pounded furiously in his chest as he fought for peace of mind. His ears strained for the sound of footsteps in the hall outside his room. Paranoia gripped him. Paranoia mixed with the shameful knowledge of his fear. He had never felt more alone.

The transition to life in the States had been difficult for many of Ron Dai's people. He sympathized but had no real way of relating to their experiences. Certainly his own family had experienced some level of racial prejudice when they arrived in Arizona. It came with the territory. His father was Vietnamese, married to a Frenchwoman. In Vietnam, his father's ancestors knew racism from the bigoted side. For centuries, they held the Indians, Chinese, Japanese, French, and later the Americans to be inferior. In Paris and, to a lesser degree, in the Tucson of his youth, his family encountered the flip side of that coin in small ways. His father and siblings were simply different in an occidental world. On the other hand, they were well-educated and from a family highly respected in the academic community. As Ron himself grew, the all-white part of his world came to respect his own intelligence as they did his father's.

Life among the boat people was radically different. Seen by many as an economic threat because of their sudden influx and ever-increasing numbers, they fought a fight that Ron Dai's family had never known. Nearly a hundred thousand of these Vietnamese and Laotian refugees had been dropped into the hungry maw of San Francisco's South Bay area. There was a demand for high-tech labor here. White junior executives and salesmen might be snorting coke behind closed office doors, but the rank and file were struggling to carve a foothold in this strange land by eating amphetamines and working double shifts.

The most recent indicators suggested that all was no longer well in the promised land. Hours and entire shifts were being cut in the face of fierce Japanese competition. There were layoffs in an area that had once enjoyed one of the lowest unemployment levels in the country. The boat people were suffering the worst of it. The nature of their drug dependencies was also changing. The fuel of ambition was being replaced by the chemical means of fighting despair. Youth crime was on the rise within the community. Heroin traffic had taken an alarming upswing.

Ron Dai was no stranger to these dilemmas. For several years now, it had been anticipated that an economic crunch might result in the pilfering of sensitive electronics for resale. His investigations were generally along this line. The FBI brought him into the SYSTEMATICS case to explore just such a possibility. They would explore other possible angles themselves, but anything else would be incidental to his own focus.

Collar upturned against the cool of a foggy evening, he parked his dented Dodge Daytona in the lot alongside a seedy tavern on San Jose's dilapidated far east side. A dozen small-bore motorcycles and a score of junkers from the sixties and early seventies made the county-owned undercover vehicle

seem right at home. In the Santa Clara Valley, the haves and
have-nots were separated by geography. The enclaves of the
movers and shakers lined the west and south rims of this vast
alluvial bowl. Executive bedroom communities like Los Al-
tos, Cupertino, Saratoga, and Los Gatos. In these towns,
heavy growths of liveoak, madrone, fir, and eucalyptus
cloaked the foothills of the Santa Cruz Mountains and their
secluded ravines. Hidden neatly away were sprawling con-
temporaries, ranch houses, and opulent interpretations of half-
a-dozen European residential styles. In these towns, the living
was easy. Streets were traveled by Porsches, BMWs, Mercedes,
Volvos and Saabs. The shopping was done in antique shops,
mini-malls, and cutsie boutiques.

Something happens along the valley floor as it flows east.
First come the solidly blue-collar and upwardly mobile towns
like Campbell, Sunnyvale, Santa Clara. They are crammed
full of apartment complexes for singles and "starter" houses
that, often as not, end up being finishing houses as well. Such
communities stretch into the central, south, and near east
sections of San Jose. Out here, the topography becomes
increasingly monotonous and uninspired. And then there is
the far east side, where the rents are as low as the prospects
for advancement. Cookie-cutter tract houses and claptrap apartment buildings are called home, the architecture squat and
uninspired. It is as though even the authors of this landscape
were without hope. This is also where most of the boat
community lives, often a dozen or more of them to a house.
They live and work with the singleminded goal of escape.
Proud people. Defiant people.

Dai could hear the strident chords of a ragtag rock 'n' roll
band as he approached the entrance to the bar. They were
struggling through the old Cream tune, "Sunshine of Your
Love." Loud. He pushed his way inside.

The joint was choked with an eye-searing haze of cigarette
smoke. And humanity. Two hundred patrons were jammed
into the tight interior. Back along one wall stood a pair of
undersized pool tables. There were patches in the faded felt.
The bar appeared to be doing land-office business. Men of all
ages stood three deep to buy drinks. Barmaids with skimpy
skirts and bared shoulders slithered expertly through the throng,
trays held high in the air. Onstage, the four-piece group set
about trying to murder "Wild Thing," slurring the syllables

of words and playing louder to cover it. To give them due credit, they *did* have the haircuts, the clothes, and the moves.

He scanned the crowd in front of the bar. There seemed to be a thin spot at the far end, outside the rest room door. He wanted a place where he could watch for faces unobtrusively. One of his gifts was a remarkable ability to recall the features of people he'd seen, on an assembly line or anyplace else. His trips up and down the line at SYSTEMATICS had been spent doing exactly that.

Ron pushed his way through the crowd, listening to the babble of Vietnamese all around him. His parents had insisted that their children employ only his mother's and father's tongues during evening meal conversations. As a kid he'd felt it old-fashioned and unnecessary. Now he was grateful. He felt completely at home with both of them.

"Hey! Bright boy. What you doing here, man?"

It came from a kid of about eighteen, his back to the bar. Dai recognized him as one of the crew of material expediters who pushed carts around the SYSTEMATICS plant, delivering parts.

"Your Mercedes get a flat or something?"

"I don't have a Mercedes," Dai growled. Attention in the immediate area was focused on him. This was just what he had aimed for, but he had to be careful here.

"The dude is a new inspection *engineer* at the plant," the kid sneered. "Joe College."

"What of it?" the detective challenged.

"Bright boys can't always afford the bread for college," the kid shot back. "Take me. I'm a bright boy"—he grinned, elbowing the man next to him—"and I didn't go to no college. Dude who looks about half Vietnamese *did* go. His mama must've bent over and let Uncle Sam take her from behind."

"My mother picks grapefruit in Texas," Dai returned evenly, keeping his cool against all inclination to tear this punk's throat out. If he could maintain an even temper, the kid was going to get frustrated sooner or later. Frustration was the thing that quickly pissed a guy like that off. "I went to college on a wrestling scholarship. So what was your problem?"

The kid was at a loss for words. He'd thrown his best verbal punch and failed to score.

"Why are you being such an asshole?" Dai pressed him.

"Because we don't like no half-white outsiders hanging around here where they don't belong."

Dai grinned. "I apologize. I guess I didn't see the sign."

He moved past to the bar and ordered a beer.

"I don't think you musta heard me, *engineer*," the kid snarled. "Go drink with your own kind."

"That's funny." The detective was smiling easily at him. "I thought *you* were my own kind." He took a sip of his beer and stepped pointedly away, pretending to watch the band.

A distraction forced the skinny young heckler to give up on him for the moment. A tiny ferret of a man with scraggly facial hair and a motorcycle jacket two sizes too big for him pushed through the throng and whispered something in his ear. A moment later, they were both easing their way toward the men's room.

Bingo. After several years in this line of work, Ron Dai recognized the bravado and territoriality accompanying a dealer's abiding paranoia. These people saw themselves as feudal barons, gunslingers, and rock stars all rolled into one. They were complex and insecure personalities without the dope. Add a headful of confidence enhancers, and all those dreams of grandeur became *delusions*.

He watched this pair disappear. There was no telling where this avenue of inquiry might lead, but Dai believed that no stone should be left unturned. As often as not, dope dealers in the electronics business turned out to be no more than just that. On the other hand, the simple observation of a primary target often led to the discovery of others. They, in turn, led to still more. When he patiently traced the strands of this complex web, he sometimes hit pay dirt. There were many tools, once he had a list of names. Records checks for previous infractions and employment where other similar problems may have occurred. It seemed a lot like looking for a needle in a haystack, but if you were methodical, and the needle was indeed there, it could be found. For the moment, until he had an opportunity to begin the same type of inquiry in the Chicano and white communities, this little bad guy would be the object of his focus. As a materials expediter, he was free to move about the SYSTEMATICS plant. That gave him access to a lot of overworked people with pressing financial problems who felt in need of a little boost.

Dai sauntered back through the crowd to the entrance, left

the bar, and walked to his parked Dodge. He checked as unobtrusively as possible to make sure he wasn't being observed and slid behind the wheel. Then he started the car, steered slowly from the lot, circled the block, and parked on the street about fifty yards from the bar. From where he sat, midway between a pair of mercury vapor street lamps, he enjoyed an unobstructed view of the front door.

The sun had set and darkness was beginning to fill in the gaps between the leaves when a Colombian DAS van pulled onto the shoulder of the road outside the cantina. Bueno was now drinking *cafe con leche*, much of the tension of the early day having melted from the muscles of his neck and shoulders. One table's domino players had since departed, but the second group lingered on. They looked up now as the federal police, a tall lieutenant and two regular uniforms, emerged from their vehicle.

Henry knew they would come. It was only a matter of when. His clothes were thoroughly soiled from the sweat and grime of his escape. The five-o'clock shadow of that morning was now the ragged beginnings of a beard. His rumpled, unkempt hair made him look vaguely wild.

The lieutenant led his two men into the place, exuding an authority he obviously expected to be respected. The old black men returned to their game, barely giving them further notice. Bueno took them in without moving as he sipped his coffee. The old woman hurried from within the *bodega*, all smiles and effusive greeting. She asked if they would like to sit and perhaps have something to eat or drink.

The lieutenant waved her off, asking instead if she'd seen a fancy silver-gray pickup truck pass that afternoon. She stood a moment, searching her memory, before reporting that she had no recollection of such a thing. He asked her of strangers, wondering if any had come through that day. She assured him without hesitation that she did a brisk business and had many strangers passing through on the way to the coast. They all looked the same to her. Their money was all the same color.

The DAS men looked around the place. One of them went inside while another approached the men at the domino table. The players were asked if they'd seen the truck or anything else out of the ordinary. Henry wasn't paying much attention to them, keeping track of the man inside the store instead. As he watched him out of the corner of one eye, the lieutenant strolled to his table and stood before him.

"Do you have identification, señor?" he asked.

Bueno shrugged, shaking his head. "No," he told the man in a perfect coastal accent. "Should I have?"

"Where are you from, señor?" the cop demanded.

"I hunt snakes in the coastal jungle," Henry told him. "I am from where snakes are."

"Do you know this man?" the lieutenant demanded of the old woman.

"For many years," she assured him. "Only he does not visit me as often as he should."

Bueno was eyed with hostility by the cop. The uniform and badge were not getting the proper response from this dirty peasant. Yet he was a white man, not an Indian or even a mestizo. A snake hunter. Antisocial by nature. He shrugged with feigned indifference and turned away. His man inside the *bodega* emerged, shaking his head. Moments later, the three of them left, climbed into their van, and disappeared down the road toward Buenaventura.

Bueno motioned the old woman back to his table and laid another two thousand pesos before her. He told her he wanted to buy those men at the other table a drink. There was also the obvious question in his eyes.

"They are fine," she told him with a grin. "A cupboard that opens to a secret room as an escape from bandits or thieves." Henry thanked her, rose from his chair, and moved back through the store to the side room. Cristina was huddled with her kids behind the false back of the armoire. He reached in a hand to her.

"They are gone. It is dark and time to be moving. Did you sleep at all?"

She shook her head. "The children did, but I couldn't. Every time I close my eyes, I see a helicopter shooting rockets into my home. I see Willie's face. I cannot even bury him. I have been denied everything."

"Except your life and your children's lives," he reminded her.

"My life would mean nothing except for them," she replied.

"Nonsense! That is not the way you felt last night. Then it was worth more than anyone was giving you credit for. Willie is dead, Cristina. If he hadn't been out somewhere getting laid, he might be here right now. For God's sake, *you* didn't have anything to do with his getting killed.''

She glared at him through the gloom. ''It all made so much sense once. I watched my mother and father live together in much the same way. That was simply the way it was. My mother would never have done what I did last night.''

''Values change,'' he told her. ''You're not the same woman as your mother. I am not the same man as my father. Much has happened in history to change the way we see who we are.''

''But where am I to go from here?'' she asked. ''I feel like I am running just to run.''

''No,'' he corrected. ''You are running to survive and so that your children may survive. I have a friend in Costa Rica. Tonight I will find someone with a boat who is willing to take us to Parrita. It is on the coast, down the mountains from the capital. If we can make it that far, we will put you and the children on a plane to Caracas. You see, even in the darkest hour, there is some small glimmer of hope.''

''But such a boat trip,'' she argued. ''Especially for fugitives. It will be expensive, and I have no money.''

''There is money enough,'' he said. ''Once we are in San Jose, I can make arrangements for more.''

143

ELEVEN

Ron Dai didn't much mind surveillance. Sure, it was a fairly static enterprise, but it gave him time to think. Sort through things and get his direction straight. In this instance, he'd been called in on this SYSTEMATICS job quite suddenly. The facts had been dumped on him in one load, and he'd been sent out to see what he could dig up with them. As an inside man who had worked the Silicon Valley underbelly for some time, he felt he was in tune with the industry and people working within it. That in mind, he was trying to figure out why something was bugging him this time.

SYSTEMATICS produced *the* state-of-the-art lap-top PC. The thing was truly portable and had big power. If an employee were in a fix for money to supply a habit or pay a gambling debt, it would make sense to steal an item readily convertible to cash on the black market. But missile guidance components? Dopers were basically a paranoid lot. It seemed to Ron that espionage of this nature was pretty heavyweight for a speed freak. Sure, you had to cover all the bases and take opportunity where it reared its friendly head, but something in his gut told him that he was barking up the wrong tree.

In the next hour and a half, patrons came and went without incident. Because of some of their ages, Dai imagined an Alcoholic Beverage Control agent would have a field day in a

144

place like this. The motorbikes, most of them of the two-stroke variety, screamed back and forth, slashing the peace like chainsaws on wheels. It wasn't the first time that he'd caught himself reflecting on the problems of cultural assimilation. If, like these kids, you were dead set on fighting the beat of your new culture instead of moving with it, you had little chance of ever learning to dance.

The obnoxious dope peddler eventually emerged from the place with a couple of cronies in tow and his gait in full swagger. They moved off to a new Pontiac Trans Am with customized flames painted on the front quarter-panels and ten pounds of crap hanging from the rearview mirror. All three men climbed in and sped off, moving southward. Dai followed, keeping that unique Pontiac taillight configuration in sight. They threaded through the worst of this suburban ghetto and headed into the Almaden area in the southeast corner of the valley.

The houses were larger and better ordered here. Yards were neatly kept and lawns clipped. The architecture was for the most part mock–Spanish in style, and the affluence level was solid middle class. He followed the Trans Am to a cul de sac, pulled to the curb on the main street beyond, and watched as the three men approached the front door of a beige split level. As soon as they'd entered, he slid out onto the street and closed in on foot.

The streets and sidewalks were well lit. There was little he could do about being seen, so he proceeded as naturally as possible. One house away from the beige one, he dodged quickly into the shadows of an ornamental lemon tree and worked his way diagonally into the side yard of his objective. A few houses away, a dog began to yap hysterically. As silently as he could, he scaled a six-foot redwood fence and lowered himself into the target yard.

Dai found himself on a patio adjacent to a curtained sliding glass door. Light gleamed from behind the curtain, giving him plenty to see by as he crossed the exposed aggregate underfoot. To the right stood a built-in barbecue constructed of red brick. Beyond it, one of those semipermanent pools had been installed with a swath of redwood decking around it. The perimeter of the patio was studded with tiki torches, colored paper lanterns strung between them.

Ron approached just the tiniest part in the curtains and

145

leaned close to peer through it. The surly kid's buddies lounged in a pair of deep, overstuffed chairs while their friend dealt with one who was obviously the main man. A triple-beam scale sat between them on a coffee table. For the moment, it was idle. Next to it, the supplier, an older, heavyset Vietnamese man, was working a spatula through a mountain of tiny pink heart-shaped pills. He quickly counted them out in tens; Dexedrine. Dai watched as his quarry's supply rose well into triple digits. Depending on how often he restocked his inventory, he appeared to be doing considerable business. His source was another area of interest altogether. A word to the county narcotics unit would set the dogs on him. The triple-beam balance tended to indicate other trade than pep pills.

Ron decided that rather than press his luck, it was time to get out of there. He beat a retreat back to the Daytona, serenaded by the yipping neighbor's dog, and waited. Ten minutes later, the swaggering kid emerged from the cul de sac to wind his way through the maze of interconnecting subdivision streets. It was getting tough to keep up at a discreet distance when they finally swung onto an access ramp and made speed along an all-but-deserted US 101 moving north. The detective had no idea what this lead might bring him, but he stayed on his tail. You didn't sneeze at this kind of immediate progress.

The Trans Am took US 280 west at its intersection and moved across the valley floor toward the foothills of the Santa Cruz range. The stunted downtown section of San Jose slumbered now, with all but the bars closed. Its squat, darkened buildings were silhouetted against the glow of suburban sprawl. Dai thought that such a massive metropolis should have more of a heart that could generate a pulse all down its arteries. San Francisco was fifty miles distant, too far away to infuse the lifeblood of culture and style a population needed to form its own self-image. Instead, the population here simply stretched across this once-fertile valley like a vast, soulless protoplasm. He had seen pictures and heard stories of this place in the not-so-distant past. It had been completely transformed into what it was today in a mere thirty years. A blink of an eye in time.

The Pontiac left the freeway in Sunnyvale, drove another mile over city streets, and came to a stop in the parking lot of a massive shopping mall. Dai was forced to stop out on the main road, unwilling to risk detection. He observed through field glasses. The three Vietnamese men waited until a green BMW pulled up next to them. Some sort of exchange was effected. The taillights of both cars lit, and they pulled away to depart in opposite directions.

Dai made a decision. He followed the BMW, figuring that he'd be able to locate the kid again any time he wanted. Rolling without his lights, he waited until he'd reached a point where he was sure his new quarry wouldn't notice them being switched on. The car traveled south on the Saratoga–Sunnyvale road through Cupertino and into the high-end suburb of Saratoga.

The community they now wound through was as affluent as the east side of San Jose was impoverished. That little pile of Dexedrine hearts had run the gamut, ending up in one of the most exclusive enclaves in the area. The high-tech elite lived here: CEOs, presidents, high-powered attorneys, and investment counselors. The detective followed the BMW to the drive of a sprawling ranch-style house, the basic seven-hundred-and-fifty-thousand-dollar variety. It was nice, but not spectacular in this neck of the enchanted forest. He noted the address and plate number of the car, decided he'd done enough fence scaling for one night, and called it quits. Roscoe Charles could get his gofers to run the accumulated info in the morning. They'd get together after work to discuss findings and any next moves. He was beat. He had to be up in six hours to go to work.

Henry handed Cristina his pistol before they set out to hike the three remaining miles to Buenaventura.

"Just in case," he told her. "It isn't smart for me to have all the firepower."

Once again, he had Rosa on his shoulders as Cristina led Miguel by the hand. It had been a long day for the kids, but at least they'd gotten some sleep. Still, they were showing signs of real fatigue, much of it emotional. Rosa was cranky, and Miguel, who had been a real trooper all day, was sniffling and asking for his dad.

Cristina took the gun and pushed it into the waistband of her skirt beneath her blouse.

"I want you and Miguel to walk ahead," Henry told her.

"If anyone wants to jump us, they'll wait until we've passed and then come from behind. Don't do anything sudden. The secret to foiling an attack is to avoid telegraphing your intentions. Watch and make your decision based on what you see."

They started off, keeping well to the side of the road. It was downhill all the way into Buenaventura, so the going would be relatively easy, but there was no moon. Henry, eyes quickly adjusting to the gloom and ears straining for every sound, moved cautiously along behind Cristina and the boy. The air buzzed with noises of insects and birds, whose jungle home pressed hard on either side of the road. It was hot, the air impossibly close and humid. A falling leaf began to rot here almost before it touched the ground. It was not a place a man would choose to live unless he had no other choice.

"I'm frightened," Cristina said quietly.

"You've got good reason to be," he assured her. "But look at it another way. You've made it this far."

When a vehicle approached, climbing up the mountain from the coast, they melted into the foliage until it passed. A DAS van, possibly even the one that had stopped at the old woman's earlier.

They were actually within sight of the city, perhaps three quarters of a mile above it, when the low, guttural voice of a man developed behind them, ordering them to stop. Two shadows took dimension, looming up from a ditch beside them, and a blinding light was played into their faces. Bueno, with the little girl on his shoulders, stood absolutely still. Cristina had drawn Miguel up close to her and stood huddled with both arms around him.

"The rifle, señor," the voice behind them said. "On the ground. Very slowly."

Henry complied.

"So what have we here?" the voice asked, amusement tinging it. "A white woman, two children, and a dog. Such children will bring much money. The fine-looking woman is something else again." When he allowed himself an outright snicker, one of his accomplices joined him. "What do you suppose they are doing? Out traveling in the dead of night. They should know better." There came the telltale click of a revolver's hammer being drawn back to the cocked position.

"Do not worry, dog. She does not need you anymore. She is in much better hands."

All the while the man spoke, Bueno focused on his voice. It told him to go to his left. He had to count on the first shot missing him.

All three of the adversaries were moving in closer now. Of the pair who were visible, one carried a pistol and flashlight while the other held a rifle. The man behind had a revolver. He knew that from what he'd heard. He also knew that he had only seconds before a bullet from it tore into him. He sprang, his hand going to his belt for his commando knife. He freed it and let it fly in one lightning move as little Rosa was sent sprawling. The revolver roared in his ear as he rolled away from the writhing body of its owner. His knife was planted deep in the man's larynx. Lunging from the ground, Henry took the feet out from under another with a vicious sweep kick to the ankles. He was on the man, delivering the blow that crushed his windpipe, when he heard the telltale clack of a rifle bolt above his right ear.

Just as suddenly, the night was split by the familiar bark of his own Walther P-5. At first, Henry assumed it was the rifle, wondering if you *could* hear the one that got you. An instant later, the rifle above him went off, the bullet flying harmlessly wide. It had been fired by a dead man.

Bueno looked up to see a quivering Cristina Faro standing above him. She'd moved to point-blank range to make sure of hitting her target. Most of the man's head was missing. Henry scrambled to his feet as Cristina just stood and stared. Miguel was clinging to one thigh, and her little girl screamed hysterically nearby. She looked down at the gun in her hands and then up at Henry.

Bueno took the pistol from her. At the edge of the ditch, he unceremoniously dumped all three assailants in and stooped to retrieve his own knife and rifle. The crying Rosa, one elbow skinned, went back up onto his shoulders.

"We'd better get the hell out of here," he told the woman. "You think you can do it?"

"I am fine," she said quietly, almost whispering. "Perhaps I should carry the baby for a while. She is frightened."

"That makes two of us," he told her.

"Three." There was a huskiness in her voice now.

"We can make the best time this way," he said. "Come."

149

They reached Buenaventura without further incident. Bueno flagged a cab and directed it to a specific hotel on the waterfront. There was nothing pretty about the place, but it was relatively clean, and he'd had dealings with the proprietor in the past. He got Cristina and the kids settled, stripped the P-5 at a rickety table, reloaded the clip, and secured the thing in his boot.

"I'm going to try to find us a boat," he told Cristina. "You keep the windows and door locked no matter what. I'm leaving the rifle with you. It's switched to twelve-gauge. Shoot anyone who tries to get in here unless it's me. I'll be back in a couple of hours."

"You look tired," she said. "Shouldn't you try to get some sleep?"

"Not until I've found a way out of Colombia," he said. "I'll try to find you something to eat."

He wandered down the docks to where the fishing boats tied up. It was not so late that the waterfront cantinas weren't still crowded with cackling whores, drunken men, and loud music. After determining who was in port, he headed for a certain bar. The Red Rose was up along the north end of the waterfront, a place where boat owners and would-be entrepreneurs congregated. These men supposedly fished, but everyone knew that the real money to be made out of a port like Buenaventura wasn't in tuna. As many dope and gem traffickers as fishermen drank in the Red Rose.

The music and laughter floating from the place accentuated for Henry just how bone-tired he was. He paused across the street, his back to the place, to stare past the boats moored in dead calm water and collect his thoughts. His gaze took in the darkened land mass across the bay and the horizon beyond. He thought of Carl Stickley and the envelope that Deputy Director Cam Stebbins had handed him that morning a short eternity ago. Jesus, things could get twisted up. They always did; it was something he could count on. He turned from the calm of an equatorial sea and strode across the street.

Ted Latham had waited until the end of the normal Washington business day to hop an Eastern flight from Dulles to Miami. Even as winter began to sink its teeth gently into the District of Columbia, a citizen unaware of the date would have had no idea, based on the weather he encountered here.

It was close to eighty-five degrees, three hours past sundown. A light breeze was laden with the perfume of tropical foliage. The locals wore shorts and light short-sleeve shirts.

The anointed patriots were, on the whole, in an uproar over Diego Cardona's recent antics. When Rod O'Doyle had warned a gathering, at the inception of their little campaign, that this particular greaseball couldn't be trusted any further than he, a pretty good-sized Irishman, could throw him, they'd chosen to disregard him. Anyone with political power down there had his finger in some sort of unacceptable pie. It came with the territory. What hadn't come with the territory, outside of Cuba, was the Red menace. *This* was what they needed a man of Cardona's audacity to help them stop. As far as the campaign went, he'd kept his end of the bargain quite admirably. There was no reason to risk seeing *their* venture abandoned now, just because of some jackass moves Diego Cardona insisted he make on a completely *different* front.

"So!" the grinning Nicaraguan major greeted him. He was recently arrived from the Caribbean and standing in the entry foyer of the Somosista headquarters in Coral Gables. One of the guards had admitted Latham at the gate after calling ahead for clearance. Now, Cardona stood holding the door for him personally. "This is a surprise and an honor, Señor Latham."

"Cut the bullshit, asshole," the CIA man snarled, pushing past him. "You've got about eight seconds to explain just what the *fuck* you think you're trying to pull. If your explanation isn't pretty good, I'm gonna pull your goddamn plug."

The ex-secret police major's face reddened. It was not customary for people to speak like this to him without suffering some fairly dire consequences. But this was a different situation. Ted Latham was integral to any hope of his regaining power in the homeland. Cardona was also surprised to learn that CIA intelligence was effective enough to have discovered his part in the recent Colombian assassination.

"We have a very simple agreement, señor," he said calmly. "I consider any of my other affairs to be mine alone."

Latham laughed in his face, removed an envelope from the breast pocket of his jacket, and handed it to him.

"Look at it," he said coldly. "It's a brief dossier on a man named Bueno. Henry Bueno. Your Italian-American shooter killed his best friend and former commanding officer in the mountains outside Cali. Carl Stickley's murder has persuaded

Mr. Bueno to come out of an early retirement and move back into the field. He is far and away the most effective agent this country has ever run in the Southern Hemisphere. He has only one thing on his mind right now, and that is to find and eliminate whoever is behind Carl Stickley's murder."

"How can you possibly know about Terranova?" Diego asked quietly.

"*Everybody* does!" Latham snapped. "Not as much as I do, but our group has members from all corners of the community. That includes Drug Enforcement and FBI. I am fully aware of your—ah—peripheral activities in the trafficking of contraband substances. The DEA seems to be even more irritated by them than I am. Then there is the FBI and their continued surveillance of a Cosa Nostra heavy hitter, put out to pasture in West Palm Beach, by the name of Jack Terranova. We took the liberty of identifying you as a Sandinista agent when it came up that you'd made contact with him."

"Jesus Mary!" Diego gasped. "You are telling me that this agent—this Bueno—is active in the field, and that he has targeted *me*?"

"You must be related to Sherlock Holmes, amigo."

"But what effect can he really have? We operated with the utmost secrecy. In the area where Stickley suffered his unfortunate demise, the army has eliminated one notorious cocaine trafficker and his family. How could this possibly lead to me?"

Latham shook his head in exasperation. "How? Jesus Christ! I've just finished describing a couple of places you've conducted your affairs in a sloppy manner. How the hell do I know what umpteen other ways you've pulled the same jerk-off shit? Bueno's on your trail, and I tell you, he's better than good. That means there's a shot at his stumbling over *our* little operation. If he does, I can't begin to imagine the problems we'd have."

Cardona turned and strode into an adjacent parlor where he poured himself a brandy and gulped half of it.

"The time is so short," he said insistently, pointing a finger at Latham past the rim of his glass. "Terranova will be kept in isolation until our operation has entered its final phase. There is no way this man will find him . . . or me."

*   *   *

The Red Rose was filled with raucous music, cigarette smoke, the din of conversation, and the cackle of forced, seductive laughter. The tough black-haired man with a wide forehead and bent nose caught the look in his drinking companion's eyes and turned to look to his right. Recognition, mixed with surprise and perhaps a little fear, crossed his face.

"Buy you a drink?" the newcomer asked.

The man looked to his companion and then back to the disheveled man he knew as Riberac. The snake hunter. He appeared to have fallen on some rough times. There was spattered blood on the shoulder of his filthy shirt.

"I am sorry, señor. I am occupied with pressing business. Perhaps another time."

The look in the snake hunter's eyes hardened. His voice, when he spoke, belied his appearance. "Now." It carried all his former strength and command with it. This hardened drinker knew many myths of the snake hunter. He was the one who walked with death, and only a fool misjudged him . . . as he had nearly done now.

"Certainly," he relented, nodding. He gestured to an empty chair.

Bueno continued to stand. He turned his attention to the man seated on the other side of the table. "Give us a few moments alone, please." It was not spoken as a request.

This other looked indignant until he caught the look of caution in his tablemate's eyes. He scraped back in his chair, threw Henry a hostile look, and stomped off to lean on the bar. Bueno took his vacated place. Now he was seated directly across from Lucho Vargas. He clapped his hands in the air with authority and, when the waiter appeared, ordered two Poker beers.

"Your boat is in port," he said at length.

"That is correct," Vargas replied.

"I need passage to Costa Rica. Before morning."

The fisherman studied Henri Riberac carefully, a slow smile developing at the corners of his mouth.

"And you have developed a sudden fear of flying, eh, señor?"

"Believe what you wish. There are three others and myself."

The beers arrived. Forgoing his glass, Bueno eased the

dew-drenched bottle to his lips and took a long swallow. He closed his eyes a moment and concentrated as the cool liquid soothed his parched mouth and throat.

"Tonight or even tomorrow is impossible," Vargas told him. "The head is torn off my engine, and the boat will not be seaworthy until tomorrow night, at the earliest. Even then, such a trip would be expensive, señor."

"You're sure you can have her seaworthy by tomorrow night?" Bueno asked it without hesitation.

Vargas chuckled. "Incentive is a wonderful motivator, señor. Just now I was talking with a man who has a pressing need to ship certain sensitive materials to Mexico. If I were to honor your request, I would stand to lose some very lucrative business of his."

"Cut the crap, Lucho. Just name your price and tell me when we sail."

The sailor took a moment to stroke his chin, feigning deep thought. "One hundred and twenty-five thousand pesos each," he said finally.

Thirty-two hundred dollars American probably seemed an exorbitant sum to him for two days work. To Bueno, even with the risk that staying an extra day in Buenaventura entailed, three grand was a small price to pay. He nodded and extended his hand.

"Done. I pay you in gold before departure. Name the hour."

Lucho scrambled mentally, trying to keep up with this unexpected good fortune. "I must locate my mechanic. He is off with some whore. Midnight tomorrow night. I will have had time to locate this man or find another."

On a hill overlooking the entrance to Willie Faro's hacienda compound, Ramon sat quietly as the rays of a dawning sun erased gloom from the valley. Behind him, parked beneath a sprawling tree off a rutted farm road, the engine of Felix Colon's Jeep ticked as it cooled. Ramon was punch-drunk from lack of sleep. Still, a mild euphoria prevailed. The past night's paranoia seemed unfounded in the light of this new day. He arrived in this place before sunup and could only now begin to make out the extent of the carnage strewn across the property below him. His field glasses were pressed to his eyes as he stared in fascination inside the perimeter of the hacienda compound.

From the look of it, the army had caught the trafficker's staff of security men totally by surprise. They would have fought valiantly at the outset, pulling back only grudgingly. But the destruction was total. The adobe wall surrounding the place had been obliterated. The big, sprawling house was utterly destroyed. It was now only a heap of rubble.

In the lane below him he saw a pickup truck gutted by fire. It had been one of those big, fancy four-wheel rigs with oversized tires and beefed-up suspension. It was ripped open like a can of sardines.

Off on a hill opposite his own position, Ramon noticed a place where the earth was scorched as if by a fierce explosion. Twisted pieces of scrap littered the area, and close by a Jeep lay wrecked and overturned.

Curious about the positioning of the pickup, Ramon focused his glasses on it again. It looked to have been caught in ambush as it arrived at the hacienda. There was no way of telling who might have been in it. He was going to have to walk down to survey it in an effort to locate some sort of identification within. It already looked like a thankless task.

He waited a bit, biding his time before undertaking this unpleasantness. Once he'd made the descent, his first attentions were paid to the truck, where he found nothing. Any occupants would have been charred beyond recognition in such an assault. He moved on to the hacienda compound itself. The dirt floor and rubble walls were all that remained of the gatehouse. The main hacienda house itself was an immense pile of broken adobe. As he stumbled through it, his fatigue made it all the harder to sustain the effort it took to perform this grisly task. He was too young to have participated in the civil war and had never witnessed such carnage. Ramon could smell the stench of what must have been corpses still trapped in the rubble. In this heat, deterioration and insect activity were accelerated. He moved away and headed out back to the scorched wreckage on the hill. Diego would want a full report on the extent of the destruction. It was not young Lopez's responsibility to determine *how* a helicopter might have crashed.

Half an hour later, Ramon Lopez wearily guided the Jeep back down the rutted lane to the highway. Even in his ex-

155

hausted state, apprehension still gnawed at him. The Colombian army was proclaiming that it had killed Willie Faro, but the man in Pitalito had told him that there were two men that night. A strange man, not Colombian. It was impossible to know whether this one was among the three dozen reported killed in the compound. News of him would certainly disturb Don Diego. The major did not like loose ends.

TWELVE

FBI agents Roscoe Charles and Peter Davis were seated with
Detective Ron Dai in the senior agent's office. Between them
lay a computerized printout of the agency's traces on the
information Dai had provided. It told them that the owner of
the house in Saratoga and the green BMW were the same
man. Gregory J. Fisk. Age: thirty-two. Born: Walnut Creek,
California. B.A. Economics, Stanford University. M.B.A.,
Stanford Business School. Occupation: controller, Gibbon,
Hastings, Mount and Ronson, Attorneys at Law.

"I don't think action against this guy would be appropriate
at this time," Dai was arguing, his comments aimed primarily at Davis.

"I don't give a rat's ass who he works for," Davis retorted
with vehemence. "The man is a suspected dope pusher."

"Take it easy," Charles cautioned him. "A nice night's
work, Ronnie," he complimented. "I think I'm with you. It
doesn't bear much on our investigation. This is more a
local police matter."

"I've been giving this whole angle a lot of thought," Dai
told him. "Something doesn't feel quite right about it. I've
seen a lot of drug-motivated pilfering and industrial espionage, and this is different."

"How so?" Charles asked, interest piqued.

The detective outlined his thoughts of the previous night.

"You don't steal a thing like a missile guidance component unless you have a specific outlet for it," he concluded. "That's my gut feeling, anyway."

"And my feeling all along," Davis interjected. "I never believed it was anyone on the production floor."

"Elaborate," Charles suggested.

"Patterns," Davis told him. "Look at the rash of incidents where national security has been breached in the past couple of years. Russians, Chinese, Israelis, or what have you. They target the most immediate guy to the source they can get their hands on. White-collar technicians and engineers. It's hard to bribe or blackmail someone at the bottom of the economic ladder. They aren't reliable, and they don't have enough to lose."

Davis might have been arrogant and condescending, but Dai was inclined to agree with him. "One thing is all but certain," he added. "We're dealing with either a broker on the open market or a hostile foreign power. Neither of them is likely to rely on a speed freak."

"But drugs *could* be a factor," Roscoe Charles cautioned. "A cocaine debt can get quite large. Some other sort of compromise might exist that could provide an opening for blackmail. It's probably a good idea to concentrate on the white-collar people, Pete. That's a good point. It's my opinion that we should start to run some banking and tax data on the SYSTEMATICS higher-ups. Identify major purchases. Significant family illnesses and that sort of thing. Anything that could indicate severe financial pressure."

"Am I still in?" Dai asked.

"How do you feel about it?" Charles asked.

Ron shrugged. "I'm here already. I know the turf."

"We'll start requesting the background data," Charles told them. "I'll want both of you to review each file. You can split them between yourselves and then trade. Don't be afraid to take any gut feeling you get and run with it."

With images of carnage still burning in his mind's eye, young Ramon Lopez gazed out the window as his plane touched down on the hard-packed beach sand of Providencia Island. Located about a hundred and twenty miles off the Nicaraguan coast, both Providencia and her sister island, San Andres, had long been disputed territories. Controlled by

Colombia, they were also claimed by Nicaragua. It had always been one of Generalissimo Somoza's dreams that one day the army of Nicaragua would attain the strength necessary to sustain an invasion and occupation of these islands for the glory of their country. Currently, they were serving as a perfect staging ground for the Somosista Contras in exile. While other expatriates preferred the safety of Florida, Don Diego traveled back and forth between the two command posts with frequency. Indeed, he was due that very morning to receive Ramon's briefing. The young Lopez was to hurry from Providencia to a surfside compound on San Andres's west coast. Cardona occupied this opulent home while plotting the overthrow of the Sandinista dog, so close across the water. He claimed that from it he could smell the homeland in the wind.

A powerboat was beached at the end of the remote runway. Ramon was surprised to see the major himself awaiting his arrival as he climbed down from the Cessna and crossed the palm-lined stretch of sand. They shook hands, unable to hear each other speak as the plane turned, taxied, and roared off into the cloudless sky.

Two armed men stood by the powerboat as they approached. Cardona ordered them away with a nod. When they had moved some distance up the beach, he peered expectantly into the younger man's eyes.

"Tell me of it, young friend. We have heard many reports on the radio."

Lopez went on to describe the scene at the hacienda, reporting that he could not conclusively identify Faro but had no reason to doubt the army's claims.

"There is one other item that disturbs me greatly," he concluded.

"Out with it," Diego demanded impatiently.

"The mechanic in Pitalito. Colon. I found him near death. He was visited by two men this past week. They asked of an American and the airplane he departed in."

The Somosista commander's eyes narrowed to slits. "Near death?"

Ramon swallowed as he nodded. "One of the men was a local trafficker fitting Faro's description. The other is a mystery. Another villager who was also shot swore that this one was not Colombian. A very large man with immense physical

159

power and cunning. He foiled an ambush they'd laid for travelers on the mountain road. Before they left, the mechanic was shot in both knees. The wounds are gangrenous. I do not believe he lasted the night."

Cardona stood with his head down. He stared at the sand between his feet, working the toe of his right loafer into it.

"A mystery man," he grunted. "Asking about the American and the Cessna. Even our friend Latham may have underestimated him."

"I beg your pardon?"

Diego shook his head, obviously perplexed. He was a man who felt most comfortable in a knowledge of absolutes. Loose ends, especially lurking and dangerous ones, disturbed him. This renegade had made remarkable progress in sniffing out Terranova's scent. He doubted if he could have picked up the trail any further than Cali, because even Felix Colon hadn't known the Turbo-prop's destination. Still, to be on the safe side he would send down a couple of his very best men to check around both Cali and Quito. If they came across anything disturbing, they would be under orders to take care of the problem discreetly.

"This man may be an unanticipated problem," Diego said distractedly. "A fly in the ointment. Now that we are aware of this fly's presence, I have every confidence we will locate and swat him before he can become a real pest."

It was developing into one of those days Maureen Counihan would rather forget. Before noon, Agent Charles dropped by to update her on Ron Dai's efforts of the previous night. It seemed that some Vietnamese punk on the production line was probably running a full-scale drug enterprise among the workers. Dai had positively identified him and two of his confederates as SYSTEMATICS employees. Then Larry Ransell, the Salvage chief, arrived in a huff, wondering who in hell this new kid they'd stuck him with thought he was, and what kind of dirt his father had on her old man to get him hired here. Peter Davis couldn't take direction, apparently. He was refusing to follow simple procedure, and all of Ransell's recent data was in an uproar of potential inaccuracy. Mo promised him that she'd call the guy on the carpet.

By two in the afternoon, when the new modem design

arrived looking like Goofy's lunchbox, she began to wonder seriously why she hadn't married a dentist and had brats. To top it off, she climbed behind the wheel of her car at the end of the day only to discover that it wouldn't start.

"Fuck!" she snarled, pounding the wheel in frustration.

"Not much of a way for a lady to talk," a voice noted in amusement from over her left shoulder.

She jerked around with a scowl on her face to find Ron Dai outside her door, grinning.

"Watch it. Your face could freeze like that. Problem?"

She sighed and turned the ignition key. Nothing happened.

"I'd say you either have a dead battery or no battery at all," he observed. "My opinion as an engineer, of course. Do you lock your car?"

"I didn't today," she admitted. "Sort of in a hurry this morning."

"Mind popping your hood?"

She released the hood from beneath the dash, and he lifted it. Sure enough, someone had not only stolen her battery but had cut through her cables rather than waste time unfastening them. Dai peered out from the engine compartment.

"The good news is that it isn't dead."

"It wouldn't be," she returned peevishly. "It was a brand new goddamn Diehard."

"Looks like you need another one. If you want, I could give you a lift."

"Please," she said, waving him off. "It was my stupidity that got me into this."

"I'm not arguing that. I'm offering to help you get out of it."

"Are you sure? It's a lot of trouble."

"If I wasn't sure, I wouldn't have offered."

She smiled for the first time. "Fair enough." Opening the door, she climbed out.

"Lock it," he advised.

"I can see where you might get to be a real pain in the ass, buddy. You always had so much common sense?"

"Since birth. Some say it's an obnoxious quality."

"If you're taking a poll, I'd like to cast an aye vote. Where's your car?"

Dai pointed to the early-seventies Dodge, parked two cars

away. It was dented, primed hastily in spots against rust, and huge.

"That?" she asked. It was a far cry from her Saab Turbo 9000.

"You got it. Courtesy of the Santa Clara County Sheriff's impound lot. Like it?" He led the way, pointedly unlocking the passenger door and holding it for her.

"What's to like about it?" she asked. "And why *this*?"

He circled to the driver's side and climbed in.

"All part of the operating image we've constructed," he told her. "If I have something sporty like you do, then I *am* one of you. The man on the production line won't let me get close to him. But with something like this crate, I'm a mystery. They ask questions about me. Good job but a crappy car. Why? Is the college boy still paying off his student loans? Is he a conscientious guy taking care of a sick grandmother? It makes me a mystery and therefore open-ended."

She studied him. "Did you think all of this up yourself?"

"Some of it," he admitted. "Everyone has to discover his own working style. I like to approach it as a sort of psychological exercise. What I'm trying to do, basically, is get inside the heads of the people I'm most likely to be around. Other people work it differently. You've got to do what feels right for you."

"I like it," she said. "The thinking man's detective."

He smiled patronizingly. "All good detectives are thinking men . . . or women. The successful ones may have different processes, but all of them have intellectual systems."

"Peter Davis?" she asked. It had barbs in it.

Dai exhaled slowly, started the car, and began to ease it back into the traffic lane and toward the street. "What about him?" he inquired.

"He's being a righteous pain in the ass. Our Salvage chief came to me today wanting to know why we did Peter Davis to *him*. Everything down there is in chaos, two days after that guy arrives. Is this his *system* we're witnessing?"

Dai sighed as he pulled out onto the Winchester Road. "I've been wondering how he was working out. There's nothing dumb about the man, but he's sort of—uh—*rash*."

"For lack of a better word," Maureen agreed.

"Ross Charles tells me he comes highly recommended by their Boston field office. This is just between us, right?"

She assured him that it was.

"Then let me put it this way. Every once in a while, I've run into a guy in this business who makes me actively wonder how he could have slipped through the shit filter. Sometimes it's nothing more than a temporarily swollen head over a good bust. All of a sudden, a guy who was pretty normal starts thinking he's a hotshot." He paused to concentrate on a turn, heading for an automobile parts store he knew in nearby Campbell.

"How familiar are you with his service record?" Maureen asked.

He shook his head. "Not at all. But he's got the earmarks of a wonder boy who thinks he's riding the tail of a comet. I *do* know that he resents this assignment to the West Coast. He expected his next stop to be D.C."

"Tough shit," she snapped, not feeling terribly sympathetic and betraying it. "He's made my life miserable today. SYSTEMATICS means too much to me and too much to my father. I'm not going to let some egomaniacal little twerp fuck everything up, because he dreams of having his face carved into Mount Rushmore. Excuse my language."

Dai was smiling broadly now. He liked this brassy woman and her no-shit approach. It was rare that he met anyone this physically appealing who also knew how to play hardball.

"No pardon necessary," he said. "It would be hard to blame you for feeling that way. I'm going to do everything I can to prevent him from getting too far out of hand. If I see something clearly counterproductive, I'll take it to Charles. You should feel free to do the same. Ross is a bright, astute pro. He'll yank the guy if he figures he isn't working out. Trust me."

They drove to the auto parts store, paid exorbitant money for a new maintenance-free battery, and returned to the plant parking lot in Los Gatos. Dai rolled up his sleeves, opened the trunk of his own car, and removed a wrench set from his toolbox.

"Always carry tools when they give you one of these babies," he told her. "You never know how much love they had in their past lives."

Mo shook her head as he went to work. A real curiosity,

this guy. Now he was talking like Shirley MacLaine about *cars*. In another ten minutes the new battery was installed, and the engine of her Saab purred like a contented cat. Dai slammed the hood and wiped his hands on an old rag.

"You're all set."

"Unless you've got other plans, I'd like to buy you dinner," she told him.

"You don't have to. But I appreciate the gesture."

"I *want* to," she countered. "You've been sweet."

"Not reason enough," he said amiably. "People ought to make a habit out of being helpful once in a while. It makes the world a better place to be."

"Then how about having dinner with me because I'd like your company?"

He glanced at his watch. "Oh, I suppose I can skip that masked ball I had penciled in. My car or yours?"

"Get in, wise guy. I've got an image to maintain."

The SYSTEMATICS V.P. had a favorite dining haunt in the foothills of Los Gatos. It was elegant in a reserved, understated way. And, because the staff valued her patronage, they pampered her there. On many evenings since she'd taken her father's job offer, she had dined there alone, with business often on her mind.

"Good evening, Miss Counihan," the maitre d' greeted as they entered the place. "A table for two?"

"Thank you, Armand. I'd like you to meet a friend. Ron Dai, Armand Giametti."

The men shook hands.

"A pleasure, Mr. Dai. Any friend of Miss Counihan's is a friend of our establishment. I hope you enjoy your dinner."

The restaurant's main dining room opened onto spectacular views of the entire valley floor. Ron and Maureen were seated at a table affording them the widest panorama.

Dai shook his napkin out and slid in onto his lap as he looked around. "What a view, huh?" he asked.

"I'm glad you like it," she said. "They treat me like family here. It would be like eating at home, I suppose . . . if I knew how to cook."

Dai chuckled. The waiter approached holding a bottle of chardonnay the maitre d' wanted them to have with his compliments. It was poured, and they sipped as the waiter handed them menus.

Maureen suggested the roast duck, raving about the sauce. They ordered minutes later and then sat with their wine, staring out at the lights of the valley.

"I guess it's time to confess that I had an ulterior motive for inviting you to dinner," Maureen said at length.

"Oh?" he asked, eyebrows raised.

"I want to help," she said.

Dai shrugged. "It seems to me that you're already being helpful."

She smiled wanly. "No. I mean *really* help. Participate. This sitting on the sidelines is driving me crazy. I'm not used to feeling helpless."

"I don't suppose you are," he mused. "You're talking like someone who already has something in mind."

She shook her head. "Not really. You guys are the experts. It galls me to have to admit it, but I wouldn't have idea number one about how to nail a spy or whatever." She was only half facing him as she spoke, the rest of her gaze on the view. Now she turned away from it and fixed him with a determined stare. "But I want to learn."

The detective was unable to suppress a grin. "Forget everything you ever saw in a James Bond movie. What we do is fairly stupefying, really. It's mostly a lot of staring at a problem until the invisible becomes visible. Right now, we're concentrating on your white-collar personnel. Their banking records, major purchases, financial pressures, family illnesses, gambling interests. The Bureau is compiling data like mad at this very moment."

Maureen looked thoughtful. "I might be able to help you there. We like to think we know our people. God knows we process them pretty thoroughly before we hire them . . . and then there's the day-to-day scuttlebutt that gets around."

"I suppose," he replied. "I mean, if you'd like. Davis and I are supposed to go over all the names together, split the files in half and then trade off. If you know these people pretty well, or some of them, anyway, you might notice something that seems out of place in the FBI's information."

"When do you start?" she asked eagerly.

"Davis and I go over the first batch of files tomorrow afternoon, and then I take my half home with me."

"So we could get together on them right off."

"That depends on your schedule."

She laughed. "If we don't catch this son of a bitch, and we end up losing the government contracts, I won't have *any* schedule. Do you swim?"

Dai looked confused. "Uh—sure."

"My place. Right after work. Bring your suit. A couple of laps to help clear the mind, and we can get right down to it. I'll pick up something to throw into the microwave."

Brightening now, he smiled at her. "Wow. A swim *and* a home-cooked meal."

Maureen ignored the gibe as their appetizers arrived. She set about attacking her escargot with shell tongs and a tiny fork.

After rubbing out the spic minister and his old lady, Jack Terranova was airlifted out of Ecuador from the same remote airstrip they'd landed at two days earlier. The Cessna Turbo-prop whisked them north out over the Pacific, across Panama, and into the Caribbean. In less than two hours he, Anna, and Luis were met by a man in a speedboat off the Colombian island of Providencia and carried the short distance over water to San Andres. Jack and the girl had been there now for a couple of days, living in the lap of luxury. That morning, he'd almost had to pinch himself, awakened by Anna coming in from a swim in the sea. She'd stripped off that wet swimsuit and crawled beneath the sheets next to him. *Caramba!* If he died from all of this humping, he figured there couldn't be a better way to go.

When they arrived, Diego had just left. Informed that he would not be arriving from a Florida trip until sometime the next afternoon, Terranova immediately set about making himself at home. After a clean, successful whack, he liked to let his hair down. Do a little drinking. Sleep late. Lie around in the sun. Eat hearty. No one on the Cardona staff had ever seen someone eat so heartily. *Three langosta* for dinner the first night. Mountains of fried *platinos*, close to a quart of black beans, and an entire bottle of rum.

Diego seemed preoccupied upon his arrival. He informed Jack that he had sent Ramon to Colombia to verify the trafficker Faro's destruction. He'd met him in Providencia upon his return and had been satisfied. Meanwhile, Jack was to be congratulated on his idea of impersonating the minister's chauffeur. It made the planting of Faro's death warrant that much easier. Luis had given him a detailed report.

Now, Jack lay staring at the circling blades of the ceiling fan in his room. The heat and wetness of his woman still lingered on him. His deliverance from a life of enforced obsolescence and self-loathing had come so quickly. Just a month ago he'd been living out to pasture among beer kegs and brassy, tennis-playing bottle blondes.

A knock came at the door.

"Yeah?" he barked.

A voice drifted thinly through the panel. "Don Diego would like the pleasure of your company at breakfast. It will be served on the veranda in thirty minutes."

Terranova reached for his watch on the nightstand, his arm gliding across Anna's tight little tummy. He peered at the thing. Ten-thirty. This Nicaraguan continued to surprise him. He even ate breakfast at a relatively civilized hour.

"I'll be there," he answered. He ran his hand across Anna's breasts and then caught her chin between thumb and forefinger. He raised up on one elbow, bent his head, and kissed her.

"Oh, yeah, little lady," he murmured. "We're gonna fuck our brains out like that, twice a day until hell freezes over. You got *such* a sweet ass."

The girl smiled at him and slid her hand down between his legs to play with his testicles. "Twice a day, Jack? That is all? I do not please you?"

He chuckled. "You're some piece of work, baby. Yeah, you please me fine."

After his shower, he dressed while Anna watched him from the bed.

"C'mon. Get ready for breakfast," he urged.

She shook her head. "Not when men talk business. You go. I will be on the beach when you have finished."

Jack found Diego seated by himself at a glass-topped iron table on the patio overlooking the Caribbean. The table was set for two only. Diego nodded at his approach, stood to shake his hand, and indicated that he should take the seat opposite.

"How are you finding the accommodations? Comfortable, I trust."

"I got no beefs," Terranova told him. "You run a top-flight hotel here."

"I was hoping you might be pleased. But it is not to ask you this that I have dragged you from your Anna's arms."

He reached to the chair beside him and handed over an envelope.

"The second half of your payment, with my thanks."

As Jack opened the envelope and inspected the contents, Diego cleared his throat.

"There is a problem."

Jack looked up. "I put thirty-two slugs in the bastard *and* his wife. What's the problem? The man ain't dead enough?"

Diego shook his head. "You remember the mechanic in Pitalito? The one whose coffee you thought so disgusting? Guillermo Faro and another man paid him a visit. They asked about an American who had recently departed there in a plane. They shot him in both knees and left him to die of gangrene."

"Faro's dead, I thought. So what's the problem?"

"Faro is dead," Diego assured him, nodding his head once. "But it is the second man we are concerned about. I had a meeting with a certain man while I was in Florida. He reports that a special operative was sent into the field to avenge the death of one of the CIA agents you shot outside Cali. There is fear that this man could interfere with the master plan we have devised."

Terranova sat back in his chair and stared out at the sea. It was yet another gorgeous day. He sighed.

"I feel for you, pal. I think I'm getting your drift, but I don't see how it concerns me. I took a job and carried it out. You might not be out of the woods yet, but how does that affect our agreement?"

"How would they have known to ask about an American leaving that place if they hadn't managed somehow to trail you there?" Diego asked harshly. "That same trail could conceivably lead to me and all my careful work. We are in this together now, my friend."

"What are you trying to say?"

Diego smiled thinly as Terranova's hostile gaze swept over

him. "I am saying that we agreed on certain further compensation. A piece of paradise for you to live out your days on. That part of the deal is tied directly to the success of my people's venture here. We have dealt honorably." He pointed at the envelope Jack held. "The money is there, in full. You have a beautiful and willing woman. Now there is a very dangerous man loose who seeks to kill both you and myself. This problem, if he turns out to be one, is both of ours."

A servant approached to refill their coffee cups. This gave Jack a moment to consider his position. He added milk to his cup and picked it up to sip thoughtfully.

"So far, I've preferred to be left in the dark. My choice," he said slowly. "I think it might be time now for you to open up a little. If I'm gonna continue to play with you, I need to know the name of the game."

Diego reached for a roll, broke it open, and buttered one half. He looked into Terranova's eyes and nodded. "You are right. There are things I must deal with today, but let us meet again for breakfast tomorrow morning. I will reveal certain information to you then."

THIRTEEN

Peter Davis was convinced that his powers of observation and intuitive understanding were going to lead him through this mountain of paper to the field agent's Holy Grail. It irked the hell out of him that he was being forced to share his mountain with some outsider. His anger strengthened his resolve to crack this thing on his own. He'd gotten a jump on the county unit detective by pulling already-prepared files from the field office the previous night. Prior to the head-huddling session he was slated to undergo with Dai, he wanted any edge he could get. There was no way any self-respecting agency man was going to share the glory with some local dick who was a wetback to boot. This one was going to be a solo tackle in the open field.

Late into last night, he'd pored over the few files he'd managed to get his hands on. A natural-born list maker, concise and analytical, he kept copious notes. The notes allowed him to reference and cross-reference once he'd completed his scan of each case. There was a personnel manager with five kids, two with braces. She had a mother-in-law confined to a nursing home and a husband who worked as a surveyor. Seasonal work, surveying. The mother-in-law had had a massive stroke that had eaten deeply into the husband's prospective inheritance. Another guy, in Research and Development, was a foreign national. Nicaraguan. Paid for his house in Monte Sereno outright. Carried no mortgage. There was a woman on the sales force who'd spent a large chunk of her income as cash with few major purchases to show for it. Another woman, a bookkeeper, had been convicted of drunk driving and had no savings in any bank. There was a transsexual in the controller's office.

At three in the morning, Pete threw in the towel. In another few hours he would be masquerading again as some jackass gofer on the dismantling squad. God, he ached to get out of the boonies and back to the East Coast. Civilization.

Now, facts buzzed around his head like gnats as he moved through the SYSTEMATICS plant. Every time he saw a face, he sought some connection to his clandestine research. Braces. Cancer. Faggotry. When he ran into the Counihan broad in one hallway, he recollected *her* file. She'd been clean clear down to the shine. Too bad she was such a bitch. Great body with nice high tits and a tight ass. He wouldn't have minded pinning something on *her*.

The meeting with Dai was scheduled for three o'clock; the two of them would be called away from their job stations for some sort of health insurance formality. They would spend a couple of hours going over the files Ross Charles brought in from the field office and then divide them up. Two days hence, if no progress had been made, they'd trade straight up and plow into the other man's lot.

Davis was seated in the company cafeteria at twelve-thirty when he noticed something interesting. He was in the middle of finishing a plate of mediocre lasagna, busy cataloging faces, when the boss lady entered. She filled a plate at the salad bar and crossed to an empty table diagonally across the room from him. A moment later, Ron Dai entered, pushed a tray down the food line, and then sidled over to join Maureen Counihan. Davis was sufficiently distracted by this bit of interaction to nearly miss what happened next.

The man behind Dai in line was tall, lanky, and deeply tanned. Unaware of the detective's direction, he, too, turned to head toward the CEO's little girl. Not paying particular attention to what was going on, he'd nearly arrived when he noticed the new inspection engineer had taken the only available chair. A strange look, much like anger, flashed in his dark brown eyes. The face was right there in Pete Davis's mental file. Philip Maldonado. Jaw set and eyes piercing in the file photo. Age: forty-two. Unmarried. Resident alien. Davis watched him as he turned abruptly and made his way to an empty table along the opposite wall. Neither Dai nor the Counihan woman even noticed him.

Davis reviewed more data he had filed on the guy. Bought his house with cash. Research and Development head. Quite brilliant. Sole surviving son of an aristocratic Nicaraguan family. Bailed out long before the leftists overran the country. In the late 1960s, actually. By all appearances, most notably the smoke pouring from both his ears, he considered the slot opposite the boss lady to be his and his alone.

Meanwhile, Ron Dai and Maureen Counihan were locked in animated conversation. From where Davis was sitting, it appeared to be more than casual lunchtime chitchat. Both made frequent demonstrative gestures. At one point, Dai pulled a notebook from his jacket and scribbled something into it. It occurred to Davis that this county prick might be trying to grab the inside lane on him.

For the next few hours, until their meeting, curiosity ate at him. They were working together. He was sure of it. Dai now had the advantage of being able to bounce the odd bit of information off a knowledgeable source. The thought infuriated him. All the attention to detail and method following in the world wasn't going to overcome a factor like that. Not unless he just got lucky. And luck wasn't the sort of thing a trained field agent wanted to rely on.

At three minutes after five, having just departed his meeting with Ross Charles and that snake Dai, Davis sat behind the wheel of his new Toyota Supra. His half of the files were on the seat beside him, and he was watching Maureen Counihan's parked Saab Turbo. There was only one way to discover just how hard they might be collaborating, and he aimed to find out. The files could wait a couple of hours. Nobody was going to rob him of his ticket out of this scum pit by getting the jump on him. Especially not some local. Hell, judging from the smile he wore on his idiot face, you'd think the guy *liked* it here.

When Maureen Counihan left the SYSTEMATICS lot and headed across Los Gatos to her home in Saratoga, Davis followed at a discreet distance. He already had the address from her file and followed only as a precaution against her going elsewhere. He eased to the curb and watched as she disappeared behind the electric garage door of a fashionable, sprawling ranch house set back about fifty feet from the street. At the end of her drive, a darkly tanned young Japanese man was loading a lawn mower up the ramp of his pickup truck. Maureen emerged out a side door and approached him with an envelope in hand. As she passed it to him, Ron Dai pulled up in his battered Dodge Daytona. The redhead chatted amiably with the gardener while the local lawman removed a cardboard carton from his trunk and joined her. Together, this curious pair moved up the front path and into the house.

Major Hardy West pulled his Ford Taurus into the parking lot of Woodbridge High School in Woodbridge, Virginia. He proceeded around to the right past the tennis courts and came to a halt twenty yards from the gate to the football stadium. It was a pleasant evening for early November in this part of the world. Balmy at around sixty degrees. Leaves all but gone from the surrounding trees, but just a bit of color lingering. He parked and locked, then sauntered down the access incline, squeezed his linebacker's build through the chained gates, and stepped out onto the rubber-asphalt running track. Latham had told him the fifty-yard line, visitor's side. He aimed for the smaller grandstand opposite the press box. A lone figure sat huddled there about six rows up.

"Evening, Ted," he called out.

"That it is," Latham responded. "Come on up and join me."

Hardy West was Lieutenant General Seymour "Jumpin' Johnny" Johnson's attaché at the National Security Council. Both men, being Marines, shared a *Semper Fi* simpatico that was rare in that nest of self-promoting vipers. The general's absolute trust in this other man was of the utmost importance to the group of which he and Ted Latham were members. General Johnson had the president's ear.

"How bad is it?" West asked.

Latham shook his head in frustration. "That little prick is really getting on my nerves," he muttered. "He thinks there ain't no way Henry Bueno could find his fucking shooter. He obviously don't know Henry like we do."

West stared out across the manicured field to the opposite bleachers. "The president gets even the slightest wind of this character's cocaine sideline and we're blown out of the water. He's declared an all-out war on drugs. This minister's assassination has really upset him. We were making some headway with the Colombians. Extradition agreements. Enforcement cooperation. If anybody discovers it was an American hitter that did this guy in, we're playing a fiddle without any strings. If we can't keep our own doorstep clean, why should they keep theirs?"

"Don't think I haven't been over all this about a thousand times," Latham told him wearily. "We're between a rock and a hard place. We need this little spic weasel until Project Alamo goes down. That means a week or two, tops. After that, we can arrange an accident. If it's done right, maybe some of his buddies will get the message and start playing by our rules."

"That'd be a first," West snorted derisively. "But I suppose we could hope, huh? So when does Alamo fall into place? The general's slated to head over for them NATO missile talks in three weeks. I'm going to need something pretty concrete for him to feed the White House at least a week before then. From what you're telling me, that could be real tight."

"The two weeks number was the worst scenario," Latham replied. "If everything goes by the current timetable, we'll be in position in eight days. That should give you plenty of time. And don't forget, once it's a go, the clock starts ticking."

West stood and stretched, then reached for a cigarette and lit it. "I know. We feed this shit to Stebbins and he goes behind Johnson's back to Admiral McNichol at the same time. We're pitting the two most arrogant peacocks in the military against each other. Both of them are going to want the first shot at neutralizing the threat."

"Just so you realize how crucial the time will suddenly become."

"I know." West took the ball, nodding. "We've gotten this far, so don't fuck it up. I won't. We're on the same side, friend."

Peter Davis was just checking his watch when he realized he had company. Dai and the Counihan broad had only just entered her place, and Davis was busy thinking about where he might go for a quick bite in this human cesspool. Up the block about thirty yards a new Lincoln Mark VII slowed and pulled over from the oncoming lane to park. Davis slouched in his seat, hoping that the glare of a low sun in his windshield would obscure the Supra's interior sufficiently to prevent his detection. He eased open the glove box, suspicious that the driver of this new arrival was simply sitting in his car and not getting out. The Lincoln came into focus through the small pair of binoculars he kept handy for just such occasions. Its occupant was partially obscured in the shadows of an overhanging liveoak. He peered harder, trying to get a cleaner edge to his focus.

Identification of the car's occupant came with the smug satisfaction of confirmation, not surprise. It was the jealous Nicaraguan from the cafeteria. Philip Maldonado, Research and Development. He was staring intently, brows knit in fury, at Maureen Counihan's house.

"My, my," Davis hummed to himself. "You *are* jealous, my man. You're screwing her, you son of a bitch."

A WASP to the core and raised in the most illiberal of that heritage's traditions, Pete Davis held a very low opinion of what he characterized as the imbalanced Latin libido. All males of Mediterranean extraction thought with their gonads. This guy, parked with hatred etched across his tanned countenance, was a perfect, if pathetic, example. He was a grown man, relatively affluent and respected in his chosen field, and here he was seething with green rage outside his lover's door. A wave of intense amusement lifted the FBI man's spirits as he continued to study the engineer's twisted features. Pete Davis, self-assured, knew that he had never been such a fool. There were willing women everywhere. This one might have a great ass and fire in her eyes, but so did a multitude of others.

Time wore on, with Maldonado continuing to sit. Davis was neglecting his own work while the county man and his lady friend were getting a jump on him inside the house across the street. On the other hand, he found it interesting that a cool customer like the Counihan babe would be sharing her bed with this hot tamale. It revealed something about her composition that she was working overtime to conceal. Once again, the old lesson about judging books and covers.

Davis was stuck at the address for five hours. Maldonado did not budge from his position across the street. Then,

175

at ten-thirty, Ron Dai emerged from the house carrying his cardboard carton. It was too dark inside the Lincoln for Davis to get much of a look at the R and D man now. He assumed that once Dai was clear, Maldonado would storm up to Maureen's front door and touch off one hell of a row. But when Dai started his dented Dodge and drove off, the Nigaraguan did the unpredictable. He followed him.

Confusion reigned in Davis's mind as he swung the Supra into a tight U-turn. How much of a hothead *was* this guy? What the hell did he think he was going to do? Challenge the man to a duel? That was no longer legal. And no matter how much he wanted to have Dai out of the picture, Pete didn't think that death at the hands of an enraged Latin lover boy was the way to accomplish that end. Damn, could this nut really be *that* paranoid?

Davis's analytical nature began to kick in. If so, paranoid about what, precisely? He was a relatively successful engineer. He'd worked his way up to a position of responsibility and economic clout after emigrating to the United States. Less than ten years ago, he purchased a house in affluent Monte Sereno for half a million dollars. No mortgage. No record of financing on the new Lincoln. Family money? His bearing was undeniably aristocratic in that greaseball, south-of-the-border way. But there was also no record of his having declared a large sum of money upon entry to this country. It seemed a bit more than coincidental that he had made his house purchase just six months after the collapse of the Somoza regime. Plenty of money left Nicaragua then, most of it shipped clandestinely into Miami banks and real estate. Maldonado could have seen some of this booty without necessarily declaring it to the IRS. Such a man might have reason to be paranoid if, screwing the boss at a company undergoing FBI scrutiny, he happened to glean that this investigation was currently underway. It would most certainly be thorough, and the results might very possibly put him in an awkward position. Davis liked this train of thought.

Maybe this wasn't jealousy he was witnessing. Maureen, in a trusting moment, may have already mentioned her collaboration with Dai. This could be something a lot more calculated than a jealous rage.

Davis quickly forgot his evening of tedious list-making. What had Ross Charles said? Don't be afraid to run with a hunch. Observation, postulation, elimination. A little blind luck. Pete knew that luck had an awful lot to do with training yourself to be in the right place at the right time. You *made* your luck.

Dai led the two cars following him to one of those ultra-ordinary apartment complexes that seemed to litter the valley floor like so many Styrofoam burger cartons. In this case, a low parking shed ran behind each of a dozen or so units. Each space was numbered to correspond with the tenant's address. Ahead of Davis, Maldonado hung back while the detective parked, dragged his cardboard box of files out of the trunk, and carried it toward an exterior staircase. Then the Nicaraguan moved forward as though he were wending his own way home. His head turned, neck craning to scan the painted numbers on the pavement as he passed Dai's Dodge.

By this time, Pete Davis was prepared to ride with the research engineer all the way to the end of the line. When he reentered traffic and drove from Dai's place in Campbell up the winding and increasingly exclusive Quito Road, Davis stayed just far enough off his tail to appear as incidental traffic. At the junction of the Saratoga–Los Gatos Road in Monte Sereno, Maldonado proceeded across and up into the foothills. The roads were twisting and thickly wooded here. Davis drove without headlights, making the going a bit hazardous but avoiding detection. Half a mile up, the new Lincoln bore left up a steep drive to a house obscured from the road. Pete pulled ahead and parked, then hurried back uphill on foot through the underbrush. Maldonado's front lawn was studded with ornamental cedar, spruce, and juniper. The house itself was single level, sprawling down a slight incline in the style of easy contemporary elegance so prevalent in these areas. A speedboat, protected by a fitted tarp, projected nose first from an open garage stall. Just adjacent, an electric door was coming down on the stall closest to the house. A light came on moments later in what looked to be the kitchen. Others came on as the engineer progressed toward the north end of the house.

A fog was crawling rapidly over the crest of the Santa Cruz mountains above him as Davis huddled in the shrubbery. He wore only a summer-weight blazer and slacks. A balmy night was suddenly turning cold on him, and he turned up his collar against it. Mists swirled down into the oak and eucalyptus. Pete decided to call it a night before he caught pneumonia. He'd spend an hour or so with Maldonado's file and do a little thinking about his next moves.

The day of their forced layover in Buenaventura had gone without incident. News bulletins on the radio were full of the government's continued manhunt for fugitives from the destruction of Guillermo Faro's hacienda. Reports of a helicopter gunship having been downed were being sensationalized by commentators. The army was unable to positively identify Cristina Faro and her two children. Henry Bueno kept the woman and her kids sequestered in the waterfront flophouse, ordering them not to show their faces when he left to purchase food and drink.

For dinner that night, Bueno had located a *cuchifritos* stand and bought an assortment of fried things along with half-a-dozen bottles of orange Fanta. They were due to rendezvous with Lucho Vargas at his boat in four hours, and night was now starting to descend. With it came the increased noise of the waterfront cafes and bars. It had been another of those oppressive equatorial days with temperatures in the nineties and humidity so high that any small movement elicited sweat. It wasn't much different in the hotel room, but the children were bearing up. They were curled together and asleep as Henry entered.

"Any trouble?" he asked.

"No," Cristina answered, shaking her head. She looked at him anxiously. "You are sure that this man's boat will be ready to take us away tonight?"

Bueno smiled. "You will find him coarse and foulmouthed, but he is the most reliable captain on the marina. We've no choice but to hope that what he said is so."

She nodded and eased herself back on the second bed. Henry produced the greasy fried food and soda.

"I'll bet you're starving. Want to wake the kids?"

"No," she decided, gazing fondly at the slumbering pair. "It has been a long day for them."

"There's not much that's any good to eat in a city like Buenaventura," he apologized. "*Chincherones* and this other stuff was the best I could do."

"You have done more than I could ever repay you for."

After a day of being dragged through dirt and another spent in a fleabag hotel in sweltering heat, she still glowed with the sort of beauty that all the artifice in the world couldn't duplicate. The image of her coming to him that night a life ago now pushed into his mind's eye. Try as he might, he was powerless to shove it out again. One day didn't make *that* much difference.

"Forget about repayment," he told her. "We're all just trying to survive. We get through a crisis only one way. One foot in front of the other."

Cristina bit down tentatively on a piece of fried pork. She looked at him thoughtfully as she chewed.

"Other men would not only hope for repayment, they would expect it."

"I guess maybe I'm not other men."

She shook her head as she picked through the food and selected another morsel. "You say this to a woman who is at your mercy. I am not certain I understand why. Not because you owed Willie anything."

"Willie Faro was far from perfect, but he was different than most traffickers I've met."

"Why?" she asked. "Because of his family? His education? Yes, he was different. But in many ways he was more like the rest of them than he would ever have admitted. He craved their respect and admiration like a drug. His mistresses and his bastards were all part of a facade he built to prove his manhood in their eyes. I hated him for that."

Henry contemplated her with interest. "And yet you grieve."

Cristina blinked back tears. "Things with us were not always so. It is hard to forget the moment you met a man. He was young, handsome, and full of big ideas then. Ambition. In many ways he was like a little boy. He was vulnerable and insecure. He would never have craved the drug of admiration if he was not forever this little boy in his heart. I suppose I am still in love with what and who he was. Not who he became."

"Have you been able to sleep at all?" he asked.

"No," she replied, shaking her head. "My mind has been full of so many thoughts."

Henry glanced at his watch. "We leave here in a few hours. Do you think I could close my eyes for a few minutes?"

"Please," she begged. "Lie down either here or with the children. I will awaken you in plenty of time."

The last thing Bueno remembered before sleep took him was the image of Cristina lying quietly on the bed across the room, her forearm thrown across her eyes and tears streaming down her cheeks. He could only imagine the things she felt. Before noon on the previous day, she'd learned that her husband was dead after seeing her home destroyed. Shortly after nightfall, she'd shot a man in the head at point-blank range. Tonight, she would leave her adopted homeland as a fugitive, widow, and mother of two small children.

Lucho Vargas and a slightly swaying deckhand stood waiting for Bueno and his mysterious passengers when they arrived on his dock. They traveled without luggage. A woman and two children. If this told him anything, the state of their clothing told him more. Once they were settled in the deckhouse of his forty-six-foot trawler, he took the man known as Henri Riberac aside to settle accounts. Payment was made in the form of ten one-ounce Canadian Maple Leaf coins.

"A very beautiful woman," Vargas commented, hefting the coins in the palm of his hand. He leered openly into the cabin.

Bueno put a restraining hand on the one holding the gold.

"Let's get something straight right here, amigo. You never saw that woman. Understood? If I ever hear different, you'll never live to spend this. Not where I will send you." He released his grip and watched the sailor snatch his hand away as if he'd been burned.

"I am also a man of my word, Señor Riberac. There is no cause to be distrustful."

"Just so we understand each other," Henry told him. "When do we get underway?"

"Immediately. The patrols have tied up for the night now."

Bueno moved off to join Cristina and the kids in the wheelhouse. It would be better to stay out of sight until they cleared port. Out on deck, Lucho's drunken deckhand struggled with the moorings, nearly falling into the water. The engine, recently overhauled and always meticulously maintained, caught and roared to life. In another moment they were proceeding from the harbor under blackout.

Two hours after Ron Dai left that night, Maureen Counihan took her second swim of the evening. There was a stiff chill in the air now, and a fog blanketed the valley. The heated pool was like a womb, which afforded her the opportunity to take a strenuous workout and think things over in peace. She had very little of any substance to analyze. Surely, they'd gleaned some fascinating tidbits about certain personnel, but nothing to set the wheels of real suspicion turning. While Dai was proving himself to be the thorough professional Agent Charles had touted him to be, she felt like her involvement wasn't helping him much.

Phil hadn't called in two days and seemed to be avoiding her at the plant. Maybe that last night they'd spent together was as unsatisfactory for him as it had been for her. She'd attempted to mask her own dissatisfaction, but things like that seemed to have a way of leaching through and poisoning an atmosphere. She had never really asked anything of him, perhaps assuming that their friendship would be more spontaneous if no pressure were exerted. And then there was something else: the challenge of not only surviving but *winning* in a man's world was still ultimately appealing to her. She intimidated most men with such an outlook. In the past two years, Phil Maldonado had been the only man determined to assail her defenses against the apparent odds. When she'd surrendered, her suppressed hunger had been enough to fill the void between them. Once he'd cracked those defenses, he seemed content to just sit inside them and gloat. It was as though he thought she ought to be grateful.

Now, as she swam back and forth in the fog, a bright, proficient and perceptive Eurasian with a great smile was gaining access the easy way. With grace, wit, and charm. His eyes and his confidence said that he was enjoying her style, that he respected the armor she wore in business. He made no overt move to suggest his own attraction, but she felt it in the air like an impending electrical storm. It gave her goosebumps to think of it. As she swam, she wondered how it would feel to have him run his hands over her.

She grabbed the ladder and hauled herself out into the

damp night air. Across her rooftop, the city lights glowed amber against the swirling mist. Her mind was on espionage and strange bedfellows as she pulled her robe around her shoulders. Maybe this wasn't going to end up as badly as she'd imagined at the outset. There were still all the files Peter Davis had. They would go through them as well, once the trade was made. Another evening of working shoulder-to-shoulder with Ron Dai on her living room floor. She licked her lips at the prospect.

FOURTEEN

"How much do you know of the recent history of my country?" Diego Cardona asked Jack Terranova. The two men were once again seated at the breakfast table on the veranda. A cool breeze drifted off the sea from the southwest. Several boats bobbed on the bright blue water near the horizon.

"Not much," Jack admitted. "Somoza got run out by a pack of commies. Our man in the White House has a real hard-on for the whole bunch."

Diego lifted his juice to his lips, sipped, and sighed. "In August of 1978, your government cut us off. Allegedly, we were violating human rights. This left us to fight the communists alone. Without the necessary military support, we failed. Because of the misled body of world opinion, it was years before any steps were taken to aid in overthrowing these dogs."

They were interrupted as scrambled eggs, fried ham, and *platinos* were served. Terranova took the opportunity to drain his fresh pineapple juice and hold out the empty glass for more. When the servant left, Diego went on.

"Together with my associates, I represent better than ninety percent of the wealth concentrated in my country before the civil war and takeover by the illegal Marxist government."

Terranova grunted with amusement. "Illegal? They're the ones with the keys to the castle, aren't they?"

Behind a frown of sudden anger, Diego reddened and waved a hand emphatically. "It will not long be so!" he snarled hotly. "What sort of popular support demands allegiance at the point of a gun? With *Soviet* guns, they waged a campaign of terror. If Carter had not cut off the weapons and spare parts, we would have crushed them!"

"And now you're fighting alongside these other Contra dudes to do just that, right?"

"Most of them are fools," Diego growled derisively. "Malcontents. We have nothing in common with men such as these. Nothing except a common enemy."

"So you think you pose a real threat, eh?"

Cardona leered now. "More than anyone might guess. With your aid, we have eliminated a man remote from the civil war we wage, but who, in death, will act to greatly bolster our fortunes in that war."

Terranova scrambled to put the facts together. "The Colombian minister . . . and this dead trafficker?"

Cardona smiled the smile of superior understanding. "Guillermo Faro was more than a dope smuggler, my friend. His operation in North America was a thing of beauty. A year and a half ago we began to destroy it by tipping the American Internal Revenue to the activities of one James 'Rocko' Strathmore. This person, with a small child and pregnant wife knew he could not face twenty years in a federal prison. Instead of taking such a fall, he spilled his guts. Faro's entire line of supply and support unraveled all the way back to the source."

Terranova held up a hand. "Whoa! Wait just a sec. If you'd destroyed him already, why did you go to all that trouble just to see him dead?"

"Read the Miami papers a little more closely, my friend," Diego suggested. "You will see evidence almost daily that a Colombian scorned is a very dangerous man. Faro's Colombian structure was very much intact. He could not move drugs, but he had an army of people who depended upon him for their livelihoods. Such men, delivered from abject poverty, are very loyal. It was only a matter of time before Guillermo Faro gathered enough intelligence to enable him to launch reprisals against me."

"That's it?" Jack asked, astonished. "Then why the hell

didn't you have me whack *him?* It would have been a whole lot easier.''

"Because, my friend," Diego explained, "it was not only Faro whom we wished to remove from the picture. What we wish to do is to alter the Colombian government's less-than-aggressive approach to the eradication of drug trafficking. Faro had only been under close scrutiny because of United States pressure to have him extradited. What does he do in his panic? He has the interior minister assassinated."

It all started to come clear to the American. A grin spread across his face. "I'll be fucked," he mused. "You're out to corner the whole market, you sly bastard."

Cardona smiled. "Fearing for their own safety and that of their families, the power elite in Colombia will move quickly to prevent further rash acts such as this. Just today we received reports of a devastating raid on one of Faro's largest competitors outside Medellin."

"Okay," Terranova said slowly. "What you're telling me is that the money you raise filling the drug void you've created is funding the fight to retake your homeland."

"Precisely. That, and to rebuild depleted cash reserves. Now, through strongholds in Mexico and Brazil, we are moving to meet demand."

Jack was impressed. "Some pretty slick shit, pal. Just like the old *capos*. And you used me down south so if something went wrong, nobody'd be able to pin it on you."

"You understand," Diego said. "And nothing *went* wrong because I got *you*. The best."

With his meaty fists gripping knife and fork, Terranova sawed off a chunk of ham and stuffed it into his mouth. While still chewing, he grinned and pointed the fork at Diego.

"I like your style, amigo. You, personally. I don't know about some of these wimps you got hanging around."

"Every man in my command has some tangible worth," Cardona said evenly. "Otherwise, he wouldn't be here."

"A little piss ant like Luis?"

Diego lifted his eyes to stare off across the sea. "Luis Ecchevarria's father was a very powerful man, señor. He may not be his father's son in all respects, but he carries the blood. You have had your little sport with him. I suggest you let it go no further. He is crucial to the success of my plans. Now, if you have finished, there is something I wish you to see."

* * *

The *Velda* plowed north through the doldrums on a heading
for Central America. The moods of the two Faro children
seemed much improved to Bueno. He sat astern, watching
them frolic amidships under the vigilant eye of their mother.
The deckhouse hatch was flung open, as were the ports on
both bulkheads, giving the interior much-needed air. They
were fourteen hours out now, moving at a steady twelve
knots. The *Velda* had quite a bit more in her if the occasion
demanded it, but her engine seemed comfortable idling along
in the mid-rpm range, where fuel consumption was most
efficient.

Cristina announced that it was time for a nap and ushered
her children back below. She reemerged ten minutes later and
crossed the deck to join Henry where he sat on a coil of
mooring line.

"They go to sleep that quickly?" he asked.

"The instant their eyes closed. This has been very trying
for them. They show better humor, but they are exhausted."

"Lucky the sea is so calm," he noted. "We don't need to
deal with seasickness. You get any sleep last night?"

"Finally. I do not think my body would have accepted any
more excuses."

They sat back side by side in the bright sun. A very
light breeze brought them some relief from scorching temperatures. Other fishing vessels could be seen on the horizon
all around them. This was a very rich ground for tuna,
protected by two-hundred-mile limits enforced by all the
Contadora countries. In two to three more hours, they would
finally be leaving Colombian territorial waters and be home
free. Until that time, a certain amount of vigilance was
required. Bueno had been out on the stern with one eye open
since sunup.

"How will your family take this?" he asked. "Are you on
good terms with them?"

She shook her head with eyebrows raised. "They love their
grandchildren but have never forgiven me for marrying a
trafficker. By now, they will believe that we are all dead.
Once the rejoicing is over, I shall be forced to get on my
knees and beg my father's forgiveness before he will accept
me back."

"What about Willie's money? He led me to believe there

was a considerable sum out of country. Do you know where he kept his records of those funds?''

She nodded. ''There is a banker named Douglas in the Cayman Islands.'' From between her breasts she pulled a small gold-plated key dangling from a tiny chain. ''In case of just such a tragedy as this,'' she said, ''Willie gave me this key, the man's name, and a numeric code to commit to memory. There are documents in a box.''

Bueno had to give it to Willie. He may have been head-strong, but he wasn't stupid. Cristina was the mother of his sole heir. Any male child of his should never want for shoe leather. If Cristina, at her own discretion, treated little Rosa just as well, a dead man had no power over the evolutionary forces at work on human sexual politics.

''What will you do once we reach San Jose?'' she asked.

''That's a good question,'' he replied with a sigh. ''The only place I can think of to go for answers is Miami. I've got another day to think about it before I know that's where I'll go for sure.''

While trying to get some sleep the previous night, Peter Davis let his speculative imagination run the gamut. It wasn't too hard to suppose a motivation if Maldonado really was the culprit they sought. With the Sandinistas almost sure to gain power in 1978, it would make sense for them to begin planning for the intrigue involved in running a Marxist power in the Western Hemisphere. As they were already known to have been courting the Cubans and possibly the Soviets back then, it might make sense to take advantage of America's blind benevolence. Political refugees of means and good family would be accepted with open arms in the United States. A man posing as a disenfranchised Somosista could worm his way into the American economic fabric and be ready when those who represented his true loyalties called. Alamo missile system parts could be some very valuable illegal tender.

Davis had accumulated some relatively sophisticated electronic gear over the years. He owned a highly sensitive directional listening dish, a telephone lineman's handset, and a Nagra tape recorder. All of these could be employed under the present circumstances without anyone being the wiser.

*   *   *

187

For the second night running, fog rolled over the mountains from the coast and filled the valley. The dampness in the air reacted with oil of eucalyptus and the rotting leaves of the liveoak. It filled Peter Davis's nostrils with a smell characteristic of these hills yet alien to his eastern roots. It was not an offensive odor. Quite the contrary. It was one of the few things that seemed even slightly exotic about this sprawling suburban wasteland.

He'd parked his car a hundred yards down the road and was now crouched next to the external junction where Maldonado's phone line came in off the pole and connected to the service inside the house. The engineer had been home now for just a few minutes. It was nearly seven o'clock, and the sun was long set. Maldonado's late arrival might be explained by problems they were rumored to be having with the latest in their series of ultralight portable PCs. This was some sort of prototype teetering on the cusp of going into production. SYSTEMATICS was banking a wad on the success of this particular baby, and a series of tests was supposed to have gone belly-up that afternoon.

The extruded aluminum cover to the junction box was held in place by one compression screw. Davis loosened it, removed the cover carefully, and unwound the leads to his handset. He clipped the leads to the terminals and cradled the set between shoulder and ear. More appropriately dressed for the fog this time, he wore a zippered jacket and jeans. In an effort to get comfortable, he eased his fanny down onto the cool earth, legs outstretched and back wedged against the house. Anticipating a very long vigil, he'd packed fortification. For starters, he unwrapped a bologna-on-Wonder and poured himself a cup of coffee from his thermos. All set for the duration, he munched contentedly, sipped, and listened.

The first call the subject made was to a health club in Los Gatos. He reserved a squash court for five-thirty the following evening. It gave Davis an opportunity to test a new gadget that captured digit tones as the number was punched in. This would allow him to retrieve the numbers dialed at a later time. It functioned perfectly.

At nine-fifteen, Maldonado dialed eleven digits—long distance. After half a dozen rings, the party at the other end answered in Spanish. The engineer spoke his native tongue in rapid-fire staccato, the conversation lasting only a few sentences before being terminated. Moments later, the phone rang on the subject's end. The voice was different, but this conversation was also held in Spanish. Davis started to get excited. They were exhibiting the classic pattern. Call an open line and request conference on a secure one. The other end calls back on the secure line moments later. The Nagra rolled, capturing it all. This time, the two parties spoke at some length, voices occasionally raised in agitation. Twice, the man at the other end actually shouted. David couldn't wait to get this stuff translated. He'd done a little deeper digging, getting a buddy in the Boston office to run requests for past phone bills and other family background on this guy. The bills were being air-expressed out and would arrive in the morning. That afternoon, his associate had been able to convey the family stuff over the phone. Nothing of consequence. At least not under this name. No immediate relatives listed as having sought residency here. This, of course, made Davis all the more curious about whom he was calling long distance now and conversing with in such familiar, agitated tones. Pete prided himself on his hunches, and he was running with this one. He smelled something rotten all over this guy.

Ron Dai and Peter Davis had exchanged their two sets of files that afternoon as agreed. That evening, Maureen Counihan was once again ensconced with the county detective in her den, the floor littered with notes and stacks of manila folders. It hadn't been a wonderful day at the office, with the SYSTEMINI compact PC III suffering performance setbacks toward the end of an accelerated production schedule. She and Dai had been cross-referencing the stuff in the FBI files against her own personnel records, and she was exhausted.

Next to her, Dai tossed his pen down and stretched.

"God, this is tedious," he groaned.

"It was *your* big idea," she mumbled, making a notation on her yellow legal pad.

"Mine?" he asked, incredulous. "Whose idea was it to make a tea party out of it?"

"Mine. Got any complaints?"

"Not after seeing you in a bathing suit."

She looked up. "You weren't so bad yourself, chum."

"And your mastery of microwave cooking is sublime."

"Now you're getting nasty."

He grinned and shook his head. "Just hungry. But could we go out for pizza or something? I can't face another night of frozen Oriental entrees."

They were in her car and rolling toward a little shopping center off Saratoga Avenue when Dai broke a brooding silence. Something was chewing at him.

"What do you know about the R & D chief?" he asked. "Philip Maldonado."

Maureen's mind had been wandering through their swim session in her pool the previous evening. She was actively engaged in figuring a way to seduce this officer of the law as subtly as possible when his question cut through her ruminations like a straight razor.

"What?" she asked, caught off guard and flustered by the unexpected.

"Philip Maldonado. Chief research and development engineer. What do you know about him? His history or whatever."

Dai didn't miss the momentary loss of color in her cheeks and the way her grip tightened on the wheel. She recovered herself quickly.

"How do you mean? He's a good engineer. Brilliant, actually."

"The file says he's a resident alien. Nicaraguan. Emigrated here permanently after completing his undergraduate work at Cal Tech."

"That's right," she affirmed. "He was third in his class or something. Electrical engineering."

"Know anything about his family or financial background?"

She frowned, confused at this line of questioning. "Just what's in his personnel file. What is it you're driving at?"

Dai shrugged, privately wondering why she seemed so defensive.

"He bought a house valued at five hundred thousand dollars just over eight years ago."

"So did I," Maureen replied. "*Five* years ago."

"I assume you have a fairly hefty mortgage."

"Of course. I didn't have a spare half a mil, and there are certain tax advantages anyway."

"Maldonado apparently *did*."

"Did *what*?"

190

"Had a spare half a mil, as you put it. He paid cash for the place."

Maureen glanced over quickly in surprise. "He did *what?*"

"He's carrying no mortgage. He didn't finance that Lincoln he's driving either. To make it all the cuter, the IRS has no record of his declaring any large sums of money when he emigrated. There's nothing in his salary history to substantiate such savings."

Maureen looked thoughtful. "I know he's told me—uh, in passing—that his family lost quite a lot when the Sandinistas implemented land reform. That meant him, I suppose, because he's the sole surviving member of his line. I get the impression that they were once quite wealthy."

"Quite possible," Dai supposed. "But were he to have brought substantial assets into this country undeclared—"

"He knows about the investigation," she said flatly.

"I beg your pardon?"

"He knows you are conducting the investigation. I told him we'd called in the FBI."

"I wondered," he said quietly.

It was her turn to be surprised. "Why?"

"The look on your face and the way you grabbed the wheel when I mentioned his name."

She winced. "I thought I was better than that. Ah, well."

They swung into the shopping center and parked with the conversation left still hanging.

"Pepperoni and mushrooms okay?" she asked, opening the door.

Dai watched her as she strode across the lot to the pizza parlor. She *had* looked great in her bikini. Phenomenal, actually. Beneath that tight corporate exterior, there was sex in her. Bottled up, perhaps, but very much aware of itself. Maldonado was a fortunate guy.

Cristina Faro sat astern, still wide awake in the middle of the night. Ten feet away, the man she knew as Henri Riberac was taking advantage of the relative coolness to put that remarkable physique through a regimen of exercises performed with singular intensity. His torso gleamed with sweat in the starlight. Even deep in her confused remorse, Cristina could not deny how beautiful she found that spectacle. Nor could she ignore the beauty of their ocean surroundings, the placid, gleaming black water and a sky crammed with billions of stars.

The children, having escaped from the oppressive heat of the cabin, were curled up on flotation cushions at her feet. She was left to her thoughts, a circumstance she was grateful for. There was still something terribly burdensome in the knowledge that she had seduced this beautiful man of mystery the night before her husband was killed. She was trying to work her way through it now. Willie was dead, and there was nothing she could do to alter that. And Riberac had proven to be such a surprise. Not in the way he'd performed in bed; she'd expected that. But afterward, through all of this. The man owed her nothing, yet instead of cutting and running he had behaved with honor, valor, and courtesy. There was never even the hint that he expected they might repeat the acts that first brought them together. She wondered what sort of man this was who had taken it upon himself to act as their protector. He moved with frightening confidence but could be solicitous of her and her children's well-being with just as much intensity.

Henry Bueno lay on his back, stomach and chest heaving with labored breath as he stared heavenward. The engine of the *Velda* thrummed reassuringly beneath him, the only noise on this tranquil open sea. He was thinking of something less tranquil, the vision of a huey breathing rocket and cannon fire down on that house he had been asleep in just minutes earlier. He knew now how a Vietnamese villager suspected of Cong sympathies must have felt.

He was finished with his exercises now and let his thoughts turn to the Somosista major, Cardona. Such a man would surely anticipate an offensive mounted by a prideful man like Willie Faro. Knowing that a war was coming sooner or later, he'd taken a brilliant step to prevent it. In blowing away the interior minister and blaming it on this notorious trafficker, he'd prodded the Colombian government into taking care of his problem for him.

Cardona was said to operate out of Coral Gables, just outside Miami. Bueno had some questions he wanted to ask a certain oracle on the Costa Rican coast. With the information this man could provide him, locating Cardona wouldn't prove too difficult. The shooter, Terranova, was a bit more of a challenge, especially if, as he suspected, the major had sent him to ground. Then again, he and Carl Stickley had a deal. Henry figured that there was still one pretty sure way of locating the hired gun. First, find Cardona and hold a gun to the bastard's balls, then ask him where old Jack Terranova might be.

Cristina appeared at his side, looked down at him, and then squatted to sit on the deck. There was a strange look in her eye.

"You get any sleep back there?" he asked.

"No," she replied. "I was thinking."

"And?"

"Hold me," she begged.

With a nod, he held out a hand, took hers, and pulled her toward him.

Maureen Counihan and Ron Dai were in her pool now, having devoured the pizza and the rest of the FBI and Personnel files. Nothing more had been said about her relationship with Phil Maldonado, even as Dai reopened and pored over the engineer's file a second time. Now, Ron relaxed in the sectioned-off Jacuzzi and watched as Maureen glided back and forth with strong, effortless strokes. She'd done at least forty laps, something that for some reason surprised him. He couldn't imagine where she got all that spare energy to burn. He was whipped and content to let jet-powered bubbles do all the work.

In time, she glided over to the whirlpool and hooked an arm over the dividing wall.

"Room for one more?" she asked.

Ron slid to one side, and she came over the little wall like a circus seal to take the seat opposite.

"Nothing like it," she said, letting out a long, satisfied sigh. Her chin sank to surface level as she found a jet to pummel her between the shoulder blades. "How do you feel?" she asked.

"Still a bit too *al dente*. Another five minutes and I'll be too limp to move."

"You're going to run some sort of number on him, aren't you?"

Dai met her gaze and nodded. "I'm going to check his

story out. You read the file. He's one of the best bets we have.''

"I'd like to say my pride isn't involved," she confessed. "But it is. It would piss me off no end to discover I've been flimflammed."

The detective shook his head emphatically. "No jumping to that sort of thing yet. You don't know that you have."

"Call it woman's intuition," she shot back. "The man has always been detached and distant. It was fine at first, because that was what I thought *I* wanted. No strings, you know?"

He smiled. "I know. When you're not ready for anything else, there's a certain freedom in it."

She wondered what she was seeing in his eyes as he spoke. If it was amusement, it didn't seem to be at her expense. Whatever it was, it made her feel more self-conscious than she had in years.

"I guess what I'm saying is that I've come to resent being taken for granted."

"We all do."

They sat for a while without speaking, the bubbles churning around them. The fog was in again, and the air was penetrating, damp, and cool. In the warmth of their whirlpool womb, it didn't much affect them.

"Where do you go from here?" she asked at length.

"I'll take it to Ross Charles. Try to get some more detailed background. They can really dig when they have a specific name to focus on."

"Surveillance?" she asked.

He shrugged. "Probably. I would sure love to get a few minutes alone inside his place."

"He's playing squash tomorrow evening at five-thirty."

Dai sat up and leaned forward. "Are you certain?"

"Pretty much. He's playing with me." Like him, she'd moved upright in her seat. She now wiggled to work into the jet a little further down her spine. With eyes closed, she arched her back, pulling the fabric of her suit tight across her breasts.

Dai absorbed this vision with delight and considered her information. He was now convinced that going into law enforcement had been no mistake. The hours were lousy, and the money wasn't all that good, but every once in a while you happened across a real pearl. At the moment, he was staring at one. She had an absolutely flat stomach, great tits, and a perfectly drawn jawline. He couldn't pry his eyes off her.

"Your bed or mine?" he asked before he could stop himself.

Maureen broke into a broad smile without opening her eyes and emitted a throaty little chuckle.

"I thought you'd never ask."

If Ron Dai had thought, for some reason, that he was tired earlier that night, he was pleasantly pleased at five A.M. to discover that any fatigue had vanished.

"I've *got* to go home and get a change of clothes," he told the woman with the mesmerizing physique stretched naked beside him. "I try to keep this up any longer, I'm gonna die."

"If you must," she replied with a phonied-up pout. "Just when I was starting to loosen up a little."

He snorted so hard his tonsils nearly abandoned ship. "Once the doctor agrees to release my erogenous zone from intensive care, maybe we can get you that close to loosening up again, huh?"

"Tomorrow night?"

He grinned. "I always was a quick healer."

FIFTEEN

Diego Cardona led Jack Terranova downstairs into the storm cellar of the island house. There was one heavy-timbered door bolted and padlocked shut on the far wall. He fit a key from his pocket into the lock, released it, and tugged the door ajar. With a yank of its pull chain, a single bare bulb illuminated the adjoining room. Everywhere in it, from wall to wall and floor to ceiling, the place was crammed with cardboard cartons.

"What's this?" the hit man asked.

"The seeds of counterrevolution," Cardona told him proudly. "Inside those cartons are components of the most sophisticated missile guidance system the United States has devised to date. Alamo."

Terranova's eyes opened wide at this information. "You're shittin' me."

"On the contrary, amigo." Cardona smirked as he said it. "I have never been more serious. Our plot revolves around a Sandinista double agent who is loyal to us and our cause. When the time is correct, he will make it appear that the pigs now holding our people hostage are preparing to make a deal for these components with the Eastern Bloc. The Russians would be eager to obtain this material and the United States, convinced of its presence on Sandinista soil, would be properly alarmed at such a prospect."

196

Terranova scrambled to keep up. "Let me get this straight. You fellas intend to plant this shit on the Sandinistas? How?"

"In just a matter of days, what you see here will be transferred under cover of darkness to Big Corn Island. It lies in Nicaraguan territorial waters, just one hundred miles west of here."

"Jesus Mother. Like I said, pal, you got balls."

"It is not so much the way you might imagine," Cardona continued proudly. "We do not work alone in this. This operation I describe is a joint effort undertaken by myself, my associates, and your own Central Intelligence Agency."

"Horseshit. Congress is all over them bumbling assholes these days."

Cardona continued to beam his patient smile. "This is not an officially sanctioned operation," he said calmly. "There are certain members of that organization and others in Washington who believe that this is the only means they have to keep the Kremlin out of Nicaragua. They work with us clandestinely."

"I still don't get it," Jack said. He'd approached a carton, pried open the lid, and was now peering inside.

"The information that the Sandinistas are preparing to make a trade with the Soviets will be leaked to high-ranking advisors in the National Security Council and to the Joint Chiefs of Staff. Your president will take military action. We who have supported the United States will be free to return and claim what is ours by right."

"And once you've got the country, you can move your dope operation to permanent headquarters," Jack said slowly, mulling it over. "What do your CIA pals think about *that* angle?"

Cardona laughed outright as he pulled the chain to douse the lights.

"They are arrogant and self-serving fools. They get what they want, and I do what I must. There would be a place for you, too, señor. Big Corn. It is beautiful and unspoiled. I have a dream for that place: to turn it into a playground for the very rich. A casino and five-star resort. Gambling. Beautiful women. It will require a man like you to insure smooth operation. In gratitude for services rendered, and as a gesture of continued good faith, I will give you a partnership in this enterprise."

Terranova followed the Somosista from the room, then stood by as he locked up.

"A paradise, huh?" he mused. "If anyone could pull it off, you could, pal. You got a different kind of balls than a man like me, but you got balls. I respect that. There ain't no reason why we can't do business together."

"Good," Diego told him. "We understand each other, amigo."

Rodney O'Doyle was under heavy pressure from his superiors at the Drug Enforcement Administration. They were demanding to know why a full frontal attack hadn't already been launched against Diego Cardona and his scumbag associates. O'Doyle was stalling them with excuses of incomplete intelligence, promising to kick something into gear within the month. He'd been saying this for over a month, and some within the administration were long past getting irritated. Over at the FBI building, Agent Conrad Burke was all too aware of the Miami DEA office's agitation. Memorandums crossed his desk several times a week now, documenting the results of his own bureau's continued surveillance of a certain Coral Gables compound. The director was getting most of this stuff. There was only so much he could safely intercept and lose. Out on the coast, things seemed to be moving with satisfactory sloth in Roscoe Charles's investigation into the Alamo guidance component problem. The last thing the anointed patriots needed was some startling development on *that* front. He found himself holding his breath a lot now and wondering when in hell Latham was going to start the goddamn ball rolling.

Hardy West had his own problems. In the wake of a recent peace initiative, Congressional support for the president's backing of the Contra effort had all but disintegrated. They needed something big to jerk them back into a nice "pinko-in-every-woodpile" mind-set. If Hardy wanted to do some whispering in old "Jumpin' Johnny's" ear, he knew he'd better have something concrete to back it up. The general could be guaranteed to go off like his namesake land mine if he had something he could rant about and shake in his counterparts' faces.

Ted Latham could do nothing but wait now. He had taken pains to orchestrate everything from his end with precision. The components were safely delivered to the Caribbean and stockpiled. It had been no easy task, but he was confident that the transfers, to Mexico, then on to the cays of Belize and deeper into the Caribbean basin, had gone undetected. Now all he had to do was persuade his confederates that the next and final step was in the immediate offing.

The four men were assembled in a hotel room on the spectacularly refurbished Baltimore waterfront. O'Doyle, by far the most volatile personality among them, had called the meeting. They were more or less the governing board of their clandestine brotherhood, the brains behind the surreptitious activities of committed men in all branches of government intelligence.

"When the fuck's this mealymouthed little greaseball gonna shake his ass?" O'Doyle demanded. He had a Rob Roy in one hand and a lit Cuban cigar in the other. His bloodhound-reddened and drooping eyes had the fire of wrath in them. "I've got some real zealous assholes trying to shove the little spic prick up *mine*. I need relief, and Ex-Lax ain't gonna do the job!"

The CIA man held up a well-manicured hand, the stone in his Duke University ring glittering on one of his widespread fingers. His face pleaded with the man to keep his cool.

"You know the setup," he said calmly. "The Sandinista captain on Big Corn has to give the all clear. They've been clearing the old road to an abandoned banana warehouse in the dead of night to avoid raising local suspicions. We're talking *days* here, gentlemen. I realize you all have your pressures to contend with, but this thing *will work*. You think I haven't got anybody breathing down *my* neck?"

Connie Burke spoke up. "I know what Rod here is going through. Our office down south has been actively onto the Coral Gables compound ever since they picked up on Cardona's meet with Jack Terranova. Terranova's disappeared. They don't like the look of that. Now they've discovered that Cardona is running half the cocaine trade in America. *Tons* of the stuff."

"Terranova will stay disappeared," Latham told him. "I have Cardona's assurance on that. Once this thing goes off and is safely in the hands of the president, we can decide what we want to do about our greedy little friend. I'm sure Rodney's superiors at DEA will be satisfied if this thorn in all our sides vaporizes in a car bombing. We *need* him now. That's all I'm saying to you.''

"What about your wild man, Bueno?" Hardy West pressed. "He's the X factor down there. You give him much more time to play with, he's going to get lucky and stumble on this thing."

"I doubt it," Latham countered confidently. "I admit that we've got no idea where he is at the moment, but some of our better intelligence leads us to believe that he might have been in residence at Guillermo Faro's hacienda the morning the Colombian army destroyed it."

Rodney O'Doyle slapped his thigh, spraying cigar ashes all over the carpet, and started to cough. It was an anxious several moments before he was recovered enough to speak.

"Somebody escaped from that attack and took down a Sikorsky motherfuckin' *gunship* in the process!" he snarled. "If Bueno is as good as they say, and he was in there, who are you gonna put your money on? Jesus Christ! Do you have any idea how hard it is to shoot a Sikorsky down outta the sky with a fucking *machine gun?*"

After nearly two days at sea, the fishing boat drifted in Costa Rican territorial waters about twenty miles offshore. Lucho Vargas pretended to fish, waiting for nightfall before taking the boat in to shore. At a bit past noon, a government patrol boat came alongside, and the commander exchanged pleasantries before moving on. With Henry, Cristina, and the children huddled below, there had been no problems. Now, they bobbed serenely in waters off the gulf of Nicoya, the surface as glassy as a millpond. Suddenly the recently reconditioned engine roared to life and was throttled down to an easy idle. Vargas had begun the journey in. At just under ten knots, it would take another two hours to reach port. In the dusk, Puntarenas was squat and glowing, a dim smudge of light on the distant horizon. Across the gulf, on the Nicoya Peninsula, tiny fishing villages dotted the shoreline. Sleepy and less vigilantly patrolled, they would provide better landfall for noncitizens wishing to enter the country unobserved.

As she sat in the deckhouse and peered toward land through an open porthole, Cristina seemed more agitated to Bueno.

The past two days had been good for her, allowing her to collect her composure in an alien environment. She would be on the run again when she stepped back onto land, and this was not a woman accustomed to running. Henry knew she was fearful. He would have been more concerned if she weren't.

At the helm, Lucho began to steer north of Puntarenas. Time crawled as the peninsula began to take on real mass in the darkness. He aimed for a spot with no lights nearby and made a beeline to a dock stretching dark and deserted out into the bay. This was another reason Bueno had sought his services. Lucho Vargas knew this part of the hemisphere like the deck of his own vessel.

The dock buckled and swayed on the water. Lucho's man, cold sober for days now, leapt ashore to tie off the bowline. Henry lifted the two children into his arms and then helped Cristina after them. When all three were safely on the dock, he turned to the grizzled skipper. Two more Maple Leaves gleamed in his open palm.

"With thanks," he told him. "Remember our deal. You never saw them . . . or me."

Vargas fingered the coins appreciatively.

"I am many things, señor," he said. "One of them is not a fool."

Henry leapt ashore, and Vargas signaled his man to cast off. The boat eased away from the mooring and out into the bay. Henry and Cristina stood holding the kids and watched in silence as it receded down the coast and out of sight.

"We made it," he said. "Puntarenas is only a dozen miles across the water." He pointed to the lights. "Once we're there, San Jose is a piece of cake. I can wire for money, and we can get you and the kids on your way to Caracas."

They'd begun to turn and walk carefully off the dock. Cristina stopped. "The children, yes. But I am not going."

"What?"

"I will send the children to my sister. There are two other things I must attend to first before I join them. One is the man named Douglas in the Caymans. I must lay claim to what is mine before he gets any ideas. And as you hunt the man who destroyed my life, so will I. I go with you."

Bueno shook his head emphatically. "No, Cristina."

Her eyes flashed with resolve and defiance.

"I am speaking of revenge. Not for my husband's death, but for the destruction of everything I fought so hard to hang onto. Security for my children. I paid for it with my dignity, and I will see those who did this to me dead. *Then* I will see Douglas and fight for what is mine by right. My children's by right."

Henry stared hard at her. He read the eyes, the quivering nostrils, the set of her elegant jaw. Saying no to that wasn't easy.

"I work alone," he said calmly. "That's the way it's always been. The kind of hatred you feel obscures judgment. You cannot carry it into a war like this one. Trust me, Cristina. I'll get him. He'll pay."

"I believe that," she said earnestly. "But it is not enough to just know. I will look into his eyes before he dies. If I must control my hatred in order to witness this man's death, then you have my word that I will. I must."

In watching her speak, Bueno saw two women. One stood before him dirty, disheveled, and torn. Weariness weighted her shoulders, pulling them forward and down. The other was a beautiful aristocrat, tall, fine-boned, and proud. No amount of dirt could dampen her fire. Without patronizing, he met the steady gaze and nodded.

"We'll see," he said.

Maureen waited for Phil Maldonado in the health club lounge. She'd left the plant a quarter hour ago, and in another five minutes the engineer was going to be late for his reservation. She sipped grape juice from the health bar and watched two athletically adept guys going at it in the glass-walled center court before her. They dove and leapt, digging out the impossible shots. If she practiced until doomsday, she knew she'd never approach that level of play. Still, she enjoyed the game. It gave her an opportunity to indulge her competitive nature openly. Phil hated the way she fought for every point, gloating over a particularly vicious kill shot or difficult placement. She couldn't help it. It was in her nature to scrap and fight to win.

Maldonado came hurrying in, still dressed in his street clothes. She rolled her eyes as he apologized for being late and rushed off to change. Five minutes later, they'd locked themselves into the little rectangular box that was court number eight and were loosening up with some tentative volleying.

"So what's it look like?" she asked. "Are we going to be able to deliver the SYSTEMINI in June?"

"We're working on it. There's too much fucking resistance in the board. I don't know. Maybe we're asking it to do too much."

"That's the point, isn't it?"

"Physics is physics," he said with a shrug. "We've run the programs ragged, and it keeps going down exactly the same way."

"I don't get it." The ball came at her, knee-high and on a direct line. She had to get out of its path and still have her racquet in position. The resulting return shot was weak and poorly placed. "Before we ever launched this thing, you guys spent six months developing the theoretical side. Everything added up."

Maldonado addressed her weak shot and blasted it viciously into the telltale. "On paper," he grunted. "We obviously missed something."

Maureen scooped the ball off the deck with her racquet and bounced it in frustration. "The trades announced last week, Phil. People buy stock based on projected activity. This thing falls flat on its face and the bottom's going to drop out."

"It's a bitch," he muttered distractedly. "By the way, where'd the FBI come up with the gook in Q.C.?"

It jarred her, but she quelled any reaction. "He comes highly qualified."

"Who do they think they're fooling with guys like that?" he asked. "Hell, nobody's even sure the reject numbers aren't screwed up somehow. Those guys will tear the place apart, and it'll turn out that there was never anything wrong."

She smiled. "They know better than that. We've got a serious national security breach on our hands, and our failure to help them locate it would amount to as big a disaster as a SYSTEMINI failure."

When she served, he quickly returned a soft shot into the right corner. She had to really spin her wheels, blast hard, and then backpedal fiercely.

"I still think they're making mountains out of molehills," Phil said out of the side of his mouth. His high, overhand swing missed making good contact, and the ball dropped into a spot she knew she could kill him from. She pounced.

"What would you have called the hole in the bottom of the *Titanic*, captain?" she asked, gloating. The shot she'd made was deadly.

During his lunch hour Peter Davis had dropped off the recordings he'd made at a commercial translation service. He picked them up at the end of the work day. The one long-distance number he'd captured tones for proved to be a temporary dead end. His buddy in the Boston field office had the phone company in Miami run it, and it ended up being a newsstand downtown. A contact number and message drop. Meanwhile, Maldonado had made a reservation to play squash at five-thirty and would be on the court at that very moment. Davis was within range of the engineer's Monte Sereno house already, heading into the foothills for a quick look around.

Ron Dai tailed Phil Maldonado from the plant parking lot to the health club just to make sure he kept his date. Satisfied that the engineer was thus engaged, he drove into the Monte Sereno foothills to find his house. The Quito and Saratoga–Los Gatos roads were clogged with commuter traffic, making the relatively short trip painfully slow going. Traffic thinned out considerably as he wound his way above the valley floor and into an exclusive enclave where property was heavily wooded and the homes were mostly obscured from view. Maldonado's road snaked back on itself at least a dozen times as it climbed a steep gulch. Dai scanned mailboxes and gateposts, looking for the number. He slowed to a crawl as the numbers started closing in. The engineer's drive ran uphill to his left after a hairpin turn straightened out. He drove well past, looking for a spot to pull the big Dodge off the road and park it out of sight.

The first turnout he came to was already occupied by a late model Toyota Supra. Ron frowned as he crawled past. There was something awfully familiar about that car: the color, spoilers, and other detailing. He pulled ahead of it and climbed out to approach the driver's side door. The owner had left it unlocked. Foolish, perhaps, unless he was anticipating a potentially rushed departure. The registration was in the glove box, and Dai located it only as a formality. He already knew

that the car belonged to the FBI agent working the case with
him. The information on the card he held in his hand confirmed it. Peter Davis. 1410 Myrtle, Apt. C-12, Santa Clara.

The detective backed out of the FBI man's Toyota and
looked up the road. There was another turnout on the other
side, about two hundred feet further up. He drove the Dodge
on up the hill, turned around in the first available drive, and
guided it well out of sight beneath overhanging trees. He set
the parking brake and waited. There wasn't much sense in
following Davis up to the house and confronting him. He'd
had the Maldonado file first and had obviously been struck by
some of the peculiarities contained therein. He was playing it
close to the vest. Early that morning, Dai and Maureen had
crawled out of her most hospitable and comfortable bed to
bring Ross Charles their own suspicions. Charles didn't
indicate that he'd heard anything about the R & D man
from another source. Unless the FBI was running some
sort of game on him, Ron could see no reason for Charles
to hide anything. Peter Davis, on the hand, could probably
be expected to play out his hand *before* he laid any cards
on the table. Trained as he'd been, he could also be expected to do a pretty thorough job of tossing Maldonado's
place.

With a slow shake of his head, Dai smiled to himself. Once
upon a time, he, too, could have been accused of overzealous-
ness. It was something you generally outgrew. He was curious to know how much Davis had already gleaned and what
evidence he was finding now to back up his suspicions.

As Phil Maldonado sweated on court number eight, he
was thinking hard and fast. This bitch was the one who had
called in the FBI in the first place, advising her father that it
was their best move. She'd been observed working closely
with the Oriental agent, carrying boxes of files into her
house. It was only a matter of time now. He'd known that
sooner or later it would come to something like this. For him,
the game was over. It was time for a change. Sit tight,
Cardona had said. Like hell.

He scrambled to return a ball, pulled up, and clutched at
his stomach. A wince of pain shot across his face.

"What's wrong?" Maureen asked, concerned.

"God!" he groaned, attempting to straighten. "Pulled something in my ab. Just heard a pop like—"

"It hurts bad?"

He nodded. "Like fire."

"You look like you're in a lot of pain."

Maldonado kept working his twisted wince. "A fucking abdominal pull. Christ. I remember hearing about Mark Gastineau's problems after he had one last year. Took forever to heal."

"You should have someone look at you."

"I'll see how it feels. Maybe we ought to hang this up, though, huh? I'm sorry."

"Don't worry about it. Maybe I can find someone to finish out the hour."

Phil forced an apologetic, glum smile and headed for the door.

"You want me to ask around out there?"

"I'll do it," she replied. "Try ice. I hear it's good for that sort of thing."

As Maldonado showered and changed, he wondered how quickly he might be able to move. Disappearing would attract attention and maybe endanger Major Cardona's master plan. As much as he hated it, he probably *would* have to sit tight for at least another week, but it might not be a bad idea to have his bags packed and affairs in order. He needed some time at home to sit and think about it.

The oncoming car speeding past him as he wound up the serpentine road toward home seemed familiar. The driver, hunched over the wheel, was obscured in darkness. He quickly searched his memory, where everything seemed sharpened by paranoia as he scanned and tried to make associations. The company lot? Maybe that was it. No . . . damn! The evening he parked outside Maureen's house while she was inside with the FBI agent. That very same car was parked opposite him. Definitely. A silver-gray Toyota Supra, distinctive in that it had the rear-deck spoiler and sport wheels. There would be a dozen just like it in the valley, but this was too much of a coincidence. And he *had* seen it in the SYSTEMATICS lot.

From the entrance to his drive and all the way up to the house, everything looked undisturbed. Phil piloted the Lincoln in under the electric garage door and parked. He entered the house through a side door leading into the kitchen. Nothing appeared to be out of place. He stood a moment, listening. Slowly, he moved through the dining room and into the foyer inside the front door. His heart slowed now as the adrenaline backed off. Everything seemed to be intact. No sign of forced entry; nothing disturbed. He loosened his tie and unbuttoned his shirt collar.

It would be late in Miami. Nearly nine-thirty. The news-stand closed for the night at ten. After that hour, getting in touch with the Coral Gables compound became more diffi-cult. Even though he had an emergency number there, it would be unthinkable to call direct. There were other routes, more circuitous. Maldonado undressed in his bedroom, chang-ing into denim jeans and a knit pullover. The major must know by now that the FBI was working on his end. It was a full day since he'd made his call to report this development and been told to sit tight. God, he hated that.

Barefoot, he padded into the den and approached the enter-tainment center with its state-of-the-art stereo and video gear. Atop a twenty-seven-inch stereo Sony Trinitron sat a sleek, four-head VCR. The engineer extended his hand, pushing his fingers past the sprung flap and into the tape cavity. His eyes widened as his fingers probed frantically. He stooped and pushed the flap back to peer within. Nothing. The little black codebook was gone.

Dumbfounded, Maldonado spun quickly around and stared anxiously at the contents of the room. In a fury, he grabbed the tape unit and flung it to the floor. There was no time to hesitate now. He had to leave this place immediately. Go to ground. Contact Florida. Then find the man who drove the silver-gray Supra before he could manage to decode the infor-mation in the book. Everything depended on it.

Ron Dai witnessed the near-intersection of Pete Davis and Phil Maldonado from the seclusion of his overhung parking place. Davis had come back from the house at a run, looking like a man ready to toss his hat in the air and shout *Eureka!* No sooner had he gotten underway down the hill than Maldonado's Lincoln appeared, moving uphill at a fair clip. At the rate both cars were moving, he was a little surprised they hadn't hit each other. He waited for the dust to settle and drove at a more modest speed to Maureen Counihan's Saratoga home. She and the engineer had been scheduled to play squash for an hour. Maldonado had arrived home quite a bit early. It also occurred to him that Peter Davis had known that the man was supposed to be away.

Maureen was another fifteen minutes getting home. She explained that Phil had pulled an abdominal muscle or something and bowed out. She'd finished her hour being creamed by one of the resident hotshots.

"Davis beat us to the punch," he told her.

"Come again?"

"He was already there when I showed up. He had to have known our man had an engagement. Pretty slick. Goddamn near got himself caught, though. It was this close." He held up two fingers with a quarter inch of air between them. "Both of them seemed to be in a pretty big hurry when I saw them last."

"He thinks you're FBI," she told him. "Asked all about you."

"Like how?"

"He was trying to downplay the problem, belittling it."

"Davis found something in there," he told her. "I'm sure of it."

Peter Davis had found the little black book when he tried to view an unmarked videotape in Maldonado's VCR. He knew now that the track he was on was going to lead to paydirt. If he could break the gibberish contained in the book and employ it to singlehandedly smash an espionage ring, he would get his transfer to D.C. Those guys were going to sit up and take notice.

He knew he had to work fast. Dai and little Miss Tightknees were in possession of the same files, but he was positive that the little book contained the number of the man whose voice had been on the tape.

He carried the transcript, along with a cold beer, to the coffee table in his living room. With the manila folder open and the typewritten pages before him in a neat stack, he picked up the first and began to read. The translation was literal, complete with invectives detailing relations with the Blessed Virgin and inferior family lineage. Other than that, the messages were crisp and clear. The first conversation was definitely with a contact. The next one put Maldonado in touch with the party he wanted. In it, he related current developments in tones of barely controlled panic. Apparently, the ''big man'' was out of the country and would have to be reached by means other than telephone. It seemed that through Maureen Counihan's own mouth he'd learned that the FBI was investigating some serious irregularities in the missile guidance component inventory. He suggested in no uncertain terms that both he and the party at the other end of the line were treading on some pretty thin ice. He was advised to stay calm, avoiding any action that might betray his concerns. The big man would hear of these developments. Maldonado didn't seem too happy about the idea of sitting tight. He'd done his job and wanted out now. The other party assured him that a solution to his crisis would be in the offing in a matter of days.

Davis completed his reading, closed the folder, and sat back on the sofa. The beer felt pretty good after his narrow escape. Damn, he'd almost hit the bastard's car on the way down the hill. Then again, it had been worth it. He had the goods and the general drift of what was going on. Now it was just a simple matter of breaking the code so he could identify this Mister Big and find out what he was up to with Alamo missile parts.

SIXTEEN

An exhaust-belching old bus filled with tourists, locals, and all manner of odd luggage bore Bueno and the shattered Faro family through Costa Rica from Puntarenas to San Jose. The hotel they found there was a quiet, family-owned *pensione* located on a back street. Henry wired his California bank for money as soon as Cristina and the children were settled. Reservations were booked on a flight to Panama City and then another to Caracas. Cristina's sister was contacted and the children sent off to her. By late afternoon, Henry was taking Cristina shopping for clothes.

One loose-fitting cotton dress had already been purchased for her in Puntarenas so that the condition of the clothing she had worn since Cali would not attract attention. Henry also wore a new workshirt and dungarees. Now they stuck to shops selling utilitarian merchandise. When they returned to the *pensione* Cristina no longer projected the image of softness she'd cultivated as the wife of a wealthy trafficker.

Bueno sat on the edge of a bed, a side table drawn up to his knees and the guts of his P-5 spread carefully across its surface. One at a time, he polished each piece with a gun-oiled rag. The door to the bath opened. Cristina had just taken what must have been her third shower that day.

Something was changed between them. An ease and famil-iarity had grown from the ordeal they'd endured and the

210

literal distance that now lay between them and Cali. As they
shopped that afternoon, Henry noticed a capacity for pleasure
in her. She'd laughed once and viewed her new clothes
proudly in boutique mirrors.

Cristina stepped into the dimly lit room. The shades were
drawn against direct afternoon sunlight. Beams of that light
streamed through cracks in the bamboo slats to fall upon her
nakedness. Henry set down the pistol reassembly and stared
at her. Wet hair hung limply, framing her face. She strode to
the dressing table, sat, and began to run a comb through her
hair. Their eyes caught each other in the mirror's reflection.
She continued to comb, holding his eyes, almost in challenge.
Something had *definitely* changed.

He stood and walked across the room. When he was standing directly behind her, watching her face in the mirror, he
put his hands on her shoulders and began to glide them gently
over her cool, silky skin. Slowly, as she watched, he slid a
hand beneath one breast, feeling the delicious weight in his
palm. When the tips of his fingers brushed her nipple, Cristina
shivered. She set down her comb and turned to face him.

"I believe you are overdressed for what I hope comes
next," she said.

There was no way Phil Maldonado could sit tight. His
agitation increased until he could stand it no longer. After
using his home terminal to access the SYSTEMATICS parking permit files, he learned that the only Toyota Supra registered belonged to a Peter Davis on Myrtle in Santa Clara. His
packed bag went into the trunk of the Lincoln, and he drove it
to the long-term lot of the San Jose Airport. From the adjacent Hertz lot he rented a Ford Escort. At shortly before
midnight, he checked into a Howard Johnson's at the intersection of the Lawrence Expressway and U.S. 280.

In the early morning, he phoned the newsstand in Miami
and gave the man his hotel and room numbers. The major
took his time in getting back to him. The phone in the motel
room did not ring until well after nine. When it did, the
engineer nearly dropped the receiver in his haste to answer.
Cardona was all syrupy confidence and calm reassurance. He
was disturbed that the man had taken such hasty action but
assured him that he simply saw it all as water under some
obscure bridge.

"Do not do anything foolish, my friend," Cardona told him. "Even if we never discussed how you would confront this problem, we all knew this time would ultimately come."

Maldonado was not nearly as calm. He was beside himself as he retorted bitterly, "I'll rot in jail. I did precisely what you asked. Now you must get me out of here."

"Do not worry. I had other business to attend to, but I am now at the New Orleans airport and on my way. You must remain calm and not do anything regrettable. Our work has gone well, and we stand on the very brink of success now. If you wish to reap your own reward from it, you must be patient. We will see to your safety."

After this less-than-reassuring conversation, Maldonado left the motel to visit a McDonald's and carry food back. He sat at a table beside the room's only window, eating. Across the room, the contestants on "The Price Is Right" gesticulated greedily on the television screen. Outside the closed curtains, he could hear the dull roar of traffic on the freeway as it thundered through this anonymous stretch of suburban limbo.

This was no game. He was no longer in an arena where a sharp tongue and inbred arrogance could carry him through a rough spot. For the first time in his life, he had no idea where to go or how to control his own fate. Everything lay in another man's hands. He knew this man to be ruthless and relentless. He was the same man who had forced him into this position of compromise in the first place, threatening to report his undeclared family money to Internal Revenue. Why couldn't he have run then? Because he'd had a good position with an innovative firm? Hell, that was lost now as well. When he had agreed to the major's demands, he had committed professional suicide in the process.

Peter Davis knew that the Salvage Department at SYSTEMATICS ran statistical data and spreadsheets on the company's central IBM mainframe computer. He had also learned through observation that certain key personnel had access to the data bank through home terminals. It wouldn't be long before Maldonado would miss the little black book Pete had stolen from his VCR. Pete knew he had very little time and had to work fast. The first thing after reporting to work that morning, he placed a call to Data Processing and explained that his boss was in need of that day's access code. He gave them Larry Ransell's company ID number, and without missing a beat, the cherry-voiced woman on the other end of the line said "Octopus" and told him to have a nice day. After recradling the receiver, he went in search of his boss to report that he wasn't feeling well and thought he should go home.

At ten-fifteen that morning, he steered his car into the lot of a nearby computer outlet and charged a new IBM PC-AT on his American Express card. In the parking shed behind his apartment complex, he unloaded the new gear from the trunk of his car and carried it across the drive to his first floor unit. It took him the better part of two hours to effect the hookup and get the thing to spit hardcopy out of the Okidata dot matrix printer. The modem that would allow his machine to communicate with the SYSTEMATICS mainframe was connected to his phone line. Before accessing the powerful company machine, he carefully input all the gibberish contained in Maldonado's book into his own unit. He was set now, and he dialed the company data bank, punching in the code word OCTOPUS.

In effect, he was turning his home unit into a "slave" machine, coupled to the vastly greater capacity of the larger, more sophisticated unit across town. With this increased speed and analytical power at his fingertips, he proceeded to instruct the bigger machine to systematically analyze the numerical and alphabetical entries in Maldonado's codebook. There were dozens of them, and this was actually to his advantage. The more items the system had to compare for similarities, the quicker it would unravel the code. Nevertheless, an exercise like this could take the better part of a day. It took him an hour just to enter his instructions. He was famished by the time he'd finished. It was getting late in the afternoon. Leaving the machine to mull over the task at hand, he went to the kitchen and made himself some lunch.

The SYSTEMATICS central mainframe computer had a backup warning system that advised the security office any time outside access was obtained. Security had a list of all personnel authorized to tap the system from their homes. A sophisticated line-checking apparatus could be consulted to ensure that the access was both authorized and coming from the appropriate location. They had encountered problems in the past when computer freaks would access the system for their own amusement and disrupt sensitive programming. This check system proved to be a big help in preventing such abuse.

When a security man noted access at 3:06 that afternoon, he routinely punched in the authorization check. The machine scanned all the authorized lines, found none of them in use, and indicated a breach. He quickly dialed the local operating company and requested a line check to determine the intruder's location and address. A phone company supervisor came on the line moments later to inform him that the line in question had been tagged off-limits by the Federal Bureau of Investigation. Curiosity piqued, the security man summoned his direct superior, and together they punched up the intruder's activity on their own monitor. They also called in the shift engineer for consultation.

Ron Dai happened to be the Q.C. engineer on duty who received the Security Office call. He arrived in their office just moments later. He absorbed the information presented by the Security chief as he scanned the screen. It took no more than twenty seconds before he was grabbing the phone and asking Maureen Counihan to get down there, pronto.

Maureen absorbed the curious information that someone on an FBI restricted line was using her machine as she watched the monitor screen in fascination.

"Code," she muttered. "Right?"

Dai nodded. "You got it. The bastard is trying to decipher."

"Beg pardon?" the Security chief asked, baffled.

"Don't worry, chief," Maureen told him. "We'll take it from here. Good work."

Henry Bueno awoke from a much-needed nap to notice that darkness had fallen outside in the city of San Jose. He could hear less street activity now and smell the crispness of a recent rain. A faint breeze reached him through the open window. Cristina lay sleeping fitfully beside him.

He still wondered how continuing on with her would color his effectiveness in the field. Much had changed in him. He was doing things and allowing feelings that would once have been unthinkable. Perhaps only time would tell him how foolish he was allowing himself to be. Then again, he had learned to view things differently in this past year. For the first time in his adult life, he'd allowed himself to loosen up some. Perhaps that wasn't all so terrible.

Right now, his body was aching to be stretched and exercised. As quietly as possible, he dropped to the floor and went through a quick half-hour routine just to maintain tone.

The security of Henri's presence allowed Cristina to sleep well and awaken relaxed. She realized he was no longer in the bed, and she heard the water running behind the closed door of the bath. For the first time in memory, she found herself wishing that a particular man *was* still there to be reached out to and touched. This man. It was hard for her to believe that anyone so physically tough and formidable could be so tender and giving.

The running water stopped, and a moment later he emerged from the bath. That hard-muscled nakedness moved toward her and paused at the bedside. A smile of amusement could be traced across that sun-etched and adversity-tempered face.

"Sleep well?" he asked.

"Yes," she replied. "You snore."

Bueno now broke into a broad grin. "So I am told. If you push me onto my side, I stop."

Cristina matched his smile. "*Now* you tell me."

"Time to talk business," he said. He sat next to her and rested a hand on her sheet-draped hip. "Other than Buenaventura, how often have you handled a gun? You said Che gave you instruction."

"My father taught me to shoot when I was ten. There is much fear of kidnapping among the wealthy families. In Cali, I carried a tiny Semmerling .45 in my purse whenever I left the house."

"How about a rifle?" he asked.

"Not since I was a girl. To shoot skeet. I was not very good. The noise and recoil frightened me."

He sighed, stood, and walked to the window to lift the shade and peer out.

"I've been trying to justify your coming along with me," he said matter-of-factly. "It's contrary to everything I've ever learned or done."

"And?" she asked coolly.

He turned back to face her. "I want you to spend some time getting acquainted with the *Tikka*," he said, nodding to the rifle leaned against the wall. "Once we get to Limon."

"Limon?"

"It's on the Caribbean coast. There's a friend there I want to speak with. He's tapped into the political situations all around the basin rim."

Roscoe Charles was preparing to leave for the day when his secretary buzzed to inform him that Ron Dai and Maureen Counihan were in his outer office. He told her to show them in, wondering what might be up that a phone call couldn't address. The door opened, and Maureen, with a look of peevish determination fixed on her face, led the way in.

"Do you mind telling me why we are being kept in the dark regarding the Davis investigation?" she demanded.

Charles registered a look of genuine confusion. "I'm afraid you're going to have to back it up a bit. What Davis investigation?"

"Of Philip Maldonado. The one he's accessed *my* computer to work on at this very moment."

"The guy you two spoke to me about? That's as far as it's gone. Our Washington people are still working on more information."

Maureen and Dai exchanged confused looks of their own.

"You don't know about this?" Ron asked.

"I'm afraid not," Charles admitted, shaking his head. "You mind filling me in?"

The detective found himself off balance. "Jesus. We thought you people were keeping us in the dark for some reason. If you don't know about this, you sure should. Pete Davis is hot on the trail of this guy. He tossed Maldonado's house last night. I was parked down the road and watched him leave. This morning Pete went home sick, and now he's tapping into the SYSTEMATICS mainframe, running some sort of deciphering program on an alphanumeric code."

Agent Charles dropped his pencil, picked up the phone, and punched in Davis's home number. When he got a busy signal, he called the operator and requested an emergency interrupt. The operator confirmed that the line was indeed engaged, but not by any party she could interrupt.

"Goddammit!" he thundered, slamming the receiver back into its cradle. "That little fucker isn't going to be able to get a job picking up papers in a county park when I get done with him!" He reached to a rack behind him and retrieved his jacket as he stood. "We'd better get over there before he does something *real* stupid. Where do we *get* these assholes?"

After learning from his phone conversation with Philip Maldonado that his coded notebook was missing, Diego Cardona had wasted no time. He dropped his New Orleans business immediately and arrived at Maldonado's motel room door at just after five in the evening.

"Let's go," he ordered when Phil opened up to him. "You have rented a car in your own name?"

"Yes," he replied.

"We leave it then. I've got another downstairs. You know where this address is? Myrtle Street?"

"I checked it out on a map," Phil told him. "It's not more than five minutes from here."

He had his luggage in the trunk of a sleek new T-bird and was seated alongside the major just moments later.

"Everything goes as planned with the things I delivered?" he asked as they left the motel, heading north on the Lawrence Expressway.

"We are on target," Cardona replied smugly. "Your work on the last load to Chetumal was exemplary. You will not be forgotten when the time comes to reward such deeds."

"I had little choice," the engineer told him, a tightness in his throat. "Now I am uprooted for a second time in my life. Everything I have worked for is gone."

"There will be other opportunities. It was your country you did this thing for. Sacrifices must often be made before glory is earned."

The apartment complex they eventually approached was one constructed in the currently popular "active singles" motif. Tennis courts. Two pools. Racquetball and health spa. Plantings of various hardy shrubs erupted in profusion behind heavy-timbered rail-tie retaining walls. The two-story buildings themselves were of a dark natural wood and brick. The unit they sought was located on the ground floor, around back on the carport side. They found the Toyota Supra of Peter Davis parked in its assigned berth.

"You remain here and keep watch," the major ordered. "Honk the horn three times if there appears to be any trouble. Be prepared to leave in a hurry." He climbed out of the car and crossed quickly to the front door of the troublemaker's apartment.

Pete Davis was getting somewhere. A little more than an hour after starting the deciphering run, the alphabetical code still remained gibberish, but the numerical portion seemed to be sorting itself out. They were phone numbers with Miami area codes. He recognized one of them as the newsstand Maldonado had dialed. He was onto something big, no doubt about it.

His doorbell rang. He frowned irritably. You got everything in a complex like this, from Jehovah's Witnesses to Kirby vacuum salesmen. He ignored it. The caller continued to buzz insistently.

"We don't want any!" he hollered.

"P.G. & E.!" came the muffled reply. "We're trying to trace a gas leak in the area."

"Don't smell a thing," Davis yelled back.

"No matter, mac. Our equipment's more sensitive than your nose. You don't open up, I gotta call a cop."

The agent punched the print button in frustration. As he stood, the machine hummed a moment, and then the printer began chattering. The solutions he'd obtained to that point started rolling out the top of the carriage. He slipped quietly across the carpet to the front window and peered out past the shade. The guy on the stoop looked like anything but the gas man. He shot a quick glance across the drive. A car sat parked there with a man in shadow behind the wheel. The head turned to look in the direction of his front door. Recognizing Phil Maldonado, Davis felt his heart leap into his throat.

He whirled, hurried across the room to the printer, and tore off the readout. He knew he was a sitting duck with no back-up. The papers were shoved down the front of his pants. He grabbed his service revolver off the sofa on the way by and spun the cylinder. The bathroom was his best bet. He locked himself in and cranked open the tiny window above the john. After kicking the screen out, he hoisted one leg over the sill and worked his head through into the night air.

The butt of a pistol came up into his face, breaking his nose and blinding him. He lost his balance and tumbled headlong into the pyracantha below. Tiny needles tore through his clothing and into his flesh. The wiry-looking Latin man he'd spied on his stoop now bent over him. The metallic *schik-clack* of a round being chambered rasped in his ear.

Nose shattered and face ripped with searing pain, Davis tried to focus through a fog of shock. His vision cleared enough to let him make out the face leering down from above him. He had never seen this man. The man was aiming an automatic at his quivering mouth. One bullet from that menacing muzzle would cancel his ticket out of this hellhole and replace it with another to oblivion.

"Federal officer," he mumbled. "FBI."

The guy above him drew his leg back and kicked him in the testicles. A wave of nausea swept over him. He almost went out.

"How much?" the man hissed. "How much do you know?"

Davis was gasping through clenched teeth. "Oh, my God," he groaned. "Don't kill me."

"What have you discovered?" the man pressed him.

"N-n-nothing. Numbers. Phone numbers. That's all."

Diego Cardona brought the gun butt down hard across the agent's temple. As the man went out, Diego straightened up, stared at the inert form with loathing, and kicked him hard in the ribs. Then he bent to search through the man's clothing. Locating the printout in his waistband, he jerked it free, unfolded it, and scanned columns of numbers. There was plenty enough to incriminate here. The number of the estate in Coral Gables. The newsstand. Other message drops. Other individuals connected with the cause. There was even a quantity of alphabetical gibberish, as yet undeciphered. A further search revealed Maldonado's notebook in the man's back pocket.

He glanced around and then back to where the FBI man lay. He was in good cover here, with bushes all around. Dropping to one knee, he removed a length of airline cable from his pocket. Each end was secured by a heavy iron ring. Working the index finger of each gloved hand through a ring, he twisted the wire around the unconscious man's neck and crossed the ends. With a vicious yank, he severed the windpipe and snapped the neck.

Blood was splattered everywhere from the agent's broken nose. Nothing could be done about this, but removal of the corpse would leave his superiors in doubt about his fate. It could buy Diego time. The computer disk and the unit itself must also be destroyed. He grabbed the dead man by the collar and dragged him around the side of the building. After assuring himself that the way was clear, he flagged Maldonado. The engineer reversed the rented T-bird, pulling up alongside him and parallel to the curb.

"Get in there and destroy his computer," the major snarled. "Kick the door in."

The engineer stared dumbfounded at the dead FBI agent's body.

"Give me the trunk key! Move!" Cardona snapped.

Maldonado came out of his stupor, pulled the keys from the ignition, and tossed them over. His mind reeled.

Jesus . . . He had slit his throat, by the look of it. There was blood all over the front of him.

The computer monitor glowed at the ready as Phil hurried into Davis's living room. An IBM PC-AT. He flipped the disk lock and snatched it from the drive. With a few quick taps, he had the menu on the screen. One by one, he deleted items from the data base. For good measure, he put the nearest dining room chair through the screen, shorting out the whole system.

The major had the body in the trunk and was slamming the lid as Maldonado emerged from the apartment.

"You drive," he commanded, handing Phil the keys and hurrying around to the passenger door.

Maureen and Ron Dai led the way toward Peter Davis's apartment complex with Ross Charles following. All three of them could think of nothing but throttling the agent's ass as they pushed through bumper-to-bumper rush-hour traffic. The Myrtle Street complex was easy enough to locate once they got out of mainstream congestion. Finding the correct address within it was something else again. They parked and convened on the sidewalk. There, Charles suggested he would try to locate the manager while Ron took a run along the parking shed to the rear. If they could spot the flashy Supra, it might save them time.

"I'm sorry, Miss Counihan," he said. "I'm going to have to ask you to stay out of this part. We don't know what the hell he's up to, and I don't want to risk getting you hurt."

"It's my car," Maureen snapped, glaring at him. "What's Ron supposed to do? Walk?"

Charles shrugged to Dai. "If you see anything, make her stay put. Please."

The detective nodded. "I'll do my best."

Maureen swung out into the long rear drive and moved slowly along the parking shed.

"It's sort of a gray. Spoilers, pinstriping, all that shit," Dai told her.

They rounded a sweeping bend to spot Phil Maldonado and another man climbing into a late-model Ford Thunderbird.

"Did I just see what I thought I saw?" Ron asked. He bent forward to pull a short-barreled Smith & Wesson .38-caliber Bodyguard from his ankle holster.

Maureen stomped the accelerator to the floorboard, and the Saab leapt ahead as the turbocharger kicked in. The man climbing in on the passenger side of the T-bird jerked around, focused, and reacted with astonishing quickness. A nine-millimeter automatic came up, level with the top of his door. He steadied the barrel, its tiny black orifice trained directly on the driver of the oncoming car, and fired.

Windshield shattered in Maureen's face, obscuring her vision. Something felt odd, as though a mule had kicked her in the solar plexus. Next to her, Dai was leaning out his window and returning fire. She no longer had control of the car; her head suddenly felt light. The Saab swerved of its own accord and smashed into the rear end of a parked Firebird. When Maureen fell on the wheel, the harsh blaring of the horn echoed off the surrounding buildings.

"Holy shit!" Maldonado yelped as Diego leapt in.

"Drive!" the major commanded.

The engineer needed no further prodding. That was Maureen's Saab back there. Somebody, probably that gook FBI man, was shooting at them.

"Stay calm," Cardona soothed as they swerved erratically

out onto the street and into traffic. "Did you recognize them?"

"The other FBI man," Phil replied. "And my boss at the plant. The big man's daughter. Executive vice president."

"What do they know?"

"She told me she was working with that guy on the personnel files. The FBI subpoenaed banking and other financial records."

"We've got to get rid of the body and the car," Diego told him. "Is there a lake nearby?"

Maldonado thought. "A reservoir off Route 17 above Los Gatos. Not much traffic there this time of year."

"How far?"

"Fifteen minutes at the most."

"Do it. We'll ditch them there."

Phil pushed the rented Ford along while trying to avoid breaking traffic laws in the process. Rush hour was beginning to wane and the going was uninterrupted once they got onto U.S. 280 and bore south at the intersection with 17. As he drove, the major busied himself with the computer printout.

"He was making progress?" Phil asked.

Cardona nodded while continuing to read.

"How much did he have?"

"Enough," Cardona grunted. "The number to the compound in Coral Gables and some other residences. I also recovered your codebook. We appear to have gotten there just in time. You destroyed everything else?"

Maldonado removed the computer disk from his jacket pocket and handed it over. "This is all that is left."

Diego accepted the data and removed a butane lighter from his shirt. He held its flame to one corner until the thing began to curl and melt.

"You did well, Felipe," he said.

Maldonado nodded with relief, eyes on the road ahead.

They approached the cut-off to the Lexington Reservoir. The T-bird swung onto an access road employed by pleasure boaters and bore east. Down the ramp of the boat launch, a crew from one of the local colleges was pulling their shell out of the water. Otherwise, the place was deserted. The two men scanned for other humanity as they continued to roll around the rim of the reservoir. On the farthest eastern shore, they pulled into the shadows of an overhanging tree and parked. A real November chill was beginning to grip the air now. Diego, accustomed to more southern temperatures, turned up the collar of his light silk jacket as he climbed from the car.

"It should roll well from here," he said, pointing down the incline to the water. A further survey of the site told him that the water level seemed to rise and fall dramatically. A high-water line of short green grass and scrub foliage stood a good twelve feet above the present level. With the rainy season coming on, the reservoir could be expected to do nothing but rise in the coming months. His little secret would be safe long past the time when Nicaragua was restored to its proper owners.

"Run down the windows and put it into neutral," he ordered Maldonado.

The engineer complied, knowing that the car would sink faster. With his foot on the brake pedal, he released the door and prepared to climb out. A loud metallic clicking came from behind him. He turned his head abruptly to find the muzzle of the major's automatic trained on his head. His eyes widened in terror.

"I am sorry, Felipe," Diego said. "You performed admirably, but there is no further use for you. There can only be liability connected to your further existence."

As Phil Maldonado made a desperate lunge for the gun, it went off in his face. The bullet penetrated his skull, killing him instantly. Cardona slid the gun into his jacket pocket and walked hurriedly away as the car, now controlled by gravity alone, rolled toward the water.

Ron Dai didn't know when he'd ever been caught so flat-footed. He lay in a bed at Kaiser Hospital, ears ringing and stars swirling before his eyes. Across the valley, at O'Connor Hospital, Maureen Counihan was in the hands of a surgical team, one 9mm bullet lodged against her spine just a hair away from her pancreas and liver. From what Ross Charles could tell him, she had no feeling or movement in either of her legs. The experts were saying that there was no apparent spinal cord injury and that there was a good possibility she suffered from a spinal column trauma called cord shock. Time—and, ultimately, a close look while removing the lodged bullet—would tell.

Dai had suffered little more than a severe blow to the head

and minor scalp laceration. He was being held for observation until the following morning. According to Charles, Pete Davis had vanished without a trace, though a quantity of what appeared to be his blood had been found by forensics people outside his bathroom window. Ron had done what he could to relay what he'd seen in the parking area of the complex. Phil Maldonado had been the one driving the late model Thunderbird, in the company of an unidentified shooter. Charles told him that a massive manhunt was on to find the engineer, now believed to be behind the missing Alamo missile guidance components.

Luck was with them on another front. The SYSTEMATICS mainframe had a special back-up installation that put a temporary lock on all data processed through it for a period of two weeks. Everything Pete Davis had been running was preserved on three-quarter-inch storage tape. As soon as Dai was on his feet, he would stand by as FBI experts took a crack at this stuff. Wherever it pointed, he was going to be on it like a bloodhound. Maureen deserved that much from him. His own pride demanded it as well.

Even in his shaken and addled state, Ron had no trouble reaching back those past few nights to touch the thing that had so quickly developed between them as lovers. He wanted revenge against anyone involved in so abruptly putting the brakes on the best thing that had ever happened in his life.

SEVENTEEN

A short bus ride took Henry Bueno and Cristina Faro through the Costa Rican interior mountains from San Jose to Cartago. From this provincial city they were able to catch a train down onto the coastal plain and into the Caribbean port city of Limon. It was a day-long journey, begun in the early hours of the morning. With the disassembled *Tikka* turkey gun stowed in a new canvas tote and both wearing their new clothes, they projected the image of a middle-income couple on holiday, heading for the miles of glorious sand and surf lining the Costa Rican coast. Cristina wore her hair back in a French braid, a look Henry hadn't seen and heartily approved of. She presented a fresh sort of beauty that had men looking furtively at him with envy in their eyes.

The previous day, Bueno's bank in Monterey, California had wired enough money to finance an extended operation. He'd replenished his belt money with a supply of one-ounce Mexican gold coins and bought more ammunition for both the *Tikka* and the Walther P-5.

Henry had first met Hector Manuel in Guatemala City in 1976. Manuel was an outspoken critic of the Honduran military government. He was a citizen of that country by birth, although he had not lived there for many years. He chose, instead, to divide his time between the New York Latin music

225

scene and the brooding political climate of Mexico City. A bright and articulate man, he maintained an ideology that had become something of a thorn in the side of his native government. His music was a powerful vehicle for exporting political philosophy. He used it to voice demands for change. His following throughout the Latin world, especially in the Caribbean basin, was immense.

On a Saturday night in May, a decade past, four members of the Honduran secret police had violated Guatemala's border with the intention of silencing this rabble-rousing balladeer. The rear door of the salsa club Hector Manuel was working had just been opened when one of the four assassins felt the thrust of the snake hunter's knife. The killer's gun went off as he began to convulse in the throes of death. Bullets spattered harmlessly into the pavement. Two more of the ambush team opened fire in confusion. A startled Manuel dove for cover at the sound of the first shots and narrowly missed being taken out in the ensuing melee. Bueno was hit once, high up on the left shoulder, in the process of killing the remaining members of the Honduran death squad. Hector Manuel paid the doctors who oversaw his recovery.

This Latin musical legend didn't play salsa publicly any longer. The political scene in Central America was just too hot. In the past ten years, another three attempts had been made on his life. In the last, he had escaped with a shattered hip. His wife hadn't been so lucky. She took a piece of shrapnel in the liver and died on the operating table of a hospital in Mexico City. Two years ago, after his wife's death, Hector had pulled up his tent pegs and gone into seclusion. He bought a small *finca* on the Costa Rican coast about twenty miles north of Limon. Now he lived a simple existence, composing music and, rumor had it, working on a book. He walked only with the aid of a cane.

The car Henry had rented took him and Cristina winding along the sea toward Hector's farm as he told her this tale. He'd visited here once, about a year ago, to see how his old friend was getting on. As remote as the place was, it was easy enough to find. Manuel was in seclusion, but not in hiding. The death of his Marta had taken the life from his struggle. Now he lived only to try to understand. Since his disappearance from the music scene, rumors about his condition had abounded. The sales of his records had gone through the roof.

* * *

The musician was in his garden, hoeing a row of lush bean vines as the car bearing Henry and Cristina passed through his gate and moved up the gravel drive toward his house. The place was a riot of flowering vines and bushes, lush and obviously very much loved. The visitors climbed out of the car into the bright sunshine as Manuel shielded his eyes in an attempt to make them out.

"Riberac!" he roared. The hoe was shifted to his left hand as he bent to retrieve his cane. Getting underway, he limped furiously toward them.

"Jesus Maria! Look what the *gato* dragged in!" His face was lit with a smile from ear to ear.

Henry clasped the man in a fierce embrace.

"It's good to see you well, *compadre*," he said. Pulling back, he looked the cloistered folk hero over from head to toe.

"And you, amigo," Hector returned. "Who is the beautiful señorita?"

Bueno introduced *Señora* Cristina Faro. Hector went into the obligatory Latin macho peacock number. Henry rolled his eyes to its conclusion.

"The shit gets any deeper here and you're going to have to provide rubber boots," he groaned. "Are we going to stand in the sun all afternoon, or are you going to invite us inside and offer us a beer?"

Hector's eyes twinkled. "I suppose the beans will be there tomorrow."

Inside the house, their host served Henry a beer and Cristina limeade he'd squeezed that morning from fruit grown on his own trees. They settled into a comfortable open room with a view out across a wide veranda to the sea. A breeze rustled with leaves of banana trees planted all along both sides of the perimeter.

"Rumor had it that the snake hunter had disappeared," Hector told them. "Yet here he is in my living room."

"A ghost," Henry told him, smiling. "The snake hunter *did* disappear. But there was a piece of unfinished business."

Manuel nodded. "Ah, yes. There is always unfinished business, no? A condition of our existence in this imperfect world."

Bueno eyed him carefully, measuring his words. "There is

a Somosista Contra who was once a major in the old general's secret police.''

Hector Manuel's eyes flashed in hatred. There was no disguising how he felt. "You speak of whom I believe you speak and you are after one in league with the devil. Diego Cardona?''

Bueno nodded grimly. "You may have seen accounts of the Colombian army attacking and destroying the hacienda of a trafficker named Guillermo Faro . . . killing him and his family in retaliation for the assassination of the interior minister.''

Manuel's eyes widened. "Yes. I took more than casual note, because I met this Faro some years. . . .'' His voice trailed off. He was staring at Cristina now. "His wife,'' he said. "I had a feeling I had seen you someplace before, señora. It is difficult to forget such a face.''

"I am flattered,'' Cristina said. "It was at least six years ago.''

"In Cali,'' he added. "Your husband invited me to your table. I am very sorry. Please accept my deepest condolences.''

"He was framed by this Major Cardona,'' she said bluntly.

"I believe that he is not only responsible for Willie Faro's murder, but also for the killing of a man I owe my life to,'' Henry said. "We seek him now. You've always kept one ear to the ground. What can you tell us about this man's activities?''

Hector Manuel related what he called an "underground history'' of recent Central American events to his friend and his friend's beautiful companion. He made no comment on the body language evident between them.

"Many people believe that the Sandinista government of Daniel Ortega has betrayed the revolution in Nicaragua,'' he began. Then he smiled and shrugged. "I do not know anymore. There is the stuff of political theory, and there is the practical matter of trying to govern a bankrupt people. Indeed, as the saying goes, power does corrupt. All men, even idealists, are human. I am sure that is at least part of the story. The fragmented pockets of purists who feel they have been betrayed have set aside their differences to fight the common enemy of their betrayal. It is ironic that once the Sandinistas did this very same thing. Now *they* wear the mantle of power, and others envy them. As you know, those the American government would lump into the Contra camp are a truly mixed bag of ideologues. Perhaps the vilest worm in the apple is the Somosista. The disenfranchised aristocracy. The man you speak of, Cardona, is one of the worst of these. As a major in the secret police, he was infamous as a sadistic murderer. His activities, if one pieces them together, make a fascinating tale of counterrevolutionary plotting and drug trafficking. They are linked.''

"How so, exactly?" Henry asked.

Manuel shrugged. "You know that a revolution costs money. Even the Somosista, with all his hidden wealth, cannot afford to wage a war of any magnitude without an influx of capital. Drugs are money. Very big money. The more you can control of the American cocaine market, the better you finance your revolution *and* increase your personal power in the shaping of a new government.''

Henry and Cristina glanced at each other.

"Willie told me that he suspected Cardona of being behind the collapse of his network in the States," Bueno said. "He thought that this guy was well on his way toward cornering that market.''

"The rumors I hear would also suggest this," Manuel replied. "Your Major Cardona has become a very big player in the cocaine game. Others have fallen besides Willie Faro. I hear of serious volume being funneled through Quintana Roo and the Yucatán and then on up to Texas, Louisiana, and the West Coast. The masterminds are not Mexican, I am assured. There is a Somosista stronghold in Coral Gables. More than a dozen of Somoza-DeBayle's highest-ranking military officers and cabinet members live in close proximity there. They have organized well, with Cardona moving freely about as their ambassador of enforcement and terror.''

Bueno sat deep in thought now. His mind wandered from this room and back to that afternoon he'd brought his boat to harbor on Monterey Bay. When Cam Stebbins had handed him that envelope, it had all seemed cut and dried. The ground had refused to stay put beneath his feet ever since. He had a direction now. Hector had confirmed everything Willie's own intelligence had gathered.

"Coral Gables," he said.

"It would make the most sense," Hector said, as if reading his mind.

"I beg your pardon?" Cristina asked.

Henry paused to explain. "If we want Diego Cardona, we either find him there or we twist one of his buddy's arms and ask him where Cardona's currently hiding."

Left eye squinted shut and right eye sighting through the scope toward a chunk of styrofoam Henry had propped in the sand, Cristina pressed her cheek to the cool walnut stock of the *Tikka* rifle.

"Try to relax," Bueno's voice came from behind her. "Think of the trigger as an avocado you're squeezing to see if it's ripe. Nice, steady, even pressure. Don't forget about any peripheral danger, but don't allow it to interfere with immediate concentration. Now, take a breath and let it halfway out."

She followed his instruction. As the air was being pushed from her lungs, the rifle suddenly jerked in her hands. The piece of styrofoam flipped in the air.

"On your left!" Henry shouted.

Her thumb was already on the conversion switch, pushing it from rifle to shotgun. A fat green coconut came laterally into her field of vision as she swung the rifle up to track it. The jarring jolt of a twelve-gauge discharge was very different from a rifle shot, but she'd prepared herself for it. As the stock rammed back into her right shoulder, the coconut exploded in a spray of minute wet particles.

"Good," Henry's calm voice came again. "Now once more. Relax."

The Styrofoam danced again, and this time a coconut exploded a dozen feet from her on the right, at head height.

Hector Manuel limped toward the pair up the beach. The tip of his cane sinking in the sand made the going difficult. Bueno moved to meet him. The breeze tousled their hair as they stood beside the surf. It was a sparkling clear Caribbean evening. The sun had fallen almost to the mountaintops behind them, and all was tranquil as far as the eye could see.

"A quick study," Hector observed.

"Looks often deceive," Bueno said sagely. "This one is a natural."

"A seaplane will take you to the other side of Cuba

tonight. A cigarette boat will pick you up about thirty miles off the Keys.''

''Quick work,'' Bueno complimented his old friend.

''I do not like this man any more than you do. Never have I entertained the pleasant prospect of sending him so formidable an adversary.'' He handed Henry a piece of paper. ''The location of the Somosista headquarters estate in Coral Gables was easy enough to obtain. There are a great many who wish you Godspeed in your quest.''

Bueno fingered the paper, looking Hector in the eye. ''It has been good to see you again, friend.''

Even with Peter Davis and Phil Maldonado disposed of, it was only a matter of time before the FBI put together something that pointed to the Florida Somosista contingent. Ted Latham would be powerless to carry his revelation to the president's close advisors if a different story had already surfaced through competitive channels. The people in Coral Gables would have to be ready to take appropriate action. Diego Cardona knew he had to push for immediate implementation on his end. SYSTEMATICS had been chosen specifically by Latham's people because it was a small fish swimming in a very large pond. Not small enough, it had turned out.

The major deplaned in Mexico City, passed through customs, and took a cab around the airport to a freight hangar on the very outskirts of the sprawling runway system. His pilot had the Cessna idling at the ready. Providencia Island was only a short hop away and San Andres a quick boat ride further.

The tiny, single-engined amphibious plane circled slowly, losing altitude over the darkened Caribbean. Henry and Cristina peered out at the black, gleaming water below them. There was a flash of light . . . and another. In the cockpit, the pilot eased back on the yoke, dropping the flaps all the way down as they skimmed the surface of the sea and settled. The plane was carried forward by momentum only now as they idled. Bueno twisted in his seat to release the fuselage door.

Outside, a short distance away, throaty engine noises announced the arrival of their next conveyance. As the inboard drifted into view, the pilot reached out to shake hands.

"We appreciate this," Henry told him.

The man shook his head. "It is I who should be thanking you, señor. Mine is the collective gratitude of many people you will never meet."

Bueno smiled and grabbed the hand. "Then wish us luck, amigo."

The massive cigarette boat came alongside, hull gently nudging the right pontoon of the plane. Henry moved to grab the gunwale with one hand and help Cristina over with the other. Hands reached out of the gloom to assist her. Their gear went next and Bueno last.

There were two men aboard the boat, neither of them much older than twenty-one or -two. Both were armed with automatic weapons. They looked Bueno and Cristina over carefully. The bigger of the two locked eyes with Henry.

"Hector's message is to help and ask no questions. We will take you ashore on a stretch of road near the Keys. You will find a car there. I would advise disposing of it before sunup."

Henry nodded, the hint of a smile in his eyes.

"How hot *is* it?"

"Before sunup," the man repeated. Turning without another word, he revved the massive power plant. The two passengers huddled below the windscreen as the boat suddenly lunged forward, the furor of its engine deafening now.

The plane that had brought them so close to the United States disappeared behind them, swallowed by the night. Pressed hard against his chest, Cristina turned from looking back for it to search Bueno's eyes. He drew a reassuring hand around her shoulders and kissed her forehead.

In the dead of night, on a remote stretch of beach, an eerie calm lay on the Florida Keys. The heavy air smelled of salt and the lush vegetation crowding them on all sides. The car Hector's friends had provided proved to be a fully loaded 1985 Corvette, gunmetal gray. Just looking at it made Henry nervous.

"Sweet mother," he muttered as he opened the minuscule trunk to stow their gear. "What do those jokers think this is, the movies?"

The plates were local, most likely from another car, or so

he hoped. He had to trust his old friend's judgment on this one. Everything else had gone off without a hitch. Still, the Corvette was a little too James Bond. With Cristina buckled in beside him, he settled into his contoured seat and fired up the car. Once on the main road, he would have to concentrate on staying within the speed limit.

They drove north, eventually crossing the causeway to terra firma at Florida City and taking US 1 on up to Coral Gables. The night was warm and balmy, the temperature hovering around the mid-seventies. At an hour after midnight, teenagers were still hanging out in front of a Burger King as Henry swung off a main drag and onto residential streets. It was a nice area that had been predominantly white for years but recently had been getting a healthy smattering of wealthy Latinos. There were wide lawns, palms, and lots of tropical foliage. Henry stopped on a well-lit boulevard to ask directions at a filling station. When the pimple-faced, spiky-haired attendant proved ignorant of local geography, he consulted the map taped to the station door. From the look of it, the Somosista house lay in a section of town where the real estate spread out a bit. The spaces between the streets grew and the frequency of them diminished. Back on the road with a sense of where they were heading, Henry had no trouble finding the area. The spaces between houses was increasing in direct proportion to the size of the houses themselves. There were thick hedges and electric gates. Henry had the Corvette at a crawl as they drifted through their immediate target area, searching for a street name.

Hibiscus. He pushed on slowly past, straining to peer down a deep cul-de-sac. There was only one streetlight and from what he could make out down there, just two gates. Another block further down, he swung around, pulled onto the shoulder on the opposite side of the road, and shut down the engine.

"I'm going in alone," he announced.

"What?" Cristina demanded.

"We don't know what might happen in there. You're going to have to back me up. We may have to get out of here in a real hurry."

"I didn't come this far to sit outside and wait," she argued.

Henry shook his head. "You're not looking at the whole

233

operation. You're only focusing on *your* motives. You can't do that now. It might get either one of us killed.''

''So *you* are going in there alone?'' she challenged. ''What are *your* chances?''

''I've done this sort of thing before, and I'm still here to tell you about it. You've just got to trust me. This is precisely the sort of thing I've been trained for.''

''He killed my husband and destroyed my life,'' she said with passion.

''And we don't even know that he's in there. Just give me thirty minutes and then pull this thing up and park it over there.'' He pointed to the corner of Hibiscus and the boulevard they were on. ''Keep it running. If I'm gone any more than ten minutes after that, leave.'' He took a small notepad and a pen from his breast pocket, jotted something, tore off the leaf, and handed it to her.

''If it comes down to your leaving, go to a phone and call this number collect. You'll get a special operator. Tell them you've got a message for Deputy Director Stebbins. Just say Bueno is down. Hibiscus Court. Coral Gables. Then hang up.''

She looked curiously at him, as if seeing him differently. ''Bueno? That is your true name or a joke?''

He reached out and brushed his fingers across her cheek.

''Might be either. I've often wondered the same thing.''

The Walther P-5 came out of his waistband. He checked the magazine out of habit, thumbed off the safety, and returned it. Without another word, he climbed out into the balmy Florida night, opened the trunk, and grabbed the *Tikka*. Dressed in black from head to toe, he completed the effect by pulling on a pair of skin-tight black leather gloves. Three extra clips for the Walther and a half-dozen twelve-gauge shells went into his pockets. He slammed the trunk, slung the rifle over his shoulder, and turned to give Cristina the thumbs up. She forced a smile.

''Under protest,'' she said.

''Just be there when I come flying down the street,'' he instructed.

Hector's information indicated the Somosista compound was at the end of the cul-de-sac on the right. Henry rounded the corner from the boulevard, staying low and hugging the shadows of dense foliage that crowded the street. It was a well-chosen location, with a clear view from the gate of any approaching traffic. From atop a small, unobtrusive gatehouse, he caught the glint of a surveillance camera as it swept the area. The gate itself, suspended between a pair of sturdy sandstone pillars, appeared to be well secured. There was no sense in attempting to gain access from that direction.

Henry pressed into the adjacent shrubbery and burrowed his way forward until he encountered a chain link fence. Carefully, he wet a finger and tapped it. No shock. That only meant that the fence proper had no current running through it. Up above, he noticed a single strand of wire, punctuated every eight feet by insulators. From his pants pocket, he removed a six-foot length of insulated wire secured at each end by alligator clips. It was nice that Hector still dabbled with amplification and recording apparatus for his own amusement. Henry scaled the fence, clipped his own wire along the length of the electrified wire, and clipped out the offensive section with a pair of diagonal cutters. Good old Hector. Henry lifted the *Tikka* over the top, gripped it by the barrel, and executed a perfect forward hand vault, pushing away hard with his hands at the apex release point with the power and grace of a gymnast. He landed feet first on a stretch of open lawn. Across it he could see a tennis court, pool, and rambling Spanish-style house with red tile roof. In the distance, a dog barked. There were several lights on in the house, and through an open garage door he could make out the ass end of a late-model Jaguar. With no time to waste, he scooted along the perimeter defined by the fence, heading for a clump of citrus trees that fronted the adjoining Somosista estate.

There was a ten-foot stone wall along this stretch. He worked it quickly, spotting two more cameras. They were purposely set out of sync to enable one to catch anything the other was temporarily blind to. Almost. There was a period of about eight seconds when both could not see an area dead-center between them. Henry gauged the wall there. With only eight seconds in which to act, it was going to take a decisive move. A running leap and decent foot plant would get him to the top of the wall. Another hand vault would get him either over it or knocked cold by the rifle slung across his back. Once on the other side, he'd have no time to adjust for a moat

235

infested with water moccasins or alligators. Worst-case scenario, as the current jargon had it.

He timed the approach with precision, hitting the wall about a third of the way up with his right foot, pushing off hard and grabbing hold of the parapet with both hands. The rifle across his back, true to anticipated form, banged him in the head as he hoisted and used his arms to fling himself over in a wide arc. There were no snakes, alligators, or watery depths. Just a wide-open, completely exposed lawn. He landed, feeling unnervingly naked, went quickly prone, and hugged mother earth. After a few seconds, he dared to lift his head and peer around. No dogs came rushing to tear his throat out.

The house was the same style but bigger than the one next door. Beyond a large swimming pool, he could make out half-a-dozen cars parked along a sweeping circular drive. All of the windows on the ground floor were caged with wrought-iron bars. Several paramilitary types stood around smoking cigarettes and looking bored. The Uzis they carried looked anything but boring.

Henry unsheathed his knife, clamped it between his teeth, and began to work his way across the lawn on his belly. His target was a terrace over a section of the house that jutted toward the pool. A pair of French doors led onto it, one of them slightly ajar behind a bug screen and revealing a darkened interior. At about twenty yards from this objective, an ornamental lime tree grew in the middle of the lawn. Henry paused in the tight shadow beneath it to study the fatigue-clad guards a moment. The one nearest the pool had a small portable radio propped atop a low retaining wall. He was listening to soft, sensuous salsa, with hips gyrating just perceptibly to the beat. His observer guessed that his mind was a long way from his job.

A second guard stood idly near the corner of the house by the driveway. He faced away from the man in back, intent on watching a pair of chauffeurs next to cars parked close by. It appeared that some sort of high-level meeting was in progress. The cars were top-of-the-line: a Rolls Corniche and a Mercedes 550SEL. Bueno licked his lips and then made his move on the preoccupied, dancing guard.

The man never knew what hit him. Henry rendered him unconscious with a blow to the base of his skull, gagged him, and bound his hands and feet with adhesive tape. Still out, he was dragged to sit propped upright atop the retaining wall. Henry wasted no time admiring his handiwork. He hurried to a ground-level window, took hold of the iron bars, and used them to climb to where he could reach the bannister of the balustrade surrounding the terrace above. Half a minute later, he stood outside the screened doors, listening.

Muffled sounds came to him from inside the house. In this immediate room, there was the sound of steady, even breathing. Someone was asleep. He tried the door to find it locked—a simple hook-and-eye affair. With the tip of his knife, he slit the screen and reached inside. The door freed, he entered silently, paused on the plush carpet underfoot, and let his eyes adjust.

A young blond woman, perhaps twenty-five and very naked, lay sprawled across a king-size bed. In the dim light, Henry had difficulty with features, but none with a round mirror that lay on the end table near her head. White powder, a razor blade, and what appeared to be a silver straw littered its surface.

Placing one foot carefully in front of the other, he moved past the end of the bed to the door. The P-5 came out of his waistband. He applied pressure on the ornate brass door lever until he heard the mechanism release. Through a quarter-inch crack between the door and jamb, he scanned the hallway outside. It was lit more for atmosphere than visibility. Fancy little prism-decked sconces glowed softly every six or seven feet along one wall. A hardwood floor was covered down the midway with a deep crimson runner. From here, voices could be heard distinctly, drifting up from the floor below. There was music mixed in with the heavy odor of cigar smoke. Bueno slipped out of the bedroom and moved off to locate the source of the merriment.

At the end of the hall, one wall gave way to the right, opening on a wide landing that ran a dozen feet to the head of a grand mahogany staircase. The thing swept down and half around on itself, arriving in a marble entrance gallery that fairly gleamed. Off it, the great double doors of a library stood open. Bits and pieces of many conversations, laughter, and glass-clinking floated up to Henry as he leaned forward to locate other adjoining rooms. Most of the conversation seemed to be in English, with either easy American vernacular fluency or heavy Latin overtones. Male voices mixed with female. As Henry hid in shadow, listening, a man in black tie crossed the gallery after leaving a powder room. A servant crossed carrying a tray of hors d'oeuvres. Henry checked his watch. Twenty-two minutes had passed since he had left Cristina in the Corvette. He had less than twenty more to determine Cardona's whereabouts before she left him hanging. Time to get close.

The *Tikka* was unslung and switched to shotgun. He gripped it by the stock, like a pistol, with his right hand as he hefted the Walther in his left. As quietly as a night-stalking cat, he slipped down the stairs and paused beside the library door.

There were nine of them in there, two of them well-heeled Americans with good-looking younger women in evening dresses parked on a nearby settee. The other five appeared to be Hispanic. Henry couldn't tell right away if one of the three males was the infamous Major Cardona. None seemed to fit the descriptions he'd been given, but he had never seen even a photograph of the man. One of the men was quite a bit older, with an elegantly coiffed head of steel-gray hair. A second was perhaps Cardona's age but heavyset, and the third was just a kid. There were two more women, one a tightly wound dowager type decked with enough diamonds and emeralds to satisfy a maharajah's wife. The other was a contemporary of the youngest male and pretty in a full-lipped, pouty way. Brandy and champagne were flowing. There must have been half an ounce of cocaine dumped out on the glass-topped coffee table in front of the settee. The two American girls were hunched over and inhaling as much as they could get their eager nostrils on.

"To our arrangement," the steel-haired Hispanic said grandiosely, raising his brandy.

The others raised their glasses and echoed his sentiment.

"May it be most profitable to us all," one of the Yanks added. "And to your Señor Cardona. It is unfortunate that he could not be here after all the work he did on this."

"The major is not a man to rest on his laurels," the heavyset Nicaraguan said. "There is much to be looked after in an enterprise such as ours."

Bueno had heard most everything he needed to know. If Cardona wasn't among the present company, he was going to have to learn his whereabouts from one of these players. The kid was clearly part of the enterprise, and just as clearly the most ill-at-ease.

The servant with the tray started to leave the room. Henry let him pass and then took him out with a knuckle punch to the base of the skull. When the tray hit the floor with a resounding crash, the assembled company looked up, startled. Their eyes locked on the menacing snake hunter, the muzzles of his two guns trained on them. The heavyset Nicaraguan went to the inside of his jacket.

"I wouldn't," Bueno snarled. "It'd be the last thing you ever did."

The man froze and withdrew his hand slowly.

"Anyone else?" Henry asked quietly. "Take my advice. A better night for acting the hero will present itself. Here, the odds are stacked heavily against you."

"What the hell?" one of the Americans demanded.

"Quiet!" Henry snapped. He turned his attentions to the kid. "Where is your Major Cardona?"

The youngster was in his very early twenties and nervous enough without guns trained on him. To be singled out and asked such a question appeared to mortify him. He glanced nervously at his two older compatriots and got stern glares but little else by way of support. He shook his head resolutely.

"I do not know," he managed.

"We'll see," Henry said with a leer. "You're coming with me. The rest of you are going to lie face down on the floor."

Outraged as the assembled company was, its members had little choice but to comply. Bueno leaned the *Tikka* against a wall some distance away, reached inside his shirt, and withdrew a fat roll of adhesive tape. He approached the young Nicaraguan and handed it to him.

"Wrists crossed behind their backs. Mouths and ankles. Let's go."

The kid looked bewildered, wondering with evident panic why he was being singled out like this. With Henry's gun to his head, he started in, doing one of the American men first. The process took about ten minutes, and Henry realized he was running short on time. Once the dowager was trussed up, he stooped to remove her jewelry, wrapped it in one of the gent's handkerchiefs, and then directed the kid toward the front door.

"Who belongs to the Corniche?" he asked.

"One of them," the youngster answered, jerking his head toward the two trussed Americans.

"Those two guys out there chauffeurs?"

"Yes."

"Good. Then they'll have the keys, and we can take a little ride."

They'd reached the big door to the front portico: massive, dark-stained oak timber with wrought-iron hardware.

"You first," he told the kid. "Hand on the knob and pull it open nice and easy, like you don't have a care in the world."

The young man turned the knob slowly as the phone at the foot of the stairs began to ring. It continued ringing incessantly as they passed outside and into the full view of the two chauffeurs and one guard in the drive.

EIGHTEEN

Roscoe Charles also suffered from the knowledge that he'd been caught flat-footed. Along with the woman's father, he now lingered outside the operating theatre of O'Connor Hospital, awaiting any word on Maureen Counihan's condition. The surgical team had been in there with her for six hours now.

The double doors to the surgical area banged open, and a tired looking pair of doctors dressed in greens emerged.

"How is she?" Bill Counihan asked anxiously.

One of the two, an orthopedic surgeon, placed a hand on his shoulder reassuringly. "We got the bullet. It was lodged against the spine but not in it. No cord damage. She's a very lucky girl."

"When can I see her?" Counihan asked.

"Be awhile yet," the doctor told him. "We've got a plastic surgeon in there closing the abdominal incision. Trying to make it pretty. She'll be in postop for a while after that. You ought to go get some rest and see her in the morning."

Ross Charles was greatly relieved as he drove his government sedan back across the valley to Kaiser Hospital and detective Ron Dai. Bad bang on the head or not, the guy was pretty shaken up about the lady's condition and would want to know that she was going to be fine.

It was pretty late and well past visiting hours when Charles

241

showed his credentials at the nurses' station and slipped into Dai's room. The detective, asleep at that point, came awake instantly.

"What's the word, Ross?" he asked anxiously.

"No spinal cord damage, Ronnie. She's going to be fine. We helicoptered down the best in the West from the University of California Med Center up in San Francisco. A plastic surgeon is closing up after him to minimize scar tissue."

"Any word on Davis or the APB on Maldonado?" Dai asked.

"Zip. They just disappeared, along with that damn T-bird. We had a partial plate and traced it to a rental agency at the SF airport. Dead end. Credit cards and ID stolen off some sap from Indiana who was visiting Disney World in Orlando."

"Did you get the computer back-up tape from SYSTEM-ATICS?"

"Not a problem," Charles assured him. "I talked to Washington, and they're flying out some hotshot agency or military code expert by sunup. We'll get it unscrambled. We know it was Maldonado on this end now, and I think Pete was heading somewhere when they got to him. I just hope the damn code will shed some light."

"It's our best shot. Maybe our only shot," Dai said, depression edging his voice.

The Bureau man frowned. "Stop kicking yourself, Ronnie. *We're* the ones who select and train these jerks."

The detective nodded in resignation. "It's just the sort of crap I worry about when I come up against a cowboy like Pete. The jackass thought he could do it all on his own. Probably bucking for the big boot upstairs. Now you've got to call his mother and tell her the kid she raised to be a hot dog might not be coming home for Christmas. I feel sorry for you."

"A shame I can't use just those words."

"Yeah, it is."

"Got any ideas how you'll want to play it from here?" Ross asked.

"Me?" Dai shot back, as though there'd been any doubt. "I'm in to the end. They want to keep me in this dive any longer than tomorrow morning, they're going to have to tie me down. Just get this so-called hotshot to work on that data.

I'll be by before noon to see how you're getting on. I want to see how Maureen's doing first.''

Diego Cardona slammed the receiver down in disgust, stood, and stalked out onto the veranda to where Jack Terranova and Anna sat.

"What do you figure's up?" the hitter asked.

"Still no answer," Diego growled. "They were supposed to be there tonight. A celebration of a new distribution arrangement with two large-quantity people from Los Angeles. It has been ten minutes since I contacted others in the area to have them try the number. They have not called back.''

Almost on cue, the phone rang. Cardona was on his feet in a flash, hurrying to answer it.

"There is no answer, Don Diego," the voice reported. "Nothing. It just rings. I have contacted the phone company, and there is no trouble with the line.''

"Then get on over there," Diego snapped. "See what the hell is going on, and report back to me. Immediately.''

He slammed the receiver back into the cradle in fury. Something was wrong, he knew it in his guts. The FBI man's computer printout had phone numbers on it. Miami numbers. The estate would now have to be abandoned for the fallback locations. If any of the big people were arrested or threatened with deportation, the entire cocaine machine could come apart on him. He needed it intact until they could return to the homeland and set it up permanently there. On top of that, he needed to attend to the Alamo shipments headed for Big Corn in the next few days. He *didn't* need any other trouble now.

The three men standing in the drive looked up as Bueno and the young Nicaraguan appeared on the front porch. The uniformed guard saw the *Tikka* rifle and started to swing his Uzi around. He was too late. Henry dropped him with a silenced 9mm shot while still covering the other two goons with the *Tikka*. They realized they were caught, didn't want to end up dead, and raised their hands.

"Real slowly," Henry instructed them. "Weapons out and in front of you on the ground.''

They complied without hesitation.

"Now, walk backward and open the trunk of the Benz, whichever of you has the keys.''

"They're in the ignition," one man said.

"Fine. Get them. You do anything dumb in the process and it'll have to be a closed-casket funeral."

When the man complied and got the trunk of the 550 open, Henry ordered both of them inside and slammed the lid on them.

"Okay," he said to the kid. "You drive the Rolls. Is there anyone manning the gate?"

"The woman of the guard you just killed," the young man replied sullenly.

"A nice smile for her," Henry warned him. "When she opens up, drive to the corner and stop."

They climbed into the Rolls Royce. The kid started it and steered toward the front gate.

"No heroics," Henry murmured as the woman appeared at the door of the gatehouse, ambled to the gate, and ran it back on its little rubber wheels. He waved as they passed through. "That Corvette just up ahead. Pull in right in front of it."

After they were parked, Bueno glanced into the sideview mirror to pick out Cristina's face behind the windscreen of the sports car. He ran down the window and waved to her.

"Now," he said, aiming the pistol at the young man's chest. "What do you know about a Colombian named Willie Faro?"

The kid's eyes widened in uncontrollable fear.

"That answers the first question," Henry said. "You're doing fine. Second question. Where can I find an American mobster named Jack Terranova?"

Those eyes widened again as the kid swallowed hard.

"This time that isn't good enough," Bueno said, shaking his head.

The kid's lower lip began to tremble as though he were ready to burst into tears. Henry snapped back the action of the automatic.

"Sensitive, this trigger." He smiled pleasantly. "It's been a long day, and I'm kind of tired. I might not even mean to, but the longer I have my hands on a gun like this, the better the chances are of its going off. By accident, of course. But then, you wouldn't be around to hear my apology, would you?"

Beads of cold sweat broke out on the kid's forehead and upper lip. His jaw muscles bunched involuntarily. He was changing color, staring down the muzzle of that gun.

"San Andres Island," he croaked. Tears welled up in his eyes. They were the hot tears of shame. He was betraying his cause, just as Henry knew he would. After years of this work, he'd learned to look at a group of men and pick out the ones who couldn't stand the idea of pain or death.

"And Diego?" he demanded. "Is he there with him?"

The kid shook his head. "I do not know. Perhaps. He went to California. San Jose."

This piece of information puzzled Bueno.

"Why?" he demanded.

The kid decided suddenly that he had said enough. He clenched his teeth and stared at Bueno defiantly. Without hesitation, Henry clubbed him in the face with the butt of the pistol, cutting him deeply across one cheek.

"Why?" he asked again.

Stoically, the young man shook his head.

With his free hand, Bueno grabbed his left wrist, jerked it back on itself, and heard something snap. The kid screamed in anguish.

"Nobody can hear you," Henry told him calmly. "This is a Rolls Royce, remember? I'm willing to bet you heard about a certain aircraft mechanic down in Pitalito. Maybe you got a good description of the poor man's knees. Now, why did your Major Cardona go to California?"

The kid gulped, glanced at the gun, and then squeezed his eyes shut. As if he were reciting a religious litany, he began to spill the beans. When he had finished revealing some startling material, he collapsed in a choking mass of self-pity. Quietly, Bueno reached for the door handle and let himself out. Moments later, he was sitting beside Cristina as she maneuvered the Corvette along deserted Coral Gables streets. She handled the five-speed gearbox expertly.

"Well?" she asked at length.

"We're getting somewhere," he said, sighing and rubbing his tired eyes. As they moved through the streetlamp-lit gloom, he related what the youngster had told him. When he finished, he reached inside his shirt to remove a handkerchief wrapped around a gleaming mass of emeralds and diamonds.

"I realize there is no true compensation," he said. "Still, I thought you should have these rather than the parasite I found wearing them."

It infuriated Diego Cardona to be forced back to Florida at such a critical time. Another high-speed boat trip to Providencia and a flight all through what remained of the night brought him to Opa-Locka at 6:05 A.M. Because he'd been unable to reach the house, he was forced to pay a cabbie to take him to Coral Gables. He was dead on his feet and extremely irritable as he emerged from the taxi on the corner of Hibiscus and approached the place cautiously on foot.

A guard who had been off duty the previous night and had arrived home just half an hour earlier now approached the gate nervously.

"Enrique. What the hell is going on? No one answers the telephone, and I am forced to fly all the way up here from San Andres."

The guard shook his head noncommittally. "I think you better go up to the house, Major. There has been trouble."

"What sort of trouble?" Diego demanded.

"A man broke in here last night, over the wall, we think. Tomaso is dead. He took Ramon Lopez."

Without further conversation, Cardona squeezed past and bolted up the drive at a dead run. The house seemed tranquil enough from the outside. The interior was anything but. As the major passed through the front door, he found people moving everywhere. Boxes were being stacked in the gallery. A weary-looking Carlos Ortiz, once Diego's commanding officer before he left the national guard for the secret police, directed the operation.

"Carlos," Diego called out as he hurried up to the silver-haired older man. "I have been trying to reach you for over eight hours."

Ortiz looked up with obvious relief.

"Jesus, Mother, Diego. We were tied up on the library floor. The phone rang often, but we were unable to answer it."

"What in hell happened?"

The old man shrugged in bewilderment. "The bastard walked right in here last night, killed Tomaso, humiliated our guests, and took Ramon Lopez. There is no telling how badly the operation has been compromised. The entire distribution agreement with the Los Angelenos has fallen through. He even stole Friedman's Rolls Royce.''

Diego was beside himself. "Who? What man?"

"We have no idea. None of us had ever seen him before. All of us were left trussed up on this floor. Tomaso tried to stop him as he left and was gunned down.''

Damn, Cardona thought, pacing the library floor. Latham had assured him the man on his trail was good, but good enough to have traced them all the way from Cali to Coral Gables? He pressed his thumb and forefinger to his temples.

"There is no sign of Ramon?" he asked.

"None. We have contacted the hospitals to see if an accident was reported. So far, nothing. This man was a master, Diego. There was nothing we could do to prevent this.''

"I do not blame you, Carlos. If it is the man I suspect, he is even better than you think. We are pushing the timetable now. Luis is directing the transfer operation on San Andres at this moment. They will be ready to leave for Big Corn on tonight's tide.''

Carlos Ortiz nodded. "We will clear out of here within the hour and withdraw to the safe house." Even as he spoke, a truck rumbled up the drive and squealed to a halt. Men began carrying cartons outside to it.

An hour and a half later, a driver held the back door of a Cadillac limousine as Diego Cardona stepped out onto the crabgrass verge of an Opa-Locka airport runway. The Cessna Turbo-Prop hunkered nose into the wind, engines idling. Carlos Ortiz peered up at his former junior officer from the recess of the Caddy's back seat.

"Be careful, my friend," he advised. "This man is like the devil himself."

"We have come too far and done too much," Diego replied, his jaw set with determination. "I will not be defeated on the eve of victory. You and the others trusted me, Carlos. I will not fail you."

The aging colonel smiled benevolently on his warrior. He was an able combatant. He had proven himself in the face of adversity many times over. A brilliant tactician and unscrupulous infighter. Totally dedicated to the glory of their Nicaragua.

"The thought never entered my mind," he said reassuringly.

Only minutes later, the Cessna climbed into the bleached blue Florida sky, winging south out over the Caribbean. Diego Cardona sat alone in the cabin, staring out a side port, attempting to assess the damage situation. Ramon had undoubtedly been tortured and killed. He had to assume that the operation was compromised. The only way he could determine the extent of the breach was to wait for its engineer to surface. This man Bueno. If a young weakling like Ramon had talked, then the man would come. While the operation moved on to Big Corn, he would leave Jack Terranova behind to do battle with him. Fire with fire, as the saying went.

Cardona knew his greatest enemy now was the clock. He could be in position in a day. For now, that was all the time he needed.

Maureen Counihan was still a little groggy from the previous night's anesthetic when Ron Dai approached her bedside in the intensive care unit. His head was encircled with a bandage, and he was feeling a little unsteady himself.

"Hi, stranger," he said, reaching down to take her hand.

"I guess I fucked it up, huh?" she asked. "God, I feel like I've been hit by a truck."

"You're alive," he said with a grin. "You should know how good it feels for me to be able to say that."

"And you're a sweetheart, detective. I guess this puts a dent in our extracurricular activities for a while, huh?"

"You just worry about getting strong again."

"They got away, didn't they?"

"Clean," he confirmed. "But maybe not quite clean enough. The Bureau has the tapes from the company back-up system. They've got code experts running them now. I'm on my way over there from here."

She focused on his head bandage with concern. "You feeling okay?"

"Well enough. I'm going to get these sons of bitches."

There was a momentary silence as they looked deep into each other's eyes. This was one hell of a way to end their ride through the tunnel of love.

"Be careful, Ron," she begged. "I think it'd be nice to be able to pick up where we left off once I get out of here."

"Don't worry too much about me not coming back. You're not going to get rid of me that easily."

When Dai left the hospital, he was driven by an FBI man at Ross Charles's insistence. He figured it was all for the best. His head insisted on spinning on its own once in a while. On their way to the FBI field office, the driver got a radio call directing him to Lexington Reservoir at Agent Charles's request. They altered course and pulled up into a group of Sheriff's Department cars, unmarked sedans, and a tow truck on the far eastern bank. Ross Charles, already on the scene, was conferring with a coroner's man as they climbed out of the car.

"How are you feeling?" he asked Dai on his approach.

"Better than Maureen," the detective reported. "What's up here?"

"Jogger saw a car go into the drink here last night. Your department couldn't do much in the dark, but they sent divers in this morning. They're down there now, hooking a tow line up to the rear axle of a new Thunderbird. There's a body behind the wheel, one bullet hole in the left temple."

Just behind them, the engine of the tow truck began to growl, and the winch barrel slowly turned, reeling in cable. A coroner's meat wagon churned up dust along the access road from the highway, hurrying to join the action. In another few minutes, the rear of the waterlogged Ford appeared, taillights first. Everyone in an official capacity moved in for a better look. Dai saw it clear enough from about six feet away to know it was Phil Maldonado in there. Why, he wondered? He'd been playing for the other team, and they'd gone and whacked him.

A combined team of county and FBI men began going over the corpse and car with a fine-toothed comb. It was another fifteen minutes before they popped the trunk and found Peter Davis with his trachea crushed. Ross Charles could now tell the dead man's mother that he would definitely not be coming home for Christmas.

"How were they doing on the code when you left?" Ron asked Ross as they stepped away from the grisly scene.

Charles wiggled one hand back and forth. "The kid had made a lot of progress already. The whole numeric code was broken. Phone numbers, almost all of them in the Miami area. We forwarded them to the field office down there for checking. The alphabetical code seems to be a bit trickier. One of the army's best is being flown in from D.C. If our guys haven't gotten it by noon, he'll crack it soon after."

Dai walked a little further with Charles.

"How strange does the murder of Maldonado strike you?"

"Curious, isn't it? We've got him down as one of the bad guys, and he winds up just as dead as *our* boy, in the same car."

"You know what it says to me?" the detective asked. "The kingpin in this little game is playing for some very high stakes. He's willing to do whatever it takes to completely wipe out his trail. They destroyed Pete's computer, and there were no disks anywhere to be found. It gives me a theory." He paused, and Ross Charles looked to him expectantly. "The bastards think they've plugged the leak out here. Maldonado was the man on the inside, so he's the only one who would be familiar enough with the SYSTEMATICS mainframe system to know about the back-up feature. Hell, I doubt if that skinny little weasel we saw at the scene knew that Davis had his home unit piggybacked with the bigger machine."

Ross Charles thought it over and started to smile.

"You're thinking pretty fast for a guy who just took a good whack on the noodle."

"All I'm saying is that we could get lucky here. Whatever that code ends up revealing, we've got to be prepared to jump all over it."

From his conversation with the young Nicaraguan the previous night, Henry Bueno had learned that there was something very rotten inside the same government intelligence network he might have otherwise turned to at this point. The kid hadn't known enough specifics to pinpoint the rot. He knew the name Latham, though, and that was a good place to start. Ted Latham was connected to Cam Stebbins, so what was the deputy director's involvement? There were unnamed others, in different walks of national security intelligence. Getting to the bottom of this rat's nest could take months. He didn't have anywhere near that kind of time. More like days. His most immediate target was still Major Diego Cardona. The kid's information had him operating from the Colombian island of San Andres, a couple hundred miles off the Nicaraguan coast. That was where they had to go, and it would mean getting Cristina some new documents.

Hector Manuel had given them an address in downtown Miami. A salsa club named Tippy's. They drove to within several blocks of it, abandoned the Corvette, and approached the place on foot. Tippy, the owner, wasn't what either of them might have expected. Six-foot-seven and black, the man was an expatriate from the Honduran coastal city of La Cieba. He spoke both Spanish and a musical English patois. His passion was apparently the cornet. There were glossy eight-by-tens of him playing the instrument tacked up all over the back office walls. Tippy also revered Hector Manuel as a hero of enlightenment and a legend in his own time. He'd been told to expect them.

After twenty-eight straight hours on the go, Bueno was dog-tired. He needed sleep before he could try to formulate a plan.

Tippy drove them out 25A to Hialeah near the racetrack and installed them in number 17 of a ramshackle two-story apartment building. Once inside, Henry collapsed on the bed without bothering to disrobe. It was close to noon when he opened his eyes.

The smell of fresh coffee and frying bacon wafted through the air. It took him a moment to focus and catch hold of the thread. He was stateside. Dead giveaways were the Kwikset knobs adorning cheap *luan* doors, low sheetrock, that cottage-cheese-type ceiling, and wall-to-wall carpeting in a baby-puke beige. This was the 1960s concept of every man's castle, mass-production style.

He threw back the sheet, rolled over on his back, and swung upright to plant his feet on the floor. God, he was hungry. He stood, padded barefoot into the bathroom, and peed. The face staring back at him from the medicine chest mirror was one he hadn't seen in the best part of a year. He hadn't shaved since being awakened so abruptly that morning by the Colombian army. Now, as he opened the medicine chest and stared at its contents, he spotted an Atra handle and a fresh pack of blades. He soaked his face, shot a little Foamy into the palm of his hand, lathered up, and began to scrape off the vanguard whiskers of a pretty decent beard.

Cristina poked her head into the room while he was still under the shower.

"Fried or scrambled?" she asked.

"I was wondering who that was in there, burning the toast."

"Not my area of expertise, I'm afraid."

"Then I'd better have them scrambled."

A few minutes later, they sat facing each other over a cheap metal dining set. Henry wolfed down his eggs, toast, bacon, and coffee while Cristina picked and looked on in amazement.

"I guess there are no complaints," she observed.

"None," he said with a grin.

"Tippy called about an hour ago. He must be at the club by two for auditions, but he will stop by here in a half hour to discuss our immediate needs."

Henry washed a last mouthful of egg and toast down with a gulp of coffee, wiped his lips, and sat back. "I suppose we'd better have some then, huh?"

"You are sure about San Andres?" she asked cautiously. It was Colombian territory, and the idea of entering it made her very nervous.

"It's where they've stored all the apples," he said. "But if you're going, it'll mean new identification. That's where Tippy comes in. We'll have to move quickly and get you documented. I want to be on a plane to Bogota tomorrow morning."

Ramon Lopez could think of nowhere to turn. It was twenty hours now since the man had left him, and at least thirty since he'd slept. He thought his left wrist might be broken. He'd betrayed the glory of a new Nicaragua. He wasn't able to stomach what he had done nor stare death in the face. He had gained nothing. Not life, not hope. From the moment the stranger saw the fear in his eyes and singled him out, he was already dead. To avoid immediate pain, he'd purchased a time of extended agony.

He stared out to the east at the sunlit Atlantic. Behind him the hulking geometric shapes of hotel after hotel loomed like grotesque tombstones. Cut off, isolated by the horror of what he had done, he could feel nothing. There was no warmth to the sand beneath him. No balminess to the breeze fingering his hair. Only the gunmetal in his hands held something he could feel. It held the coolness of death.

Ramon stared blankly, mesmerized by the tiny void receding back into the muzzle of the Browning automatic as he lifted it shakily to his mouth. With parched lips encircling the barrel, he begged his father for forgiveness and pulled the trigger.

Ron Dai pointed excitedly at the monitor as Spanish instead of gibberish marched past for the first time that day. Beside him, the army code expert flown in from Washington eased back in her chair.

"Easy money," she said. "You look at a designation like this and think it's nonsense." She pointed at the words:

QUINTANA ROO

"That's actually a Mexican state on the border with Guatemala. Then 'Chetumal' starts making some sense, because Ciudad Chetumal is the capital of Quintana Roo. Look it up. On Chetumal Bay. You've got your man talking about the Mexican Caribbean, just a stone's throw from Belize and the Cayman Islands."

Dai was beside himself. "That tan. The son of a bitch claimed he'd gotten it on vacation in the Yucatán. Hell, to people like me, everything down in that part of Mexico is the Yucatan. But he was *south* of there. Just a hop and a skip from his old home."

The code expert, a wiry little wisp of a black master sergeant, shrugged and nodded. "Quite possible. If I were you, I'd check airline records and credit card charges to see if he made it as far as Vera Cruz." Again, she was pointing to the monitor. "Right here you've got a notation for Agua-Aero Vera Cruz. It's a pretty good bet that is some sort of local, private seaplane service. There aren't many good roads down into Quintana Roo, if my memory serves me well."

"It seems to be doing pretty damn well so far," Dai marveled. He turned to the hovering Ross Charles. "Does this start to make a little unorthodox sense to you?"

"How so?" The agent was obviously still bewildered.

Dai frowned, one hand stroking his jaw. "I'm not saying it's all come together, but look at it this way. Phil Maldonado was a Nicaraguan national who appears to have played a big part in a conspiracy to steal sophisticated missile guidance technology. Now we've got him talking about a Mexican city and bay just a stone's throw from the home country . . . in *code*, no less."

As Charles absorbed this, one of his agents approached to summon him to the phone. He crossed the room to pick up and, after a few muffled words, listened intently. His participation in the conversation took the form of sharp queries and a lot of listening as the others in the room stood patiently by. After close to ten minutes, he hung up and returned across the room, now deep in thought.

"That was Miami," he told them. "And you're onto something, Ronnie. When they ran those phone numbers down there, one of them turned out to be an estate in Coral Gables that we've had under surveillance on and off for the better part of a month now. It seems that a former major in Anastasio Somoza's secret police lives there. Not on the ownership papers, but they've been tailing him, and he seems quite at home there. And get this: he's a principal player in both the cocaine game *and* the Somosista Contra movement."

The information sank into Dai's admittedly rattled brain.

"A Contra?"

Charles nodded. "One who spends a lot of time flying in and out of this country in a fancy private plane. Three and a half weeks ago, he contacted a retired Syndicate shooter, and that's what put us onto him. Now, here's the real kicker. That house and every other one on the phone number list is vacant. Neighbors reported seeing trucks leave those locations *this morning*. Major Cardona's plane was reported leaving Miami –Opa-Locka just two and a half hours ago. Several other big names in the Somosista fund-raising and lobbying efforts appear to have gone to ground."

One of the other field agents in the room shook his head, still staring at the computer monitor. "This is fucking *weird*," he snorted. "What in God's name are they *up* to?"

Ron Dai was staring at the same information, struggling a bit with his high-school Spanish but managing to filter out what appeared to be names associated with those remote Mexican places. There were names in Chetumal, a cryptic number in Belize City, and a phone number with an unfamiliar national dialing code followed by the word "San Andres." Where the hell was *that*?

NINETEEN

Henry Bueno sat in Tippy's battered Ford van, parked at the curb outside a storefront on Biscayne Boulevard in North Miami. The area, only a mile from the causeway to the exclusive Bay Harbor Islands and Bal Harbor, was glutted with chic boutiques, specialty shops, and salons. The pink and green neon sign in the window across the sidewalk dubbed this particular establishment:

SO-HO HAIR DESIGNS LTD.

There was a twenty-seven-inch Sony Trinitron monitor in the window facing the street. At that very moment, a sheepish-looking Cristina Faro, sporting a new, iridescent platinum hair color, sat under the watchful eye of a video camera as a beautician in tri-colored Mohawk put finishing touches on her.

Henry watched in amazement. The cut was short to the point of severity, shorn high above the ear on one side and left vaguely loose and floppy on the other. The beautician seemed to be explaining what she was doing, step by step, as she painted Cristina's eyes.

"Vanity, thy name is woman," he mumbled to himself. Then he yawned. The sleep he'd gotten had only just begun to do the job, and it was starting to look like another long night. Once the transformation was complete, they had to get Cristina to Tippy's place for a meet with his document expert. He'd told them they could expect overnight delivery if they got there no later than six.

Twenty minutes later, Cristina emerged from the shop after almost three hours in the chair. She'd spent two hundred and thirty dollars, but the effect was startling. No one who knew the old Cristina Faro would suspect that this was the same woman, even from up close. She hopped into the front seat.

"What do you think?" she asked breathlessly.

For a moment, he just stared at her. "I think I've been in the jungle too long."

"You hate it."

"I didn't say that. It's just . . . different. It'll work, though. No question."

They drove south along the shore into Miami as rush hour began to stymie the flow of traffic. Things got a little better once they turned left onto Seventh and passed the Orange Bowl, where some sporting event was just getting underway. The rest of the trip west to Tippy's was a breeze.

All eyes in the place moved with Cristina as they pushed through the crowd. The music on the sound system was really cranked. Henry held off one happy-hour drunk who made a grab at her.

Another man waited with Tippy in the cluttered back office. He was white, massively assembled, with myriad tattoos on his stovepipe forearms and sporting a profusion of scraggly red facial hair. Once he peeled his eyes off Cristina, Tippy made introductions.

"This is Alfie. He's the best there is in the whole Southeast. Cristina and Henry."

Alfie gave them a curt nod hello. "French, right?" he asked.

"That's right," Bueno affirmed. "As good as this one." He extracted his passport from his hip pocket and handed it to him.

Alfie held up his hands, shaking his head, and dug into his pockets for a pair of rubber surgical gloves. "No offense," he told them. Reaching out, he took the offered document and thumbed through it thoughtfully.

"Excellent." He examined it approvingly, pausing over

the photograph, studying the mounting detail and embossed seal. "Very neat work. Good grade of paper. Domestic?"

Henry shook his head. "Oriental."

"Ah." The man nodded.

"I'll need a current U.S. entry visa. Tourist," Bueno told him. "Same for the lady. And we'll both need Colombia. Thirty-day."

Alfie nodded matter-of-factly. "And the lady's particulars?"

"First name Simone," Henry returned. "Born Lyons, February 19, 1949."

Alfie jotted this information down. Glancing up at Cristina, he mumbled to himself. "Hair: Blond. Eyes: Brown. Height?"

"One hundred seventy-one centimeters," she answered.

"Weight?"

"Fifty-two and a half kilos."

Alfie grunted as he closed a little black notebook. "Five thousand for the Frog passport. Another hundred and a half for the Colombian thirty-day, and three for the U.S. ninety. Fifty-four fifty. Cash. Half up front."

Bueno reached into his pants pockets and extracted the dozen gold Mexican coins contained there. Counting out seven, he stacked them in front of Alfie on Tippy's desk. Alfie picked them up gingerly and hefted them, eyeing Henry with fresh curiosity.

"Been a pleasure doin' business with you. If the lady'll sit down here and watch the birdie a sec, I'll have these things in time for you to catch a plane out in the morning."

Before leaving the office, Alfie rolled up his pant leg and stuffed everything into his right sock. A quick-release, spring-loaded commando knife was strapped to his ankle. Tippy turned to them when he'd gone.

"Your flight is an Avianca 747 leaving Miami International at nine and arriving in Bogota at noon. You have thirty minutes to catch the connecting flight to San Andres. If you want, I can drop you at the apartment now and pick you up in the morning, say seven-thirty?"

The speedboat bearing Diego Cardona nosed into its slip behind the sprawling San Andres hacienda. There was already a deep-sea fishing rig moored alongside. Half-a-dozen shirtless men were busy shuttling cartons out to it from the house. Diego leapt onto the dock and hurried across the beach and lawn to where Luis Ecchevarria stood. The younger man was directing the evacuation operation from here, deferring to his commander now with a crisp salute. He pointed to a clipboard.

"We are all but loaded, Don Diego. Ready to sail on the evening tide."

"And the men on the other end?" Cardona asked. "They have confirmed?"

"In position," Luis reported. "They expect our arrival at three A.M."

Diego turned to survey the fifty-five-foot oceangoing trawler tied to his dock.

"There are factors that conspire to defeat us," he said, bitterness in his voice. "We have no more time. You must be prepared to leave for Washington immediately. Latham has said all along that they will want you there to testify, if need be."

Luis nodded. "There is a flight to Bogota tonight and another that will get me into Dulles at seven tomorrow morning."

Diego locked eyes with the younger man, his eyes expressing approval. "Our moment of truth, my friend. Where will I find Señor Terranova?"

Luis jerked his head toward a spot down the beach. A man and woman played in the surf there about a hundred yards away. The pain of the shooter's abusing him in Ecuador still spoke volumes in the young man's hateful glare.

"She acts as though she enjoys it with him," he muttered.

Diego came close to smiling as he watched them. "You are young yet, my friend. She was a teenage whore, doomed to grow old and wrinkled with a cock in her mouth. In this one gringo she sees more power than she ever hoped to encounter. She would do it with a dog now if it meant maintaining the spell she has cast over him."

"He is poison."

"No," Diego countered sternly. "He is grateful. Look at him there. His social graces are not to our liking, Luis, but we are under siege. We need an ally with his special skills. A contented ally. One who sees *us* at the core of his rejuvenated will to live."

Jack Terranova knew something was up. Things had been jumping around the place all day. Cardona was off-island,

259

and he wouldn't give a twerp like Luis Ecchevarria the satisfaction of either dispensing or withholding information. If Cardona wasn't around, any action had to have been previously scheduled. Nobody in his right mind would entrust a wimp like Luis with anything as complex as decision making.

Jack and Anna played on the beach all afternoon while six sweating greaseballs ferried the cartons he'd seen in the basement out to a fishing boat moored to the dock. That morning, the girl had been all over him, sticking that hot wet thing in his face, teasing him up and balling him raw. Damn, what a sweet piece she was. He'd never known a woman who fucked like that. Like she *enjoyed* it. She worked it around on him like she had a hornet's nest shoved up her ass. Hell, no matter how played out he might think he was, all she had to do was pull her dress over her head and he found himself getting all bothered *again*.

Diego showed up in the early evening while Jack and Anna were still in the water. Later, once they'd returned to the house and Jack was grabbing a quick shower, one of the housegirls came to the door to inform him that Don Diego would like to see him on the veranda.

Jack found Diego about ten minutes later, a rum and tonic in one hand, watching the sun go down beyond the activities aboard the fishing trawler. He turned to him, reached out a hand in greeting, and asked him if he wanted something to drink. The hit man requested a Scotch and water. As he pulled up a chair and sat, he wondered if he was picking up something out of the ordinary about the skinny spic. He'd always found Cardona amazingly self-confident for a guy so light in the ass. This evening, the look in his eyes, sort of dull and uninspired, spoke of a step or two lost on the world.

"What's up?" he asked. "Good trip?"

Diego sat a moment, apparently considering the question.

"Not such a good trip."

"No?" Jack was smelling trouble now like a dog smells fear.

"The FBI broke our operation in California. It was all finished but for a man we should have removed sooner. They pilfered his house, and we believe they recovered a document that could be most damaging to us."

"How damaging? You mean a threat to what's going on out there?" He nodded toward the fishing boat.

Diego shrugged. "Perhaps. Much of the information was about our operation in Florida, and that has been moved. But not soon enough, I'm afraid." He told Terranova about the attack of the lone mystery man the previous evening, concluding with the abduction of Ramon Lopez.

"That *kid*?" Terranova shook his head. "If you're thinking what I'm thinking, your mystery man is the same special talent who's out there looking for the CIA man's killer."

"You are supposing the worst," Diego countered defensively.

"I've stayed alive forty-eight years doing exactly that, amigo," Jack said evenly. "You told me yourself that this Latham character says he's the best. Get used to the idea. He's already squeezed Ramon. You can bet on it. That means only one thing. He's headed our way."

Diego sighed. "I'm afraid this is probably true. I have an entire operation to attend to, one that must go off like clockwork."

Jack sipped his Scotch, set it down, and chuckled. "Don't worry, pal. I know what we're really talking about. You go about your business. I'll take care of your cockroach problem. Just remember me come Christmas." To his practiced eye, Diego appeared to relax.

Diego Cardona *was* relaxing. In a willing Jack Terranova, he had his warrior. It might be the assassin's greatest challenge, waging war against an unknown enemy. But Ramon could not have known that they would accelerate the timetable. The man would seek them out here, on San Andres Island. Terranova would at least have the advantage of expecting him.

Ron Dai moved past beds where patients stretched out in all manner of grotesque distress. There was a lot of noise in the intensive care unit, something that surprised him.

Maureen looked better this evening than she had in the morning. A lot of the color was returning to her face. Her eyes, now hours out of anesthesia, sparkled with that characteristic intensity again. The smile she gave him made his heart soar.

He sat on the edge of her bed and took her hand. It had more strength now as it returned the pressure he applied.

"You're looking good," he said softly.

"I missed you," she replied. "It's boring as hell, lying in a bed all day. You ought to try it."

He grinned. "I think maybe I will, as soon as you're feeling frisky again."

Her smile matched his, and for a while they were content to maintain their happy contact in silence.

"I've got to go away for a while," he said at length.

Maureen's smile disappeared. "I don't understand."

"The Bureau flew an army code expert in. She broke Phil's word cipher. It was in Spanish. Everything points to a little port city in Mexico on the Belize border. I don't quite get it, but the FBI raided Somosista Contra headquarters in Miami. Those were the phone numbers we found in the program. Maldonado was a Nicaraguan. I've got a couple of vacation weeks coming, and I'm going down there. Tonight."

"Why?" she asked. "Why you? Let *them* take it from here, Ron."

"I can't," he told her, shaking his head. "I've come this far with it. I can't leave it half-done."

Conrad Burke sat behind the wheel of his Ford Taurus in the parking lot of a Burger King in Annandale, Virginia. At evening mealtime the place was more crowded than he would have liked, but this was an emergency. Ten minutes after he emerged with a Whopper, an order of fries, and a cola, Ted Latham pulled in, three cars away, and hurried over.

"What is this?" the CIA man asked in agitation after climbing in.

Burke washed down a mouthful of burger with a little soda and reached for a document inside his jacket.

"The entire Alamo pilfering operation and the participation of the Contras in it has been ripped wide open." He handed the folded papers across the console. "This stuff came across my desk this afternoon. It documents the murder of an FBI agent in Santa Clara, California, and the Miami field office raids on five Coral Gables estates, one newsstand, and an all-night convenience store."

Latham scanned the material. "They didn't find anything specific in Florida," he mumbled. "Damn, if Maldonado was shot in the head, who killed this Davis guy?"

"You wanna make any wagers?" Burke asked sarcastically. "I knew that goddamn Cardona was out of control the minute I set eyes on him. First, one of *your* team outside Cali, and now one of *my* team on fucking domestic soil!''

"They're moving the stuff tonight," Latham said, trying to appear calm. "I got word just an hour ago on the Company wire. The Ecchevarria kid is due in on an early-morning flight. He'll be carrying pictures of the actual electronics."

"What the hell good do you think it'll do?" Burke exploded. "The Bureau is going to dump all over the guy's bullshit story as soon as he tries to tell it. Hell, we might even *arrest* his ass!"

Latham held out a calming hand. "It's not down the tubes yet. While the Bureau is still stumbling around trying to figure out what they've wandered into, we'll have hard intelligence saying the Sandinistas are on the verge of dealing away top-secret electronics to the Soviets. No one in the FBI can deny that the stuff is missing from where it's supposed to be. The man in the hot seat is going to have to make a decision *fast*. I say we've still got a real good shot."

Connie Burke groaned. "God, I hope so."

The task of moving nearly a ton of sophisticated electronics across a hundred miles of open sea in a fishing boat was the easy part. Getting it ashore would be a lot tougher. A steady stream of cartons being offloaded into the back of a truck in broad daylight would surely arouse local curiosity. Big Corn Island was, in fact, not big. It was only a few square miles of sand and tropical foliage. The inhabitants, primarily black, English-speaking fishermen, saw any change in the daily routine as a curiosity. Life there was extremely slow.

With arrival in Nicaraguan waters set for as close to three A.M. as possible, they were to make landfall in the darkest hours of early morning. Now, with the boat already en route, Diego sat astern in his own powerful motor launch. He plowed across light seas at a speed in excess of forty knots, bearing down on the target island. Salt spray stung his eyes and glistened on his rubberized slicker. The forecast called for a fast-moving squall to pass around midnight. While his boat would in all likelihood arrive well ahead of it, the fishing boat behind was going to get tossed around a bit.

After three hours of deafening progress, Big Corn loomed off to the starboard, and the helmsman cut the engine back to proceed at a more dignified pace. Their arrival was not out of the ordinary, as pleasure boaters from all up and down the Caribbean rim regularly used these islands for recreation. There was a resident patrol craft that made irregular sweeps of the area, but no official customs house.

A reef had to be negotiated before they gained the placid calm of the lagoon on the windward side of the island. Most of the inhabitants were asleep at this hour, preparing to rise for fishing before dawn, when the air was cool. There were already several other pleasure boats in the rickety marina as they eased up to the main dock and tied off. A couple doing some late drinking astern of a sailboat from Louisiana raised their glasses to the major and his helmsman as they came ashore. Cardona smiled and waved back. His stomach growled, and he realized he'd neglected to eat before setting out. There was no time to satisfy his hunger now. It was more than a mile's walk from the marina to the tiny army outpost he was headed for.

Jack Terranova had watched from the veranda as the fishing boat sailed on the tide, and twenty minutes later he saw Cardona follow in his big fiberglass-and-mahogany powerboat. Before leaving, the major dismissed all but two of the house staff, retaining only a maid and the groundskeeper. Jack, Anna, and six Contra soldiers were all who remained behind as the rear guard. Jack privately wished that these six ragtag soldiers had also gone. If some sort of superhuman bogeyman was really on his way, Jack preferred to keep it nice and personal. One on one. The fewer heroes around to take credit for removing this one-man army, the greater the debt incurred.

Diego had left him a box of his best cigars. Cuban, proving that a good smoke knew no political bounds. Jack snipped the tip of one with a pair of clippers and rolled the end of it around in his mouth. A man might be able to get a fairly decent hand-rolled cigar in the States, but not like this one. With Anna beside him, he sat on the veranda, letting the cool Caribbean breeze blow over him. The girl had Tito Puente playing softly on the stereo and was gently swaying with it. Jack picked up the table lighter off the tray in front of him and fired up. He worked his cheeks in and out, sucking air through the perfectly compressed leaves. A machine could never roll a cigar like that. He didn't know why; he just knew it.

"When do you think this man come, Señor Jack?" Anna asked.

Jack smiled wanly. "Soon. Not tonight, I don't think, but maybe tomorrow."

"Why no tonight?"

"Not enough time," he said sagely. "He was in action just last night. Late. A careful man allows himself enough time to rest and study his next move. The way I got it figured, even if he squeezed Ramon, it'd take him a day to get down here, and that'd be fast. Once he hit the island, he'd have to check the lay of the land. Reconnoiter. Tomorrow night, I think. I ain't a gamblin' man, and even I'd put dough on it."

Anna gazed at him all doe-eyed and submissive. Her body still swayed unconsciously to the salsa beat. She leaned close to take one of his big hands and slip it inside her blouse to a breast. Jack felt the nipple get hard beneath his touch.

"Mmmm," she moaned.

"I want you to stay in a hotel the next couple of days," he told her.

"No." She shook her head and pulled back.

"I want you to be out of danger. If I'm worried about you, I can't keep my mind on the job at hand."

She smiled wickedly now. "But not tonight, right, Señor Jack?"

"No, baby," he agreed, grinning broadly. "Not tonight. Tonight we're gonna fuck our brains out. And a couple nights from now, once I dust this mosquito that's bothering everybody, we'll do it all over again, right?"

Her hand moved up his thigh to his fly and tugged the zipper down.

The night on Big Corn was touched by a light, balmy breeze. The nearly full moon, setting behind the treeline to the west, bathed the woolly clouds of the gathering storm with white luminescence. Diego and his helmsman strode purposefully along the dusty shore road toward the military outpost. No more than a dozen regular army troops were stationed at this lonely duty, commanded by the loyalist captain involved in the present conspiracy.

Ahead, the simple compound loomed. Outside a low barracks, the Sandinista banner fluttered at the top of a painted wooden pole. The sight of this symbol made Cardona's blood boil.

Captain Arturro Velasco was still seated behind a battered metal desk in the command building when the two visitors entered. He rose quickly and broke off a snappy salute. Cardona returned the formality.

"Does everything go as planned, Major?" Velasco asked.

Diego nodded. "The boat with the components aboard will arrive in the early hours of morning. It will lay off until the driver of your truck signals it ashore. Our man left for Washington this evening."

The captain digested this information. "The warehouse is ready. The truck will be at the estate pier just after midnight."

"Very good. My man and I will need transportation to the Ramirez estate."

"I will drive you myself," Velasco replied. "The less any of my men see, the better."

"But you say they are loyal, yes?" Cardona asked.

The captain smiled. "To me, Don Diego. Because I make the life here easy for them. And they are loyal to your money."

The Ramirez estate was the last real estate holding of a Somosista loyalist who had elected to stay in-country rather than flee. He was too aged to endure the hardships of expatriate life in a strange country and was willing to live out his remaining life in obscurity. His wife, of a less enduring mind, had left him early on in his reclusion. He was providing food and shelter for the former secret police major and his men until the work of liberation could be completed.

"It has been a long time coming," the old man said. He and Cardona were enjoying a glass of wine after the hungry major's late meal. "We have suffered the indignity of these pigs too long."

"And with admirable patience," the major added. He was feeling much better with some food in his belly and wine to warm his weary mind. "Your sacrifice will not soon be forgotten, my friend."

The old man bowed his head graciously. "You flatter me,

Major. I was too old and weak to fight nearly ten years ago. Today, I am a man who cares too little for his remaining days to obstruct those who build for the future. There is nothing else in this life that could satisfy me now.''

Outside, a truck rumbled across the property and down toward the dock. Diego rose.

"I am the one who is flattered," he told the old man. "Now you must excuse me so that I may check on the captain's preparations."

Three and a half hours before dawn, the fishing trawler from San Andres emerged from the gloom and glided toward the pier of the overgrown estate. The Nicaraguan military truck was parked nearby, with Captain Velasco's men ready to load it.

Diego Cardona and the captain stood together on the weed-choked lawn of a once-glorious garden, watching as the crates came out of the hold and off the boat.

"This time, the gringos will listen when we plead for help," Cardona said bitterly. "They will see what we have done as a great favor. Their own national security is at stake here."

The captain fished a pack of cigarettes from his breast pocket, shook one out, and offered the pack. Diego took one and bent his head to the match the junior man held for him.

In another hour, the truck was loaded and the boat pulled away westward toward its home port of Prinzapolca on the Nicaraguan mainland. For this fragment of the loyalist faction, the job they had been called upon to perform was finished.

When the truck pulled out to traverse old Ramirez's estate, Diego and Velasco followed in the captain's Jeep. Their route took them along a rutted road running inland off the shore road for about a quarter of a mile. Ahead, the truck had already pulled up in front of a barbed wire fence and rusted gate. Inside this enclosure sat a sagging, dilapidated tin warehouse. One of the soldiers had the key to the lock and was working to swing the gate open.

"You have done well," the major told the Sandinista captain.

"Rotting burlap," Velasco said proudly. "Untouched for

over ten years. The owner is thought to have fled to Brazil. It is all as I reported, no?''

"It is excellent,'' Diego replied.

Together, they approached the big entrance doors on foot as the truck was backed around into position. Two of the soldiers lit camp lanterns, illuminating the cavernous interior. It looked just as in the pictures the captain had sent. The same pictures Luis would show his interrogators in Washington.

TWENTY

Ron Dai was dead weary after the all-night flight from San Francisco to Mexico City via Los Angeles. His head hurt like the devil, and he found himself wanting sleep a lot more than before the accident. At least he hadn't had too much difficulty falling off during the flight. That was something he'd found impossible on past plane trips.

The prospect of a bus ride down the mountains from Mexico City to Vera Cruz didn't sit too well with him. He wasn't sure he was ready for some hot-dog Mexican driver taking all those hairpin turns on two wheels. On the other hand, he didn't want to rent a car because there was no telling whether he'd be returning that way. The coastal city lay about two hundred miles distant, and even though the road was good by Mexican standards, the route was anything but what a crow might fly. It was going to take him the better part of a day.

Outside the main terminal, basking in torrid heat and breathing some of the worst air in the civilized world, the detective flagged a cab and took it to the downtown bus depot. A luxury coach was preparing to leave almost as he inquired at the ticket window, and a dead run got him to the gate in time to beat the closing door.

Dai had been to Vera Cruz once many years ago with some college pals from the University of Arizona. They'd done almost the same trip, arriving in the coastal city and spending

the night in an inexpensive *pensione* before striking out for a
Caribbean paradise crawling with bathing beauties. Now,
some fifteen years later, everything but the city and the route
had changed. His bathing beauty was lying in a hospital bed
with her guts sewn closed. One of the men who had caused
her such pain was dead, but another was down here somewhere. He had seen him, and that face was etched in his
memory. Ron didn't consider himself to be a violent man.
Even though his job demanded that he carry a gun on his
ankle, he never thought he might have occasion to use it.
Now, he wondered if he could hold himself back if the target
presented himself.

He thought ahead to what he might do with the remainder
of the day once he arrived at his destination. He craved sleep,
but if he could get the seaplane service to fly him to Chetumal
City, he would probably wait to take a room there. The code
Davis had input into the data base had a name associated with
Chetumal. Rosario Esparza. It was Dai's bet that the man
with this name owned a boat. After a good night's sleep, the
man with a boat wouldn't be too hard to find in so remote a
place.

The United States Customs and Immigration officer who
scanned the French couple's passports stamped them without
a second glance. Alfie, good to Tippy's word, had represented top-of-the-line craftsmanship. Upon Henry's own close
scrutiny, the document created for Cristina appeared identical
to Henri Riberac's.

Even after he'd had a night to get used to Cristina's new
look, her appearance was still astonishing. Last night's experience with this strange creature had been undeniably erotic.
The body may have been the same, but the aura seemed to
have changed. In her new persona, much of her own residual
inhibition was evaporating. She was acting the part of the
siren, and the animal in him was responding to it with unbridled passion.

Their Avianca flight to Bogota was full of upper-class
Colombians returning from shopping vacations to the con-
sumer capital of Latin America. The customs lines were
snarled with color televisions, VCRs, dishwashers, and mi-
crowaves. This was a virtual high-tech exodus. Bueno and
Cristina, with their neat little pile of Louis Vuitton luggage,

seemed almost out of place when they landed at the Colombian capital and waited in a shorter line processing foreign nationals. Ahead of them, a nervous-looking American kid with expensive sneakers, a silk jacket, and a turquoise belt buckle tapped fingers against his thighs. Trafficker, Henry thought. It was written all over him. He'd seen a thousand guys just like him over the past decade. More balls than brains. The Colombian and American jails were full of them.

This was obviously a trying time for Cristina, even in her new persona as Simone Riberac. She stood clutching Henry's arm, digging her nails in, as the DAS man looked at their visas, their photos, and finally at them.

"Destination?" he asked crisply.

"The Caribbean," Bueno answered smoothly. "San Andres Island."

"Purpose of your trip?"

"Pleasure. A vacation."

"How long do you and your wife intend to stay in Colombia, señor?"

Bueno smiled pleasantly. "Not as long as we'd like, unfortunately. Only a week."

The uniformed man nodded curtly, stamped their visas and scribbled something illegible across them.

"Have a pleasant stay," he told them, handing back their documents. He then looked Cristina directly in the eye. There was nothing in his gaze but pure male appreciation. He actually allowed himself a small, self-conscious smile.

The next leg of their journey was undertaken aboard an eighteen-seat, prop-driven aircraft. The atmosphere aboard was festive, with most of the travelers being fun-seekers off on holiday. This was a crowd bent on the simple pleasures of snorkeling, waterskiing and windsurfing, not the ferreting out of murdering thugs.

"I wonder if they have confiscated our house," Cristina said wistfully. She was staring out at the island as they circled above it, preparing to land.

"Your house?"

"At the south end of the island. On the beach. Willie loved it here. It was his great escape."

"Then this has got to be rougher than I thought. How are you holding up?"

She glanced over reassuringly at him. "I'm fine, I sup-

271

pose. Everything has happened so quickly that I haven't really had the time to think it all through. This is definitely strange, being here now.''

He supposed it was. At that moment, it was feeling a bit strange for him as well. In the past, he, too, had sought refuge on this little-known, out-of-the-way place. He would avail himself of the seclusion afforded by a tiny *pensione* on the water above an inlet called Caleta Schooner. It was a cove of no more than a half mile in diameter with a little crescent of white sand around it and a view west across the sparkling sea. The Pensione Las Palmas was a place he knew and one that knew him. This was where he would take Cristina for the duration of their stay here.

Washington, D.C. was not unfamiliar to Luis Ecchevarria. When Luis was a child, his father had served for eight years as Nicaraguan ambassador here. His movements were confident now as he arrived at Dulles on a connecting flight from Miami, collected his luggage, and caught one of the city's unmetered cabs into the heart of the District. His reservations were at the Four Seasons, a hotel his father had seen as the *only* choice when visiting here. By the time he'd finished checking in, tipping the bellhop, and settling in his room, it was early afternoon. By now, everything would be in place on Big Corn Island. He had the photographs of the Sandinista captain's prepared location and of the electronics themselves. If Señor Latham was to move, he would need to have these immediately.

At the same time as he contemplated these logistics, Luis thought of his stomach. He detested commercial airline food and had not eaten the garbage offered him. He'd tried to doze to catch up on sleep lost in the shuffle of making an all-night series of flights from San Andres to Bogota to Miami to Washington. He was not as sharp as he might desire and felt soiled with the griminess that always accompanied air travel. He was ravenous. Lifting the receiver of the bedside phone to his ear, he dialed room service and ordered a late breakfast. Then he began to undress, confident that a shower would make him feel much better.

While lingering beneath the hot, needlelike spray, Luis tried to loosen the kinked muscles of his neck and shoulders. Throughout his journey north, he'd mentally avoided confronting the responsibility that rested upon him now. There could be no escaping the implications of the task at hand. His childhood friend Ramon Lopez had been faced with the prospect of pain and possible death and had failed. Not only had he failed the counterrevolution, he had failed his ancestors and his blood. Luis also feared pain and death. He thanked the Virgin that he had not been forced to face such a test. Those few days in the company of Jack Terranova had left him with no doubts as to his capacity for enduring the threat of physical harm. His knees had not stopped shaking, and it seemed that nothing could stanch the flow of fear-induced sweat.

Luis knew his own task was different. The surroundings were commonplace. He functioned in this world with confidence. This man Latham's father had graduated from the Office of Strategic Services after the Second World War to a job with the American intelligence network being assembled to fight the Cold War. Most importantly, Raymondo Ecchevarria-DeBayle had been his roommate at West Point in the late 1930s. When the Nicaraguan brigadier was named to the ambassador's post in Washington, the two men renewed a friendship that went back many years. Little Luis, just an infant, had eaten Thanksgiving dinner with the teenage Theodore in his family's Potomac home. It was five years since Luis Ecchevarria's father had died of a broken heart in exile from his beloved homeland. The twenty-five-year-old Luis had been enlisted to renew an old family acquaintance. Theodore Latham had followed in his father's footsteps and was, at that very moment, eagerly awaiting his call.

Winter's early nip was in the air, and Luis pulled the collar of his light coat up as he sat waiting on the retaining wall outside a building housing something called the Painters and Allied Trades Union. Ted Latham had named this location for the pickup and was now late. Luis was just not accustomed to such a change in climate. His wardrobe was also inadequate, and he was freezing.

The copy of *The Miami Herald* he had purchased in his hotel lobby was clutched in shivering hands as he attempted to catch up on South and Central American football results. From them, he worked his way idly into local Miami news. The tiny half-column article hit him like a hammer.

NICARAGUAN EXILE'S DEATH RULED SUICIDE

Miami Beach—The shooting death of Nicaraguan exile Ramon Lopez, 23, has been ruled suicide by the Dade County Coroner's Office. Lopez, believed to have been residing in the Coral Gables area, was found by bathers at midday on Miami Beach, shot once in the mouth. The weapon, a 9mm Beretta automatic, was found next to the body. . . .

As he swallowed hard in an attempt to stop the trembling of his lower jaw, Luis scanned the rest of the piece. No known relatives. Funeral arrangements pending. Question of motive. There was no note left at the scene.

Ramon was dead, and the fact that he had taken his own life confirmed Major Cardona's worst suspicions. The operation had been badly compromised. They'd moved quickly to avert total disaster, and Luis now had the fate of his country tucked away inside his coat. God, he wished Latham would get there. While he waited, he prayed silently for Ramon Lopez's soul and for the success of his own mission.

AGUA-AERO VERA CRUZ, the big sign, painted on the side of the boathouse hangar, proclaimed. Ron Dai's head hurt like the devil as he contemplated it. This part of the Vera Cruz waterfront, removed somewhat from the city, was accessible by short cab ride or long walk. He'd chosen a cab.

Dog-tired, head throbbing, and his neck really starting to stiffen up, Dai stepped onto the access dock, carrying his light grip. The place appeared to be deserted. He wandered to the end of the building where its mouth gaped on the water and peered inside. The sea lapped the pilings of an oil-stained interior, now empty of anything significant. Junk littered a workbench on the back wall. All around the inside perimeter the maintenance area was strewn with steel drums and various tools. The smell of gasoline was in the air. Even though it was shady in there and the detective had held some hope of curling up in its relative cool to nap while he waited for the tenant's return, he chose the open sun of the dock instead. The hastily packed grip went beneath his head as he stretched out and closed his eyes. He had no hat to shade them, and the fierce sun burned a bright blue behind his lids. Thoughts of Maureen occupied him as he tried to nod off.

The crackling roar of a single-engine aircraft tore through the weary detective's fitful slumber and brought him bolt upright from his bed on the dock. An aging seaplane, brightly festooned with green and red paint, bore down on his position from the open Caribbean. It did not pull into the hangar but bumped alongside the dock as a teenage ran out of nowhere down the planking, past Dai, to moor the plane. A moment later, the pilot and his passengers began to disembark. The passengers, two American couples in beach wear, babbled excitedly as they said their goodbyes in mangled Spanish and headed for a rented car parked on the road above. The pilot shuffled past Dai without appearing to notice him, reached around the front wall of the hangar, and retrieved what appeared to be lunch. Ron got to his feet, feeling little better for the nap, and nodded to the man.

"I'm looking for someone to fly me to Ciudad Chetumal," he opened the negotiations. "Are you available for such a trip?"

"One hundred and fifty thousand pesos," the man returned.

Dai calculated quickly. It was nearly a five-hundred-mile trip, and the pilot was willing to fly it for less than a hundred and fifty dollars.

"When could you leave?" he asked.

"As soon as I eat and gas up."

Ron went to his wallet, extracted a hundred and a half in U.S. green, and held it up. "This okay with you? I have pesos, too."

With the ever-plummeting exchange rate between the peso and dollar, the pilot's eyes lit up at Yankee green. He held out his hand.

"One hour." He turned to flag his young helper. "Pedro! Gas it up. Check the oil. Move your lazy ass!"

In an hour they were scuttering out across Vera Cruz harbor, the pilot at the controls and Dai seated next to him. The plane found enough speed, and the air sucked them skyward with a sickening lurch. The altimeter began a slow sweep upward once its master tapped the glass encasing it. The airspeed indicator had them moving along at about a hundred and twenty knots. It would be evening by the time they reached Chetumal. He had one or two pointed questions he wanted to ask this guy but thought it might be better to reach his destination before posing them. For the moment, he would sit back and amuse himself with the scenery.

When Cameron Stebbins was informed by his secretary that Ted Latham wished to see him and that he was with a young Nicaraguan named Ecchevarria, a dull day turned suddenly bright. He'd been wondering what the hell was taking Ted so long in coming up with the goods on this Sandinista missile guidance piracy. He was confident, based on the Latin liaison's intelligence, that the leftists had planted people inside the Contra movement and were using them to create trouble now.

"See them in," he barked, releasing the button on his intercom. Latham had finally brought him a warm body. Someone he could march in front of the director and his Joint Chief buddy, Pete McNichol.

The door to his office swung open, and Ted Latham entered, leading a disappointingly young fellow of barely apparent Latin ancestry.

"Ted?" Stebbins greeted, the question in it pointed toward the liaison's companion.

Latham didn't lose a beat, importance and authority in his voice as he made introductions.

"Deputy Director Stebbins, I'd like you to meet Luis Ecchevarria-DeBayle. Luis is the son of the former Nicaraguan ambassador to the United States, General Raymondo Ecchevarria. The general and my father roomed together at The Point."

The deputy director's demeanor changed as he listened to this young fellow's pedigree. "I assume this is not a social call, young man," he said, shaking his hand. "Please, take a seat."

When Latham and Luis were situated, the agent held out a hand, and his companion placed a manila envelope in it.

"You're aware of our investigation of the Alamo thing and our intelligence on where we thought the pirated electronics were headed," he began. "Luis here is part of a network of contacts we maintain to help us keep an ear down in the area. Yesterday, he contacted me with word of evidence collected by a loyalist captain in the Sandinista army. This captain managed to get photographs to the Contra faction Luis is part of.'' With this pronouncement, he opened the envelope, removed a sheaf of eight-by-ten black-and-whites, and handed them across the deputy director's desk.

Stebbins picked up the stack of pictures and began pawing through them. Cartons of electronic equipment. A dock behind a dilapidated estate. An overgrown road. A decrepit warehouse situated inside a rusting barbed wire compound.

"Fill me in," he urged them.

Latham nodded to Luis, who cleared his throat and leaned across the desk to point as Stebbins placed the shots, one by one, onto his blotter.

"This shows the actual cache of stolen Alamo missile guidance parts," he explained, touching the edge of the first glossy put before him. "The rest of these photographs depict the location of this cache. All of the places are on Big Corn Island on the Caribbean coast. This one"—he touched the second shot—"is of the boat landing where the equipment came ashore after the trip south through Mexico and Belize. It is a good dock on an old plantation estate located on the island's north coast. The overgrown dirt road in the next photograph leaves the coastal road near here and progresses inland to the abandoned banana warehouse. The Sandinista army readied the warehouse under cover of night to avoid arousing any local curiosity. There is a loyalist captain keeping us informed, but he has no information as to when the exchange with the Soviets is to be effected. Everything is in place, and we fear the time is very short."

Stebbins perused the pictures after the youngster had finished. This was good, hard stuff. Concrete, it would appear. McNichol and the director were sure to be very pleased. For all the time that "Jumpin' Johnny" Johnson had tried to curry favor with the Oval Office with his bombastic conspiracy railing, the bastard had never been able to deliver the actual goods. The Joint Chiefs would get a little lead time to present an actual plan of action now, instead of endless hot air. McNichol would have a SEAL team briefed and standing by to go in and destroy the national security breach. The president would have all the evidence he needed to justify invasion.

"Nice work, young man," he said quietly. "You've done your valiant cause and your father, God rest his soul, proud."

*   *   *

Christopher Newman

The sunsets visible from the Pensione Las Palmas were often spectacular, as the crimson-drenched clouds of Pacific storms shredded over the Central American isthmus. Earlier that afternoon, Henry Bueno had suffered the ebullience of Señora Friedlich, the proprietor, as she fussed over her old guest and his new woman. An expatriate Swiss national who'd come to the island as a tourist twenty years ago and ended up marrying a local, she had lingered on long after losing her gigolo beach-boy mate in a swimming accident. Diminutive in stature, dark-haired and green-eyed, she cut a handsome figure at forty, still glowing with youth and frantic enthusiasm. In times past, she'd made it abundantly clear to the big snake-hunting Frenchman that she was available for whatever recreation he might have in mind. He never got around to taking her up on it, and as they were being shown to their room he didn't miss the way she gave Cristina the once-over. Even considering the task at hand, it felt good to be back here.

"What do we do tonight?" Cristina asked.

The two of them were on the little private patio adjoining their room, facing toward the fading sunset. In an hour, the sea would be overhung with clouds of stars. Off on the horizon, it looked as though a squall might be headed their way.

"You've probably heard of the places I want to visit," Henry said. "Clubs where the island hustlers and gigolos hang out to compare notes and show off their most recent conquests. In a while, I'll walk over to Cueva del Morgan and ask around. If a crowd of Nicaraguans has been operating on the island, they'll know something about it."

"I shall come along, then."

Bueno shook his head. "Not this time. You've seen some of those guys. If I go into one of these places, I'm going to need a clear head. I can't be worried about them hassling you."

While she didn't want to admit that she might not be able to look after herself, Cristina didn't fight him now. Something in his voice told her not to contest this one. She told him about a restaurant she knew instead. It wasn't far, and the seafood they served was sublime.

*   *   *

Cristina sat on the edge of the bed and watched as Henry dressed in sneakers, loose-fitting khaki pants, and a short-sleeved shirt for his little fact-finding expedition. Before they left Miami, he'd taken pains to contrive concealment for his handgun and knife. The rifle had been no problem. He carried it in a case, right out in the open, as a hunting weapon. No one batted an eye. Now, with the solemnity of a biblical warrior girding his loins for battle, he stooped to strap the knife to his right ankle.

"You will be careful?" she asked, voice edged with concern.

"Always," he assured her. Straightening, he stepped to her and reached down to run his thumb gently across her cheek. "We're real close now. I've gotten so I can smell it."

When the man she knew now as both Riberac and Bueno departed their room, Cristina continued to sit in her chair looking out over the breeze-tousled sea. She was no longer sure of exactly what it was she was doing, or what her feelings were about this man. There was something she could not touch in him, an unpleasant weight he seemed to carry in some deeply private place. As a lover, he was never anything but kind to her, but even this seemed sometimes spooky. The quality of that kindness felt to her as though he was trying to make up for lost time.

From and through him, she found strength of a sort she'd never known she possessed. Taken at face value, both the tenderness and strength of conviction he showed her were things too long absent from her life. She was now grateful for them and for his patience, no matter where this thing led.

The Agua-Aero seaplane made a slow, sweeping pass around Bahia Chetumal. The sun had long since set, and Ron Dai had traveled the last hour of his journey in darkness. Now, as it was about to end, he shifted in his seat and eyed his pilot. The man was concentrating on the water coming up below them, aiming toward the lights of the small coastal city that was their destination.

"You have done business recently with a friend of mine, I think," he mentioned conversationally. "That's how I got the name of your company. He is a Nicaraguan named Philip Maldonado."

279

The pilot's eyes flicked quickly in his direction, a scowl forming on his face.

"An arrogant and demanding man, your friend. He would have gotten nowhere with that attitude if I did not do much work for the one who runs his organization. Major Cardona paid me well to carry your friend's precious boxes. Double the usual price."

Dai was scrambling mentally. Cardona was a new name to him. The arrangement he seemed to have with this guy sounded like trafficking talk. Double the usual price had to mean they did a fair amount of business, and "precious boxes" weren't the usual cargo.

"Those boxes were very important to them," he tried.

"*Everything* is important to such men," the pilot retorted. "And to you as well, no doubt. But do not think I am ungrateful. Do not *tell* Cardona I am ungrateful. I have a woman and six children to feed. If the gringos insist on killing themselves with the drugs, I cannot begrudge you profit from providing them with their amusements. I am thankful for such steady business. You tell your Major Cardona this."

Damn, Dai thought. He'd heard reports connecting the Contras with dope trafficking, particularly cocaine. To get the electronics south, they'd simply reversed the flow of their pipeline. But why? And was this Major Cardona some sort of partner of Phil Maldonado's? Was he the same skinny character who'd eventually put a bullet into Maldonado's head and killed Pete Davis? The one who'd shot Maureen? To what end? The man was most likely a simple profiteer. Drugs for money. Pirated electronics for money, to the highest bidder in a very competitive international market.

The plane hit the water with a jolting splash, bounced, settled, and began the slow run in toward the outskirts of town.

"I will be sure to tell the major of your gratitude," Dai told the pilot as they nosed into shore.

"My thanks, señor," the man returned. "I am afraid you will have to get your feet wet here. There is no dock I can approach. Safe travels and many thanks."

"Do you know where the fishing fleet ties up?" Dai asked.

"Toward the city. About a kilometer from here."

Dai removed his shoes and rolled up his trousers before

climbing down onto the pontoon and stepping into the shallow water. The immediate beach area they'd landed against was dark and appeared deserted. He wandered up onto it and stood watching the plane as it turned and taxied back out across the bay. He knew a lot more than he had known just hours ago, and he was even more exhausted. Finding Rosario Esparza didn't look like it would be much of a chore, and he needed sleep more than anything else right then. He walked in the sand until he located an out-of-the-way spot. His grip had an apple in it, and he ate that before placing the bag under his weary, aching head and dropping off.

CIA Director Randolph Blake was ensconced in the study of his Georgetown residence with Cam Stebbins and the Navy Joint Chief, Admiral Pete McNichol. All three smoked cigars and drank port as they talked. The atmosphere was charged with the excitement of the recent intelligence Stebbins had just shared with them.

"That asshole Johnson is going to shit his britches when we pull an end run on him," McNichol gloated gleefully. "I can have a SEAL team mounted and in the starting gate by midmorning. We dump this in the president's lap and present him with the most immediate option at his disposal. There's no way he won't go with the boys I got chomping at the bit."

Blake nodded agreement. "If we let Johnny Johnson have his head with this thing, he'd just trip all over it and maybe lose us crucial time. Nice job here, Cam. A beautiful piece of intelligence gathering."

"And how," McNichol echoed him.

Stebbins faced his two comrades in government service, coloring slightly with their effusive compliments. McNichol, the bigger and rougher-tongued of the two, was an indispensible ally to have in making such a play. They'd been friends a long time, but you still had to have the goods to support any strong position you wanted to take. Cam had delivered them.

McNichol rose. "Thank you, gentlemen," he said. "I can think of no stronger vote of confidence than yours. Once the SEALs go in and confirm this stuff, then Jumpin' Johnny and the rest of them can have it, and we've still done our jobs. There are some people up top who aren't likely to forget that." The admiral heaved his considerable bulk out of his comfortable wing-back chair and made his apologies. "I've gotta get this ball rolling, gents. There's a crackerjack lieu-tenant commander I've had my eye on, stationed in Norfolk. He's my team leader on this baby. We'll need to do some briefing within the hour, and that means I get a move on and catch me a whirlybird down there. What time you got in mind to hit the commander-in-chief with this?"

"Right after he's had time to take a shower and read the morning paper," Blake suggested. "Think you could make that?"

McNichol chuckled. "Wouldn't miss it for the world."

TWENTY-ONE

The slickly polished backbeat of a reggae recording thundered through the sound system of an open-air club on the outskirts of Cueva del Morgan. The place was jammed with bobbing, jerking bodies; the pungent odor of marijuana was thick in the air.

"With a little more luuuh-uv, my brother. With a little more luuuh-uv, my seesters . . ."

Bueno had heard an awful lot of reggae in these parts over the years. He still liked the infectious rhythms, but the lyrics, as social commentary, left a lot to be desired.

As unobtrusively as possible, he emerged from the shadows of a nearby alley and edged his way to the bar. A small opening developed next to an extremely fat black man with a full beard and hair in the mandatory knotted dreadlocks hanging well below his shoulders. When Henry flagged the bartender, this big man, heretofore distracted, suddenly noticed his presence.

"Eh, mon. You lookin' fowa ganja?"

Bueno forced a smile as the man behind the bar approached. He ordered a beer from him. "Not tonight," he told the fat man, shaking his head.

"Den why you heah, mon? Lookit dis place. Black mon. Rasta mon."

Henry looked around. "I hadn't noticed."

"Boolsheet, mon."

Sipping his beer, Henry eyed him. "Whatever you say, big guy." He pushed off the bar and picked his way through the crowd to a low retaining wall along the far side of the dance floor. Finding a vacant spot on it, he sat.

Out on the floor, directly ahead, a tall and heavy-muscled black man in a red, yellow, and green wool cap danced energetically with a thin, raw-boned blond woman. Henry guessed Scandanavian by the cut of her hair and clothes. Obviously affluent, five-nine or -ten, with great cheekbones and eyes like the ice of a frozen fjord. As they moved together, the big man had his hands all over her. He was bare-chested, glistening with sweat, and appeared to have her mesmerized. Bueno smiled when she splayed her fingers and ran them over his well-defined pecs. A vacation in the islands could really loosen up those northern European inhibitions.

A short, wiry man with a mountain of thick, knotted hair approached him.

"Ganja, mon?"

Bueno shook his head. "Tell me," he asked, "who's the big wheel around here?"

The little guy puffed out his chest and got a scowl of disdain working. "You lookin' at 'im, mon. You need de ganja? De coke? You come to Maw-tee."

The music stopped. The blond and the big Rastafarian turned to leave the dance floor. The woman noticed Bueno watching her with interest. The muscleman saw the two of them eye each other. Without hesitating to consider his move, he stepped across to Henry and grabbed the front of his shirt. Bending to glare straight into his eyes, he bared stained teeth and smiled wickedly.

"What de *fok* you tink you lookin' at, mon?"

"You just might be the man I'm looking for," Bueno returned calmly. "You always so friendly?"

"Fok you, mon!"

The woman, a little frightened, stepped up. If a look could have blackened an eye, the one he threw would have broken her nose as well. Those big blue eyes of hers widened in alarm as she backed quickly out of harm's way.

Neither man's position had changed. The big black man continued to glare while holding a bunch of Bueno's shirt in his fist. In the next instant, Henry had a fistful of the man's hair and five inches of high-carbon steel wedged up under his chin. Both men's eyes, registering comprehension of the sudden shift of power, remained locked.

"Don't swallow too hard," Henry advised quietly. "It could be real painful."

Unable to restrain himself, his adversary gulped. The tip of the knife bit into the skin of his neck just above his Adam's apple. A tiny droplet of crimson formed over the puncture. The knot of onlookers around them had quickly become a crowd. Behind them, the thump of a new tune worked to electrify the atmosphere.

"Rockin' time . . ." the singer howled.

"Let go of the shirt," Bueno suggested.

Quickly, the sweating Rasta released the loose cotton. On him, the musty odor of dancing exertion was being overwhelmed by a different smell. The smell of fear. Henry smiled into the face.

"Tell me what you know about the Somosista Contras," he said.

The man looked genuinely puzzled. "Wot?"

"I think you heard me."

The guy thought hard. "Dey fight de Sandah-neesta, mon. Every mon know dat."

"I don't know anything," Henry snarled. "Educate me. What about here? On the island."

This time, when the man gulped, Henry withdrew the knife a quarter inch. The eyes before him squeezed shut in anticipation of pain that failed to materialize. They opened in surprise.

"Der be a place, mon. Named El Cove. To de sout'. Beeg house. No mon go near der now."

Bueno studied the man's face as he spoke. Satisfied that he was being straight, he smiled. "You ought to be more friendly to strangers," he said. As he started to stand he pulled the head upward with him by the hair. As he released it, he stooped to replace the knife in its sheath.

The big, rangy Rasta wasn't quite finished. Bueno knew this even as he released him. The man was embarrassed in front of his acquaintances and the woman he was working to impress. There was a nearly imperceptible tensing of the muscles, followed by a quick little flex of the planted leg as he launched a roundhouse kick aimed at Henry's head. He had excellent form, good quickness, and power. If Henry hadn't known it was coming, it would have taken his head off. But when he suddenly shifted the intended target, the kick swept harmlessly through the air. From the floor where he'd dropped, Bueno shot a heel upward into the man's exposed groin. As momentum carried the Rasta through his roundhouse motion, he was lifted off the ground by the force of the blow. His eyes, wide with the reflex of surprise, rolled back in his head. His legs gave way, and he crumpled. Just as quickly as Bueno went to the floor, he was now back on his feet. The crowd backed off a quick step, stunned.

Slowly, Henry backed out of the place, leaving his attacker unconscious on the edge of the dance area.

Before delivering Luis Ecchevarria to Cam Stebbins, Ted Latham had used his miniature Minox camera to shoot a duplicate set of the photographs Luis carried. After returning the kid to the Four Seasons some hours later, he'd had the film processed by a buddy at the Langley lab and then delivered the prints to Hardy West. The opposing prong of their two-pronged assault on the Oval Office was now being activated.

General "Jumpin' Johnny" Johnson was a wiry, diminutive leatherneck of the old school. With a steel-gray crew cut and a face as grooved with weather as the Marlboro cowboy's, he saw himself as built from the stone of Stonewall Jackson's wall and cut from the whole cloth of Old Glory. Hardy West sat across from him now in the library of his Potomac, Maryland home. Johnson had been born to South Carolina tobacco money and could afford the finer things in life. Beautiful Thoroughbreds romped the pastures of this palatial manor in the D.C. suburbs. The two men drank antique Armangnac from an even older cut crystal decanter and smoked the finest hand-rolled Honduran cigars.

"This shit is pure dynamite, boy," the general growled as he hunched over the photographs. "You say you connected with it through your associations with Contra factions?"

"That's correct, sir," West affirmed. "A real stroke of luck, if I might say. These people have come to depend on and trust us."

"They'd be shit outta luck if we'd left it entirely up to Congress," Johnson grumbled. "Glad we had the foresight to have you make the rounds and maintain contact. Tomorrow,

I'm takin' this stuff to the president. Hell, that shithead Ortega and his crew are just as good as rollin' out the red carpet, and I mean *red*, for the fuckin' Rooskies.''

West chose his next words carefully. "You understand, sir, that there is no guarantee that mine are the only hands these things have gotten into."

Johnson glanced up, eyes squinting in concern. "What are you sayin', son?"

"Just that these people are desperate, sir. They seek aid from any quarter that might be able to offer it, and they have a lot of very influential friends now."

"If *we* can't deliver on this, no one can," the general said insistently. "You couldn't convince 'em of that?"

"I did my best, sir. I believe in the corps. After what we did in Grenada, we have the confidence of the American public. The president knows that."

"First thing, then," Johnson growled. "There ain't no son of a bitch gettin' the jump on Johnny Johnson. No way in hell."

The hike from Cueva del Morgan, across the island, and then north again up the coast road to El Cove, took Bueno a little more than an hour. When he was near the Somosista stronghold, he took another hour to work his way into an observation position. He'd gone all the way past and was now watching the house from the northeast. The two sentries he could see on this side of the place were well positioned but poorly disciplined. They smoked and moved about restlessly. Because of how they were situated, Henry was sure there would be more of them, spread at equal distances on a perimeter.

In the course of the next two hours, he made one complete circuit, moving down the incline from the road to the beach, along the sand under cover of a retaining wall, beneath a sturdy pier, and then back up to the road on the south side. There were six men in all around the house. They wore fatigues and were armed with what appeared to be Valmet M-76 automatic rifles. Henry had also observed something inside the house through an open, lamplit window. There were two people in view: a big, heavyset white man and a scantily clad younger woman. The girl was flaunting everything she had, and the guy was eating it up. There was a

287

heavy gold chain around his neck, a gold Rolex on one wrist, and another gold chain around the other. The shooter, Jack Terranova. It *had* to be him. He was too big and Sicilian-looking to be one of these others. Henry had watched him walk out of view, with the girl following. The man had that side-to-side Brooklyn meatball street swagger.

There was no sign of anyone who could have been Major Diego Cardona. If the kid in Miami had spilled the straight dope, the kingpin was probably already on the Nicaraguan island, triggering his operation. San Andres was his second line of defense. They knew that someone had broken into their Coral Gables setup, killed a guard, and leaned on the kid. It made sense that they'd be expecting him. Terranova and his men were there to take the brunt of this potential assault. They were waiting for it, but they obviously weren't expecting anything tonight. Bueno had carried only his pistol to the reggae club. A wise move then, but unfortunate now. With his rifle and some minor attention to the ragtag perimeter guard, he could have had a clear shot and been on his way. Tomorrow night they were sure to be a bit more attentive, and he was going to have to do it the hard way.

The whore looked bored, sitting there in the living room of Conrad Burke's Watergate apartment. The guys didn't care. Just as long as she continued to sit there in her sequined g-string, creamy white skin contrasting with that mass of flaming red hair. She looked like she was made for action: small but perky tits, thin hips, and a tight little ass.

Rod O'Doyle worked on the wire cork cage of a Dom Perignon magnum bottle. Across from him, Ted Latham and Hardy West were boastfully recounting their exploits of that afternoon and evening.

"All I'm gonna tell you two," O'Doyle said, interrupting West while still fiddling with the bottle of bubbly, "is that the minute this thing comes off, I'm gonna crawl up your pal Cardona's ass with a fistfull of fishhooks. I don't care if I gotta take him out behind the shed and shoot him in the head, my boss wants to see him taken down, and I aim to make him happy."

"I love a man who loves his job," Burke quipped. He pointed to the whore. "You wanna go first?"

O'Doyle was glancing over at the all-but-naked redhead

when the cork came loose and champagne foar... onto his big, meaty paw. He jerked the bottle out over the five waiting glasses and started to pour.

"Hang on a sec," West protested to Burke. "Ted and me got us a full head of steam up after our go-rounds with the big boys. Ain't there any reward for front-line service?"

"What're you sayin', Jarhead?" O'Doyle growled. "You want her first, the bedroom's thataway. I'll just make sure she rinses her mouth out with Drano when she's finished. God knows where that thing of yours has been recently."

With a scowl, West stood and walked over to the whore with his hand outstretched. "Let's hit it, Bambi, baby. Hate to spoil all your fun right up front, but with these three spaghetti dicks in line, the show's gonna be over after you've had your Marine."

The other three guffawed, slugged back the sparkling wine in their glasses, and quickly headed for refills.

"To tomorrow," Latham toasted, holding his glass out and up. "Ain't that little prick Ortega going to be surprised?"

"And ain't Bambi gonna be surprised by Hardy's little prick," O'Doyle snorted and guffawed as he touched his glass against the other pair.

The Marine major had just reached the bedroom door and was standing back to let the woman pass before him. "No more surprised than your wife was, *Rod*-ney," he shot back.

The night had moved well into the wee hours of predawn as the fat man from the reggae club found himself on the road above the isolated, sprawling beach house on El Cove. He had summoned a doctor for his friend and then hurried here, afraid of what the Nicaraguans might do if they learned Rikki has passed on information about them. Strange rumors surrounded this place. Comings and goings in the middle of the night. Boats tying up here from off-island. Most recently, there was a story about a big white man and a beautiful young girl who had been seen making love right out on the beach.

Some time ago, one of the locals had tried to burglarize the place. His body washed up three days later at Punta Sur, to the south. It was riddled with bullets. Later, a mortician saw that the man's tongue had been cut out. Word got around, and nobody had messed with the Nicaraguans since.

The fat man decided that it would be safest to attempt hailing the occupants of the house from the road. *"Hola!"* he hollered. *"Buenas noches! Hola!"*

From out of the deep gloom a man appeared with a nasty-looking automatic rifle pointed at his chest.

"What do you want?" he asked.

"I be Isaac," the fat man returned nervously. "I come wit' de message for de mon who be in charge heah."

"Who is it?" a voice growled from ten yards further away.

"De name be Isaac, mon. I come wit' de warnin'."

Jack Terranova stepped into view with an automatic trained on the man's huge head. "What sort of warning, pal?"

"'Bout de white mon. Very bad white mon. He come askin' de questions 'bout dis place. Near to kill me brother Rikki."

"Questions?" Terranova asked.

"Ya, mon. 'Bout de place heah. Where it be. Talkin' 'bout de Nik-a-rogwan. He be fost, mon. So fost he be like de lite-nin'."

"And you're telling me all this out of the goodness of your heart, right, fat boy?" Terranova sneered as he said it.

A look of confusion crossed Isaac's face. "I don' know nottin' else, mon. I swear it. Isaac don' lie."

Terranova laughed outright. "And little fishes don't swim. Tell me everything, fat boy. Hair color. How tall he was. What language he spoke."

"Eengleesh," Isaac said. "Wit' de brown hair, and tall. Dunno, mebbe de two meters. Beeg mon."

"And why did he try to kill your friend?"

The big Rastafarian shrugged. "He jest mean, mon. Bad."

"And nobody told him nothing, right?" Jack asked, sneering.

"Thot be right, mon. Nottin'."

Terranova shook his head and clucked his tongue. He steadied the pistol on the target and pulled the trigger. As part of his skull exploded in a bloody pulp, Isaac crumpled to the ground. Jack gestured to the soldier on his right, and grunted with disgust.

"You and your buddies throw this tub of lard in the water. Then get your asses back up to your positions. No more smoking. He's here. He could come any time in the next twenty-four hours."

* * *

Ron Dai didn't sleep as long as he wanted to, but considering his exposure on an empty beach, it was probably just as well that a playful stray dog licked his face a few minutes before the sun came up. He figured he must look awful, his clothes rumpled and his face unshaven and unwashed. The morning was warm enough, though, and the bay glowed orange before him with the first light of half a sun. A swim seemed like as good an idea as any, and it appealed to the brindled mutt as well. When he stripped and dove in, the dog bounded in right behind him. He swam out fifty yards or so with long, sure strokes, paused to tread water, and scanned the shoreline in toward the city. Already, a dozen fishing boats had left their berths and were moving down the bay toward the open Caribbean. He knew that if he wanted to catch up with the decoded name connected to this location, a Rosario Esparza, he'd better get a move on.

The dog followed him as he walked down the coast road toward Chetumal. A change of clothes felt good. He was in loose-fitting safari shorts and a Hawaiian-style shirt now; his gun was stuffed into his waistband at the small of his back. Dressed like this, and in sneakers with no socks, he could have been any crazy gringo vacationing on the cheap. Even at six-thirty A.M., the day was already getting hot. His stomach complained of being famished with a series of nasty growls.

The captain of a fishing vessel could pretty much work the waters up and down this coast as he pleased, Dai imagined. The next sovereignty encountered to the south was Belize, formerly British Honduras and currently an impoverished independent protectorate. Travel through that country's waters would be unhindered. Picking up a load somewhere in the area and ferrying it to Mexico to be flown north by Agua-Aero Vera Cruz seemed like it might be a fairly low-risk enterprise. Ron hoped this Esparza was not one of those dozen he'd spotted who saw fit to set sail before sunrise.

There was a cantina that looked inviting just a stone's throw from the wharf area. Ron managed to persuade his stomach that food could wait a little while, and he marched stoically past. A moment later, he was thanking heaven for his high school Spanish and a sheriff's department refresher course as he began asking around the boats for Rosario Esparza.

The boat pointed out to him was a fairly recent vintage

deep-sea rig, maybe forty feet in length, low and squat amidships with upswept bow and stern. Unlike many of the others, she was outfitted with radar and a sophisticated antenna mast. The paint on her was fresh and gleaming white. There was no visible rust on her riveted steel hull. If Dai had been harboring any doubts about Maldonado's buddies being traffickers, they quickly vanished. He strode down the pier with as much nonchalant confidence as he could muster and hailed anyone who might be on board.

A grease-smudged face appeared over the access hatch to the engine compartment just behind the deckhouse.

"What is your business?" the heavyset Mexican asked.

"Let's just say you were recommended by a friend," Dai replied. "Phil Maldonado told me that for the right price, you might take some more cartons to the previous destination for us."

Esparza scowled. "I was told those he brought were the last. Why have I not been informed differently?"

Dai shrugged. "Major Cardona is a busy man. So is Señor Maldonado. That is why they sent me."

"How soon?" Esparza asked, sighing with resignation. The mention of Cardona's name seemed to have an effect on him. "My engine is running poorly and needs attention."

"We need to get them there within the day," Dai pressed him.

Esparza snorted derisively. "San Andres is seven hundred miles from here, señor. It would take the day to get them there if we were to set sail as we speak. I have a faltering engine, and you would still have to bring the boxes."

San Andres was all Dai needed to know. One of Maldonado's coded entries suddenly made sense. The Bureau had pinpointed the single number with a Colombian exchange to be on San Andres, a Caribbean island. He had to get to this place a lot more quickly than a fishing boat could carry him.

"I beg your pardon," he said. "I meant within the day once the cartons *arrive*. They are still in transit near Guadalajara. It will be at least three more days until they arrive here."

"Why didn't you say so in the first place?" Esparza growled. "If I am given twelve hours notice once your cargo is here, there will be no problem. Major Cardona's business is something I value highly."

Dai bet it was. He said his so longs and got out of there. San Andres, according to the small regional atlas he carried, was a tiny island controlled by Colombia but situated closest to the Nicaraguan east coast. How to get there quickly was a question he'd have to find the answer to in a hurry.

While wolfing down a quick breakfast at the cantina adjacent to the wharves, Ron studied the atlas, looking for a solution to his problem. The country of Belize was just a stone's throw from where he sat, and the capital city of such a place had to have an airport, no matter how small. If he could get there by fast boat, a trip of just over eighty miles, he could charter a plane to fly him the remaining five hundred air miles to the little island. There was a problem of possessing no Colombian visa, but he'd solve *that* in Belize City.

Further up the beach toward the city itself, he could see a marina crowded with pleasure craft. He beckoned to the wizened man who had waited on him and asked if such a place would be where he might hire a ride in a powerboat. The man agreed that if such a ride were to be found thereabouts, the marina was the place he should go looking for it.

The director of the FBI had scheduled an early breakfast meeting to discuss a matter of some concern that his San Jose, California and Miami field offices had combined to uncover. In the private dining room of the Justice Department, he sat across a table from the U.S. attorney general and the secretary of state.

"Let me get this straight, Larry," the secretary of state said when he'd finished his briefing. "DEA confirms your suspicions that these Somosistas are running quantities of cocaine through a well-established network. Your people have further documented their contact with a notorious East Coast syndicate shooter who has since disappeared. Now, if I read it right, you've directly implicated these same men in an effort to subvert U.S. national security through a plot to steal sophisticated missile guidance components."

The director sighed and nodded. "That's correct. And it's too damn cut and dried to just shrug off."

The attorney general held up a hand. "Hang on a sec, fellas. Just stop and think what it is we're saying here. This is a cornerstone of the president's foreign policy we're talking about. It turns out there's some rotten apples in the barrel, but for God's sake, think about what blowing the whistle on them could mean to everything we're trying to do down there.''

The director looked him straight in the eye. "One of my agents is dead, Ed. Garroted in cold blood, for crissakes. This administration has launched a full-scale war against drugs, and these guys wind up looking like Golden Triangle warlords. How much slack are you willing to cut them?"

"Larry's got a point," the secretary of state said quietly. "The Contra effort is on pretty weak legs as it is, and we all know what something like this could do toward strengthening Ortega and Sandinistas' position. Then there's the question of what sort of integrity we stand for as a government. I'm inclined to let the president make up his own mind on this one. It's too big for us to sit on."

The attorney general sighed with resignation. He was known as a team player in spite of his public image as a hard-liner.

"You want to take it to him or leave it up to me?" he asked the Secretary.

"Let's both do it," State replied. "It'll give him a bigger sounding board."

TWENTY-TWO

Henry Bueno woke to light streaming in through a high overhead window. The sea rumbled onto the beach outside, stirred up by the squall that descended shortly after he returned from his night of reconnoitering. Cristina was still asleep beside him as he slipped from between the sheets and pulled on a pair of swim trunks. Outside, in the cool of the early morning, he walked barefoot across the sand to the water's edge, stretched, and plunged headfirst into the surf. With long, powerful strokes, he made straight for the horizon. The water was rough but warm, a perfect seventy-eight to eighty degrees.

His aim was to exhaust himself. He would clear his mind and review the picture objectively. That was the sort of focus he needed right now.

Back ashore after swimming a hard half mile, Henry bent over with his hands on his knees to catch his breath. He felt as good as he had in weeks, dripping sweat and sea water into the sand. Just down the way, he noticed a small skiff under an all-but-rotted tarp. As soon as he could walk again with any ease, he inspected it for seaworthiness. Not more than eight feet in length and constructed of aluminum, it looked as though it might still float. He sought out Señora Friedlich and asked about it.

"That thing?" she scoffed. "It was my husband's, and I

don't believe it has been in the water in six years.'' She stopped and thought a moment. ''No, there was a boy about three years ago who took it out. Be my guest. There are oars around here somewhere.''

By the time Cristina stumbled sleepy-eyed out onto the beach, Bueno had the tarp off and the skiff dragged down to the water. With surf sloshing around his ankles, he scooped lard from a can with his fingers and applied it liberally to a set of rusted oarlocks.

''Good morning,'' she said, rubbing her face.

Henry glanced up from what he was doing. ''Sleeping beauty. Feel rested?''

''Fine,'' she replied. ''What have you got there?''

''An assault craft disguised as a mild-mannered rowboat.''

''Lard?''

''One squeak could mean the difference between life and death,'' he explained. As he spoke, he worked the pins back and forth in their slots. The rust slowly broke down until the action of the locks was smooth and effortless. Removing them a last time, he applied one more glob of fresh lard to each.

''Go for a test run?'' he wondered. ''I'm curious to know if it floats.''

She smiled. ''I don't suppose it would be much good if it didn't, right?''

Together, they pushed the boat into the surf and scrambled aboard. Henry set the oars and leaned into them, pulling away from shore. About forty yards out, they noticed their craft taking a little water. A tiny hole in the starboard gunwale was admitting a steady flow under the stern seat.

''There's our answer,'' Bueno said. He turned the boat toward shore. ''Let's make sure it's the *only* one.''

They searched about under both seats and could find no other breaches in the hull's integrity. Once again, the boat was beached. After dragging it well up onto dry sand, Bueno went off in search of a suitable plug.

Jack Terranova was reasonably satisfied with the defense of his perimeter. Midmorning, he toured each man's position and inspected it a second time for field of vision, concealment, and contact with the positions on either side. Any attack would have the advantage of a moonless night. The perimeter guards were going to have to be extra alert and vigilant. The way he saw it, there were five approaches to the house: sea, air, the road above, and from both north and south along the beach. He himself would remain in a position where he could respond just as well to an attack launched from any direction.

After making the circuit, Jack returned to the house. Anna had steadfastly refused to leave him. He found that he could not sustain anger with her. Now, taking her in hand, he looked sternly into her eyes.

"This afternoon you are going down into the basement until this is over," he told her. "You will stay put until I tell you it's safe to come out. Understood?"

"You will be careful, Señor Jack?" she asked anxiously.

"Always, baby. Careful is my middle name." He reached out, pulled her to him, and cupped a hand over her ass. "Ain't no way I'm gonna let some shithead stop me now, mama. You and me are gonna run an empire together. I promise you that."

She got his favorite look in her eye and pushed close against him.

"Jesus," he groaned. "Not now. I got work to do."

The morning started off with a bang in the Oval Office when the attorney general and secretary of state laid out their tale of subterfuge stretching from Contra Florida strongholds to the drug-producing regions of South America. The president was still reeling from this dismal picture when NSC Chief Johnson and Joint Chief McNichol arrived almost simultaneously an hour and a half later. It was no secret that these two men, ostensibly from sister branches of the armed services, loathed each other. McNichol had spent a sleepless night in Norfolk briefing an elite SEAL unit. He was bringing to the White House not only the problem but a first step toward its solution. Finding "Jumpin' Johnny" Johnson there surprised him. Learning that the marine general also knew of the problem and had come with his own solution shook him to his shoes.

"The SEALs are damn good, I admit that," Johnson was saying to the president. "But they ain't been into any real action since Nam. The corps's got the invasion of Grenada just a few years back. This sort of thing is exactly what we do best."

Both the secretary of state and attorney general were still on board. The commander-in-chief held up a hand and looked to them.

"Gentlemen? How do you see this thing?"

The attorney general hopped in first. "Mr. President, the way I look at it, we've just stumbled on a way to save face over what these jackass Somosistas have been up to. Before the press can even get wind of their dope treachery and the dead FBI man, we've gotta take up the gauntlet and go on in. Here's the proof the American people have been demanding. This is a classic; we can snatch victory from the jaws of defeat."

The president set *his* jaw. "Mr. Secretary? You're a steady-as-she-goes type. You with him here?"

The secretary of state sighed, staring down at the intertwined fingers of his hands. "For a change, I am, sir. These bastards have stabbed you in the back. Hell, we've compared them to the founding fathers. This is a foreign policy fiasco we have staring us in the face."

"I can't afford that," the president admitted. "Details will have to be worked out, but the way I see it, the Marine Corps is best prepared to establish a beachhead on the west coast below Managua and then launch a full frontal invasion on the capital. Backed up by the Rangers and the 101st Airborne. Pete, your SEALs will invade Big Corn Island and put a lock on the Alamo components. We can't fail there. That stuff is what we're going to need to show the world. Top-level national security breach, Soviet collusion and all that."

"The marines could do it all, sir," Johnson protested hotly. "A brigade of Jarheads could roll over that little sandbar and lock it up tighter'n a drum."

The secretary of state stepped in. "One problem with that, General. The intelligence looks cast in concrete, but what if something goes wrong? Do we want a division of marines on foreign soil, egg all over their faces, or a small team of in-and-outers?"

"That's pantywaist thinkin', sir!" Johnson bristled. "We oughta gone in there ten years ago. We're gonna do it now, then let's do it right."

"Gentlemen," the president said, and there was silence for a moment. "Admiral, I want your SEALs on Big Corn Island tomorrow night. General, get to work on the details of a red-alert standby for a fully supported beachhead invasion force. We'll talk to the army and air force in a full meeting of the Joint Chiefs this afternoon. Instead of sitting here debating, we'd better get cracking. No?''

As Admiral Pete McNichol left the White House in the back seat of his staff limousine, he was thinking about his old Annapolis classmate, Cam Stebbins. The man had really come through for him on this one. When the smoke settled, he was going to get Cam awarded the Navy Cross.

The powerboat bearing Ron Dai surged into the swampy marshland canals that were the delta at the mouth of the Belize River and the surrounding terrain of Belize City itself. On the way in to a dock area in the heart of the little city, the detective spotted three different seaplanes moored on the outskirts. Aside from procuring a Colombian tourist visa, Maureen was also on Dai's mind. He needed to locate an overseas exchange and call.

Ron had made fine time that morning, arriving here in Belize before noon. He had hopes of getting to his Colombian island destination before nightfall. What exactly was going on over there remained a mystery to him, but he could feel himself closing in on the skinny Nicaraguan major. The more he learned about him, the hotter his hatred burned.

The Mexican boatman left him on an antique wharf skirting what appeared to be a main boulevard. It was hot as hell at this hour, and most of the population was off seeking shade. Even finding a policeman took him half an hour, and that man had to search out one of his brethren before Ron could be pointed toward the Colombian Embassy. At the embassy, he explained that he wished to fly over to San Andres for what he heard was excellent deep-sea fishing. The clerk was happy to issue this American lawman a thirty-day tourist visa. Hungry again, he took a break to eat lunch at a cafe, where he asked the jovial proprietor if he would recommend a tourist seaplane service. The man mentioned two that tied up just to the south, within walking distance.

To plug the leak in his boat, Henry found a small screw to fit through the hole and a nut and washer to secure it from the other side. With a screwdriver and pliers borrowed from the Las Palmas handyman, he tightened the nut down on a gasket of chewing gum until it was snug against it. Crude but effective. In addition to lard, the oars were further muffled by wrapping rags around the shafts and knotting them in place. Once slotted into the locks, they moved soundlessly. He took time to go over every inch of the hull once more, searching for any reflective surfaces and dulling them with sand rubbed hard against them. No matter how small, anything that might catch stray light could mean disaster. Before departing for his objective, he would take pains to blacken his own skin.

Bueno and Cristina stood together on the beach now. Darkness had descended two hours earlier. Aside from two lights burning in isolated windows, the *pensione* above them was quiet.

"You don't have to do this," he said to her. In the absolute dark of a moonless night, he held both her hands and stared hard into her eyes. He had tried every way he could think of to convince her to stay behind, but she was having none of it.

"I will do exactly as you say once we are there," she promised. "But I *must* go."

Without another word, Henry took hold of the skiff and shoved it into the surf. With Cristina aboard, he clambered in. The gear was already stowed. Rifle, ammunition, and the plastique and detonators Tippy's friend Alfie had supplied.

The mile-long trip down the coast to the seas beyond El Cove took about half an hour. Bueno checked his watch as they rounded the little point of land bracketing the inlet. It was eleven-fifteen. Two hundred yards from shore, he let the boat drift as he handed the oars to Cristina, along with his pistol.

"Give me fifteen minutes," he whispered. "There's a guy dug into the sand just beneath the boat dock. I take him first, and then you come straight in, hugging the pilings. I'll hook up with you there."

Face, torso, and legs blackened with greasepaint, he slipped noiselessly over the side and into the water. "Fifteen minutes," he hissed before disappearing in the gloom.

Watching him go gave Cristina gooseflesh. Something about Henry had changed that afternoon. He'd gone off somewhere inside himself, excluding her from his thoughts. There were no hesitations in his movements now, nor had there been for hours. He was in a very exclusive element, and it frightened her to see how at home he was.

At the end of the long pier, Bueno used the pilings for cover as he inched his way toward the perimeter man's foxhole position. At one point, about fifteen yards out, the man was staring straight into his eyes and seeing nothing but wet barnacles.

With the knife gripped in his teeth, Henry filled his lungs with air and submerged. Once beneath the water, he pulled hard for the beach. This was a full frontal approach. Immediately in front of the sentry he launched himself from the water. In the instant before the man could even cry out, this human killing machine was upon him, clamping one hand over his mouth and driving a knife into his heart with the other.

Jack Terranova sat up on the veranda, his back to the wall of the house. With a semiautomatic twelve-gauge shotgun resting lightly across his knees, he stared out over the water at the horizon and a heaven filled with stars. It was another one of those perfect island nights with a light breeze carrying the scent of tropical blossoms. Below him, the Caribbean rustled like the train of a satin wedding dress dragging on church steps.

He removed one of Diego's Cuban cigars from his breast pocket and ran it slowly back and forth beneath his nose. Dispensing with any notion of using clippers, he bit off the end of the smoke, spat it out, and wet the butt.

His mind, while still on what he felt to be an imminent attack, had drifted home. He thought of Maria with her mobster's wife arrogance, everything about her life in the lap of luxury taken for granted. And those young upstarts in the organizations back home. They'd all turned into pussy-whipped candy asses, running scared from some glory hound U.S. attorney in downtown Manhattan.

"Screw you, Maria," he grunted to the wind as it moved northeast. "You never could fuck worth a damn anyway." Grinning around the stogie, he struck a match and lit up.

Bueno hunkered in the sand, waiting for Cristina. A match flared up on the patio by the big house. As it died, he could make out the faint glow of a tobacco ember as it brightened and faded with regularity. Jack Terranova was one confident son of a bitch.

Behind him, he heard the light thump of the little boat's gunwales against the dock. Quickly, he slid down in the water and sidestroked to the point where Cristina sat clinging to the edge of a cross brace. He grabbed the bow painter she threw, clamped it in his teeth, and towed the boat beneath the pier toward shore. The water, shallower here, moved in and out of the pilings with the surge of surf. Cristina worked to make sure the boat didn't crash into the uprights. Bueno's feet eventually found sand, and he dug in and pulled until he was waist-deep where the pier approached a beachfront retaining wall.

"Terranova's up on the veranda," he whispered into the void. "I've taken care of the closest man here. First the rifle, then the explosives and my handgun."

Cristina handed him the weapons slowly, one item at a time. Then she crawled over the side into the shallow water and tied the boat off. Five yards further inland she found herself on hard-packed sand squatting next to Henry. He handed her the *Tikka* rifle and slipped the knapsack full of explosives over his shoulders.

"Give me five minutes," he said. "Then work your way north along the retaining wall to the steps through it. There's good lateral cover there. I'll have taken out the nearest sentry. I'm going to work my way all the way around and then into the house. You're my safety valve. Don't shoot unless you actually see him coming your way."

Cristina reached out and traced the contours of his face with her fingers.

"Be careful, Henry."

He patted her arm and disappeared.

Terranova's perimeter men, for all the sophistication of their Valmet assault rifles, were not trained for this sort of work. Against an unseen enemy moving with the freedom and soundlessness of a light breeze, they offered no resistance. One by one, Bueno eliminated them as he worked his way in a circle. Not a shot was fired nor a groan of anguish uttered. Henry had become, once again, a machine with a purpose; he was oblivious to the horror his hands now wreaked. In the realm of that reined-in consciousness, his only focus was Jack

Terranova. He knew that in this place, the two of them were the same, trained in the same mechanisms of denial and response, cause and effect. Morality ceased to apply.

He came to the sixth and final perimeter guard on the down side of the breeze, putting on shadows like a succession of garments. In this instance, as with the first man on the beach, the best approach was head on. Henry moved to within five yards of where this soldier was dug in. The knife he carried was now slippery with blood. He took a moment to wipe it carefully on the side of his swimsuit before hefting it with deep concentration to locate the exact balance point. A small chunk of driftwood lay close at hand in the sand. He picked it up and lofted it in a high arc over the guard's position. It landed in a bush behind him.

In one motion, the man chambered a round in his rifle, rose to a crouch, and whirled. Henry's knife caught him in the throat just as he opened his mouth to challenge a phantom. In the throes of death, the guard's finger jerked spasmodically on the trigger of his weapon, unleashing a burst of automatic fire that ripped the quiet night apart.

Bueno cursed under his breath as he ran pell mell for cover by the side of the house. Above him, on the patio around on the beach side, Terranova roared in fury. It was the first time Bueno had heard American English since Miami.

"What's the matter with you fuckin' pussies? Call out your positions! Report in!"

Nothing but silence answered him. With it, Terranova himself suddenly became very quiet.

Henry knew how the eerie silence must affect his adversary. Jack was operating on the theory that at least some of his support would survive an initial onslaught. Those were the odds . . . generally. By now, the hit man knew he was all alone up there. If holding the high ground inspired any confidence, it was countered by the knowledge that his opponent had just dispatched six armed men. Each of them, until the last, had gone without a sound.

From where he crouched alongside the house foundation, Henry had a straight run under cover to the seawall where Cristina was concealed. He scurried along in search of her.

The sight of him brought her immense relief.

"I heard gunfire," she whispered.

"He's alone up there now," Bueno replied. "I'm going to

try to get into the house, and you're going to have to keep him busy."

He took the *Tikka* from her, switched to the rifle selection mode, chambered a round, and eased up with it until his eyes were level with the cobbles of the lower terrace. On the patio above, the glow of the cigar had been extinguished, leaving him no telltale red cherry to sight on. Immobile in his stance and concentrating fiercely, Bueno watched. After almost five minutes, his eyes caught something off to his left. A glint of light as something metallic moved ever so slightly.

Through the scope, he could make out an irregular shadow behind a large planter to the right of a pair of French doors. The shadow shifted; it was nothing more than a deep darkness intruded upon by a deeper one. Henry's finger closed slowly around the trigger. The shadow sat squarely in the crosshairs now. His breath ran out evenly as he squeezed.

The report of the rifle split the night, the muzzle flash most certainly giving away his position. Bueno pulled the gun back without pausing to gauge the effect of his shot and grabbed Cristina by the hand. They moved off down the wall together in a hurry. He knew he'd hit him but had no idea to what effect. They pulled up at the inland bend in the wall. Henry started up from his crouch to take a look.

The shadow he'd seen was no longer where it had been. He waited for his eyes to adjust to the deeper darkness of the veranda. Movement, ever so slight, caught his attention. The shadow hugged the ground now; the glint of a weapon extended before it. Henry tapped Cristina on the top of the head and beckoned her up.

"It's okay," he whispered. "Slowly."

In another moment, she stood beside him. He could feel her knees tremble alongside his own.

"Those glass doors on the right," he told her. "I'm going to get behind him. He's stretched out flat on the cobbles there and still very much in action. Aim for that big planter so you avoid shooting me, all right?"

Cristina turned her head to him fearfully. Search as she might in this enveloping blackness, she could not find his eyes and the confidence they could impart. She could barely breathe. With great effort, she nodded.

"Work your way back and forth along the wall here with

every shot,'' he instructed. ''And for crissakes, keep your head down.''

Without another word, he was gone again, and she was very much alone. What seemed like an eternity passed while she absorbed what was happening. This was the bloody part of the revenge she'd pledged in righteous anger. The clarity of her purpose was darkened now. The blood on him had glistened black in the night. While her knees shook, he moved with deadly competence.

Move! Somewhere from the back of her brain, a little voice screamed it at her. The urgency in it was ferocious. Nothing mattered now but her survival and the survival of the man protecting her. She swung the rifle up, aimed quickly at the planter, and fired. Seconds later she was hunched over and running north along the wall. Behind her, a rock exploded in a shower of sand and fragments. Terranova was returning fire for the first time. The thunderous report of his shotgun echoed in the night air.

As he made his way cautiously along the coastal road in absolute darkness, Ron Dai was surprised by the report of a rifle followed seconds later by that of a shotgun. He had crossed a rise and was descending a steep hill now. The rifle report came from the beach. The shotgun seemed to be returning that fire from inland.

The coded number for San Andres had included the words ''El Cove'' alongside it. A local map obtained at Customs made locating this designation easy. It indicated an inlet here on the west coast where he now walked. Seven hundred miles from Chetumal and just another stone's throw directly west across the water to Nicaragua itself. In some way that Dai was still trying to fathom, it added up to make as much sense as this exchange of gunfire did not.

Continuing along the road, he stuck to cover now, his pistol clutched in one hand. About a hundred yards from where he'd heard the first exchange, he heard another, all but identical. The roof of a sprawling beach house loomed below him. There was a muzzle flash down near what appeared to be a seawall, followed instantly by the shotgun's roar from either inside or just behind the house. From a crouch, Dai started over the verge of the road and down the steep incline. In the darkness, he didn't see the foxhole and tumbled headlong into it, coming to rest up against something soft but firmer than loose dirt. As his hand reached out and touched the face of a lifeless human being, the reflex reaction almost made him vomit.

With Cristina keeping Terranova pinned down and occupied, Henry took time to pick optimum access to the house. Several times during his search, the quiet was shattered by reports from the *Tikka* and return shotgun fire. Twelve-gauge, by the sound of it.

Along the south side of the house where the land fell away toward the sea, he discovered basement storm doors. They were secured by a chain and padlock. Because of its exposure to sea air, the wood of the doors themselves was in far worse shape than the contrivance securing them. He waited some forty seconds for the next exchange of gunfire and ripped one panel off its hinges barehanded.

The basement was pitch black as he inched his way inside. He paused to let his eyes adjust and thought he heard movement. It was just the slightest noise, like a quick intake of breath. There was someone down here with him. In the next instant he was prone on the floor, pistol extended in front of him. Nothing happened.

Slowly, as his eyes became accustomed to this deeper gloom, he sorted through the shifting densities of darkness. In one corner, huddled down almost at his floor level, there was a unique thickening of shadow.

"In two seconds, I'm going to shoot you on the spot," he said calmly, drawing bead. "Hands in the air."

Two thin, spidery shadows grew from the top of the huddled mass. Bueno got his feet beneath him, eased upright into a crouch, and advanced. He was nearly on top of his prisoner when he realized it was a girl.

"Por favor!" she whimpered. "Do not kill me. Please!"

"Against the wall," he snarled. Spinning her brusquely, he pinned her with his forearm and hastily patted her for weapons. "Why are you here?"

"I am told to hide here until it is over," she said sullenly.

"Unbutton your blouse and take it off."

When she hesitated, he shoved the barrel of his pistol against her head. Slowly, she moved to comply, bewildered and fearful. Once she was out of it he tore it to shreds, shoved a wad of cloth into her mouth, tied a gag with another, and used the sleeves to bind her hands and ankles.

"Don't try to scream," he warned, backing slowly away. "All of the men guarding this house are now dead, and you are still alive. Think about it."

TWENTY-THREE

The clip of the dead man's rifle was full. A quick sniff of the barrel told Dai that it hadn't been fired in days. The exchange of fire from the beach and the house continued as he lay on his back collecting his wits and trying to assess the situation. Something was coming apart here, and it was very possible that he was too late to affect the outcome. He had to get closer and try to determine what the current situation was.

The firepower of the strange automatic rifle was appealing. Dai reinserted the clip, slapped it home, and cleared the action. He replaced his pistol in his shorts and advanced with the rifle carried down low, his finger on the trigger. A seawall began to emerge from the incline down toward the sand; it appeared to wrap around the entire bottom terrace of the beach estate at about head height. He stayed with it, figuring it would afford the best immediate protection. There were sprawling lawns above the north and south ends of the wall and a cobble patio in between that served as a wide access to a substantial boat dock.

A muzzle flash and the sharp crack of a rifle told him that one of the two combatants was located some distance from him along the sand. The thunderous reports of the shotgun were coming from the second-level terrace above and not from the house itself. He maintained his position and waited.

A minute passed before the rifle bearer shot again, from a

different position this time, some thirty yards closer to his own. He heard heavy breathing coming in his direction and the muffled thudding of running feet in sand. The shotgun erupted again while, out of the gloom, a thin, platinum-haired creature emerged to set up, rise, and fire over the wall toward the house. Dai crouched, riveted in shock. It was a woman. She lurked not a dozen feet from him, oblivious to his presence there. Still breathing heavily, she hastily loaded additional rounds from her pockets into the rifle, set, and ran off back in the opposite direction.

There were no lights on in the house. Still, compared to the gloom of the basement, the room Bueno now entered seemed well illuminated. Outside, Cristina and Terranova could be heard maintaining a steady exchange of fire. He moved stealthily across a vast living room, staying as far away from the hit man's position and as close to the walls as possible. His eyes quickly scanned from wall to wall, reading the layout. A second pair of French doors, unseen from the beach, also opened on the veranda. A large bamboo shade had been rolled down outside them, probably as a shield against the earlier sunset. Terranova's next shotgun discharge came from a good ten feet to the left of the visible pair of doors. Henry had no idea how badly he'd hurt him with that first beach shot, but he seemed to be doing all right for himself now.

Slowly, staying low, he crept toward the shaded doors, noticing, when he got close, that one of them was already propped just slightly ajar. Just beyond, through the slats in the shade, he could make out the long, low planter he'd observed earlier. When Cristina's next shot came, he heard the slug thud into it. It was comforting to know that she was still operating according to instructions.

Bueno had a pretty good fix on Terranova's exact location now. He was setting to make his move on it when the intensity of his quarry's fire suddenly increased. He reacted.

Jack Terranova was madder than hell. First the son of a bitch clips him in the *butt*, down low in the fleshy part of his right cheek. Then he spends the next ten minutes scurrying back and forth down there like some sort of carnival target, keeping him pinned here the whole while. His anger kept him from realizing up until now that the intervals between the bastard's shots were nearly identical. A minute between each, give or take ten seconds. Never two shots a few seconds apart and *then* an interval. Always a run of twenty or thirty yards up or down the beach.

"Fuck you, pal," he muttered under his breath. "Good, huh? *Lucky* fuckin' shot, I say. Try this on!"

Down the terrace from where he was operating, a series of wide, shallow steps led to a lower terrace and the dock beyond. After his opponent's last shot, Jack figured he had a full forty-five seconds to run headlong down to the dock, drop, and draw bead on this puke. The twelve-gauge was fully loaded as he came up out of his crouch, cranked off three quick ones to keep the other team honest, and made his break beachward.

He'd once been fleet of foot for a big man, and he still thought he was making good speed. His fanny burned like eternal fire with every stride. Then, out of nowhere, a slamming blow, lifted him clear off his feet and knocked him sprawling. The sharp crack of a pistol shot reached his ears from the direction of the house. His momentum carried him forward and down hard onto the cobbles, just a half step short of the pier.

Out of the corner of his eye, he spotted the flash of something below him on the beach. A head of platinum-blond hair. A fucking *woman's* head. The motherfucker'd suckered him with some goddamn piece of *fluff*!

The bile of incensed machismo boiled inside him. Badly hurt, he still found the power to clutch the shotgun, lurch forward, and dive for the bitch. One fist clubbed down hard on her fleeing form as he went over the seawall and into the sand. It caught her up high, between the shoulder blades, and sent her headlong into the sand. He landed half on top of her, fury fueling his movements. With the fast-numbing arm on his bad left side, he jerked her around by the shirt and shoved the barrel of the shotgun up under her jaw. Their eyes met and held, both of them panting, as footsteps, coming hard, approached from above.

Ron Dai wasn't at all sure what he was seeing. Directly ahead of him, a big man, badly wounded in one shoulder and bleeding profusely, had just overtaken the rifle-wielding blonde. As he managed to get her jerked around and his shotgun wedged up under her chin, a second man appeared above them on the dock. He held a pistol extended in a combat stance and zeroed on the wounded man's head. It was a classic standoff, by all appearances. Then, suddenly, when the men spoke, it was down-home American English.

"Hi, Jack," the man occupying the high ground said quietly. "She didn't shoot you. I did."

The wounded man chuckled hoarsely, still out of breath.

"They said you were good, asshole. Not good enough to save your girlfriend here *and* get me, I'm afraid. You want to even hope she might live through this, you'll clear off and let me and her work it out."

"What's to prevent you from killing her anyway?"

"Not a thing, pal. But you and me are gringos. Your beef's with the skinny spic, and he's cleared outa here. Let's call it a draw. I go off and lick my wounds, and you think about what a yellow fuck you are for using a woman to try and get me."

"Yellow? You remember a thickset Company man you ambushed last month? Cali?"

"The nose tackle."

"My former commanding officer for three nasty tours in Nam. A goddamn good friend."

The skinny spic who'd cleared out *had* to be Cardona. The big guy was some sort of American hired gun employed by him. Ron Dai no longer questioned which side he was on. Either way the man on the high ground chose to play it, the wounded fellow would blow the blonde's head off. Some sixth sense told him that. The guy with the pistol trained on his quarry's head was probably thinking the same thing.

Without thinking further, Ron began a flanking maneuver. Staying low to the sand, he skirted the pier pilings until he had a straight rear approach on the shotgunner called Jack. When he'd stolen up within six feet of his objective, the guy above caught him out of the corner of his eye. Ron stopped in his tracks and held his two hands palms upward in a sign of peace. His pistol was visible in one and the other was empty.

"Fuck you, hotshot!" the man in the sand snarled. "I've got a tense trigger finger, and I wouldn't mind taking a fine-lookin' piece of ass like this to kingdom come with me. What's your move?"

Dai's mind-set became that of the 147-pound wrestling champion he'd been at the University of Arizona. Low crouch, the quick snatch, lightning quickness. He had moved so close that he could reach out and touch the man now. The shotgun was angled up to the frozen woman's head from the right. He switched his revolver to his left hand, set, took a deep breath, and pounced on the exhale.

When this new arrival made his gesture of nonaggression, Bueno knew that he had only this option left. It felt strange to be relegated to the bleachers. From deep center field, he watched the interloper, who heretofore had moved ever so slowly, launch himself into a sudden blur of action. His right hand shot out, caught the twelve-gauge by the barrel, and jerked it away from Cristina's head a split second before the hit man's surprised reaction triggered it. The thunderous discharge went wide, as the shotgun's recoil jerked it free of both men's grasps. Without hesitation, the human blur brought the same hand down and around Terranova's head, twisting it away from Cristina as his little snub-nose thirty-eight was jammed with his left hand into Jack's left ear. The gunshot was muffled considerably by the brain matter that exploded with it.

The sheriff's detective from Santa Clara County, California, the ex-CIA agent from neighboring Santa Cruz County, and the Colombian trafficker's widow sat together on the little patio of the Pensione Las Palmas. Ron Dai and Cristina Faro, both splattered earlier with blood and gore, had taken a swim in the sea and changed clothing. Bueno had showered to remove the black greasepaint and donned more comfortable cotton. There were beers on the table in front of them, and the only light at that late hour emanated from their room.

"They actually think they can persuade the United States to invade?" Dai asked incredulously. "That's balls!"

"Balls, but a pretty good bet," Bueno replied. "The climate in Washington is perfect for something like this. One thing the administration has failed to come up with, for all the rhetorical hot air, is the absolute proof of Soviet collusion. Those missile parts from your friend's company would be just the ticket."

Cristina was having a difficult time keeping up with these two as they spoke in their native tongue. She was glad enough to be alive after her ordeal and pretty much content to let them clear up their strange intersection as they saw fit. She knew one thing, though. She would be dead if it weren't for this other man. He was of an ethnic origin she couldn't quite figure, handsome in an exotic way, with those deep laugh lines on either side of his mouth and his chiseled cheekbones. Now she knew what it had felt like for Willie to have another man save his life. The debt of gratitude was not describable.

"I want in with you," Dai told Henry, "when you go over there. You have your motivations and I have mine."

Bueno shrugged, unable to deny the man his desire. "I suppose you have, friend. Just be aware that we might be walking into the teeth of a full-scale invasion, or *some* such shit. The kid told me that the seeds were all but planted. They were just hours away, and that was three *days* ago. Time is short."

"So what's your ETD?" Ron asked.

"How do you feel?"

"No better than you do, but what the hell. Like you say, we're wasting time here."

Bueno smiled. A little sleep would be nice, but there was a time for everything. He could think of no better hour than this for procuring a boat.

"There's a nice beachfront hacienda about a quarter mile over that way." He stood and pointed. "They've got a nifty ski boat tied up at the dock. One of those high-performance Chris-Crafts from the fifties. All mahogany, and a monster Chrysler inboard that'll push it at around fifty-five knots on smooth water."

Dai realized that this big, battle-scarred artichoke farmer was talking about *stealing* that boat. There was something uncanny about the guy's absolute confidence. Then again, if he wished to succeed down here, this sort of strength and confidence was just what he needed to ally himself with.

"I've heard rumors that you CIA types are big believers in the five-finger discount," he said with a grin.

Bueno snorted. "You don't know the half of it, copper."

Lt. Commander Gus Stackhouse USN was relaxing at the tight little mess table of the USS *Galveston*. His current command, comprising four highly trained young navy SEAL commandos, lounged on the benches beside and facing him. The Los Angeles Class Trident submarine they sailed aboard

Christopher Newman

was moving at top submerged speed on a southwest heading, a hundred miles into the Caribbean beyond Jamaica. At that rate, they would be close in off the coast of this Big Corn Island by an hour after nightfall tomorrow. After the approach, it was going to take them another hour to get ashore in their rubber boats.

A map of the island was spread out on the table, and the five men casually studied topography while drinking coffee. They were already plenty familiar with the objective, each man having committed the entire island to memory some hours ago. Even so, Commander Stackhouse was a stickler for mental rehearsal.

The warehouse, marked with a red X, lay two minutes forced march from the beach. The garrison support on this little sandbar was reported to be at joke strength. Washington was calling this a cakewalk. Gus hated that kind of confidence. Sure, the mission looked simple enough: capture and confirm. Then again, looks often deceived. He didn't care how many generals, admirals, and the like were lined up with sweaty palms itching to press the big panic button. In fact, he couldn't give a rat's ass about the politics involved. His job was twofold. First, he had an objective they had to reach. Then he had to get his men out of there alive.

The weapons, ammunition, and explosives were stowed in the Señora's skiff. Bueno and Dai dragged it into the surf, helped Cristina in, and then clambered aboard. They crossed the bay under cover of deep morning darkness.

If the owners of the Chris-Craft employed a watchman, he was asleep. The tank of the boat turned out to be only half-full, but they discovered three full jerry cans stacked together on the dock inside an unsecured locker. When two simple wires were stripped and touched together, the big inboard coughed, sputtered, and roared to life. With Ron manning the moorings and casting off, Henry swung the launch into a wide, sweeping arc and headed out to sea. His compass bearing was west by southwest.

It was dead in the middle of the rainy season now, and at least once a day a squall could be counted on to really dump some moisture. About an hour out from San Andres, moving at thirty knots to conserve fuel, they encountered heavier seas

314

generated by strong westerly gusts. Dead ahead, they could see thick clouds looming against the canopy of stars. They had a hundred miles of open water yet to cross.

Forty minutes later, the rains came, accompanied by eight-foot seas and howling wind. Bueno knew that there was only one way to play this sort of weather in a boat like this. He headed her straight at the oncoming swells, pushed the engine wide open, and ran at it. Within minutes, they were drenched. Dai looped a spare painter under Cristina's armpits and around her seat, lashing her in. He then hung on for dear life himself as his new partner actually came up out of his seat and rode the helm bent-kneed. Spray broke in buckets over the bow. It was impossible to maintain their heading. They would deal with correcting it later. Henry was more worried about their ammunition staying dry.

When, in twenty minutes, the squall passed, they settled back onto their course. Henry used the stars, once again visible, to reckon how far they'd been blown off it and adjust. They were headed almost due west when he'd finished, with about fifty miles to go.

Fighting the storm had really taken it out of him. He told Ron as much over the roar of the engine.

"We want to get ashore under cover of predawn fishing departures," he hollered. "I don't know about you, but for me it's been a long day. Once we get on the beach, I want to hole up somewhere and catch a couple hours shut-eye."

Dai laughed, eyes twinkling. "I'm glad you said it and not me. I was beginning to think I'd hooked up with the Bionic Man."

At three-thirty A.M. on Big Corn Island, Diego Cardona was unable to sleep. He'd left his bed and was walking an overgrown path of the estate, along the seawall. Less than an hour ago, a squall had hit and passed, leaving the air fresh and alive with the fragrance of myriad flowering plants. Behind him, the house was dark, and two men patrolled the grounds in shadow.

He could not help but wonder how it had gone for Luis in Washington. Latham was to have picked him up and walked him along all the proper channels. Then there would be conferences as decisions were made. They would either send in a confirmation team here or go for the whole thing. Either way, they would now find exactly what they looked for. Then it was on to Managua.

He smiled at the open sea. It had been hard, dangerous work. But it was all worth it. His moment had come, and his power was consolidated. The old fools in Miami would be forced to pay him heed. They would have no choice.

Even in his agitated, sleepless state, there was nothing he could do now but wait. He removed a small glass vial from his shirt pocket, tapped a tiny mound of cocaine out onto the back of his hand, and consumed it with a quick, satisfied snort.

Several dozen fishing boats dotted the water off the leeward shores of Big Corn Island. The sea and sky were rose-flushed with the color of the recent storm. Hungry sea birds wheeled in the sky, diving and squabbling over fish. Trees and rooftops along the shoreline sparkled and steamed even in these long, weak early rays of the sun. The little island gleamed in the midst of the surrounding sea, an emerald on azure velvet. Like many of these minor islands, it had not yet been spoiled by money and politics. Greed marched toward it with ugly inevitability, but today it was paradise.

Bueno eased the boat as unobtrusively as possible through a break in the reef and into the lagoon beyond. He was taking his time, barely running the big engine above idle. Inside, he was busy analyzing the landfall he saw, searching it for the best possible mooring. Big Corn was barely two miles in diameter at its widest point, and the cover it could afford was minimal. As Henry saw it, the best way to hide was to blend into the heaviest concentration of activity and act as if they belonged there. That way, they could simply tie up and walk away. Cristina had no more than a small handbag now, while he and Dai would carry canvas grips and the *Tikka* wrapped up along with some fishing rods conveniently stowed aboard the boat. They would look like day trippers up from Costa Rica on a pleasure boating expedition.

Inside the lagoon, the water was as smooth and glassy as a millpond. Henry wove his way through the loitering commercial rigs and several other pleasure craft. It was fortunate that the politics of Washington, Havana, and Moscow didn't play to much of an audience out here. This was the same island culture as could be found all around the rim of the Caribbean basin. Locals fished, hustled, and scraped by. Rich people from neighboring countries poked in and out, cavorted in snorkling gear, and drank rum. The sun shone brightly, it never got cold, and the living was unhurried.

Half-a-dozen foreign pleasure craft were moored among the rickety wharves he nosed the boat up to. Three were from the American South: Corpus Christi, Galveston, and Port Arthur. All were completely shut down and bobbing quietly, their occupants most likely sleeping off hangovers at such an early hour. The mahogany inboard gently nudged the dock. From beside him, the California detective leapt ashore with the grace of a ballet dancer to grab the bow line and tie them off.

Before being ceded to Nicaragua, the Corn Islands had been owned by the United States. The decaying, ramshackle construction typical of such American intrusion was still in evidence. Unlike the British, who generally built in brick, the Yankee colonial outbuilding was designed and built as though creeping doubt was the primary architectural influence. Such structures do not stand the test of time. Nevertheless, even now they appeared to serve a very real purpose. Despite peeling paint and rusting tin roofs, the locals had converted them into useful shelter. Around them, the streets were no more than packed dirt, the sidewalks sand. The contrast of these buildings against truly stunning natural beauty was arresting.

The three new arrivals hurried toward the outskirts of the tiny town looking for a place where they could hide the rifle and explosives. About a half mile on, they entered a dense stand of trees and pressed on until they reached a clearing.

"This'll do," Bueno told Ron and Cristina. "After that drenching, we need to strip down the weapons and clean them. Then we should take a quick nap just to get us thinking straight."

"How do you see us moving from here?" Dai asked.

Bueno smiled. "We wander into town looking naive, pay a little money to somebody who looks like they might know something, and take our chances. The odds aren't stacked very heavily against us in a place like this. Combined, these people are bound to have seen most everything."

With Dai assigned to work over the *Tikka*, Bueno had Cristina clear a little area where they could sleep, and then settled down with the P-5. An automatic pistol of this precision and accuracy was a thing of wonder. Henry made it his religion while in action to clean it daily. He could strip and reassemble it blindfolded. Just as he suspected, there were tiny, encrusted salt deposits all through it from the storm. Just when he was thinking he would have to run off in search of some petroleum solvent like gasoline, Dai produced a tiny squirt-can of gun oil from his grip.

"The anal-retentive tendencies of a former Eagle Scout," he confessed. "I brought it to clean my revolver."

"Nice to have you aboard, scout," Henry chuckled.

Ten minutes later, all three of them were stretched out on the ground, heads on their arms or on a change of clothing, trying to get a few hours of shut-eye.

This was it, Bueno thought. Jack Terranova was dead, and though he had not done it himself, he hoped Carl, wherever he was, had had the pleasure of seeing it. Back in the old days, nobody had thrived on a tense moment like old Stickley. Now they were in Major Diego Cardona's back yard. No matter where he was on this island, they could reach him on foot in an hour.

Cristina had fallen into a deep sleep almost immediately, but Henry knew he would not sleep. Grateful for at least a little down time, he watched her. That face was so relaxed in sleep, as if there were nothing at all to worry about. Who they were to each other was still something that confused him. They didn't talk about it. He wondered if they ever would.

The sun was bright in the sky when the other two responded to Bueno's stirring, sat up, and stretched. It was time to think about their stomachs and about locating the warehouse the kid in Miami had spoken of.

Back down the road in the little beach town, they found an open-air cafe serving fried *platinos*, fish, and eggs. While Cristina and Dai ordered for the three of them, Henry crossed the street to a small *bodega*, entered, and smiled at the old woman minding it. He asked her to direct him to the person selling Cordoba on the black market. Every town in Latin America had at least one such hustler who made fortunes on the margin between the artificially deflated official rate of exchange and the true street value of the currency. He'd chosen this place because it looked the most properous of any on the main drag. A good bet.

The woman looked him up and down before addressing him in that curious Caribbean English so pervasive in the region.

"Dollah you 'ave, mon?"

Henry shook his head. "Gold, mother."

She studied him again before demanding, "Let me see."

When he withdrew his hand from his pocket, it held a single shiny new Mexican one-ounce coin. Her eyes lit up with pleasure as she glanced quickly back and forth before beckoning him into the back room.

"Who send you heah?" she asked. "Fat mon on de beeg boat?"

"That's right," he replied. "Said you have the best rate."

"That we do, mon," she said, pushing a curtain back. "That we do."

A man of roughly the woman's age was revealed sitting at a small desk, a ledger at his elbows. The old woman explained the transaction to him and departed. The man beckoned, holding out his hand. Henry placed the gold coin in it and waited while the wizened character put it through its paces. Satisfied, he looked up and nodded.

"Fowah hondred fitty-tree dollah today on de Lon-done mawket," he pronounced. "Cordoba value at ten, even in de Managwa."

"That's the *official* rate," Henry agreed. "What can you do for me?"

"Elebben an' de half," the man replied.

"Give me a hundred bucks worth and the rest in U.S. greenbacks," Henry told him.

The old guy shook his head. "No good deal de udder way, mon. I geeve you fowah hondred to de ounce, top."

"Fine," Henry shot back with a grin. "Business been good lately?"

"How so?" the black marketeer sniffed, suddenly wary.

"Just heard there's been some new action around. Some of the old guard coming back through."

"An' wot if dey do?" the man demanded angrily. "Fo' my mon-ee, de whole fokin' con-tree gone to hell since dey left."

"No skin off my nose either way," Henry told him. "I'm just a dude with his eyes open for opportunity. Got me a big

319

boat tied up down in Tortuguero. A cigarette that goes like hell. Always ready to pick up a little action.''

The petty profiteer relaxed visibly. ''Why don' you say so, mon? Been de roomah floatin' roun' dese pawts dat dere be some changes in de wind. Be interestin' if de old re-jeem be ready to move bok, eh?''

''Might,'' Henry agreed. ''I tend to doubt they can pull it off, but who am I?''

The old guy shrugged. ''Dere been de roomah.'' He removed used Cordoba notes from a metal strongbox and counted out eleven hundred, laying the last fifty on top with a flourish. Next to it, he laid thirty U.S. twenties. Bueno picked up the money, folded it separately, and put it into two different pockets.

''Pleasure doin' business with you,'' he said. ''I'm going to have me a little breakfast across the street. Food good?''

''Edible,'' the man replied.

''And after that, I'm going to do a little nosing around to see if anyone hereabouts can use the services of a fast boat. You mentioned rumors. Anyone hear them better than the rest?''

The man flashed him an all-but-toothless grin for the first time. ''Right dere wheah you be eatin', mon. He be holdin' court bout dis tahm of de day. De nem be Hor-hay. Beeg mon.'' A hand shot out to touch Bueno on the wrist. ''You do de beesnez wit' dis mon, you 'member ol' Awgustus, no?''

''You bet,'' Henry told him. ''If I can find any reason to keep me here, I'll be back.''

TWENTY-FOUR

Ron Dai pushed his plate away and sat back to drink his coffee. Outside in the street, many fishermen had already straggled back into town after their predawn forays onto the sea. They talked and laughed with gusto. It seemed that fishing cultures everywhere were the same: hard lives lightened by hard drinking, boisterous camraderie, and easy laughter. The cafe had begun to fill up. Beside him, Cristina toyed idly with her food while Bueno watched the crowd inside the cafe, searching for something.

Henry scraped back his chair, picked up his coffee and carried it over to an adjacent table. A large Hispanic had for some time now been holding court there. The others in the place seemed to defer to him as they discussed some upcoming soccer game, the previous night's storm, and the sweet ass of a young woman who happened by in the street. He was being addressed as Jorge.

The man looked up as Bueno's shadow fell across his table. Bueno had an easy smile and employed it now as he nodded to this stranger.

"Mind if I join you?" Bueno asked him with his perfect Spanish.

Jorge shrugged. "Why not?"

"The name is Riberac," Bueno extended his hand.

Jorge took it and shook. "Everyone calls me Jorge, Riberac. What can I do for you?"

"I've been sitting across the way there," Bueno told him, "having my breakfast with friends. I've noticed that you seem to be the man around here."

Jorge continued to smile good-naturedly, looking pleased with himself. Another at the table spoke up for him.

"He is elected representative to the National Council," the man said. "The only such man from Big Corn."

"It's a pleasure to meet a man of your distinction," Bueno said. "You may be able to help my friends and me. You see, we're interested in helping stimulate the economy hereabouts. This is a beautiful island you've got. We ask you to think about how many more of those rich Americans you could lure here in their boats if you had, say, a nice restaurant and maybe a bar. Some people we represent have sent us here to scout around, you know? To see how local people with influence might take to the idea."

Dai watched the man look over at him and Cristina, nod sagely, and put on his politician's face.

"We are a simple people," he said cautiously. "We enjoy our lives as they are."

Bueno grinned a big one and waved reassuringly. "Wouldn't change it for the world. Believe me. We just want to enhance the beauty. Create access to it. And I'm not talking about Miami Beach. Just a few creature comforts to entice the gringo ashore so you people can take a little of their money off them."

"And how would you need my help?" this Jorge asked Bueno.

Ron rolled his eyes at Cristina, who smiled her own amusement in return. Henry was working this guy like a snake oil salesman.

"We'd never move ahead with a deal like this without enthusiastic local support. Other than renting a couple of warehouses from the government and moving in a few supplies, we haven't done a thing here yet."

The big man was unable to mask his sudden look of surprise and concern.

"I am aware of no such arrangement," he said cautiously. "Warehouses?"

"We didn't want to alarm anyone before we could talk to

you people and let you know that everything is going to be just fine," Bueno told him. "The folks in Managua thought it might be best if we moved the stuff in at night, you know. Anyway, I'm going to be around for a few days with my friends, staying on the boss man's boat out in the harbor. I want you on our side. Please, think long and hard about this, okay?" He stood and held out his hand. "No rush now, and I *mean* that."

This time, Jorge shook with much less enthusiasm. As Henry sat back down between Ron and Cristina, the local politico was busy gathering his cronies close around him. The tones of conversation were hushed now. Out of the corner of an eye, Dai watched the proceedings while pretending to be engrossed in his coffee. It appeared that one of the men might know something specific that the others didn't. He was speaking rapidly and gesturing off toward the north. A moment later, Jorge pushed back from the table and descended to his Jeep in the street. Firing it up, he set off out of town in the direction the man had pointed toward. Henry turned to his companions.

"I think that's all we need to know," he said.

Captain Arturro Velasco was visiting the warehouse compound to give his men some last-minute instructions. There were two of them, the pair he felt he could entrust with the greatest responsibility.

"You would be foolish to offer them any resistance," he was saying, his foot up on the front bumper of a Jeep parked around back in the shade. "Any men the gringos send will be part of a very elite unit, highly trained and very lethal killers."

"What would you have us do, Captain?" one of the two asked.

"Surrender," he suggested. "There is a better chance of no harm coming to you this way."

Behind them, they heard the angry growl of a Jeep fast approaching the front gate of the compound. The driver, encountering the obstruction of the perimeter fence, began sounding his horn incessantly. In irritation, Velasco turned and strode across the hard-packed earth to the gate. Hands on his hips, he scowled at this man.

"Silence!" he roared. "What in the Holy Mother's name do you expect to accomplish with that?"

The captain recognized the driver as a local politico named Jorge Arellano. The fat man remained seated behind the wheel.

"I demand to know what is going on here," he growled.

"That is military business," Velasco replied, trying to sound equally disagreeable.

"I hear different," Arellano challenged. "There is some Managua plot to develop Big Corn behind the backs of the local assembly. As their elected representative, I will not stand for this. We want some answers."

"I have your answer right here," Velasco retorted, grabbing at his crotch.

Jorge Arellano colored. "I demand to see the contents of that warehouse."

"How will you get through this gate?" the captain asked, amused now. "You are the butt of some joke, señor. The contents of this compound are a military concern. You have my word that they have no bearing on this fantasy development of Big Corn that you speak of. I suggest you go back to your rum and your friends."

Jorge sat where he was and stared at the old warehouse. Velasco's two soldiers were now in position on either side of the big main door, brandishing automatic rifles. It would appear that he was not going to get what he wanted in this manner.

"I, too, have friends in Managua," he announced importantly. "This is not the last you will hear of this."

"After we radio back to the sub," Commander Gus Stackhouse briefed his team, "all we've got to do is maintain a lock on the location. As soon as they get the word, Rapid Deployment will send up a pair of Chinooks with two Ranger companies from the Canal Zone. The local garrison is reported to be so weak that we shouldn't have any problem holding them off. The Rangers will help fend off any reinforcements the Sandinistas might send from the mainland."

"Ain't the mainland army gonna have its hands full?" an Alabama kid named Wilson asked. "They's talkin' full beach-head over on the west coast."

"Probably," Stackhouse answered him. "But we take no chances. This shit in the warehouse is the whole ball of wax.

The president's got to be able to point to it when them mangy dogs from the press start gnawing on his trouser cuff.

The four faces stared resolutely back at him from their positions around the tiny staging area. "That's it, then, gentlemen. Now comes the hard part. Sitting and waiting for the green light. Try to relax. It won't be long now."

The island turned out to be crisscrossed with footpaths. Once they'd retrieved the *Tikka* rifle and explosives, Henry, Cristina, and Dai had set off, angling northeast up onto and across a low central ridge. From the top of the ridge, they were able to identify five different warehousing complexes lining the interior flatlands along the north shore. In two of them the roofs of the main buildings had collapsed completely. One other was all but entirely overgrown with small trees and creeping vines. That left them with only a pair of possibilities, and they looked to be nor more than an eighth of a mile apart. They reached the first of these in less than ten minutes and discovered that it had seen no human activity in many years.

The few hundred yards between their first and second objectives proved to be a bit of a rough go. There were no convenient footpaths, and the trek over densely overgrown terrain took them nearly fifteen minutes. The sun had reached its zenith by the time they arrived at the rear fence of the compound perimeter. All three of them were feeling the intense, wet heat and were grateful for any obstruction that forced them to rest. Dai was just opening his mouth to suggest they split up and follow the fence in opposite directions when Henry held a finger to his lips and cupped the other hand to one ear. Slowly, he led the way east along the fence to where it turned a corner and moved off at ninety degrees to the north. There were voices in heated conversation near here, the words still indistinct. At a point near the end of this north–south fence, Henry held them up and slowly peeled back the fronds of an overgrown banana tree.

The heavyset local politician known to them as Jorge sat in his Jeep in front of a large, locked gate. He was apparently involved in some sort of standoff with a uniformed soldier conversing with him from inside the compound. It was forty-five minutes since they'd watched the fat man climb into his wheels and motor off in a huff. It was not difficult to imagine that he, too, would have had to spend a bit of time searching out this specific location. His presence there now was a pretty good indicator that they were on the right track.

"The guy inside the gate is a captain," Bueno whispered. "You see the bars on his collar?"

"I suppose you've checked out the two goons on the door," Dai murmured back.

"Soviet AK-47s," Bueno told him. "It'd be convenient if those two were all of it."

They sat and watched as Jorge apparently made no progress. He sulked a moment before bending to switch on the ignition. The engine coughed to life, and the fat man steered the thing around in reverse and spun his tires as he roared off.

"The one they're guarding looks like it's had some recent repair work done on it," Dai said quietly.

Bueno nodded as he continued to watch the captain, who returned to his men and huddled to talk something over. All three of them drifted around into the shade of the east side, closer now and in plain view. The captain handed around cigarettes, then bent his head to accept a light from one of the men.

"There's nothing we can do until sundown," Henry whispered. "It looks like those three are all they've got watching the goodies. Once it's dark, we can move in and blow the big building. I suggest we find us a nice little nest and relax."

One of the soldiers began to move away from his partner, heading for the gate. At the same time, the captain strode back around the south end of the barn and disappeared. The soldier at the gate began unfastening the lock and chain securing it as they heard the sudden roar of a Jeep engine other than the one visible to them. The captain, at the wheel of this second vehicle, emerged suddenly from the unseen west side of the complex and steered through the now-open gate. The guard saluted as he passed.

After an agitated Captain Velasco left the beachfront hacienda, Diego Cardona paced the floor of his host's living room. Someone on the island had observed the offloading of crates, and now the abandoned warehouse had been visited by some local petty bureaucrat. He'd told the captain a wild story about developers purporting to have the green light from

Managua. Whatever *that* meant. And no matter, really. The operation was exposed.

Cardona was trying to remain calm and rational. He told himself that the Americans would make their move no later than tonight. Even now, they were off the coast somewhere, awaiting the cover of darkness.

He clapped his hands together, summoning the man who had piloted the speedboat over from San Andres. On his appearance, Diego nodded curtly.

"Radio the seaplane," he ordered. "I want it standing by. Tell them to be ready to move tonight, at a moment's notice. Once the Americans land and the warehouse is breached, I want that plane ready to take me to Honduras to join our troops."

Lucien Wilson and Stanley "Peaches" Beauregard were assigned to the primary landing boat. The commander, along with Tony Watkins and Greg Boyce, wouid come ashore a couple of minutes after them in the second boat.

"You ready, Georgia boy?" Wilson asked his partner.

Both men were superbly tuned physical specimens. Wilson was the shorter and stouter of the two; Beauregard was built more like a power forward. Because he was tall and had the better leverage, the Georgia Peach was doing the rowing while Wilson and his Barrett Light Fifty machine gun rode point in the bow.

"I been waitin' six years for this shit, and you're wonderin' if I'm ready?" Beauregard replied.

Above them, a deck hatch was suddenly flung open. A pair of submariners tugged the first inflating rubber boat canister out on deck and triggered its release mechanism. Instantly, the fiberglass shell popped away as the compressed boat within began to unfold in a hurry.

"All right, you guys," Gus Stackhouse growled. "Get your fannies up there and go. We'll see you on the beach."

Because he was occupying the more stable stern position, Peaches flew up the ladder first. Wilson was right on his tail. The two of them had a long history of friendly competition throughout every aspect of SEAL training. They pushed each other but also felt comfortable with each other's abilities. Wilson couldn't run the hundred in ten flat or dunk a basketball, but he could pin Peaches to a mat in *better* than ten flat.

"What do you see?" Beauregard asked as he began pulling for shore from nearly a half mile out.

"Water, Georgia boy. Just row."

Shortly after nightfall, Henry left Cristina and the detective to steal down into the compound solo. He wanted a little more information about the layout before they launched any sort of offensive. At the moment, the two soldiers guarding the place still occupied the north side of the main warehouse near the big doors. He took advantage of their inattention to noiselessly divide the plastique and plant it with detonators at a dozen strategic structural junctures. This big building was definitely the place. All the smaller ones on the premises were in bad shape; most had gaping holes in their roofs and chunks of siding fallen away.

"All set," he told his waiting accomplices.

"What's the plan?" Dai asked.

Henry pointed up toward the front corner of the building on the east side. "You're going to step out and cover our two friends when you hear a pebble rattling on the tin roof. That'll distract them and mean that I'm in position opposite. Make sure you move far enough out in front so that the angle you have on them would mean hitting the front door instead of me, huh?"

"Got it," Dai answered.

"What about me?" Cristina demanded.

Henry handed her the P-5. "There's a jerry can strapped to the back of their Jeep. I want you to get it while we're taking care of the guards. The explosives are already set, but I want to splash a little gas around inside to make sure we get a real hot fire when the place goes."

The two soldiers were drinking beer and listening to a low-volume radio squawk mainland news when Ron Dai appeared out of the gloom, his little snub-nosed .38 sweeping slowly back and forth between them.

"Don't do anything heroic," Dai advised them in his best refresher-course Spanish. "Hands behind your heads."

They slowly complied, sheepishly glancing at each other. Bueno appeared as well, the *Tikka* switched to twelve-gauge and held on them at hip level. They were relieved of their ordinance and made to lie face down on the ground.

There was a heavy padlock on the two main doors. Henry rattled it.

"Who has the key?" he asked.

Dai prodded one of the soldiers with the barrel of a confiscated AK-47.

"Our captain," the man said sullenly.

Henry grunted, stooped to reach into his boot, and extracted the lock picks he'd last employed at the country club outside Cali. It took him another five minutes to get the lock open and swing the big doors ajar.

"Cristina!" he called out.

Laboring to lug the full five-gallon can of gasoline, the spiky-haired platinum blonde appeared, to the astonishment of the prostrate soldiers. Bueno traded her his rifle for the silenced Walther and the can. Just as he began to splash gas around on the stacked cartons inside the barn, he thought he heard a wire snap.

Wilson and Peaches, as the first two on the beach, had made sure it was secure while the rest of the team came ashore. The intelligence on the place was pretty accurate. Nothing greeted them but a host of bananas and coconut palms. As they grouped up just below the beach road, each man checked his weapon.

"Wilson, assume your point position," Stackhouse growled. "We go in nice and slow. No noise."

The five-man team strung out twenty feet apart and skulked along in the shadows of the road shoulder until they came to the spot where the warehouse access road was supposed to cut inland. There was a fire-gutted and overgrown beach house on the opposite side of the road: their landmark. From the condition of the vegetation along the verge here, you could have fooled anyone with the suggestion that there was a road close by. Wilson began probing the foliage until he located a place where just a few overgrown fronds gave way to a vegetationless void. He signaled the team forward and began picking his way along a narrow, rutted trail.

Less than four hundred yards in, the trail abruptly widened into a clearing that fronted on a fence and gate. There were voices dead ahead, speaking harshly in Spanish. Wilson called the column to a halt. Stackhouse hurried forward to crouch down and scan the area through sensitive infrared binoculars.

329

What he saw inside the compound confused him. Two soldiers were lying flat on the ground while a well-built blond woman and a nonuniformed man covered them with rifles. The woman was holding a weapon he couldn't identify, but the guy definitely had a Soviet AK.

"What the fuck?" he muttered.

"Sovs?" the sharp-eyed Wilson wondered.

"Maybe," the commander mused. "So why are they playing it like this? Them soldiers on the ground are supposed to be their comrades."

They squatted on their haunches together while Stackhouse mulled it over.

"We're gonna split the team," he said at length. "Wilson, you and Peaches take it over to the right about twenty yards and clip yourselves a hole in the fence. The rest of us'll go left." He looked at his watch. "Give it exactly five minutes and then come at 'em straight across the front of the second building over there. Let me be the one to tell 'em it's party time, and you two just hang back in the shadows."

"Move and we blow your fucking Rooskie heads off," a voice told Dai and Cristina. Both of them froze as three men bearing some menacing-looking automatic armaments materialized out of the gloom to the east.

"No Rooskie heads here," Ron said calmly.

The casual southwestern U.S. accent caught Commander Gus Stackhouse by surprise. "I want to see them weapons go real slowly onto the ground. Then I want you to tell me just who the fuck you are, boy."

Dai and Cristina stooped to cautiously place their guns in the dirt. Straightening, Ron looked this muscular, greasepainted military man in the eye.

"Have one of your men check my hip pocket, friend," he said calmly. "You'll find a detective's gold shield in there. Santa Clara County Sheriff's Department. That's in California."

"Fuck you, wiseass," Stackhouse snarled. He nodded his head to one of his men, indicating he should do as the captive had suggested. Sure enough, the wallet in his hip pocket carried the I.D.

"Who's she?" the commander demanded.

"Friend of a friend," Dai returned.

330

"You mind telling me what the hell is going on here?" Stackhouse asked.

Ron jerked his head toward the gloomy interior of the warehouse. Bueno had disappeared somewhere in there, and the fumes of dumped gasoline were now heavy on the air.

"The contents of this warehouse were stolen from a company in my jurisdiction," he said. "Until a few days ago, I was assigned on loan to the FBI field office investigating that theft. As I'm sure you know, national security is involved."

"Jesus Christ!" Stackhouse muttered. "This ain't no covert operation. It's a fuckin' three-ring circus. What in God's name is that heavy smell of gas?"

"We were preparing to destroy that stuff when you showed up. Got a match?"

"Like hell, boy. I got orders to hold that crap till doomsday, if that's what comes first. Soon as I make a little radio call to a certain submarine, this whole fuckin' island'll be crawling with army Rangers inside two hours. Just think, you'll be here for the party." The Commander waved over his man with the radio. "Get the *Galveston* on the horn, soldier."

"I wouldn't," Henry Bueno's voice boomed.

Slowly, from its direction, the bound and gagged figures of Wilson and Peaches shuffled forward. Henry was carrying a leveled AK-47 right behind them.

"Nice weapon, this," he said casually.

As Stackhouse and the two remaining men in his command bent slowly to place their guns on the ground, Dai and Cristina stooped to retrieve their own.

"Who the hell are *you*?" the commander growled.

"Just an old warhorse who used to carry the trident himself," Bueno replied. "Among other things. Next time you cut a hole in a wire fence, don't forget to muffle the snap with a rag or something, okay?"

Bueno kicked one of the two Nicaraguan soldiers still lying on the ground.

"Get up," he told him, switching to Spanish. "You and your *compadre* are going to take a little walk with us." He turned to Dai, reached back into his waistband with his left hand, and extended something to him.

Dai took it, a printed circuit board.

"That look like the goods to you?" Henry asked.

"Close enough," Dai told him. "Mind if I keep it? I know a particular lady and her father who would be awful glad to see it."

"Suit yourself," Henry told him. "I soaked all the boxes. You think that'll do the trick?"

"Should," Dai replied. "Those silicon chips ought to melt down into one big low-tech puddle of glass."

"Keep G.I. Joe and his friends covered," Henry told him. "I forgot one thing."

He hurried back inside the barn to grab the empty gas can, carried it across to one of the main support timbers, and leaned it against it. There was a pod of plastique planted just on the other side of the wall. When it went, the fumes at critical mixture inside the can would turn it into an ideal incendiary device.

Outside, he worked with his two partners to get the ragtag group lined up in tight single file. That done, he positioned Ron to one side and Cristina to the other. After making a search of each SEAL to relieve them of knives and the like, he took up the rear. Slowly, they started the little file down the access road toward the beach.

"What are you doing with us?" Stackhouse demanded en route.

Henry chuckled. "I ought to send you to Ortega as an early Christmas present," he told him. "But lucky for you, I've got a soft spot in my heart for your particular branch of the service. When you get back, tell Admiral Jack Hunthausen that Henry Bueno says hello."

When they reached the coast road, Bueno stopped the column and cut the two Sandinista traitors out of it. From deep in a front pocket, he extracted a tiny electronic plastique detonator and held it up in their faces. A tiny red light glowed on the top of the device. Adjacent to it a green one remained unlit.

"When I flip this little switch here," he explained, "that warehouse you were supposed to be guarding turns into the biggest fireball this island has ever seen. I want you to think about the fact that we could have left you inside to burn to death. But we haven't. We're going to let you run off down this road to good health and a long life. And you're grateful, right? So grateful that you're eager to tell us where we can find Major Diego Cardona."

As the five Navy SEALs, guarded by Dai and Cristina, watched in confusion, the two soldiers glanced quickly at one another. One of them licked his lips, eyes moving back to the tiny transmitter held in his big captor's hand.

"You will let us go?" he asked nervously.

"That's right," Henry replied. "Just tell us where to find Cardona."

"There is a large hacienda on the sea just a short distance from here." He pointed along the road to the west. "Less than a quarter mile. The only one of its kind. The gardens are overgrown. It cannot be missed."

Henry nodded, smiled, and stood aside to gesture them off down the road to the east. Both men stood riveted, questions on their faces.

"Move!" Henry snapped. "I'm all out of engraved invitations."

With no need for further encouragement, the pair turned tail and ran down the road, disappearing into the night.

"Now," Henry said, addressing Stackhouse, "where have you gents hidden your boats?"

"Fuck you, boy," the commander spat back.

With that, Bueno swung the butt of the *Tikka* he'd traded Dai for, catching the big SEAL officer hard in the solar plexus and doubling him over. As the Commander started going to his knees, a big blond guy with a crewcut and massive greasepainted arms made a quick half step forward. Like lightning, Bueno had the Walther stuffed up under his chin.

"No, sweetheart," Henry growled. "I think you know better."

The big guy swallowed hard and backed off. Stackhouse was down in the road making retching sounds. Henry squatted on his haunches next to him and explained the facts of life.

"The U.S. government's been flimflammed, friend. This whole warehouse full of goodies is a maverick CIA plant designed to prod that jelly-brain in the White House into invading. Save yourself for a war that's worth fighting. If you find one, you'll be luckier than I ever was. Paddle back to the submarine you came on and have a nice trip home."

He stood and nodded to Dai and Cristina. They'd taken pains to stack the SEAL team's entire supply of weapons inside the warehouse. Once the switch was flipped, the commandos would have no means of standing and fighting, even if they chose to. Henry, Dai, and Cristina began backing away down the road to the east, leaving the four bewildered SEALs gathered around their gasping leader. Above them, off to the north, they heard the drone of an approaching aircraft.

Major Diego Cardona was staring out along the seawall of the hacienda, awaiting the arrival of the seaplane he could now hear. The flash of an explosion lit the entire night sky, and for an instant the landscape was frozen bright as day. The major, startled by the intensity of the blast, whirled to stare inland in astonishment. Then he began to calm down and smiled with satisfaction. The Americans. They never did anything halfway when an opportunity came to expend a little ordnance. It would only be moments now before the thunder of Chinook transports and Sikorsky attack helicopters filled the sky. The drone of the seaplane grew louder on the heavy night air. It was time to be away from this place.

Out on the coast road, Bueno, Dai, and Cristina paused just short of a sprawling, heavily overgrown beach estate. Before them, a red-tiled adobe hacienda occupied a vast stretch of square footage for at least two hundred running feet. Beside and behind it, an extensive garden area ran down a slow incline to the sea itself.

Above them, the plane they'd heard approaching now swept low over the water. From out along what looked to be a seawall, someone in shadow flashed a lantern.

"You see that?" Dai hissed. "It's coming here."

Henry was already moving quickly toward a low wall that fronted a citrus grove on the east side of the house. They scrambled over it and into the trees, keeping to long shadows cast by floodlights from a pool cabana. Beyond the grove, it was obvious what the Sandinista guard had meant by overgrown. Nothing had been tended in years. Bananas, date palms, weed-choked lawn, a bed of roses in full wild bloom. The heady fragrance of it all floated up on the light sea breeze.

They were on their knees, crawling through this tangled shrubbery, when they spotted a soldier in camouflage fatigues hurrying across the lawn toward a dock. He carried two heavy-looking leather valises. A second man soon followed, bearing a rugged, impact-resistant plastic gun case and a large, bulging canvas duffel. The noise of the light plane had grown louder as it banked into a long, sweeping turn. Its pontoons touched down and skimmed the water.

A third man exited the house with a fourth, much older man beside him. The older man was stooped and shuffled painfully until they stopped, and the younger, wiry man hugged him fiercely. All three observers felt their pulses quicken. The younger man had thin, hawklike features and a short, clipped beard. He stood no more than five and a half feet tall and weighed no more than a hundred thirty pounds. There was commanding self-assurance in the way he moved. He was a man convinced of his own destiny who moved full steam ahead to fulfill it.

Henry lifted the *Tikka* and slipped a triple-aught buckshot magnum shell into the breech. From the range at which the man was going to pass him, and considering how proficient he was with the gun, the shot was going to be easy money.

Dai's hand shot out, gripping Henry's bicep.

"I want him," he growled.

"Sorry, friend," Henry countered. "You already got one of mine. I get the other." He was on one knee; the elbow of his gun support hand was on the other.

The single-engined seaplane was down and coming around on the water now at high revs. It had to taxi about a hundred yards to the pier.

The major's head came into focus in the crosshairs of the *Tikka*'s scope. Henry began to let his breath out slowly when he was distracted by movement to his immediate right. Cristina was suddenly on her feet beside him; in her hands was the AK taken from one of the warehouse guards. With a look of hatred and absolute determination in her eyes, she jerked the trigger, spraying back and forth at waist level.

The Somosista leader twitched spasmodically as a hail of lead tore into him. His knees gave and he went down, convulsing on the ground by the pier as his two henchmen stood in shock. One of them swung into action, bringing an Ingrahm machine pistol up and into firing position. Henry wasted no time putting the triple-aught magnum load intended for Cardona into his thigh. It nearly tore his leg off. The second man took a .22-caliber Remington slug in the shoulder as Bueno automatically switched modes and fired again.

The seaplane was nosing in toward the pier.

"Come on!" Henry shouted, already up and running toward it. At the dock, he picked up one of the suitcases and started to wave.

Dai and Cristina were behind him with more baggage when the plane came to rest. Henry hurried to the cabin door, yanked it open, and shoved the P-5 into the pilot's face.

"A little change of plan," he told him. "I've got this sudden itch to fly a seaplane. Get out!"

Minutes later, as Bueno took the plane airborne, he turned in the cockpit to regard Cristina as she rode quietly beside him. Dai, in the seat behind was grinning from ear to ear.

"Even the best can get beaten to the punch," he ventured.

"I guess so," Henry murmured. He'd begun to smile at her, too.

TWENTY-FIVE

It was the Wednesday morning before the long Thanksgiving weekend. Los Angeles International was jammed with travelers. Henry Bueno and Ron Dai, in search of fortification after clearing customs, sat at the bar of the lounge most convenient to their next departure area. Bueno was having a beer, while Ron had ordered black coffee and a shot of bourbon. When it came, he dumped the latter into the former and sipped his concoction slowly. They were awaiting a connecting flight to San Jose Municipal. Dai had already offered Bueno a lift to his home on the beach side of the mountains, and Henry had accepted.

A big color television above the bar carried the "Today" show from New York. As they watched, John Palmer launched into the news segment leading each half hour. All sorts of accusations were flying in the wake of the FBI breaking open a Contra plot to implicate the Sandinista government in the sale of stolen U.S. military secrets to the Soviet Union. The Sandinistas were reporting that one of the men named in the conspiracy had been found shot to death the previous night on the Nicaraguan island of Big Corn. This same conspirator was named by the FBI as the man responsible for the death of Agent Peter Davis in California. Identified as Diego Cardona, a former major in the Somoza secret police, he had also been under investigation by the FBI and DEA for suspected involvement in a large-scale cocaine smuggling operation. Who had shot and killed him remained a mystery.

"Go figure," Bueno grunted.

Dai shook his head. "What do you suppose will happen to this guy Latham and the other guys in our government? Nothing?"

"They've got serious egg on their faces," Bueno said. "They've done more than just lose some credibility with their superiors. Vouching for dogshit intelligence like the stuff they delivered can have a real damaging effect on a career ladder."

Henry reached into the hip pocket of his pants and extracted some folded pieces of paper. Without comment, he handed them to Dai.

"What's this?" Ron asked. He unfolded and flattened two official-looking certificates on the bar.

"Letters of credit," Henry told him. "Payable to bearer on the National Bank of Panama."

"Each one says a hundred and fifty thousand dollars," Dai murmured.

"You got it, friend. I took them off Terranova after you blew his brains out. Thought you should have them."

Ron stared at Henry and then back at the small fortune in paper on the bar. Neither of them said anything for a while, each lost in his own thoughts.

"I wonder how she's getting on," Bueno said at length.

"She's getting on fine," Dai replied. "Did you see the look on that banker's face?"

Henry chuckled. "I got the feeling that one A.M. was a little early for regular banking hours. But then again, the lady's dead husband was a large depositor. Once he learned who she was, he was most accomodating."

"The fact that she was accompanied by a pair of automatic rifle-toting desperadoes couldn't have hurt her case any," Ron added. He paused to take a sip from his cup. "What's next? Between you two, that is."

Henry thought about that one for a while. Then he sighed and shook his head. "Your guess is as good as mine, friend. She's got two little kids to raise and a whole lot of shit to sort through. I gather her family isn't too high on her recent life choices. Not that she should care what they think. A couple hundred million bucks shouldn't hurt her notions of independence any. I've got no idea where I might fit into that, if at all.''

"You'll see her again in the not-so-distant future," Dai told him confidently. "I saw how hard it was for you to leave each other."

"Maybe I can get her to bring the kids up here." Henry mused. "I'm sick and fucking tired of everything about *down there*."

Dai finished his coffee and glanced at his watch.

"Drink up. We've still got one more plane to catch."

Henry followed him out of the lounge, and they strolled side by side down the wide corridor toward their gate. Halfway along it, Henry stopped in midstride.

"Hang on a sec," he told Dai. Then he turned and pushed his way into the men's room.

He chose an empty stall, closed the door, and latched it.

The photograph on the passport stared back at him. His face. His eyes. Henri Riberac. Born: August 15, 1947. St. Etienne, France. He gripped the thing between thumb and forefinger, tore it violently twice, and dropped it into the commode. When he kicked the flush lever with his boot, an eager rush of water turned it into sewage. Henry Bueno watched it disappear. Now, *mañana* stretched out before him. Someone else could hunt and kill the snakes. He was going sailing.

ABOUT THE AUTHOR

Christopher Newman lives in New York City. He is also the author of MIDTOWN SOUTH and SIXTH PRECINCT.

Read Christopher Newman's bestselling police novels.

MIDTOWN SOUTH

THE KILLER: The leather-clad owner of a fancy townhouse that looks like a porn parlor, a very wealthy man with one devastating obsession.
THE CASE: Brutal, terrifying murders of prostitutes who bear an uncanny resemblance to one another.
THE COPS: Rosa Losada, straitlaced, by-the-book detective with her own private reason for entering the department. And Joe Dante, undercover detective, fresh from five years in the city's seamy drug culture, ready for the easy duty of life in a precinct. But when the precinct borders on Manhattan's Times Square, there's no such thing as easy duty—and this case is as hard as they come.

SIXTH PRECINCT

Millionaire art collector Oscar Wembley is hacked to death with a kitchen knife, his priceless paintings slashed to bits, his blood used to paint vicious epithets on the walls of his Greenwich Village townhouse...

Fat-cat neurosurgeon George Scully is slapped with a killer malpractice suit that could ruin his practice, destroy his marriage to a WASP princess, and expose his cozy setup with shapely blond cokehead Fiona Hassey...

Brilliant detective Joe Dante, now assigned to the Sixth Precinct, is tracking down the maniac who probably killed Wembley when an even more bizarre and baffling murder forces him to question everything and everyone he knows...

MIDTOWN SOUTH

and

SIXTH
PRECINCT

by Christopher Newman
are available in bookstores,
or use this coupon to order by mail: